A Weave of Starlight

SYDNEY WINWARD

A WEAVE OF STARLIGHT

SUNLIGHT AND SHADOWS BOOK 6

A Weave of Starlight

Cover Design by MiblArt

Published by Silver Forge Books

Paperback ISBN 978-1-960461-14-8

Digital ISBN 978-1-960461-13-1

www.sydneywinward.com

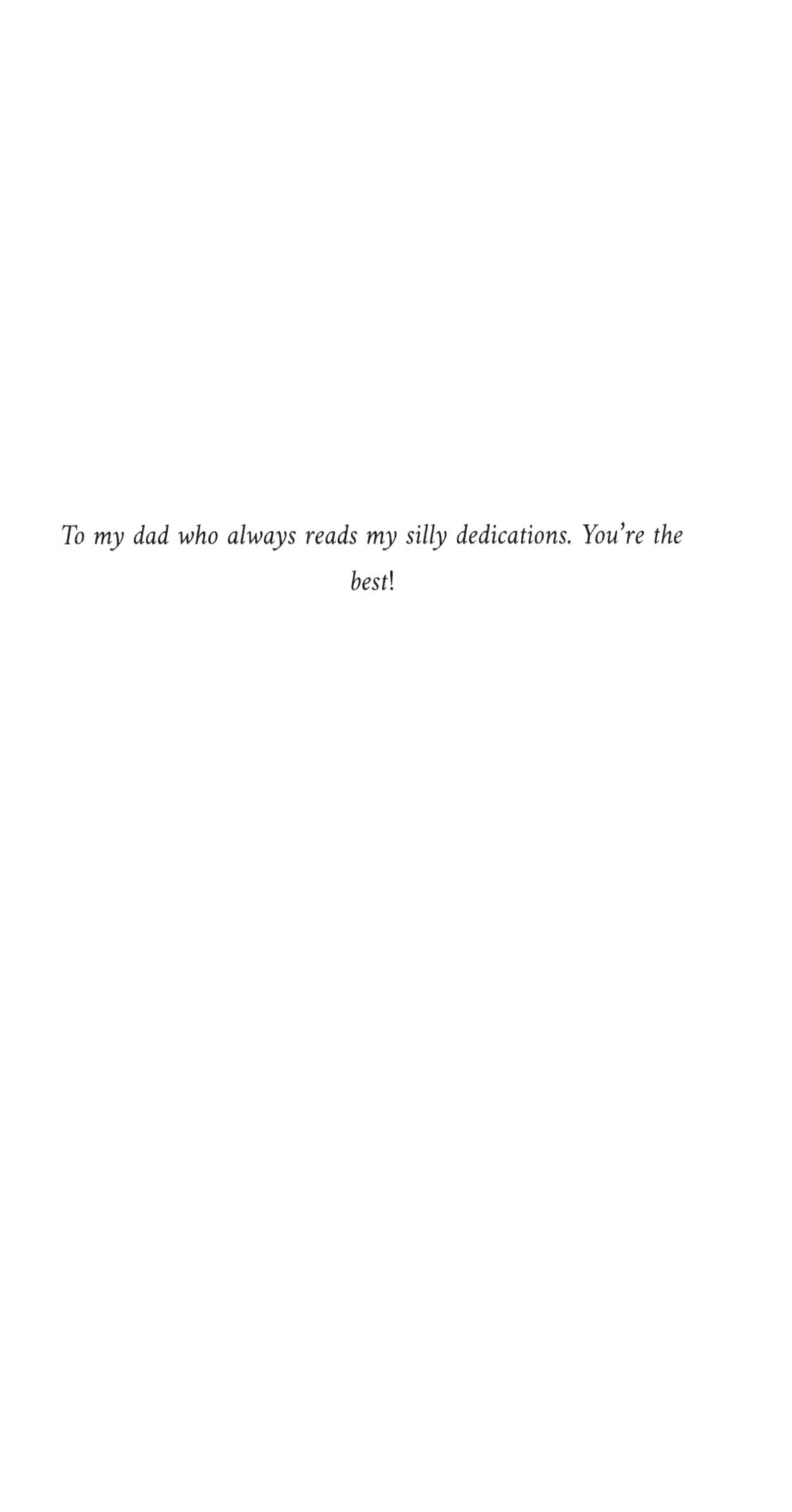

To my dad who always reads my silly dedications. You're the best!

BOOKS BY SYDNEY WINWARD

The Bloodborn Series

Bloodborn

Bloodbond

Bloodscourge

Bloodbane

Bloodcurse

Bloodheir

**Sunlight and
Shadows Series**

A Breath of Sunlight

A Taste of Shadows

A Glimpse of Music

A Kiss of Embers

A Balm of Healing

A Weave of Starlight

Letters to Love Series

Yours, Sterling

Forever, Mirabelle

Always, Ivette

Charles, With Love

Lord Death Series

A Waltz with Lord
Death

Novellas

Venom Kissed

Through Wylder
Meadows

Root Brew Float

On Silver Wings

Bloodmoon

Selkie

A Wingless Hope

AVRA NASSAKI HAD GROWN to dislike the scent of
incense.

The woodsy burn filling every breath she took followed
her through each ritual, each tradition, and each
responsibility resting heavy on her shoulders as next in line
for the Infernal Matriarchy.

Today was no different as she sat cross-legged on a
woven rug for the recurring ritual of taking her mother's
mantle for herself. Of course, it was only symbolic, as her
mother was still alive and well, and Avra wouldn't become
the Matriarch until her death. But every time the two moons
of Crotona in the lower realm reached their peak each new
cycle in the sky, her family and the Elders of her clan
performed the ritual.

She tipped her head to the side as she tried not to nod
off, the golden jewelry around her long, curled horns

tinkling with the movement. Across the room of the dim hut, candlelight flickered across her brother Theo's bored expression, his blue-gray skin a similar shade to hers melting him into the background of the shadows. The red, striated marks across his skin pulsed with a crimson burn when he noticed her attention on him, and he feigned hanging himself with a noose.

Her own stripes pulsed with amusement, the smallest giggle escaping her mouth. But one darting glance from her *Ikshwa*, Yianni, and she immediately sobered.

The current Matriarch, her own mother, and two Elders circled her, chanting in the Infernal tongue as they shook their rattles in a synced rhythm. The incense burned stronger in the air, and she forced herself to hold in a cough. This part of the ritual always seemed to drag on when one of the older Elders, Antonis, was long winded and seemingly oblivious to the passing of time.

Surreptitiously, her gaze landed on Yianni, his skin a darker shade of obsidian and his stripes a muted crimson when his emotions were more level than hers and Theo's. He was her guardian. Her partner. Always at her side. They'd been bonded since the day of her birth, and together for nearly two years now since she'd come of age.

Her *Ikshwa* was always a constant shadow. A steady presence. Forever at her side. Ten years her senior, he inspired no feelings of joy or attraction in her But she respected and trusted him. That was enough.

Her head tipped to the other side, the tinkling jewelry around her horns momentarily falling over her eyes. With the sharp tips of her ebony fingernails, she swiped it out of her face and studied her *Ikshwa* across the hut.

Yianni never spoke much, but when he did, his title alone commanded a room. People listened to him. He was one of the fiercest—if not the fiercest—warriors in the clan. He'd earned his spot as her *Ikshwa* by competing for her hand by killing other Infernal opponents. The vertical crimson stripe from collarbone to navel had appeared only after killing another Infernal. Among their people, it was a badge of honor if acquired during a duel.

One of the Elders stopped before her and smeared the blood of the sacred *gheshti* across each cheek. The dark-blue, pointed-eared creatures often lived in warm ponds close to external heat sources like volcanoes or heated rocks, and they were never killed needlessly.

Her mother stopped in front of her and smiled, running a gentle, motherly hand over her hair. "You have grown so much, my little one. One day, when I am gone, the Matriarch power will pass down to you." Although Avra had heard this dozens of times, she listened with rapt attention. "It will only unlock when you are ready for it. Until then, you must prepare yourself to the fullest extent to be the vessel for that power."

"I will be ready," Avra murmured with a dip of her head. "I dedicate my life, light, and soul to protect our people from harm."

The shaking rattles grew more insistent, picking up their rhythm, the incense growing heavier around her.

Again, Theo caught her eye across the hut and feigned struggling to keep his eyes open and his head up. She clamped her mouth shut to keep from laughing and shot him a glare. If he wasn't careful, she would make *him* an Elder one day just to teach him a lesson when she eventually reigned over the clan. No one could refuse such an *honor* bestowed by the Matriarch. Not even her brother.

A rumble shook the ground, startling her upright. Theo and Yianni leaped to their feet, hands flying to their weapons. The rest of them remained still and listened.

"What was that?" she whispered, searching for reassurance in her mother's eyes. But they remained hard with an air of uncertainty.

The red stripes across her mother's skin heated and burned as she harnessed the power of the Matriarch, the power of their ancestors. But she continued to stand still. Listening.

That's when the screams began.

Everything happened so quickly that Avra only managed a single blink as Yianni darted forward and stood protectively over her, his sword raised.

Someone stumbled through the door, another Infernal. But black blood coated his short male horns sticking out of his hair and seeping into the threads of his guardsman uniform.

"M-matriarch," the man gasped, swaying dizzily on his feet. "Hawkers. Dozens of them. You must...you must..."

Before the guard finished his sentence, he pitched forward and crashed to the ground, laying unmoving on the floor.

Screams, the metal strikes of weapon against weapon, and guttural growls filled the air outside, followed by the scent of ash and fire. They were under attack.

"How did they get past our scouts?" her mother shouted, but her words quickly sounded far away as fear latched onto Avra's soul and crushed. Harder. Harder. Harder. Until she felt immobilized.

Intense ringing drowned her ears as her world seemed to drift away as if something dragged her backward through a tunnel, and the light at the end became smaller with each passing second. Her breaths escaped as rapid bursts. Her limbs froze, making movement nearly impossible.

Hawkers.

The word echoed in her mind, striking fear straight through her chest like a sword ripping out her heart and throwing it into a blazing fire. One Hawker mercenary was capable of taking down at least ten Infernal warriors. But dozens of them?

"Why are they here?" she rasped through the fear tingling through her lips, her gaze darting from her mother, to her brother, to Yianni. "How did they break through our borders?"

"They've never been so brazen before," Yianni said in a deep, growly voice as he strapped extra weapons on his person.

Theo took her elbow and dragged her to her feet, tucking two daggers within the coiled ropes of her waistband. He started to tuck a third in when Yianni clamped a hand around his wrist.

"She needs no weapons. She has me. I'll keep her safe."

This wasn't the time Avra wanted to tiptoe around her *Ikshwa's* delicate pride, but she found it difficult to form the words to speak out for herself.

Thankfully, Theo spoke on her behalf. "Just hope she won't have to use them. But she should have them regardless."

Yianni didn't argue.

Her mother ushered them toward the back exit of the hut, a steely look on her face. "Get her out of the village. Should I perish, she will be their next target."

"Mother, no."

She grasped onto her mother's hand and held tight, just as her mother's own *Ikshwa*—not her father when he was long dead—ran his sword through a Hawker attempting to shove his way into the hut.

Avra's throat constricted as her gaze fixed on the black curse mark peeking out from the man's armored chest, the very one non-Infernals received after killing one of their kind.

Killers. All of them. Those mercenaries were surely here for her and her mother's heads.

"Go!" her mother cried, stooping low and placing one hand against the ground. Her crimson stripes climbed up her skin and turned translucent in her core as she called upon her Matriarch magic. Heat burned its way to the surface of the earth, a simmering steam wafting up from the ground. But before she managed to unleash its raw power, something crashed through the wall.

Dirt and debris rained over their heads, momentarily blinding Avra. She cried out and lifted her hands over her head to shield herself from the destruction. Red moonlight entered through the caved-in wall. A warm breeze climbed up her arms like sharp barbs. And then a fierce growl sent what remained of her small amount of bravery to her toes.

An Infernal Minotaur stood within the cavity of what used to be the western wall of the hut, a blood-thirsty creature commonly captured, trained, and controlled by Hawkers to do their foul bidding. And impaled on the minotaur's wickedly sharp horns…

Avra gasped, her heart clenching with unimaginable ache as she watched her mother's body slide further down the horns. Black blood coated her entire torso and dripped down the beast's face in rivulets.

Her mother turned her head, choking on her own black blood as she mouthed one word. *Run.*

And then the light of her stripes flickered out.

Numbing shock coursed through Avra, giving her no time to grieve the sudden and unexpected loss of her mother as Yianni grabbed her by the waist and tugged her out of the back exit with Theo following in their wake.

Avra's lips parted in shock at the red and black smoke permeating the night skies, filling the atmosphere with a nightmare haze. Hawkers and minotaurs battled against her people, dropping some of them like imps exposed to Infernal poison magic.

Heartache burst through her chest at watching her people fall to the Hawkers, but she didn't witness it for long as Yianni pulled her along with one hand while carving a path forward with his sword with the other. Theo flanked them from behind.

Yianni shoved her down out of the way of a swinging sword, and a sudden realization pulled the warmth from her face at the absolute worst time. She was the Matriarch now. She had to survive. No matter what, she needed to live.

As if other Hawkers recognized her decorated horns and came to the same conclusion, they began circling in like vultures intent on feasting on their kill. Ten of them. She counted ten.

Desperately, she searched within herself for the power that her mother had possessed, but in her terror, she couldn't locate it. She was going to die, too.

With shaking hands, she pulled her daggers out of her corded waistband, readying herself to fight. When a Hawker moved close enough, she swiped with her blade, slicing her target from elbow to wrist. She hardly saw faces. Only curse marks, weapons, and vicious snarls.

As if marking Yianni as the biggest threat, the Hawkers began surrounding him. He took out three of them before some of them turned toward her. She and Theo sprinted away, her previously immobilizing fear now transitioning to a panic to flee.

She glanced over her shoulder only long enough to watch as one of the Hawkers sliced Yianni's arm. Another stabbed him through the chest. Yianni fell to his knees, and then his side until the sight of him was swallowed up by the enemy.

No! she internally screamed. Her *Ikshwa* wasn't supposed to die. This wasn't supposed to happen!

If her mother could fall, if Yianni could succumb to death, then none of them stood a chance. Especially not her.

This was a massacre. It was not likely she would escape alive.

Still, Theo grabbed onto her hand and pulled her forward. She stumbled after him on stiff legs, fear threatening to petrify her.

She gasped for each frightened, labored breath as she sprinted through the darkness of the streets. Flames blazed through village huts on all sides of her. Screams lifted into the skies that burned scarlet from the streaks of red clouds overhead. The crimson, striated marks in her skin pulsed with a glow, her poison magic burning and ebbing within her, ready to be released should she need to use it.

It felt as if hours had already passed, but it might have only been minutes. The Hawkers had descended on them so quickly and without warning.

"We're almost there!" Theo shouted as he tugged her by the hand through winding streets filled with chaos and bloodshed.

Two Hawkers jumped out from behind a larger hut and lunged at them with curved swords, and they skidded to a stop in the dirt.

She reacted from instinct alone as her weary body moved with the quick grace of her people. She ducked beneath the swing and thrust her obsidian dagger into the man's chest. Blood sprayed her face, momentarily blinding her. Before she could remove her dagger and sprint away, the singing of metal from a sheath reached her ears, giving her enough warning to sidestep.

She wasn't fast enough.

Something sharp stabbed through her side, and she cried out at the burning agony that followed. Her head swayed with dizziness. The world tilted one way and then the other. But as she'd been taught growing up, she never relinquished her grip on her weapon as she endured the pain and spun around.

The red stripes on her skin glowed as she called upon her own magic, and with a desperate burst of energy, she struck her hand against the second Hawker's chest. The green, wispy poison of her power smashed into him. He screamed as his body crashed into the dwelling behind him, her poison eating into his flesh until he slumped to the ground and lay still. Most Hawkers were immune to Infernal poison, but this one clearly wasn't.

When she pivoted on her heel to face the next attacker, she found three Hawkers dead in the street while her brother stood over their bodies, his blade bloodied red and his crimson stripes pulsing with power. One of his short black horns was halfway broken, and she might have lamented with him at the devastating loss if their lives hadn't been at stake.

"Come on." He reached for her again, and despite the agony roaring through her side, she stumbled after him as they finally reached the gnarled black trees surrounding their village. Branches wove tight around one another, creating thick walls difficult to navigate for those who hadn't grown up in Crotona and played in these forests as children. They were relying on the fact that they were less likely to get lost than their human and fae enemies who pursued them.

Together, they wove in and out of the trees, ducked beneath gnarled branches and twisting vines. Shouts echoed behind them, followed by swiping blades and distant curses.

Hawkers were following them.

With their depleting magic and energy stores, they likely stood little chance at survival. Judging by the tick of Theo's jaw, he believed it, too.

Still, they hurried through the forest at a brisk pace until they reached the hovel they used to play in as children, crafted of woven branches and makeshift furniture of rotted bark.

The moment her brother released her hand, she groaned as she sank to her knees and clutched her wound. Her fingers came back bloodied black. All she wanted was to lay down and rest. Just for a minute.

"Stay conscious," her brother ordered as he lightly patted her cheek. "Stay with me, you hear?"

He didn't wait for an answer as he turned and rummaged through shelves lined with a variety of glass jars and vials. Through bleary eyes, she watched as he laid out a series of dried herbs and oils in the shape of a circle.

After he smashed a vial filled with lilybane extract onto the ground directly in the middle of the circle, he murmured several words under his breath to activate the portal.

The circle lit up with orange and red light like fire. But instead of the orange embers burning them, they provided a sense of hope through the pain and devastation lying in wait the moment they closed their eyes.

Without a single moment's hesitation, she took her brother's hand, and together, they jumped through the portal.

For a moment, it felt as if they were thrown upside down like being tossed beneath the ocean by a strong wave. A rush of chilly air raked across her body as black roots and branches transitioned into lush green forests and chokingly humid air.

She clutched at her throat when she suddenly found herself unable to breathe. The upper realm was too light and cold and humid when she preferred the heaviness and warmth of the lower realm.

A similar orange and red portal to their own opened up several paces away, not giving them the chance for their bodies to adjust and to catch their breath.

Again, they scrambled in the opposite direction, each running as fast as their weary legs could carry them.

The Hawkers' portal wouldn't be able to sustain more than a couple men at a time, which gave Avra and Theo the advantage. If they could find a safe place to hide, they could still escape them.

But she was so exhausted…

Keep going, Theo seemed to say with a single glance of his lightly glowing eyes, and with the encouragement, she found enough strength to run through the darkness of the forest, across two rivers to help hide their tracks, and over the rough, rocky terrain of a cliffside before they entered forest once more.

Finally, they collapsed on soft grass beneath the shadows of several leafy trees. She clutched her side once again, wincing when she found her ripped and torn clothing covered in sticky blood.

Her head spun, and she felt like retching as the memories of the past horrifying hour assaulted her mind. Fire. Screams. Death.

Rather than waiting to catch his breath, Theo began dragging branches and foliage closer to her, clearly to hide her from view.

"What about you?" she asked with trembling breaths when all her concentration lay fixed on keeping the darkness in her mind at bay.

He rested another leafy branch beside her and unsheathed two daggers. "I can't let them take you. You're our last Matriarch."

"And you're my brother."

Slowly, he shook his head and blinked sad orange eyes. "It matters not anymore. My duty is to you as my Matriarch, and not as my sister." He gave her arm a gentle, reassuring squeeze. "Stay here," he ordered in a gruff tone. "Don't move until I return."

"What if you never come back?" she whimpered.

"I will. I swear it."

And then she watched with a heavy heart as he rushed away from her and was swallowed by thick green and brown trees.

By the minute, her body grew colder even as her lungs adjusted to the uncomfortable upper realm atmosphere. With each passing moment of terrible silence, her wound ached more and more as her shock slowly dissipated into worry.

Tears streaked down Avra's face what felt like hours later as she hunched within the shadows of the bushes, still trying to conceal herself from view. Her brother hadn't returned, even though the sun had long since disappeared, replaced by the burning silver sphere in the sky so different from the two red moons from her own realm.

She clamped her hands over her mouth to keep herself from shouting out to the darkness in her growing panic.

If her brother hadn't returned by now…

She feared he was dead.

The slightest scuffle down the path reached her ears, and her entire body froze, alarm clamming up in her throat. She dared not take a single breath, even as her pulse hammered through her veins and her lungs screamed in protest.

They were going to find her. And just like the rest of her village, they would kill her, too.

Someone rounded the corner of the path with another scuffle of their boots. She released a muffled scream and scrambled backward until her shoulders hit the tree behind her.

A chill shot through her blood and straight into her chest, immobilizing her as her fear finally won. Each of her limbs froze, and her head suddenly became unbearably light as she struggled to remain conscious when her body wanted to succumb to darkness.

But the person who stepped into her line of sight wasn't a hunter. He was…well, she wasn't quite sure what he was. She hadn't seen one before.

The man stood tall, towering high above her with pointed ears, blond hair, and blue eyes that contained a slit-like pupil, similar to the desert serpents back home. A pack rested over one shoulder, and he held a book beneath his other arm as he stared down at her with brows furrowed. It was as if he could see well in the dark, his gaze honing in on her immediately rather than scrambling through midnight shadows for her form.

"By the shadows," the man gasped in the upper realm language, dropping his pack to the forest floor. "An Infernal. I've never seen one before in the flesh." He grimaced. "Ah, forgive me. It was not my intention to be rude."

He held a hand out to her, but she flinched away, hissing as the movement pulled on the wound in her side. His gaze immediately jumped toward the black blood seeping through her clothing. It surprised her that he spotted that, too. She trudged through the pain as she picked up her knife and held it in trembling fingers.

"Stay away!" she warned in his language, having learned it in intensive studies with her mother and tutors. Although most of her magic had long since flickered out, a small amount managed to break through her exhaustion. The red stripes on her arms glowed, and green wisps traveled down her arm, over her hand, and wove around her blade. A single slice would poison him.

But instead of scrambling away from her, his mouth pulled up into a soft smile as he crouched and held out a palm to her, his long fingers open in invitation. "It seems as if you've suffered through something terrible. Let me help you."

"I don't need your help," she said through chattering teeth. "My brother is coming for me."

He seemed to see straight through her uncertainty, as his expression fell into one of sympathy. "Where is he?"

"Fighting off our enemies. They...they..." She gritted her teeth as anger and fear consumed her. "My village was attacked. My family is dead. All I have left is my brother."

Why was she pouring herself out to this man? This...this...stranger? She knew nothing about him. But... He exuded kindness and safety. And she knew if she stayed out here hiding any longer, she might catch sickness or infection.

As if coming to the same conclusion, he said, "I can shelter you from your enemies, and then we will find your brother. I promise." His soft smile returned. "My name is Killian Graves. I'm a Shadow fae, and my school, Darkest Star Arcane, is a safe haven for all magical beings and creatures alike. Come with me, and my wife and I will provide you with food and shelter."

Avra stared at his offered hand before her gaze jumped to his face. The man looked to be ten or fifteen years older than her, and she detected nothing but honesty and sincerity in his tone.

He was safe. And she had no choice but to blindly trust him when the alternative would be far worse should her enemies catch her.

The magic in her hand cut off abruptly from her supply, leaving her desperate and destitute. With trembling fingers, she tucked her dagger away before placing her hand into his.

With a strong heave, he helped her to her feet, shrugged off his long, black coat, and draped it over her shoulders. The lingering warmth from his body seeped into her, but it still wasn't enough to eliminate the chill from fear and blood loss.

"You'll be safe with me," he murmured. "I promise."

"How?" Her teeth chattered through every word. "Someone will recognize me for what I am."

"Our first order of business is to take care of that wound. And the second…" His mouth quirked up at the side. "We'll find you a suitable glamour to hide your identity."

When he offered his hand again, she didn't hesitate this time as she gripped his fingers. And like a sudden whoosh of breath leaving her lungs, a ripple of dark magic exuded from his body, similar to that of some of her Elders from her village when they shadewalked.

They melted into the shadows, became the shadows, and with uncertainty following in her wake, she left the pain of her past behind.

2

"WE DID IT, POPS," Nox Klaver whispered under his breath as he clutched the vial holding his father's ashes within his palm. "We made it."

He stood on top of a bench at the Darkest Star Arcane, a magic school for fae and humans alike, and turned in a full circle to take in his surroundings.

An enormous fountain lay in the center of the courtyard surrounded by cobblestone walkways and tall buildings consisting of classrooms, lecture halls, and male and female dormitories. A variety of plants and trees dotted the landscape with foreign, ethereal beauty, almost as if the headmaster had made sure to hunt down at least one species of each to include in the backdrop of Darkest Star.

He spotted several plants that glowed within the nighttime atmosphere, and far more that he recognized from his years of traveling over the fae kingdoms.

He extracted the chalk pencil from behind his pointed Shadow fae ear and opened his sketchbook, quickly tracing his view with several dozen fast, expert strokes. One picture for every place he visited to document his travels with his father and his sort-of sister and friend, Leni, both who had always wanted to see the world.

A pit of guilt formed in his stomach at the thought of Leni. After his father's passing, he'd left her to fend for herself. He should never have abandoned her. But what choice had he had?

He pushed thoughts of her from his mind and focused on his surroundings.

The corner of his mouth quirked up in a grin when several ladies passed by beneath the blue light of a glowing orb resting within a tall brazier. Two of them had long, pointed Sun fae ears while another had long ears with a slight droop to mark them as a Forest fae. They glanced at him, then at each other, and giggled as they hurried on their way toward one of the lecture halls.

Hopping down from the bench, his grin lingered as he stared after them, excitement alighting in his chest. So many female students and so much time to woo them. Well, at least until he finished what he came here to do. Until then… It was going to be a *fun* year.

Dozens of students trailed one after the other toward the lecture hall, and Nox finally followed when he had his fill of the landscape. It felt surreal to find himself surrounded by hundreds of magic users like himself. Not only to get accepted into the school located in Skaad, one of the ten provinces in the Shadow Kingdom, but to also join a class or two taught by the Lord who ruled over this particular province.

Lord Killian Graves.

He flipped his black curls away from his forehead and stuffed his sketchbook in his bag as he filed into the large building with the other students. The entire structure hit him with its magnificence.

High-vaulted ceilings. Black and silver embellishments on the furniture, walls, and hundreds of seats. A masterpiece painting emblazoned on the ceiling.

He took a moment to appreciate the fine brush strokes depicting the original ten Lords of the land standing in a circle and sharing a swirling black mass of power between them. The lines... The expressive details... The sheer *talent*...

Although he had no idea what he wanted to do with the rest of his life, he thought painting the world didn't seem like such a bad idea.

Just as he found a seat, a girl across the room wiggled her fingers in a coy wave, her Shadow fae slitted pupils growing larger with interest. At first, he thought she was waving at someone else behind him. But then she blew a kiss, and a pink heart created from magic floated across the room and poofed across his face. A lingering perfume filled his nostrils with the light impact.

In response, he grinned back, planning to catch up with her later to learn her name. He normally enjoyed a good chase, but the ones who chased him were enjoyable for a short time, at least, before he often grew bored.

The excited chatter in the room died down suddenly when all the seats filled, and Nox snapped his attention to the front of the room to find a tall, blond Shadow fae approaching the lectern on the stage. Everything about him exuded confidence and excitement from the sharp way he dressed in a black suit and red neck cloth to his squared shoulders to the intense blue stare that seemed to miss nothing as he scanned the crowd.

He couldn't help himself as he gazed up at the headmaster in awe.

Professor Killian Graves. One of the most powerful Shadow fae to walk the entire Shadow Kingdom of Katalle.

"Good evening, students," Professor Graves addressed the room at large with a smile, "and welcome to Darkest Star Arcane."

Whistles and cheers lifted into the air, and Nox clapped excitedly along. No matter the underhanded means in which he'd applied to the school, he'd earned the right to be here, and he couldn't wait to show off what he could do with his magic.

Continuing, the headmaster said, "This is our second school year since opening, and we couldn't be more excited for another successful season of magic and academics. Some of you may be more adept at one area over the other, but rest assured, we will provide a large variety of education to meet each individual need of our students."

Nox's gaze was drawn to a woman with copper hair, using her hands to translate with sign language in the front corner of the room while a one-year-old boy played with toys near her feet. Although he'd never seen her before, he already recognized her as Professor Graves' wife. Apparently, she was an Ocean fae. A mermaid. Legs on land and fins in the sea.

Lyyli Graves, if he remembered correctly. Mer were more difficult to discern from other races when they took on similar outward characteristics as humans. Although she looked like a human, she was anything but.

The faint whispers of a story came to mind. He'd heard she'd been cursed and couldn't speak for most of her life. Until Professor Graves broke the curse. Or something like that. It explained why she knew sign language so well when she wasn't deaf and no longer mute.

With so many people in the room, the temperature rose a bit too high. He rolled his white sleeves up to his elbows to reveal one of the black designs rolling across his skin. It was permanent like a tattoo. But rather derived from ink and needles, it was born from a curse.

The mark drew several curious stares when a few people seemed to recognize it for what it was. But he wasn't ashamed of it. Rather, it made for a good, if not embarrassing, story stemming from when he'd broken off a relationship with a witch. In her anger, she'd forever cursed him to speak in rhymes every time he defeated a foe.

The curse mark on his chest, on the other hand...

He clenched his jaw and returned his attention to the front of the room, not wanting to miss a single word from the headmaster's mouth.

Professor Graves gestured to the room at large.

"I know it may seem silly to some, but one of the things we make a priority here is sleep. Some of your professors will be nocturnal, like myself. Others will be diurnal. The school will be constantly in use from morning till night. That's why..." He held up what appeared to be a smooth black rock with a white symbol etched into its surface. "We will provide each student with one of these, called a Kip Stone. Once activated, it will block out all sounds outside your immediate space. Very useful for sleeping and even studying." He gave them each a stern look. "Which I expect all of you to do."

Everyone in the audience laughed, and Nox couldn't help but chuckle along. So far, he liked the headmaster. The man wasn't as no-nonsense as he'd expected, but he did expect a certain amount of responsible autonomy during their time at the academy.

He went over the rules at the academy such as no hurting others unless during combat training where a Sun fae healer would be present. No bullying. No racism toward others. Those who received low grades would have chances to improve and receive plenty of help from professors, but in the end, a lack of effort could result in someone losing their spot at the academy.

When he mentioned that men and women would have separate dorm buildings and that sexual relations were not permitted, this rule received plenty of groans and lamenting.

Nox snorted, knowing full well that it would happen anyway no matter the board's best efforts. And judging by the defeated look in the headmaster's eyes, he likely knew it couldn't be wholly prevented.

The man continued, "Members of the opposite sex are allowed in the dorm rooms, but not after curfew. We encourage use of our library and grounds for studying and group projects."

After going over several more rules and explaining classes, buildings, and schedules, he gripped either side of the lectern and offered a beaming smile. "And with that, I welcome you all to Darkest Star Arcane, and I look forward to seeing many of you in my class."

The audience cheered and clapped. Excitement alighted in Nox's own chest at the numerous possibilities that awaited him, at the chance to become anything and anyone.

At the chance to put his past forever behind him.

After his assignment was finished.

He reminded himself that he wasn't a student here. Not truly. But it didn't mean he couldn't pretend for a short while.

He stood from his seat as the rumble of voices, laughter, and excitement bounced off the wall and into his ears. Classes started tomorrow, and he already looked forward to finding his dorm room, meeting his roommate, and beginning yet another new adventure.

Making his way down the aisle, he glanced up, and it was as if the entire world halted as his gaze landed on a gorgeous woman with her arms crossed, a leg propped against the wall behind her. She already wore the school uniform with a navy blue pleated skirt touching below her knee and a white button-up blouse beneath a blue blazer. Her shoulder-length brown hair curled lightly at the ends, which accentuated the soft curve of her jaw and the plumpness of her lips. The intense blue of her eyes watched everyone warily, her body language guarded.

A challenge.

And he very much enjoyed a good challenge.

But before he managed to approach her, she slipped out of the room and outside into the darkness.

His jaw clenched with determination as he weaved in and out of the crowd, ignoring several ladies waving to get his attention. The cool night air entered his lungs as he glanced wildly around for the woman.

There!

He found her walking briskly around the fountain and toward the female dorms, but her short stride was no match for his long legs. He crossed the distance between them in only a few paces.

"Was it just me, or were you eyeing me across the room?" he said with a grin, trying to reach for his natural charm while keeping pace with her. He expected her to stop and refute him, giving him the chance to go in for the kill. But…

It was as if she hadn't heard him and kept on walking.

"Excuse me, miss." He placed his hand on her shoulder.

Unexpectedly, she spun around with lightning fast speed and slammed her fist into his gut. He choked on his next breath and doubled over, momentarily seeing stars in his vision. For a moment, he couldn't draw air, and his ears rang incessantly. But not quite enough to drown out the vicious, mocking laughter surrounding him and the quiet, hurried footsteps as the woman darted in the opposite direction.

He glanced up to find the tail end of her skirts disappearing around the bend while dozens of people stared at him, laughing and pointing and whispering amongst themselves.

Another male student guffawed and slapped him on the shoulder. "She really got you good, didn't she? An ex-lover?"

Nox's lips curled into a snarl to hide the fluster and humiliation crawling up his neck. Anger and annoyance created an even hotter burn as the flush grew warmer across his skin. He didn't even know the woman and she'd managed to make him look like a fool in front of many of their peers. Without a single apology, too. What had he done to deserve a sucker punch to the gut?

After a moment, the other student asked, "You all right?"

"Fine," he wheezed, trying to straighten when he wasn't sure if he was going to pass out or retch. He tried to take a deep breath through his nose to hide his discomfort. Unfortunately, she'd known where to punch him for optimal damage. He needed to lie down. And maybe vomit and sleep. Not necessarily in that order.

When he tried to casually walk away as if nothing had happened, the other student fell into step beside him as they made their way toward the male dorms. "You're Nox, right? I overheard someone saying your name in orientation. I'm Hans. Looks like we're roommates."

Hans held out a piece of parchment with a list of his classes and his room assignment at the top. The room number matched his own. He held back another groan of humiliation. This was not the first impression he'd wanted to make.

The moment the stars at the edges of his vision faded, he took in his new roommate with renewed clarity. The man was a Shadow fae, like him, with chin-length, blond wavy hair and ice-blue eyes. However, the slight length and droop to his ears suggested he was part Shadow fae, part Forest fae.

They shook hands, and it took all his concentration not to keel over and vomit in the bushes. Who in shadow's glory knew how to land a punch like that?

As if reading his thoughts, Hans explained, "No one knows who she is aside from her first name. Avra something or other. Professor Graves took a shining to her over the summer and took her in. I have nothing of note about her other than she's odd."

"You don't say," he ground out through clenched teeth. If only to himself, he admitted it irked him that she was on the headmaster's good side already. What had she done to deserve his recognition? "How do you even know all of this? Didn't you just get here, same as the rest of us?"

"I've been here for a couple weeks already," Hans said with a shrug before stuffing his hands into his pockets. "My talent is remembering people. I know who most everyone is by connecting an attribute to a name and face. I recognized you immediately."

"How?"

"Your curse mark." He gestured to Nox's arm. "People talk. I don't know anyone else who has one of those."

Nox kept the fact that he had two to himself. Surely, if they were to be roommates, Hans would find out about it soon enough, anyway.

"And this girl? She really just came out of nowhere?"

They reached the male dorms, and while the laughter and goofiness and ruckus in the hallways would have enticed him to join in, his head still swam with embarrassment and an overwhelming sense of injustice.

Climbing the stairs to the second story, Hans unlocked their dorm and they stepped inside. The room was a simple setup with a wall separating each side for privacy, a bed tucked in the corner, and a desk resting below the window overlooking the fountain. A single portmanteau rested beside the bed, and he quickly opened it to make sure all of his weapons were stashed inside. Thankfully, he found nothing missing in the heavy mountain of his daggers, potions, and knives, and his sword even lay across the desk, seeming relatively untouched. At least the staff members had delivered his belongings here as promised.

He reckoned he would spend very little time in his room, as his need to move and train and travel prevented him from staying in one place for too long.

Finally, Hans answered, "Sure did come out of nowhere. No family as far as I can tell. I wasn't even positive she was fae at first, as I've never seen the shape of her ears, but I witnessed her doing magic in the hallway. I think. So, she can't be human, surely. Some strange magic it was. I don't know what the blazes she is."

"Well, whatever she is, I don't care. She can go on her merry way."

Hans snorted. "You sure you don't want to try wooing her again? It worked so well the first time."

Nox cut his roommate a scathing glare before picking up his sword and unsheathing it halfway to inspect the blade. The weapon had aided him on more than one occasion during his travels, and it looked as if it needed a bit of time with the grinding wheel.

A grin spread across his face as he glanced out the window at the people milling about on the school grounds. It was time to accomplish what he'd come here to do. Only then could his father truly rest within the injustice of his ashes.

He wouldn't rest until the Infernal Matriarch was dead.

AVRA RAPPED QUICKLY on Headmaster Graves' door leading to his office, stopping only for a moment to grimace at the foreign sight of the pale hands and stubby fingernails of her glamour. The blue of her eyes shocked her whenever she passed a mirror. Her lack of stripes, the foreignness of her brown hair, the absence of a tail and horns… There was a wrongness to her body that caused her skin to crawl. She felt naked and exposed, confident that everyone could see through the lie to what really lay beneath the deception.

She knocked again, this time louder, tapping her foot impatiently when Killian didn't answer the door. She tapped her cheek next and frowned when her curved, human-like fingernails grazed her skin in the most unsatisfying way. Until now, she'd never known that such a small thing as losing her sharper black Infernal fingernails would fill her with grief.

Lifting her hand to knock again, she jumped when someone reached past her and unlocked the door. She spun around to find a grin spread across Killian's pale Shadow fae face.

"I wasn't in the office, in case you were wondering," he jested, opening the door wide open for her. "I've been in the lecture hall."

She sighed. Of course. After his orientation speech, she should have known he wouldn't have sequestered himself in his office so quickly.

He shut the door behind them, rummaging through piles of parchment instead of taking a seat at his desk. He rarely sat, she noticed. He was always busy. Always on the go.

"Did you need something?" he asked.

"I can't stay here!" she blurted, warmth burning her face when the stripes hidden beneath her glamour heated with her rising emotions. She recalled the way that man had grabbed her outside the lecture hall. Her first instinct had been to protect herself. When she'd punched him, everyone had laughed. Back home, no one would have *dared* to laugh at the Matriarch. This culture in comparison was confusing and disorienting and she hated trying to adapt to something completely foreign. "I should be out there looking for my brother."

She gestured toward the window. But even as she did, an intense fear climbed up her spine at the thought of facing those Hawkers again. Her mother had died. Her *Ikshwa* had been killed. She stood no chance.

But if her brother were still alive? If some of her people had survived?

Lord Graves offered a sympathetic yet sincere smile as he briefly glanced up from his stacks of parchment he now sorted into several different piles. Each time he set a paper down, the scent of new parchment lifted into the air, creating a nostalgic feeling deep in her belly for her books back home. "I understand how you feel, Avra. But considering what happened in Crotona… It's dangerous for you to leave. My soldiers are doing their best at trying to track down your brother—"

"And I appreciate it more than you know. But they've found nothing."

The expression on her face must have been absolutely pitiful for Killian to set his papers aside and give her his full attention. "We can only do so much in the upper realm. We'd glean more information in Crotona, but visiting the lower realm could kill my men by simply being exposed to the harsher environment without a way to protect themselves. *Yet,*" he added. As a master at concocting potions, he'd tried solution after solution without success. Whatever method Hawkers used to breathe and adapt to Crotona air, they certainly kept the secret close.

"You really want that alliance with our people," she jested feebly.

He chuckled. "We hardly know anything about Infernals aside from nasty rumors that I know aren't true." He cleared his throat. "Well, after meeting you, that is. I know you don't actually eat children for supper or bathe in rivers of blood."

She almost rolled her eyes. *Almost.* "Are those the lies the Hawkers are spreading about us?"

The Hawkers were blasted mercenaries who specialized in killing creatures in the lower realm, including Infernals. They'd never before dared to conduct such a large-scale attack on her people. When they were motivated by coin, she could only guess someone had paid them a great deal to attack like that. But why? And who was behind the deep coffers?

"After what I've heard from you, I genuinely think that's what the Hawkers believe of your kind."

Someone knocked on the door, and Lyyli, Killian's wife, slipped inside with her one-year-old boy sitting on her hip. She glanced between the two of them and offered a radiant smile to her husband. "I hope I'm not interrupting. I know you haven't eaten all day, love, busy as you've been. I brought you something to eat."

Lyyli set a box down on the desk. Killian cupped her cheek, pulled her closer, and placed a lingering kiss on her lips. Avra couldn't help but stare. Fae culture was far different from that of her own. In Crotona, they bonded to those who showed strength and resilience. She didn't know anyone who actually loved their partners. Not in the same way Killian clearly loved his wife. The idea of love was foreign...

But wholly beautiful.

Her cheeks burned as she forced herself to glance away from the sweet display of affection.

Killian continued to hold Lyyli's hand even after the kiss, foreignly unapologetic for giving into the weakness of the heart. "I ask you to be patient for a little while longer, Avra. We'll find him. But in the meantime, it may be beneficial for you to attend classes at Darkest Star Arcane and get to know other fae."

Avra massaged her temples as frustration deeply vexed her. This air. This body. Not knowing the fate of her people. How could she stay here safe within the borders of the school while her people may be suffering?

Unfortunately, Killian was right. It was too dangerous for her to leave. She had to trust him. "All right," she agreed. "Does that mean you will give me a roommate?"

Lyyli laughed and shared an amused look with her husband. "Judging by that tone, I'd think we'd have better luck housing a field mouse with a Shadow horse."

Killian shook his head. "We won't change your living arrangements. You'll still have your own room. But classes start tomorrow, and I hope you'll attend."

"I will." The ache in her head only seemed to grow worse by the second. This felt like a waste of time. But what choice did she have?

With a dip of her head, she exited the office and made her way toward the library. Surely, there was something she hadn't yet found in the thousands of tomes at her disposal. Perhaps there was something she'd missed.

The first day as a student was nerve-wracking. Everything was different here. The people. The culture. The atmosphere. And Avra found it difficult to navigate such foreign obstacles. From the way people spoke to their ranges of their hierarchy threw her off balance. To read about these people in books was far different from seeing them and living among them in person.

As she sat in the library with a book open on the desk, she flipped quickly through the pages on the chapter about magic used to locate someone. Her own poison magic was limited, but with the right potion and the correct spoken words, she could imitate what others could do with innate ability.

Out of the eight different methods on the page before her, she mentally checked off number six when dreaming of

Theo's location last night had not worked. But number seven… Surely, this would work.

She lifted her attention from her book and glanced around the room. Several small groups of fae lingered in the library, waiting until the start of their next class in just a few more minutes. She was getting better at recognizing them for what they were by the shape of their ears. Forest fae had long, droopy ears. Sun fae sported long and straight ears, and many had tattoos ranging in colors from gold to bronze to silver. Shadow fae had short, pointed ears, their eyes containing slitted black pupils like a snake. Humans and mer were more difficult to tell apart on land, as they both had legs and rounded ears. But the humans were far more awkward than the graceful and bubbly merfolk.

Many types of fae and humans sat at desks or spoke quietly to one another in corners. No one glanced her way.

Taking a deep breath, she pulled out a handkerchief from her bag and carefully unwrapped it to reveal several preserved herbs within that she'd clipped from the greenhouse or had scavenged from the garden. And then she thoroughly copied the list from the seventh method in the book, trying to be as exact with her ingredients as possible. Even the smallest deviation could ruin a potion.

Pulling out a small knife tucked safely into her blazer pocket, she used the sharp end to strip a piece of bark into the vial. The scent of nutmeg greeted her nose, lodging a pit of nostalgia in her throat. Some of the bark in Crotona smelled like this, too.

Next, she added a few beads of lavender, crushed amber leaf, and a solution made of equal parts morning dewdrops and goldenflower extract. The only thing remaining…

A drop of blood from the person she wanted to locate. She didn't have that, so she used the next best thing.

Again, she glanced over her shoulder, making sure no one noticed her actions before she pricked her finger with the knife and dripped a speck of her own black blood into the mixture, watching as it bubbled and hissed within the vial.

She quickly sucked on her finger to hide the color of the blood, her stripes heating beneath her glamour with momentary fear. Hawkers hadn't found her yet, but she didn't want to do anything to give herself away, nonetheless.

For a moment, she glanced with panic down at her arm when she thought her glamour might have slipped. It hadn't. She wasn't sure why, but she'd thought for certain her blood would have been red to aid her glamour. It wasn't. Which meant the glamour only showed on the surface.

When the panic refused to abate, she mentally counted the days since she'd taken her last glamour potion. Eight days. It usually lasted around two weeks, and she still had two more in her pocket before she needed to seek out Killian for more. They were complicated to make, and she couldn't risk messing it up and risking exposing herself.

When her finger ceased bleeding, she corked the vial and shook the ingredients within. When the potion transitioned from a muddy brown to a dark purple, she unstopped the vial and lifted it to her face, wafting the fumes beneath her nose.

According to the book, the fumes were supposed to incite a vision of the person she was scrying for. But as the seconds passed into minutes and nothing happened...

Defeat slumped her shoulders as she tucked the vial away and ran her hands through her hair—an uncomfortably foreign sensation without her horns creating an obstacle for her fingers.

Mentally, she crossed method seven off her list. Using her own blood had been a stretch, but still, she'd hoped...

Method eight consisted of using a Sun fae's right ear and the carcass of a fox, and she wasn't about to hunt those down unless Killian was certain such a method could work. She'd try anything at this point.

"Have you seen that new Shadow fae in room 305?" a girl tittered to her friends across the room as Avra packed up her belongings. "Do you think Nox will give me a chance?"

"You are hopeless, Maya," one of her friends said.

"And engaged," another supplied.

"Oh, hush," Maya said with a flippant hand gesture, showing off the bronze tattoo on her wrist in the shape of a swirling flower. "Brody doesn't have to find out. It's only a bit of fun."

Avra's eyebrows furrowed as she tried to wrap her mind around such a casual attitude toward courtship. In her culture, her *Ikshwa* could be put to death for being unfaithful. Were other cultures so flippant about relationships? Or was Maya a special case?

Shaking off the uneasy feeling, she finished packing her things and strode toward the exit. But then she internally cringed and tried not to squeak in mortification when she noticed a human sitting at a desk and writing in his book. Actually writing! Defiling the pages with his ink and sloppy handwriting.

She bit her knuckle and turned away quickly to keep herself from interfering. The poor book was already desecrated. There was nothing she could do to save it now.

Clutching her own book close as if that could make up for what she'd just witnessed, she walked down the hallway leading to her first class of the day. She passed a mirror within an ornate gold frame to her right and quickly glanced away, not liking what she saw when the sight of her reflection created discomfort in her belly.

Sure, Killian had helped her find a suitable glamour that still looked like herself but in a more fae-like form, but she didn't like the color of her skin or the absence of orange in her eyes.

It's only for a short while, she reassured herself as she released a long breath. Until she found a lead on her brother, she was good and stuck at the academy. She was immensely grateful to Killian for allowing her to stay. It was the only place she could possibly feel safe when Hawkers were out for her blood.

At the thought of Theo, she clutched her book tighter to her chest as she hurried to her first class, if only to blend in with the rest of the students at the academy and not draw unnecessary attention to herself.

Upon entering the room, her heart sank when she realized Killian had not yet arrived. Rather, several students surrounded a desk, talking and laughing with one another and casting wary glances in her direction.

Back home, her peers would have inclined their heads or touched their fingers to their lips in fealty to their new Matriarch. But she received no such greeting here. She was an outsider. A nobody. Despite how much she longed to fit in, her goal wasn't to make friends. It was to find her brother and save what was left of her people.

It's too late, her mind whispered miserably. *I am only one person against dozens of Hawkers.*

She took a seat near the back of the room and unpacked her bag, neatly stacking another book on top of the first. When she next reached for her bottle of ink, she gasped when someone bumped into her desk, sending her books flying and crashing to the ground.

Her gaze darted up to find the man she'd punched yesterday smirking at her with revenge burning in the dark depths of his green eyes.

"Whoops," he said, though his expression told her it was anything but an accident. "I didn't see your desk there."

Without another word, and certainly without picking up the books he'd scattered on the floor, he joined a group across the room, charming each person immediately with a strategically placed phrase from his pert little mouth. The group laughed, and one of the girls flirtatiously touched his arm.

Fury blazed in Avra's eyes as she glared at the back of his dark curls, remembering last night's incident all too well. He'd grabbed her. What had he expected after grabbing a woman in the dead of night who was already paranoid about being hunted? That he would walk away without getting punched?

Perhaps she would have apologized to him, now that she knew he wasn't a Hawker, but he didn't deserve it. Not anymore.

After another dozen people filled the classroom, Professor Graves finally ambled in with a frazzled look on his face. "Excuse my tardiness," he said as he pushed his blond hair out of his eyes and set his briefcase on the desk. "I'm usually very prompt, but my child just took his first steps tonight. I've missed so many firsts that I couldn't possibly pass up the opportunity to experience this one."

Avra smiled softly at the conjured image while other women "awwed" at the sentimentality. Killian had told her he owned several properties and had lived at one of them for most of his life, but ever since opening the school, he had lived here mainly with his wife and child.

Not one to dally much, Killian took the roll before standing at the front of the class with a book open in his hands.

"Nox, can you tell me the difference between those born with magic and those who learn it? This is from the required reading material stated in the syllabus that everyone should have read over the summer."

Several whispers filled the classroom, followed by a few quiet groans. Nox's mouth pinched, giving away the fact that he hadn't read it along with seemingly many others in the class.

"Today is the first day of school," Nox said instead of answering with a casual shrug of his shoulder. "I'm not sure anyone is prepared to answer such a question."

Nods of agreement accompanied his words, the sheep around him following him to the slaughterhouse. He was a natural-born leader. Charismatic. Charming. But stupid. How could she possibly have thought he was a Hawker?

"I don't know…" Avra mused, meeting his hard gaze unflinchingly. "For someone spending a pretty farthing on their education, you would think one would take the welcome packet and syllabuses a little more seriously than treating them like a flimsy piece of parchment."

"Oooooh," the room chorused, glancing back and forth between the two of them.

Nox turned more fully in his seat to better face her. "And I suppose you read everything required in the syllabus? What, do you have nothing better to do with your time?"

The man beside him snorted. Others laughed. Avra refused to be cowed.

Honestly, she was only here for the short-term as she tried to locate her brother's whereabouts. She hadn't read anything in the syllabus, as she wasn't supposed to be a true student, but that didn't mean she didn't know the answer to the question.

Turning to the professor, she stated, "Those born with magic have a more intuitive ability to draw upon their power while those not born with magic have to develop those instincts by practice and discipline."

Killian nodded. "Very good. This is where I would like to start. Let's talk more about..."

His voice faded to the background as Nox's nose twitched, his glare intensifying by the second before he turned back around in his seat and didn't glance back again.

It looked as if she'd already made an enemy when she was supposed to blend into the background. And he wasn't even a Hawker. But it was no matter. She hated people like

Nox. And every now and again, they needed to be put in their place.

Unfortunately, she had a feeling this was only the beginning of their battle.

"We shouldn't skip class," the girl whispered, her gaze darting over Nox's shoulder to the students passing around the corner of the Magical Creatures class building. The shadows from the nearby trees shielded them from prying eyes. He couldn't remember her name. Sadie or Sophie. Sandra? "We'll get in so much trouble."

"You only get in trouble if you get caught." He gave the girl—Sandra, he decided—what he knew was a charming smile and leaned close enough for her to get the idea that he'd crossed the line of friendship. Her eyes widened, and her breaths became stilted. *And* he hadn't even touched her yet. Too easy.

She would give him *exactly* what he wanted. Information.

"If only there was someplace we could be alone," he continued with the faintest pout of his bottom lip. He traced a slow circle on the back of her hand, and that was all it took to push her over the edge of her indecision.

"I know a place," she breathed. "But you mustn't tell a soul. My mother would kill me."

When she turned her back to him, he couldn't help but grin triumphantly, especially as she led him around the back, into the dark interior of the building, and down a flight of stairs to the basement. The musty air attacked the first breath he took, and his eyes watered at the relentless scents of hay, fur, and dung. Sandra was the daughter of the Magical Creatures professor. Students weren't allowed in the basement with the dangerous animals, which was exactly why he wanted to search there for the Matriarch. Anywhere off limits was exactly where he wanted to be.

The Hawkers had tracked the Matriarch to the school. They knew she was here and that she hadn't left. Due to the wards outside, no one could get in but students and guests. And, well, he was young enough to pose as a student. Justice was close enough to nearly grasp it in his fingers. He could feel it.

"I apologize for the smell," Sandra said as she took him by the hand and led him down a path with barred cages on either side of him. Several beasts were small and unrecognizable huddled within their shelters. Another looked like a cross between a monkey and a crazed squirrel. And when they came to a cage blocked by a steel wall rather than bars…

"What's in here?" he asked, rapping lightly on the metal.

Instantly, a screech echoed inside, followed by a vicious snarl and something that sounded like a whip of a sharp tail. He'd know that sound anywhere. He'd fought an agrazi with his father deep within the Shadow Kingdom. A cross between a lizard and a spider. Vicious creatures with tails that could stun with a single strike.

"Agrazi," she confirmed. But she seemed far more concerned about *him* than the creatures hiding within the basement. She led him several steps farther before pinning him against the wall and looking up at him beneath fluttering lashes.

Perhaps another day, he might have sought female company. But today? Distraction was the last thing he wanted when he had a goal in mind. He needed to take control of the situation.

Using her smaller stature to his advantage, he reversed the roles and pinned her against the wall instead, grinning at the hitch in her breath. He leaned closer and trailed a finger down her chin.

"This is quite the collection of beasts." He traced the droop of her Forest fae ears next, stunning her into complete silence. "That agrazi tail is sharp. Though, are there any beasts in here with horns? I'd like to see...*more.*" He emphasized that last word, raking his gaze down her body in a suggestive manner. The poor girl latched onto his arm as if struggling to stand. He might have felt bad for using her if his end goal wasn't so important.

She shook her head, her mouth opening and closing as if trying to find the words. Finally, she spoke, "This is all we have down here. Usually poisonous creatures and others more on the violent side. Headmaster Graves used the agrazi venom a couple months ago in a healing tincture. But I'm not sure why. It doesn't work on fae. It would probably kill them instead."

He perked up with interest. "What does it work on?"

"Well..." In the darkness, he noticed her cheeks flaring with color as she briefly glanced toward the agrazi cage. "You'll think I'm insane."

"I won't."

Releasing a deep breath, she answered, "I overheard the headmaster talk about Infernals with one of the healers, though I'm not sure who the healer was. I've only ever read about Infernals in books. I'm not sure they even exist."

Nox's fists clenched, and it took every ounce of his self-control to keep his smile from slipping. He'd had no idea Killian Graves was involved in this. He was a powerful mage. A Shadow Lord himself, one of the most powerful mages in the Shadow lands.

He needed to tread carefully.

The agrazi let out another screech, loud enough for his ears to ring. He pushed away from the wall and flipped his dark blue blazer over his shoulder. "You're right. We shouldn't skip class. Besides, that agrazi is going to give us away."

Disappointment pulled on Sandra's features, and he almost felt bad. *Almost.* But then he reminded himself of the bigger picture as they exited the building, and he made his way to his next class alone. From what he'd uncovered, the Matriarch had been here, injured at one point. She likely was still here, as the Hawkers waiting outside the academy gates had not seen her leave. And even worse, Headmaster Graves was likely hiding her. But where?

He shook the issue aside as he made his way to the outdoor training field, glad he had an outlet to move and distract his burdensome thoughts. Professor Gray—a human who insisted they just call her Gray—split them into twos outside in the training field, pairing him with another man who appeared a few years older than himself.

The scents of leather, metal, and practice wood filled him with excitement, along with clanging swords and shouted orders. He'd missed the years he'd spent training with his father and Leni. Training to fight. To use his magic. To hunt and fish and track. Rarely was there a moment where they sat down to do anything but sleep or eat, as they were always on their feet, always ready for the next adventure.

He swallowed the hard lump of the reminders of his past as he concentrated on fighting against his opponent with the spear. His partner clearly had very little training with the weapon, as he kept dropping it and fumbling with his grip each time Nox struck. Nox could have killed him twelve times over by now should it have been a real fight.

With a huff, he glanced around the field at his peers to find out if anyone could match his level of skill to keep things interesting. Several of the students looked as if they had some semblance of knowledge about what they were doing, but everyone else seemed absolutely hopeless.

His heart dropped to his toes when he spotted a familiar face approaching Gray. Avra's brown hair was tied back into a pigtail on either side of her neck, bringing attention to the intense blue of her eyes and the soft pink of her lips. Her face shape was more prominent than ever without the strands of her hair curling around her shoulders. However, her hair still covered her ears, making it impossible to know what kind of fae she was.

Likely not a Sun or Forest fae, as her ears would probably be poking out of her hair. Her round pupils revealed her lack of Shadow fae heritage, and it was highly unlikely that she was a human. Could she be...mer?

He fisted his hands, annoyance burning brightly within him at his fixation on this woman. He'd despised her since the first moment they'd met.

"Ah, Avra," Gray said as she handed the other woman a spear. "You will be my partner today."

Nox's attention became distracted as he half-heartedly defended against his opponent's flimsy attacks and watched the other two out of the corner of his eye.

"I've never had spear training," Avra said as she smoothed down her black training attire, similar to his own. "I'm used to fighting within closer quarters."

"No matter, that's what this class is for. We'll train with spears for the first couple of weeks and move onto another weapon after."

Avra glanced over her shoulder, her gaze scanning the tree line around the edge of the field. But when her eyes landed on him, she glowered. He glowered right back. Infuriating woman.

The next hour consisted of teaching the basics of spear fighting. Block, block, block, and more blocking. This wasn't what he'd signed up for. He wanted to fight like his life depended on it with others who matched his level of attention and skill. From the look of it, very few of these people knew how to simply hold the spear. Especially Avra.

Her stance was all wrong, and her center of balance was disadvantageous at best. He could likely blow her over with a single breath and she wouldn't be able to catch herself.

His opponent stabbed toward his head, and even with half his attention, he managed to lift his spear to block the attack and then swung his weapon toward the back of the other man's knees. In a single well-aimed swoop, he threw his opponent's legs out from under him, and the other man crashed to the ground on his back.

Gray clapped slowly before gesturing with her head for him to join her at the front of the class. "Who taught you how to spar like that?"

Everyone ceased their fighting. All eyes turned in his direction. With a grin, he spun the spear around his hand and gripped it between his fingers. "My father taught me everything I know."

"Well, then. Show me what you can do."

Cutting in on Avra's training might have filled him with guilt should it have been anyone else. The professor momentarily left the field to retrieve a better spear, and Nox delighted at the humiliation dusting pink across Avra's face as he shooed her away. "Playtime is over, little girl. Let the adults take over."

The surrounding laughter bolstered his confidence, and he even winked at another student giving him a sultry smile while batting her eyelashes at him. Maya, if he remembered correctly. He could use a little fun tonight. And she was pretty enough to catch his eye.

When Gray returned, they faced off with one another, finding the correct stance for the weapon they wielded. And in a blinding motion, the professor attacked.

In a swift movement, Nox blocked with his spear and shoved her backward before they became a dance of strikes, swings, and blocks. He couldn't hold back his grin at the excitement of finding an opponent who could match his skill, who could keep him from growing bored on the field. Even if she was a teacher and a human at that.

After a few more minutes of fighting, Gray held up her hand to signal them to cease their skirmish. In all honesty, they likely could keep going for longer. He was genuinely curious about who would win in a fight between them.

She pointed at him. "You. See me after class. I want you training with our elite fighters."

And then she walked away, leaving him staring after her with a smug grin on his face. This was exactly what he'd wanted. To prove himself capable with a weapon in his hand. To attract the headmaster's attention. To win others' confidence and gain access to places he otherwise couldn't. He had to do this. For his father.

Maya approached and hung on his arm, batting her long eyelashes at him. "Rain and sunlight, you fought so well!"

"Oh, I don't know." He rubbed the back of his neck with mock uncertainty. "I could have done better." But then he placed his fingers on top of hers and squeezed lightly. "Maya, right? They're treating us to a special Sun fae delicacy in the cafeteria tonight. And as it is... I don't have a companion. How about it?"

"Meet you by the fountain after classes?" she asked breathlessly, and he almost laughed. It was too easy.

"See you after classes then." He grinned from ear to ear as he dropped her hand and walked backward. "I'll make sure to—"

He cried out as he tripped, and unable to catch his fall, he flipped over the obstacle and landed on his back. The grass padded the impact enough to keep himself from getting hurt, but the air still whooshed from his lungs, and for a moment, he choked on air, similar to when…

He shot to his feet, only to glare down at Avra who was crouched low to the ground, fiddling with the laces of her shoes. He pointed a menacing finger in her face. "You tripped me on purpose."

"What?" she asked a little too innocently with those large blue eyes and a slight pout to her lips. "I was only tying my laces. It's not my fault you don't watch where you're going."

"My situational awareness is unparalleled."

The innocent pout to her lips only grew more prominent as she stood at her full height, her head only reaching the top of his shoulder. "So it seems."

When she glanced around him, he followed her gaze to find the two girls whispering to one another and giggling, too far away now to hear their conversation but close enough to have seen what had happened.

Avra lowered her voice. "I suppose you two deserve each other."

Nox rolled his eyes and scoffed. "What are you going on about?"

"The girl you successfully wooed. She's already engaged." She flipped her pigtail over her shoulder and turned away from him. "I never thought you'd stoop so low in your conquest for female attention, throwing yourself away for easy sport." She paused only long enough to snub him with a lift of her nose. "I hope whatever you're looking for is worth it."

Without another word, she sauntered in the opposite direction, and rather than glancing back at Maya, his gaze couldn't help but watch the way Avra's hips swayed as she walked, the way the strands of her hair ruffled with the breeze, the way her confident posture drew more gazes than just his own.

His fists clenched at his side as he forcefully tore his attention away from her. He hadn't known Maya was engaged. Besides, the way Avra spoke to him sounded as if she had him all figured out. What did she know? She hardly knew a thing about him.

However, as he fixed his gaze on Maya, she suddenly seemed gray and dull and lacking when she'd been full of color only minutes prior.

"Ugh!" he hissed under his breath as he snatched his belongings from one of the benches. "I can't let her get under my skin. She knows nothing."

Then why did that seed of doubt plant within his mind and begin to sprout? Was he truly throwing himself away because...

A shuddering breath escaped him as he forced himself to finish the thought.

…because of what happened years ago?

He clutched the necklace hanging from his neck and lifted his gaze toward the afternoon skies. He often chose easy women because he never stayed in one place for long. But was that what he thought he deserved? For something light and fun and quick. Never anything real?

"I hate you," he muttered under his breath as he stalked away from the field, only taking a moment to glare over his shoulder at Avra, who now conversed with a Forest fae male, standing far too close to one another as if they already knew the other. "You know nothing of me."

Although he knew he needed to put thoughts of Avra to rest…

His stubborn mind refused to let her go.

TWENTY-FIVE.

The number stared back at Nox from where it rested at the top of the exam paper, emblazoned red like blood. As he flipped through each piece of parchment with a shocked, slack jaw, he found most of the answers marked in red.

Twenty-five correct. Out of *one-hundred.*

He'd failed the exam.

"I missed one," Avra muttered in a disgruntled tone behind him. "Professor!" She raised her hand, and before Graves could make his way toward her, she stood from her seat and approached the front of the room. "I don't agree with this mark. The question asks what type of magic shadewalking derives from. It is not only limited to Shadow fae. It is an art practiced by…"

She trailed off and glanced over the classroom. By now, she'd drawn every eye in the room with her silly outburst. Nox couldn't help but glower. She already had a ninety-nine. A perfect score would make little difference to her overall grade.

Smoothing down her hair, she lowered her voice, but he still caught what she said. "I've read somewhere that shadewalking is an art perfected by many Elders in the Infernal realm."

A cold chill rushed through Nox's blood at the mention of Infernals. His heart slowed. His limbs froze. Each breath trudged through thick sludge and shook through parted lips. Slowly, his stiff arm somehow managed to lift, his fingers shaking as he placed his hand over his heart, right where his curse mark lay beneath his clothing.

Infernals…

His father had been killed by an Infernal. That nasty, cold-blooded killer had taken the very last thing of meaning from Nox's life. They had stolen the light and joy and carefree happiness from him.

They had taken his father from this world, and had left him with nothing.

Breath struggled in and out of his lungs in barely controlled gasps as his hand moved from his heart to the necklace corded around his neck. He had to leave. Before he broke down. Before someone noticed him.

"Huh…" the professor murmured before taking her exam and striking out the question entirely. "It's not every day I get corrected by a student. I will have to look into this further. Until then, I will add a single point to everyone's grades for this exam alone—"

Nox stood abruptly from his desk. "I'm late for something."

With hurried movements, he scooped up his offending exam, shouldered his bag, and escaped the stifling room. The walls seemed to close in on him as he walked briskly down the hallway. Dark flashes of memory assaulted him around every corner, between greeting after greeting from his peers, and they even managed to follow him into the indoor training hall located on the bottom level of building one.

He pressed his back against the cool wall and closed his eyes, allowing the clamor of steel on steel, of wood against wood, to drown out the panic and grief taking root in his body.

For several long moments, he focused on taking deep breaths through his nose and out through his mouth. Just as his father had taught him when faced with the turmoil of his emotions in battle.

Slowly, the panic dissipated, and anger crawled down his body, into his arms, and curled into his fists. When he opened his eyes again, he couldn't stop the fury from blazing in his eyes.

The last thing he'd promised his father was vengeance.

To make things right, he had to kill the Infernal Matriarch.

Weeks had passed since school first started, midterms quickly approaching. And although Avra thought she might have found a sense of safety as the time passed without getting discovered, she found she only became antsy and worried. Somewhere out there, Theo might still be alive.

Today, she had a plan. It was a risky plan, especially when it involved leaving the academy gates. Thus far, her locating potions had not worked. But what if her magic, and perhaps even her blood, was muted because of the glamour?

Even as she thought the words, her hands started trembling as she recalled sharp blades and enemy faces, screams and death. The Hawkers could be waiting for her. But she had to try.

Holding out one of her hands, she turned it every which way, feeling the glamour begin to slip. She had to be strategic about using this potion and quickly consuming a glamour elixir afterward lest one of her peers see her in her Infernal form. She had minutes at best before the glamour would drop.

Across the field, a group of men in the weapons class burst into laughter, drawing her gaze as they pushed and shoved each other in their little pit of chaos. Naturally, her gaze was drawn to the most infuriating among them. She couldn't help but watch the way Nox's face split into a wide grin as he shoved his friends back.

Her attention lingered on the way he fixed his messy hair with the brush of his fingers, to the way he planted one confident fist on his hip. She didn't get it. How did everyone like him so much when he had questionable morals? Was it the infuriating dark curls brushing against his forehead? Or the confident glimmer in his green eyes? Or perhaps it was because he always knew the right thing to say when he was naturally charismatic? Surely, one day his facade would slip, and everyone would see him for who he really was.

Before she managed to ponder on him further, Professor Gray handed each of them a real sword within its scabbard. The weight of it inspired a frown to her lips. She hardly knew how to use a sword when she had regularly trained with daggers.

"Yes, class," Gray called out. "It's a real sword. Sharp, too. So be careful. Today, I'm going to teach you how to patrol. Some of you might end up as guards or soldiers for nobility, or perhaps the world of traveling might find you. But either way, learning your surroundings and how to navigate them and search for possible threats is a boon no matter the situation." She held up a sheathed sword of her own. "When we leave the school grounds, like we will today,

I am required to give you a real weapon for safety reasons. But we should run into no issues so close to the academy."

The forest outside the gates suddenly seemed like a shadowy mass of sinewy magic ready to grab hold of her ankles and pull her into the Infernal abyss in the lower realm. Her throat clogged with fear, and her trembling fingers struggled with strapping the weapon over her hips.

"Scared?" Nox laughed and cast a shadow over her with his bulky, arrogant form. "I can strap it on for you if you're too terrified to step into the spooky forest."

"Shut it, Nox," she warned as she finally managed to secure the strap in place. "I'm not afraid of the forest. It's nothing compared to what we have back home."

"Yeah? And where is back home?"

Not for the first time, she caught his gaze lingering on where her ears were covered by her hair. He was clearly still trying to figure her out, and she enjoyed not giving him the satisfaction of confirming what her glamour was.

She was supposed to be an Ocean fae. Killian had come up with it himself, as he'd figured it would be best when she'd be unable to showcase Shadow, Sun, and Forest fae magic to her peers. If posing as a Freshwater fae, she'd easily be exposed as a fraud when spring and bath water would inevitably fail to show off the shimmers of her supposed mer form. And as she could opt out of visiting the ocean not too far from the school, no one could expose her lie when only seawater would normally affect an ocean mer.

She looked like a human as all mers did but posed as a creature of the sea.

However, she was far different beneath the paleness of her glamour.

She quickly hid her hand behind her back when the red stripes of her natural skin seeped through the enchantment. The movement didn't go unnoticed by Nox, as he continued to stare at her with scrutiny.

"I'll place you in the middle of the pack," he said, stretching his arms behind his head, his large muscles rippling with the movement. "Weak as you are, you're in no shape to protect anyone."

Her jaw clenched, and in response to her anger, her hand heated behind her back as her crimson stripes threatened to release noxious fumes in his face. Just because she wasn't proficient in many types of weapons didn't mean she couldn't hold her own.

Even so, she knew she was lacking, and she didn't know how to fix her shortcomings when training in a group filled with many other people who were also lacking didn't help one bit.

"And I suppose you're going to take up the rear? Careful, Klaver. If you can't see over your own ego, how will you protect anyone?"

"From what?" He stuffed his hands into his pockets as he gave her that irritating grin she hated so much. It was strikingly handsome yet insincere. No matter how hard he might try, she would always be immune to his charms. "You heard Gray. It's a training exercise. Nothing is going to jump out at you."

"How shortsighted, *little boy.* This is the Shadow Kingdom. If anything is going to jump out at us somewhere, it would be here."

He snorted. "Please. I grew up here. I can see in the dark forests, unlike you. Nothing can take me off guard. I'd have my sword at their throat before anyone had a chance to scream."

Clutching her hands to her heart, she feigned relief. "I feel safer already!"

"As you should."

He lightly chucked her chin and sauntered off, leaving her both bewildered and irritated beyond belief. He'd never actually touched her before, and she tried to ignore the way the simple action caused heat to bloom on her face in its wake.

Immune to his charms, she reminded herself with a huff. Nox Klaver was as smooth as they came, and she refused to fall for his act.

Gray called everyone in the class into a circle, reviewing rules and procedures. They would be graded on how quietly they could walk, how effectively they could communicate, and how well they could react to surprises. She'd set up several obstacles on the course ahead for the drill, and would only be there for protection purposes while the rest of them delegated amongst themselves.

Naturally, Nox stepped up as a leader, along with a few other people in the class. Avra internally berated herself for not doing the same. Among her people, she was supposed to be a leader. She was supposed to take up the mantle to guide and protect. But at the moment, she didn't feel like a leader. Rather, she felt small. Useless. Weak.

Whether to demean her or irritate her further, Nox placed her in the back of the group near him, another blow to her fragile pride. At least she hadn't been placed in the middle where many weaker candidates currently huddled together, still with no clue on how to wield a weapon.

Her heart shot to her throat as the black steel gates surrounding the school opened, and they stepped outside.

A shiver ran down her arms as if the air dropped twenty degrees in the matter of seconds. The world outside the gates felt far too large with too many trees casting shadows around them. Strange sounds from strange creatures echoed in the boughs overhead as they began their patrol.

But then a shaky breath escaped her when she glanced down at her hands to find her glamour slipping even further. The red stripes were even more prominent on her skin, though they could easily be mistaken as shadows cast from the sunlight overhead.

Minutes remained at most before she needed to consume her next elixir. She only had a short window to use the locating potion.

But...

Surreptitiously, she glanced over her shoulder but quickly realized she wasn't as sneaky as she thought when Nox's gaze immediately landed on her. His characteristic grin made its appearance right on time, and she glowered back. Surely, his scheming mind was already coming up with new ideas on how to humiliate her in front of the class.

What was he planning next?

"Oh no!" Gray called out with terrible acting skills, and the group quickly surrounded a pair of man-made animal tracks, as the grooves in the mud didn't quite reflect the creature they belonged to. But it was a good replica. "Looks like something dangerous is prowling these woods. Quick! Someone tell me the beast who made them."

Avra glanced over her shoulder again, searching for a gap in the trees she could slip into to perform the spell without a watchful audience. She didn't want anyone asking questions.

However, she found none when the group leaders tucked them in like children ready to nap.

"No one?" Gray sighed. "I had hoped your Magical Creatures class would have given you some insight about what we face. No matter. It's a—"

"Harpy," Avra called out, unable to help herself. But then she internally cringed when every eye in the class swiveled in her direction. She made a show of fixing her hair to hide the stripes likely beginning to appear on her neck. She could only rely on the shadows to obscure her for so long.

"Very good. And can someone tell me what to do after a harpy sighting?"

Nox's deep voice reverberated in her soul directly behind her, far closer than expected. She fought the urge to glance over her shoulder. "Hunt it down and kill it?" he jested, followed by laughter from the rest of their peers.

"Is that really your first instinct?" Avra scoffed. "To hunt innocent creatures? The harpy probably has a nest somewhere nearby. It won't hurt you unless you venture too close."

"Hence, hack and slash."

More laughter.

But before Avra managed a retort, Gray stepped in to explain the procedure when coming across territorial or nesting beasts. Avra couldn't listen when the heat of anger pumped through her blood and drowned in her ears. Surely, even Nox couldn't be so cold-hearted as to kill an innocent creature rather than finding a way to live in harmony.

"Are you always so terrible?" she hissed, keeping her voice low to avoid attracting the attention of her peers. "You honestly wouldn't care if an innocent creature got hurt?"

"I would care if *you* got hurt," Nox replied. But he wore that same insincere grin that contradicted his own words.

"Oh, please. Save it for someone who believes it."

"What's wrong?" he shot back. "Can't have a little fun?"

"Fun?" she squeaked, eyes wide. "Is that what you call dallying with a woman bound for marriage? Was Maya your idea of a little fun?"

His infuriating grin only widened. "Someone sounds a little jealous."

She snorted quietly and rolled her eyes. "I could never be jealous of someone who earned your cheap affection. Have you no honor, Nox?"

His eyes hardened, and she realized she'd struck a nerve. Good. Especially when his grin fell into a scowl.

He pointed a finger between her eyes. "Did it ever occur to you that I never took Maya out? I don't dally with taken women. I do have a few morals, mind you."

Avra's heart jolted in surprise. "Why didn't you say something before?"

"You never asked."

Her gaze traveled to the put-out woman in question. Maya crossed her arms over her chest, wearing a pout on her lips as she glanced their way across the trail.

"Besides," he said, stuffing his hands into his pockets as he continued to glare at her. "I don't see you getting involved with anyone. Perhaps I'm a little more free with my affection, but at least I don't carry a stick up my arse.

No one could get close to you even if they tried, what with your prickly coat and whatnot."

"Prickly?" she scoffed, tuning out Gray's lecture entirely. "In my culture, we take courtship seriously. We don't court casually, and arranged marriages are more common than not. Perhaps I don't get close to anyone because there is no one worth getting close to."

He opened his mouth as if to retort, but the professor raised her voice to gather everyone's attention.

"Let's move on, class." Gray motioned them forward, and her peers started on the path again.

With irritation burrowing a hole through her mind, she followed the group, trying to ignore Nox's looming presence behind her.

It was next to impossible.

Panic raced through her when her glamour dropped even further as her red stripes burned brighter. She stepped into a patch of sunlight to obscure herself from Nox's eyes. He may be able to see in the dark, but as a Shadow fae, he couldn't see well in the light.

"I need to relieve myself," she lied when he remained behind with her rather than continue on with the group. "I'll catch up soon."

He crossed his arms and rolled his eyes. "You couldn't have gone before the exercise? If you leave, you'll fail the assignment. And if I let you leave, *I'll* fail the assignment."

"Sounds fair to me." She grinned when her statement inspired his scowl.

He glanced from her to the group moving farther out of sight, clearly trying to decide whether he wanted to stay with her to "protect" her as a group leader or leave her behind to "protect" the others.

"Make it fast." And then under his breath, he muttered, "I'm not keen on the idea of failing another class."

"Don't worry." She rolled her eyes right back. "I won't get you failed if that's your concern. I'll only be a minute."

She ducked her head and rushed into the trees, slipping into the sunlight just as the remainder of her glamour dropped. Her pale skin transitioned to blue-ish gray with red stripes. Her horns spiraled out of either side of her head. Her tail whipped out behind her, the sharp tip slicing into the tree bark and leaving a gouge mark in the wood.

Another shiver raced down her body at feeling so exposed. Yet, at the same time, she momentarily rejoiced at having herself back. She was no fae or human but an Infernal, and she'd most dearly missed her own skin and her horns and her tail. Her sharp claws...

What was she to do? She couldn't hide behind the face of a fae for the rest of her life. But how could she not?

Acting quickly, she pulled out another vial of potion and dripped a single drop of black blood within. She shook the vial until the liquid turned a dark purple. And then she uncorked it and inhaled its pungent fumes.

Her vision spun with obsidian webs. Her head slammed backward, nearly hitting the tree trunk behind her. The scent of smoke and sulfur choked the breath from her. And then images attacked her like bees striking with barbed stingers.

Red moons. Black soil. Volcanic mountains. And then the images transitioned to a lush green forest. Hardly any sunlight filtered through the thick leaves. A slow river marked by two large boulders stood out in the vision, resting next to a bush boasting of yellow and crimson leaves.

Her heart raced when she spotted the flicker of the Infernal cords of Theo's attire. It was all she managed to glimpse before the vision slammed her back to the present in a wave of dizziness and disorientation.

Theo! She'd caught a glimpse of his location. She was sure of it.

A breathy snort startled her attention upward, and her entire body froze when her gaze locked on two spheres of glowing red.

Her heart stuttered in her chest, her eyes growing wide as she took in the large frame three times her size, the muscled black and red skin, the bull's head with horns sharper than an Elder's wit.

A minotaur. The very creature that had killed her mother.

The beast charged forward.

And Avra screamed.

5

THAT WAS NO "I almost urinated on a bug" scream. That was a real, earth-shattering, terrified bellow that caused his insides to quake.

Nox's instincts drove him forward as he drew his sword and rushed toward the sound of Avra's scream. The sunlight blinded his senses as he stepped into a smaller clearing surrounded by trees so bright in his vision that they appeared like thin silhouettes. But what he did manage to make out through his hazy vision twisted his stomach into little knots of fear as his gaze traveled from large, muscled legs to the horns sticking out of the head of the enormous beast.

That was no mere harpy.

An angry snort escaped the beast's large nostrils as it pawed at the ground with its hooves and wildly shook its mane of black hair. However, the creature wasn't trying to challenge *him*. It was after Avra.

Through his hazy vision, he spotted her silhouette backed against a tree, two daggers held in either hand. One of the blades dripped blood, and he glanced back at the beast to find its neck matted with the sticky liquid.

And then the beast charged.

Nox stepped in between Avra and the raging minotaur. He planted his feet, squared his shoulders, and harnessed his magic. A beam of purple burst out of him and smashed into the creature, hard enough to throw it backward. It landed on the floor with a ground-shaking boom.

With his left hand raised, ready to release his magic again, he lifted his sword in his other hand as he prepared for a second attack. Minotaurs were not known to flee a brawl. Rather, they would keep fighting until they lost every limb on their body and found themselves unable to move or until they died.

To prevent himself from getting mauled, he needed to end this quickly and efficiently. No room for mistakes. Just like his father had taught him.

Rather than waiting for the beast to regain its feet, Nox charged forward and stabbed his weapon directly through the creature's chest. The minotaur bellowed loud enough for his ears to ring. He gritted his teeth as he pulled the blade free, realizing his weapon had missed its heart when it had shifted at the last moment.

He ducked beneath the swipe of the minotaur's sharp, vicious claws. He jumped to the side when it snapped at him with pointed, drooling teeth.

Another opening allowed him to stab his weapon through its chest once again. He cursed under his breath when the strike missed its mark a second time.

When the beast swiped at him, he leaped backward and reached for his magic. Purple tendrils of shadow shot out of his fingertips, and just as the minotaur lunged forward, his magic wrapped around the beast's body, restraining it and keeping it from attacking again.

The magic tightened its grip whenever the beast moved. It thrashed and roared and snorted. Unfortunately, his magic wasn't strong enough to keep the beast in its hold.

The minotaur broke one arm free from its magical bindings, and in a blindingly fast movement, it swiped its claws toward Nox's face.

Years of training took over, and his body seemed to move on its own as he ducked and weaved and moved closer. With a powerful swing of his weapon, he cleaved the monster's head from its body.

And then the forest fell into an eerily silent hush as the minotaur fell to the ground dead.

"Oh, minotaur, you now lay dead. If only I could have said off with your head!" he shouted loudly without his own consent, but immediately clamped his hands over his mouth, his gazing darting toward the tree Avra had stood beside moments earlier, only to glimpse the shadow of her form on the opposite side of the trunk.

Heat climbed his neck and settled in his pointed ears. Had she heard the rhyme? His silly little curse had never bothered him this badly before—the curse marking his arm in black, to be precise. But for the first time in years, mortification burned a hole through his pride when faced with Avra's ruthless opinion of his character.

Had she heard?

How badly would her gibes become if she had?

When Avra uncharacteristically said nothing about his cursed rhyming after felling an enemy nor about the defeated minotaur, he rushed in her direction and rounded the tree.

Only to find her on the ground, clutching a hand to her stomach.

She was covered in blood.

"No!" Avra cried out, panic racing through her at the amount of black blood staining her clothes. Her elixir had barely started working before he'd rounded the tree, concealing her identity beneath a false mask, but it did nothing to hide the color of her blood. "Don't look at me!"

"But you're injured!"

"Oh, really?" she asked sarcastically. "And whose fault is that?"

Well, it was her own, really. But if his job really was to protect the "weak" in the group, then he'd failed miserably.

She cried out again as pain rippled through her. Black blood coated her torso and her fingers where she clutched at the wound. Thankfully, daylight likely prevented him from seeing her wound well with those Shadow fae eyes of his. She wouldn't be surprised if he mistook her black blood for red beneath the bright light of day.

Instead of pushing him away, she clutched onto him when he leaned closer. Her fear for him was replaced by her fear of others seeing her. He'd saved her life instead of allowing her to die. He'd proven she could trust him. "Don't let them see me. You have no idea the trouble I'll be in. I need you to take me to the headmaster."

"Graves?"

"Yes!" she cried, fighting against the burning pain in her abdomen.

When he didn't move as if stunned and frozen, she attempted to climb to her feet but immediately collapsed when her legs refused to hold her weight. Only then did Nox spring into action as he stripped off his shirt and pressed it to her wound.

A hiss escaped her mouth, but she managed to smother the scream wanting to emerge when he jostled her as he effortlessly picked her up and cradled her in his arms.

Pain warred with fluster when her gaze dipped to his bare, muscled torso, at his warmth seeping into her body growing colder by the second. Of course, his fitted tunics had left very little to the imagination, but with his entire chest on display...

Her cheeks grew even warmer as her gaze couldn't help but dip downward again. He could likely crush an acorn between his pectoral muscles if he tried.

Professor Gray burst through the foliage, took one sweep of her surroundings, and demanded to know what had happened. Avra found herself barely lucid as Nox briefly explained the situation before rushing her back toward the school.

"You need a healer," he said in a gruff tone.

"I can't trust a healer!" When her wound jostled further, she focused on taking deep, steady breaths through her nose. "I can only trust Killian."

"That's a lot of blood. You could die!"

"I will be fine. Just get me to Killian."

His grip tightened on her, and she was hardly aware of her passing surroundings as she focused all her remaining energy on keeping Nox's shirt pressed to her wound to staunch the bleeding. If she lost too much blood, not only would she be in danger of losing her life, but someone might see it was black.

Because if the attack in the woods from an Infernal Minotaur proved anything...

The Hawkers knew she was here.

They burst through the doors of the staff dorms, and Avra hissed against Nox's shoulder when he turned a corner too quickly. She squeezed her eyes shut and focused on breathing deeply for a few moments before Nox adjusted her in his arms and rapped quickly on the headmaster's door.

When no one answered, he knocked again. Finally, the door flew open to reveal Lyyli Graves on the opposite side. Her wide-eyed gaze darted from the two of them to Avra's bleeding wound. She used her hands to sign something, but then shook her head as if forgetting she could speak out loud.

"Come inside," she gasped, stepping aside to let them in.

Nox set her down on a cushioned chair, and with agony in every movement, she attempted to shift away to hide the color of her blood from him. When his eyes were likely still adjusting from stepping from daylight and into a dark room, she had only moments to act before her blood revealed the truth.

She attempted to reach for a blanket to shield herself, but cried out in agony once more when the movement tugged on her wound.

Killian rushed out of his room, hurrying to buckle his belt in his half-state of undress as he strode toward her. "Avra! You're bleeding. This is bad." His gaze darted from her wound to Nox hovering over her with hardened eyes. "Does he know?" he asked in a low voice.

Avra shook her head, unable to do anything more when the agony of her wound seared her from the inside out. Poison. The minotaur's horns had been poisoned. Thankfully, she was resistant to most poisons. But it explained why it burned so blasted much.

Killian turned to Nox. "I'm afraid I'm going to have to ask you to leave."

"What? No! I'm staying."

"You have to leave."

"But..." Nox trailed off, catching her pained gaze.

The headmaster stepped in front of her to shield her from view and gestured toward the door. "If you must help, fetch Healer Mari from the infirmary, and only her. Speak to no one else about this."

Not a single protest left his lips as he rushed out of the room, leaving her alone with Killian and his family.

"What happened?" the man demanded as he rifled through a series of vials within one of his wicker cabinets, taking them out one by one until four lay on top of the table. Lyyli squeezed Avra's hand, offering a small amount of comfort in the face of agony.

She grimaced as she lifted the shirt pressed to her wound long enough to spot the deep gouge mark in her torso. "An Infernal Minotaur poisoned me with its horns outside the academy walls." A gasp blew from her mouth when the poison set in deeper. Her body could handle this. But it wouldn't be easy. "Killian, they know I'm here."

His mouth set into a grim line. "That's what I was afraid of."

"My glamour was down. That's how the minotaur found me."

If it was possible for his mouth to thin any further, he managed it. "Glamours sustained for the long term are tricky. You may need a stronger dosage to keep it up."

After retrieving a wooden bowl from another cabinet, he began adding several drops from each vial, mashing them together with a few sprigs of herbs and water for dilution. When it resembled runny sludge, he bade her to drink it, and she did so without hesitation.

The bitter properties of the mixture cooled down the burn from the poison, but it also caused her own magic to waver within her. As long as the elixir remained in her system, she reckoned she would have limited access to her powers.

Minutes later, the Sun fae healer rushed into the room wearing High Healer, fingerless gloves on both hands with sun stones on each knuckle. Outside, Nox protested against Killian refusing him entry, but soon enough, the headmaster managed to shut the door in the other man's face and locked it behind him.

Healer Mari set her bag down before approaching. But when she lifted Nox's blood-stained shirt, she gasped and dropped it in her shock. "She's an Infernal."

Killian dipped his head, his gaze darting toward the closed door. "Your discretion. Please."

"Of course, m'lord."

"I'm not titled at school. You may call me Headmaster or Professor."

She dipped her head. "A hard habit to break."

When the immediate shock seemed to have worn off, Mari hovered her hands over Avra's wound. A golden light shot out of her fingertips, bathing her torso in a warm sunshine glow.

Relief spread through her as the magic threaded her wound back together. She exhaled a long sigh and leaned back against the chair as she allowed the healing to take effect.

Finally, the light flickered out. Mari spent several minutes inspecting the healing job as well as taking her vitals before she nodded her head in satisfaction.

"Anything else, m'lord. Erm, Headmaster Graves?"

"That will be all."

With a dip of her head, Healer Mari packed up her things and exited the room, not asking a single question about the incident, although she'd clearly wanted to.

The moment the Sun fae left the room, Avra turned to Killian. "I saw a location in a vision while scrying for my brother. I don't know where it is, but I believe it to be in the upper realm."

The man's eyes hardened into a more serious note. "Describe what you saw."

And so she did, trying not to leave out a single detail from the color of the leaves to how many trees shaded the riverbank.

He nodded. "I know of several places that fit that description, though we'd best start near the area where I first found you. I'll send my men to search."

"Thank you," she breathed. For the first time in months, she finally felt a sliver of hope. But then she sobered at the thought of what had happened in the woods outside the school. "I'm not safe here." She stood and stretched her tight skin where the wound had healed over without leaving a scar. "And I don't want to put anyone here in danger. But I have nowhere else to go."

Lyyli placed her arm around Killian's waist and leaned into his shoulder, almost as if the action were second nature. A surprising pang of longing squeezed Avra's chest as she watched their interaction with one another. It was nothing like her relationship with Yianni. It was gentle. It was loving. It was pining and happiness. And for the first time, she found herself wanting that. She wanted to know the warmth of affection and the tender touch of love.

But then she shook the irrational thought away. Her culture was just different, and love was not usually in the cards for a Matriarch.

Lyyli said, "Darkest Star has a lot of powerful mages. They can reinforce the boundaries surrounding the school. At least until the danger is gone."

Killian nodded his head in agreement as he pushed his blond hair out of his face to reveal his Shadow fae black-slitted pupils. Similar to Nox's…

Stop thinking about him!

But he'd saved her life. Without him, her skull would have been crunched beneath heavy minotaur feet, and she wouldn't have survived the attack.

"I would be a fool to allow the Infernal Matriarch herself to go on her merry way when I can help. Especially when I do enjoy the possibility of a future alliance between our people."

"Killian!" Lyyli lightly smacked his arm. "Her life is at stake. Politics can wait."

He grimaced. "Ah, yes." He cleared his throat, tidying his vials in the cabinet as he spoke. "It would do you well to have a bodyguard. At least for the time being. And I promise you, I will use whatever resources I have at my disposal to aid you in your predicament."

Yes… But he'd already exhausted plenty of resources with very little to show for it.

She shook her head and stepped behind a folding screen to change into Lyyli's borrowed clothing. She didn't want to risk anyone else seeing the color of her blood on her way back to her dorms to change into her own clothing.

"Keeping a bodyguard with me will attract more attention than I want. I cannot risk it."

"Fair enough."

When she returned to the main room, she threw her old clothes into the hearth, watching as the orange flames burned her blood in green wisps of fire due to her Infernal heritage before catching onto the fabric and eating away at it slowly.

As for Nox's shirt...

She held it in her hands, her thumbs brushing the only corners not soaked with black blood. Should she have died today, whatever was left of her people would have no leadership. It would be the end of them.

Killian's voice escaped muffled through the wicker cabinet. "Might I suggest something else entirely? Your weaponry skills lack...mmm...*finesse*, I should say. What if you had someone to tutor you? Not only would you gain valuable knowledge on how to better protect yourself, but you will also have this *tutor*," he emphasized the word with finger quotes, "with you plenty enough to keep you safe. A bodyguard disguised as a tutor, if you will. They wouldn't even know they were guarding you."

"And…" She bit her lip as she continued to stare down at the dirtied fabric in her hands. "Who would you suggest?"

"I think it should be your choice. Who do you trust?"

Finally, she threw the shirt into the flames and watched as it, too, momentarily burned green before giving way to the rising flames.

She took a deep breath and let it out slowly. "I want Nox Klaver."

6

THERE WAS NOTHING worse than getting called to the headmaster's office and not knowing why.

Well, Nox had a decent idea of *why* after the minotaur incident in the woods yesterday. But he couldn't be entirely sure when he could also count on two hands what this possible berating might be about. They hadn't caught wind about him pranking one of the human students in the dining hall, had they?

Just to be sure the message was meant for him—despite how many times he'd already listened to it drone back to him—he touched the small blue ball of light hovering in front of his face to replay the summons.

The female voice speaking to him was clear and crisp and unmistakable in what she wanted from him.

"Nox Klaver, please come to the headmaster's office immediately. There is a matter that needs to be discussed."

No, the message is certainly not for me, he thought sarcastically with a roll of his eyes. Although still sweaty from his post-nap physical exercise, he changed his clothing from something comfortable to his school uniform. But this time, he didn't forgo the blazer when he wanted to make a favorable impression with the headmaster. He even took the time to fix his hair and make sure every bit of the fabric from his uniform lay smooth and aligned against him.

His attention caught on the bloodied trousers shoved into a corner of the room. Black blood. He'd stabbed the minotaur several times, so he wasn't surprised to see it. However, the sight shocked him, nonetheless. An Infernal Minotaur. Surely, this confirmed the Matriarch resided on campus somewhere.

He pulled his attention away and hid several knives and other small weapons on his person before he exited his dorm and stepped into the darkness of night.

Each of his strides exuded confidence and calm, but inside, his entire being trembled with anxiety. What did the headmaster want? What was he in trouble for? He'd tried his hardest to blend in with his peers as he searched for signs of the Infernal Matriarch on campus, but what if he'd slipped? What if someone found out the reason for his attendance?

Taking a deep breath, he took a moment to steel his nerves as he stood in front of the office building on campus and stared up at its formidable height. The centerpiece for the Darkest Star Arcane with a large nine-sided star glowed like stained-glass in the sunlight. Imposing. Beautiful. Enough to strike uncertainty into his soul.

And then he stepped inside.

The woman who had the same voice as the one inside the orb message ushered him through a set of hallways and guided him toward a large room with the door wide open, waiting to swallow him whole.

Nox frowned as he entered the office, glancing back and forth between Professor Graves, who sat behind his desk with his hands clasped together, and Avra, who stared into her lap from where she sat across the desk and refused to meet his gaze.

Her injury seemed much improved. The healer must have taken good care of her.

"What is this about?" Nox's frown deepened when the door closed behind him, making him feel like a trapped songbird unable to break free from its cage. "I already gave my statement on the minotaur incident. Otherwise, I didn't do anything. I swear."

"I'm sure you didn't." Graves tipped his head to the side, scrutinizing him with a careful eye. "Why don't you take a seat?"

He eyed the empty chair beside Avra and crossed his arms over his chest, putting his muscles on display. Of course, he doubted the other Shadow fae would be intimidated by a show of brawn, especially when he could likely inflict internal or even external magical torment with the snap of his fingers if he wanted to. But he hated feeling trapped and helpless, and it was the only thing he could do to control the situation aside from throwing the window open and escaping into the fresh air.

"I'd rather stand."

"Suit yourself." Graves shuffled a stack of papers, his eyebrows drawn as he pushed several of them toward the edge of the desk —Nox's previous exams, showing offensive red ink striking out many of the questions. "I take magical academics very seriously, Nox. And I have to say that you have less-than-satisfactory grades in each of your classes except Magical Adaptiveness and Weapons Education. In those, you exceed your peers."

The blood drained from his face as he clutched his father's vial in his hand. If his father had still been alive, he'd be most disappointed if he managed to get himself kicked out of school due to poor academic performance.

His jaw clenched, his gaze darting briefly toward Avra. Fluster climbed his neck when he realized he didn't want to have an audience for this discussion. Especially not from *her* of all people. "I have not had the privilege of a formal education, Professor. I'm trying my best."

"You are trying your best in the areas in which you succeed," he corrected. "I am apt to believe you try very little to listen to lectures and finish your assignments on time."

Again, Nox's jaw clenched, and his grip tightened around the vial. "Are you kicking me out then? Is that what this," he gestured to the room as a whole, "is about?" And how did Avra factor into all of this? Had she tattled on him? The little snot.

Professor Graves shook his head. "As it is, Miss Avra is failing abysmally in Magical Adaptiveness and Weapons Education while she excels in all areas of academics."

"I wouldn't say *failing abysmally...*" she murmured under her breath, to which Graves rewarded with a warm, sympathetic smile.

"You excel in some areas of magic and dagger training. But it's not enough."

Nox realized with a sudden clarity what the headmaster was getting at. *Why* he and Avra were in his office at the same time. And he didn't like it one bit. "I'm not tutoring her. She's intolerable."

All right, so she wasn't entirely intolerable. Rather, she was intriguing and drove him entirely mad every time she opened that sweet little mouth of hers. But he had a Matriarch to hunt down and kill. He didn't have time to tutor another student.

Avra stood from her seat and squared off with him, a glare in her eyes. "And you think you're any better?" She poked him in the chest, which was followed by surprise dissolving her previous disgruntledness before her glare returned at full force. "I find you detestable and irritating."

He rolled his eyes. "Keep going, why don't you?"

"Arrogant. Full of yourself. Rude. And utterly despicable."

"Look in the mirror, love."

As expected, his insincere term of endearment was enough to drop her defenses and fill her cheeks with color, enough to flounder her to give him the upper hand in the argument.

He turned to Graves once again. "I find this arrangement unacceptable."

The professor glanced between the two of them with an apologetic grimace. "Miss Avra has already agreed to the terms. She will tutor you in academics. You will tutor her in weaponry training. I suggest for you to agree as well if you want to keep your coveted place at this school."

"That's not fair."

"It's in the terms outlined in your acceptance papers. You must maintain a passing grade to stay at Darkest Star. And I say this to both of you."

Nox released a stream of angry purple magic from his nose as he glared at Avra. He was torn between telling her off and upping his charm to the headmaster himself.

He decided to lay on his charm.

His arms dropped to his sides, and he leveled the headmaster with an apologetic smile. "If you'd like me to find a tutor, I can find one on my own. I swear I will get my grades up this semester."

Avra shared a concerned look with the professor, which boiled his blood even more. It took all his effort to keep his temper under control. What were they hiding from him? Why were they being so secretive?

"I have already made my decision," the professor said as he gathered several papers together and tucked them into a briefcase. "These are the terms for both of you to stay at Darkest Star." He started toward the exit but stopped briefly in the doorway. "I suppose this is as good a time as any. I am pairing you two together for a project that will be announced in tomorrow's class. You must replicate something in nature using your magic, and sustain it within a classroom setting. The project is due by the end of the semester."

And then he stepped out of the room, leaving Nox alone with the one person he detested the most at this school.

"I am not working with you," he hissed. "It's bad enough to have to tutor you. But also complete a project with you? I would almost rather be expelled."

"Go on then." She gestured to the door. "Walk away from the school."

A growl escaped his throat over his frustration at his situation. If he'd only sought help sooner with his academics, he could have avoided this mess altogether. "Fine then! But I'm doing the project on my own. You can stay out of my way."

"Professor Graves isn't dimwitted. He'll know immediately you did it by yourself, and you'll only receive a half grade."

"I don't want to work with you!" he shouted.

The room became deadly silent, the tension sharp enough to cut glass.

Avra lowered her gaze to the floor rather than fighting back like he'd expected. Silently, she gathered her belongings, avoiding eye contact. But he swore he noticed a sheen in her eyes, and the red growing on the rims of her eyelids only confirmed his suspicions.

He'd made her cry.

Guilt slammed into him, dropping his defenses immediately. He lifted a hand, wanting to say something. To say *anything*. But his throat clammed up, his tongue refusing to work.

"I should have known you were not equal to this task," she murmured, her back to him. "This is not Killian's fault. It's mine. I personally asked for you to tutor me. It was my mistake." She paused as if to gather her emotions. "I will ask for someone else."

Before he could find his voice, she slipped out of the room, leaving him staring dumbfoundedly after her, completely speechless.

She had asked for *him*? Why? And why not someone she got along better with?

His attention returned to the test scores marked in red. Pride battled duty within him as he contemplated what this meant for him. Midterms were over, and the end of the semester crept closer and closer with each passing day. The Matriarch was still here, the Hawkers waiting outside the school told him as much, though he wasn't sure where she was hiding. If he was kicked out of school before he found her…

Then his father's soul would never rest, and Nox's heart would never find peace.

But Avra? Of all people?

She was the only person who made him squirm. The only person who battered his pride while singlehandedly creating an unquenchable desire for something infinitely out of his reach.

Releasing a huff of annoyance, he stuffed his offending papers away in his blazer. If he didn't keep his grades up, he'd never get a chance to avenge his father. But he'd already made an arse of himself. How could he salvage this?

He blinked slowly when he realized he was in the headmaster's office. Alone.

Glancing toward the open door to find the outside hallway empty, he wasted no time as he strode across the room and carefully shuffled through Professor Graves' drawers and cabinets, careful not to disturb anything enough for it to appear tampered with. Parchment. Ink. Quills. Administration documents. But no devastating secrets as far as he could tell, and nothing remotely mentioning Infernals.

After several minutes of quietly searching the room, the only things he learned was that one of the humans was here on scholarship, the cost of the star emblem on the main academy building had cost a small fortune, and a Sun fae student wore magic-suppressor gloves because his magic was too powerful.

Interesting. But not relevant.

With a huff, he placed everything back where he'd found them and slipped into the hallway just as someone from the front office turned around the corner, her attention on the stack of parchment in her hands. She didn't even glance up when they passed one another, and no one stopped him as he exited through the front door of the building.

It was time to take another approach. If he couldn't find the Matriarch, then he'd have to smoke her out.

But how?

7

"I'M SORRY," Killian murmured, giving Avra's shoulder a brief, comforting squeeze. "We managed to find the location stated in your vision. But... It's all we found of him."

She stared at the piece of fabric woven from black nettle leaves, an indigenous plant from Crotona. Hesitantly, she took the impossibly soft fabric from the headmaster and brought it to her nose, inhaling the unmistakable ashen scent of her brother.

A sob escaped her throat, but she managed to swallow the second down when shock drowned out all other emotion.

"Now, keep in mind," Professor Adler, a Shadow fae who taught Magical Adaptiveness, hurried to say, "that no body was found. He's still out there somewhere."

What the woman *didn't* say was whether or not Theo was still alive.

She inhaled her brother's scent one more time, not finding any trace of blood. But it didn't mean he wasn't injured or dead. "And the surrounding area?" she hesitated to ask. "Were there signs of a struggle? Blood? Weapons? Magical traces?"

The two professors glanced at one another, and Killian grimaced as he nodded. "We found magical signatures several months old, and the foliage that grew back over those months have made it next to impossible to tell if there had been a struggle."

Professor Adler cut in next as she tucked her short, chin-length gray hair behind her ear. "We found traces of Infernal blood, though we don't know if it was your brother's or someone else's."

A shaky breath trembled what remained of Avra's frayed nerves. But she needed to know. "Can we track him?"

Killian gestured to the other fae and allowed her to answer. "We don't know as much as we'd like about the Infernal realm, though we suspect he traveled through a portal, due to the high amount of magical traces left behind. We don't know how to follow him, nor if we should…"

"I can make a portal," she declared, rising to her feet. "I just need the correct ingredients."

Such things had always been Theo's specialty, and although she'd never practiced such a feat, she knew how it was done.

"And then what? By acting rashly, you don't know what will await you."

She stood and threw her hands in the air in frustration. "And if I do nothing, Theo could die!"

If he wasn't dead already.

Before either managed a reply, she turned to Killian and begged. "You have soldiers. A lot of them. If you lend them to me, we could fight for my brother. We could fight for my people."

Because she refused to believe they were all dead. It would destroy what little remained of her hope.

The Shadow Lord offered a look of sympathy. "My soldiers are yours, Matriarch Avra. But I cannot send them to face an uncertain doom. I recommend we gather more information before acting."

"How?"

"First, we need to know the layout of the realm and figure out how my soldiers can survive in Crotona. We are not built to traverse such a place for long periods of time. My soldiers would die of dehydration or quickly become useless in your plight."

"I've managed to adapt to the upper realm. Surely, they could adapt to the lower realm."

He nodded thoughtfully. "Perhaps." His brows furrowed as if deep in thought as he took several moments to add several drops of flowery liquid to an empty vial sitting on his desk. "You may need to go first. To scout out the land and the situation. And once you find a favorable opening, we'll transfer my soldiers to your realm."

Hugging the piece of her brother's shirt close to her chest, she nodded. "That's fair. And what would you like in return for your aid?"

This was not a mere student-to-teacher discussion. This was between two rulers in vastly different lands.

She bit her lip, realizing her predicament. She had not yet come into her Matriarch magic and wouldn't until she spoke the words to take up her mantle over her people. Her power was locked away deep within herself, and she wasn't ready. Because what people were left? How did she know if she had any people to rule over? And she didn't want such a hefty responsibility. She wasn't ready to lead her people to further destruction.

But with Lord Killian's soldiers and his help? Perhaps such a feat was possible.

"Hmm..." he mused as he combined two vials, causing the liquid to hiss, sizzle, and foam before lying still once more. "I would like some time to ponder your request. Though, gaining access to your indigenous plants and species is high up on that list."

"Anything you want, consider it yours."

Currently, she had nothing to give. But if he helped her with this, she would owe him the world.

He nodded in satisfaction before swirling the liquid in the vial, placing a stopper in the glass, and pushing it across the desk toward her. "A stronger dose of your glamour elixir," he explained before sitting back in his chair and leveling her with a contemplative stare. "I'll send word to my captain to prepare the soldiers for battle in a dry climate. When you give the word, they'll be ready." He rummaged through his drawers, pulled out a fist-sized box, and unlocked it. Inside lay several glass orbs with swirling black shadows within their core. He handed one of them to her. "Keep it safe. Once you break the glass, it will create a portal to wherever you are. My soldiers can aid you when you need them."

"Thank you," she breathed, touching her fingers to her lips and dipping her head as a show of the utmost respect. "I have the means to create a portal to Crotona for myself, but I will need to grow an herb first. As quickly as possible."

"Professor Laugen can aid you in the greenhouse." He paused for a moment, his mouth pressing into a thin line. "I trust him. I really do. But he has a talkative mouth. You'd better be careful with what you share with him."

"I will." She scooped up the elixir in her hand, tucked the glass orb safely in her pocket, and made to leave but paused at the door. "How do you do all of this?" She gestured to her surroundings as a whole. "You're a Shadow

Lord. You're the headmaster. You have a family. How do you balance it all?"

Killian chuckled. "Oh, I thrive off of keeping myself as busy as possible. My school and family are my passions, and I take my duties as a Shadow Lord seriously. It's exhausting, absolutely. But rewarding in every sense."

If only she could feel the same way about her own responsibilities.

She stepped into the hallway and glanced down at her brother's shirt in one hand. She had to believe he was safe. Perhaps in hiding. But somewhere out there, she believed he was still alive.

"Hold on, Theo," she whispered. "I can't find you now, but I will. I promise. Just hold on."

It wasn't entirely her lack of weaponry skills that slowed Avra down and made her clumsy, she decided. It was this blasted upper realm with its humid, chilly air. It filled her lungs with clog and rot. It gave her the worst headaches. It slowed down every movement with exhaustion and fatigue.

Gripping her sword in her hand quickly depleted her strength as she sparred with a Sun fae from her Magic Adaptiveness class. He instructed her on footwork and swings, but each time she failed to follow his confusing, disorderly advice, he grew visibly frustrated to the point where he started shouting at her when she faltered.

She clenched her jaw as she refrained from spewing hate right back. How dare he disrespect the Matriarch! In Crotona, he would have been flayed and then locked up while children threw ox dung at him between the bars.

But here in Skaad, she reminded herself that she was nobody. Just a student unable to fight well with a sword.

An ache traveled from her wrist, up her arm, and into her shoulder, and she took a moment to rest the tip of the weapon against the ground to give her muscles reprieve.

"I didn't tell you to put down your weapon," the other student growled, stomping in her direction. "We still have to—"

A blur of movement shifted quickly in the corner of her eye, forming a tall Shadow fae with black curls and a snarl on his face. Avra barely had time to blink before Nox shoved the other fae by the shoulders.

"Get out of here," Nox demanded, and the Sun fae visibly shrank before his height and bulk.

"Wh-wh-what?"

"I said leave. I'm her tutor. Not you."

A smug grin of triumph twitched at the corners of her mouth, and she scratched her chin in an attempt to hide it.

The Sun fae protested not so much as a single word as he packed up his weapons and raced out of the field, not looking back in his haste to flee.

Nox rounded on her, crossing his arms as he leveled her with a disgruntled stare. "I can't believe you tried to replace me." He gave her a mock pout. "So quickly, too. I'm hurt."

A weight lifted from her shoulders and filled her with relief. In the forest, Nox had stood between her and death without even a second thought. He'd handled the threat with confidence and prowess. After the incident...

She trusted him.

Of course, she refused to fluff his arrogant feathers by telling him as much. He could do with a bit of pride battering now and again to humble him.

"It's just a sword," she said nonchalantly as she inspected her nails. Short and pale. She missed her sharp, black fingernails more than she ever thought she could. "Anyone could teach me."

"Anyone?" he spluttered, now staring at her with a miffed expression. "That filthy dog had no idea what he was doing. Besides, a teacher who can't hide their frustration toward their pupil isn't worth their weight in shadows."

"Fine then." She lifted her sword. "Show me how it's done."

"First off, you can't hold your sword like that." He stepped behind her and gripped one hand over hers, lifting it higher. "If you hold it straight out, your muscles will tire faster. The weapon will become too heavy for your arm over longer periods of time."

"Huh. Well, that explains my aching muscles."

"Obviously."

Rather than finding offense with his manner of teaching, she forced herself to hide the grin probing at her mouth, threatening to appear in his presence. She refused to give him the satisfaction.

"Where is your sword?" she asked, noticing he only carried a couple of knives and a dagger on his belt, peeking out beneath his blue blazer.

He cast her a disbelieving stare, his eyebrows lifting into the shadows of his dark hair. "You can't train with someone until you have this," he gestured from her head to her feet, "figured out."

"What are you saying?" she huffed.

With a shrug, instead of fighting her, he showed her a surprising amount of patience to his teaching. "Let's work on your stance."

"My stance is fine."

"Your stance is sloppy." He pushed her shoulder, and she stumbled backward, barely able to catch herself from tripping. When she huffed again, he guided her back to her previous spot and demonstrated the correct way to stand while wielding a sword. "No one can knock you down if you center yourself. Keep your dominant leg slightly behind the other. It helps keep you sturdy and centered."

He pushed her again, but this time, she rocked into the movement rather than stumbling backward. She lifted her sword, and again, he corrected the angle in which she held it.

"I've seen you fight with daggers before." The clang of weapons from other skirmishes on the field filled the momentary silence as he stuffed his hands into his pockets and studied her. "You're decently proficient in those. Why skip over the sword?"

Speaking of her culture could prove disastrous, but… She wanted to share at least a little bit of home. "In my culture, when we reach ten years of age, we spend one week with each weapon. By the end, we choose what weapon we feel fits us best, and train with only that. For me, it was dual-wielding daggers. It just felt…right."

He nodded, his expression turning thoughtful. "In a way, it mimics hand-to-hand combat. You are comfortable with close-quarters fighting then."

"It's where I excel."

"Uh huh. Right."

Before she managed to react to his slight, he struck out with his palm and shoved her in the shoulder. This time, she found it impossible to catch herself as she stumbled backward and crashed onto her side in a heap of metal and tangled limbs.

She spat a piece of grass out of her mouth and glared up at him. "I thought you were supposed to be teaching me. Not battering me around."

"I *am* teaching you. More specifically, showing you that your balance is off center."

"Well, how can I find it when I'm missing my—"

Immediately, her mouth clamped shut and she averted her gaze. The glamour took away her horns and tail, making it impossible to find that sweet center of balance she had known all her life. A few months in a fae body wasn't enough for years' worth of training.

"Well, whatever it is, you need to do without it." He reached down, and with an effortless movement, he pulled her to her feet. Her cheeks warmed when she found herself standing close enough to catch the masculine scent wafting off his skin, close enough to witness the way his slitted pupils widened from thin lines to almond-shaped darkness. The lone curl at the corner of his eye brought attention to the full, thick dark lashes shadowing his green eyes.

She blinked herself out of her confusing daze and stepped backward, tightening her grip on the hilt of her sword. Tucking her hair behind her ear, she said, "Stance and weapon position aside, what else am I failing abysmally at?"

"Don't look at it as what you are failing at. Approach it as what are you going to improve today?"

"Who taught you all these things?"

He cleared his throat and turned his attention toward the tree line outside the school property. "My father."

The way he clutched the necklace in his hand spoke volumes of what she suspected might have happened to him. "Where is he now?"

For a moment, she thought he might not answer when the silence became long and unbearable between them. But then he released a long breath and said, "He was killed by some terrible people."

She ducked her head, her heart aching. Not just for him, but for herself as well. "I suppose we finally have something in common. My parents, too, were killed by terrible people."

"I'm sorry."

"Same."

His attention seemed far away, his eyes dazed as if trapped in the memories of his past. Usually, he wore a confident, take-on-the-world expression. But now? He was vulnerable, and she wasn't sure what to make of it.

"And what of your mother?" she asked gently.

"I never knew her. Some high-born Shadow fae in the Inuwa province." Another long breath before his mouth quirked to the side. "My father was a rogue. They courted in secret. She birthed me in secret, handed me to my father, and never spoke to him again. Never sought me out." He shrugged and stuffed his hands into his pockets. "It's better this way."

However, she detected the hurt underlying his words, the hurt of long-repressed emotions over the parent who had never wanted him.

Before she managed to reply, he glanced at her from the corner of his eye. "So… Are we doing this or not?"

Her mouth twitched, her spirit soaring exponentially as she gripped the hilt of her sword and lifted it to practice again. "I suppose we are."

Seconds turned into minutes and minutes into a couple hours. Despite the ache of her muscles and her body screaming at her to stop and rest, she found that she didn't want to. She wouldn't dare admit it out loud, but she enjoyed Nox's banter and each time he touched her, whether to fix her stance or correct her hand placement on her weapon. She felt…safe with him. If a Hawker were to attack her, she knew she could rely on Nox like she had once relied on her *Ikshwa*.

Yes, she was placing a lot of faith in him. But faith was all she had when the rest of her world had fallen apart around her.

"Nox!" someone shouted across the field, startling them apart.

She lowered her sword and spotted the outline of a male student wearing his dark blue uniform, waving Nox down from a distance next to several other male and female students.

With an apologetic smile, Nox gathered his belongings and paused, jerking his thumb over his shoulder. "I have to go. I have plans."

"Don't forget our study session," she called after him as he backed away. He raised a hand to say he'd heard her, but then he joined his friends. Laughter trailed after them as they made their way toward one of the buildings.

Avra couldn't help but watch longingly. When she'd been the future Matriarch, she'd had very few friends. Less, now, when some of them might have been killed. She desired the easy friendship Nox had with his peers. She longed to join them and to find out what a few hours without the hefty responsibilities of the Matriarch felt like.

Her lips thinned, and her shoulders drooped as she returned the heavy sword to its stand. Alone. For once, she wanted to be a real student. Just an average young woman who worried about classes and grades and graduation. And perhaps...

Her face heated at the thought of love. She wanted to learn what it felt like. To have something like what Killian and Lyyli had.

With a sigh, she packed her own belongings and ventured toward the library. When the world was heartbreaking and confusing, at least she could find solace in her books.

8

"THERE YOU GO," Avra whispered as she tucked the lilybane seeds into dry, withered earth. Although parched, the soil was filled with all the nutrients the herb needed to grow. Only one thing was missing…

She glanced over her shoulder, making sure other students in the greenhouse were occupied before she reached for her magic. It raced down her arm and through her hand, escaping her finger as a puff of green smoke before the poison seeped into the soil to aid the herb in its growth.

The poisonous plant shouldn't affect any of the others nearby, but just in case, she labeled the pot and set it away from everything else beneath the warm light of a sunbeam created by Sun fae magic to replicate a hot, desert sun.

Soon, she would return home. For better or worse, she couldn't hide anymore. Especially when Theo wasn't coming back.

"Grow quickly," she urged as she folded her arms on the warm table and rested her chin on top. "I'm depending on you."

For the plant to fully mature, it needed two to three weeks beneath the right temperature and consistent nutrient balance in the soil. In the upper realm, she wasn't positive it would grow. But currently, no way to return to her homeland existed other than to create a portal herself.

Thoughts of her people's suffering disheartened her. Surely, it was too late to save anybody.

A whiff of ash drifted past her nostrils. Her heart shot to her throat, and her head snapped toward the source of the Infernal scent in time to catch the tail end of someone's silhouette drifting behind rows of plants, trees, and flowers, effectively blocking her view.

Her fingers trembled as she placed her hand on the dagger beneath her blazer, slowly advancing toward the shadow. Quickly, she rounded the corner, only to find Professor Laugen bent over a rare species of berry. He squinted at the plant, took off his spectacles to clean the dirt from the lenses, and squinted again.

Behind her, someone dropped a potted plant and swore, nearly startling her right out of her glamour. She snatched her bag from the tabletop and quickened her pace, not daring to stop for a single moment. Fear seized her, climbing into her throat and clogging it like cotton in a pipe.

Her breath quickened. Her surroundings became hazy. For a moment, she was unaware of where she was going, only that she needed to escape, to find safety.

She ran past the fountain reflecting the colorful lights of dawn and down the cobblestone walkways of the gardens. When she glanced over her shoulder, she found nothing chasing her except her own paranoia and—

"Ah!" she cried out as she tripped over something in her path and crashed onto her hands and knees on the cobblestone. Her skirt protected her knees from skinning, and her palms received painful scratches. But they didn't bleed. It was a small comfort when she still felt as if she were being watched.

"Are you *trying* to hurt yourself?" an obnoxious voice asked moments before a strong arm hefted her to her feet.

With a huff, she glared at Nox as she brushed the dirt from her clothing. "Are you *trying* to injure me? Assuming it was *your* foot I just tripped over."

However, the sight of him filled her with relief and a sense of safety. Never in her life would she have thought she'd have the urge to throw herself into his arms, for his presence to calm the terror racing through her veins. But she couldn't do that, so she settled for his presence of safety alone.

"How was I supposed to know you weren't going to stop? You were supposed to meet me here, remember? You're late."

"Ah, yes. I needed to do something first." Pain still throbbed through her hands and knees, and she tried to quell at least some of it by brushing away the small rocks lodged into her skin. Before she tended to the second hand, Nox snatched it and brought it closer to his face.

For a reason entirely opposite of fear, her heart thundered in her chest, and for a moment, her body felt as if it floated on clouds.

Stupid! she internally cried to herself as she tried to push down the heat quickly rising from her toes. *He doesn't affect me. I'm not one of those girls.*

He carefully picked off the lodged rocks in her skin and blew gently to scatter the dirt on her palm. The heat she'd unsuccessfully shoved away climbed into her face and refused to abate. Nox was charming with all women, and the poor saps fell for it. She spurned the idea of getting caught in his web of insincere flattery and attention like everyone else.

She snatched her hand back and sat on the bench behind the one where his things were situated, so they were back to back rather than side by side.

"Open your book to page twelve. We can start there."

Nox sighed dramatically. "All work and no play? You're no fun at all."

"Studying is not meant to be fun. It's supposed to be a contemplative exercise for the mind. Stretching it beyond even its own capabilities. Practicing mastery and restraint and pushing away any and all distractions until the exercise is complete."

Rather than opening his book, he opened his mouth and released a long yawn, slumping on his bench and resting his head against the back of it. "It's late for me. Dawn is when I get some shut eye."

Dawn was the only time she'd had available for tutoring sessions. She'd tried to pick a time that also worked for a nocturnal Shadow fae, but no learning would happen if he was too tired to cooperate.

"What are you?" he murmured, and she turned her head to find him pinning her with his intense green gaze. He lifted a hand toward her, and she held perfectly still as his fingers brushed loose strands of her hair near her ear.

She leaned away from his curious hand, smirking at the way he pouted, jutting his lower lip comically forward. "I'll never tell," she teased.

Unexpectedly, he unstopped his waterskin and splashed it into her face. She cried out at the chill of the water and the rude and unnecessary attack. She barely managed to hold her book out of the way to prevent the water from dripping down her face and landing on its fragile pages.

"Whelp… Looks like you're not Freshwater mer." He lifted one finger at a time. "That either leaves human or Saltwater mer."

"You arse!" she cried, taking the liberty of reaching over the back of the bench, grabbing his arm, and using his sleeve to wipe the water from her face. "Could you have done anything other than rudely accosting me?"

"Excuse me?" he scoffed, feigning hurt by placing his free hand against his chest. "I was not accosting you. I was simply using the *contemplative exercises of my mind* to conduct this very important experiment. How can I trust my tutor if I don't even know what species she is?"

She angrily tucked her hair behind her ear to show off the rounded curve at the top. "If you want to know so badly, then fine! Saltwater mer."

At least, that was her glamour. But he didn't need to know that.

"Interesting." A grin pulled on his mouth, and once she released his arm, he rested it on the back of the bench, his hand nearly touching her shoulder. "What color is your skin when you swim? Your fins?"

"You are avoiding studying," she pointed out.

"Oh, just humor me. What color?"

The genuine sincerity staring back at her through green eyes momentarily shocked her. He wasn't using his constant, ingenuine charm. If just for this moment, he actually wanted to know.

Therefore, she told the truth. "My skin is blueish-gray. My fins," or rather, stripes, "are red."

"And your hair?" he murmured. "In this form, it's brown. But what about your other form?"

"Black," she whispered. She held her breath, wondering how he'd react.

"Obsidian black or ashy black?"

"Ashy."

Slowly, his lips crept upward, and she wasn't sure whether she would get charm or sincerity. However, the underlying smirk he usually wore lay hidden beneath a shockingly genuine smile. "You sound gorgeous. I can't wait to see your other form."

A puzzled frown worked its way through her confusion. He usually mocked and belittled her. What had changed?

A pit of anxiety churned in her stomach as the realization hit her. The minotaur attack had changed things. It had been the first time he'd looked at her with worry rather than disdain. The first time his defenses had truly dropped when he hadn't wanted to leave her side. Adding the brief camaraderie during his tutoring session with the sword…

It felt as if they weren't quite enemies anymore. Though, the middle ground felt loose and uncertain, almost as if she might fall through an unforgiving chasm at any moment.

Therefore, she stepped onto the strange middle ground with him. "You don't find *this* form gorgeous? I'm offended."

"Hah! If only you knew." But he didn't expand, leaving her puzzling over his words. Just as she opened her book once more, he leaned closer and nodded over his shoulder. "You could have it worse. You could be a human."

She snorted when she glanced at the human in question making large, laughable gestures with his arms. But no matter how hard he tried, no magic escaped him.

"Oh, give him a break. He's trying his best."

"Clearly." And then his devilish smirk returned. "I heard Professor Graves only accepted his application out of diversity pity."

This time, Avra slapped her hands over her mouth to keep her laughter from bubbling up her throat. Humans could learn magic, but they were never born with it. And by the looks of it, some humans had to study a little harder than others.

"Look out, everyone," Nox said under his breath. "Here comes the next headmaster of Darkest Star Arcane."

This time, Avra burst into laughter, unable to help herself when Nox's teasing became too much. She hated laughing at another's expense, even if they *were* human, but she failed miserably to keep herself in check this time around.

When she glanced back at Nox, she found him staring at her mouth, and her body reacted on its own as a warmth spread through her cheeks. "What?"

He shrugged, lifting his gaze to meet her eye. "I didn't know you were capable of laughing."

Her lingering smile immediately fell. She reached for his waterskin on his bench, and before he could react, dumped it over *his* face.

He coughed and spluttered, blindly snatching the waterskin back from her before opening his eyes to glare at her. "Fine," he said as he grabbed *her* arm and used her sleeve to dry his face. The blush in her cheeks only grew worse. "I deserved that."

"You *did* deserve it. Now open your book. We'll start with magic in different cultures and move on to magical compounds by next week."

Something between a sigh and a groan escaped his mouth. "How are you so smart? Who taught you all of this?"

A despairing ache settled in her chest as she thought of home and the people there. Or who used to be there. The Elders. Her mother. Her tutors. Her brother. It had been her job to learn everything. Literally. As the next in line as Matriarch, she needed to be ready to rule over her people.

Now she wondered if everything had been a waste of time in the end.

"I had tutors of my own," she finally answered, trying to remain vague. "And I enjoyed learning."

"Surely, you like to do something else aside from learning and studying. What do you do in your spare time?"

The thought of her home and their customs finally inspired happiness rather than despair as she recalled her people's chants and dances and rituals. As Matriarch, she would have presided over all their events, being one of the first, if not the very first, to participate in them.

"I enjoy dancing," she replied, a soft smile lifting on her lips as she remembered all the many hours she'd spent practicing footwork until she'd gotten it right. "My companions would tire before I did, but they humored my passion." And then the sadness crept in as her memories turned sour with blood and screams and fire. "My bonded partner spent a lot of time indulging me, and I respected him for it."

Silence stretched between them, and she lifted her head to find Nox frowning at a tree in the distance, his brows furrowed.

"You're married."

"*Bonded*," she corrected, now staring in the distance opposite him. "But not anymore." The official title of her partner was *Ikshwa*. "I was bonded almost since birth, as was customary among my people." She didn't want to divulge more information, lest she give herself and her origins away. She trusted Nox. But not enough to confide in him about *this*.

"What happened to him?"

"He's gone." And she wanted to say nothing more. It did no good to dwell and lament over the past. Her Elders had taught her that. To brace herself for the future. To look to each new sunrise.

And then she lightly smacked his arm. "You are very good at putting off your studying. If you stopped distracting my thoughts, then we could actually begin our work."

His characteristic grin returned as he tipped his head to the side and gave her a charming smile. "I was hoping you wouldn't notice. I could have kept you talking for the entire hour, and then I'd be off the hook."

"Your D-average grade would suffer as a result."

"Don't bring down my mood with your pessimism."

She laughed again and rolled her eyes. "Page twelve!" she said loudly, refusing to allow him another tangent if she could help it. "Let me show you the tricks I use to help me remember information."

FOR THE FIRST TIME in his life, Nox found that he was enjoying studying. And he wasn't entirely sure what to make of it.

Perhaps he found the content interesting. Or…

More likely, he found the company stimulating.

No one challenged Nox like Avra did, either in academics or wit. She battled his pride, matched him for wits, and kept him coming back for more like a starving, salivating man in the presence of a feast he could look at but not touch. All while doing it without the expectation of a relationship or tryst. In fact, she seemed to have no interest in him at all.

"Ha," he muttered miserably as he trekked across the school grounds, staying within the shadows while keeping his weapons close to his side. "It's as if that's a good thing."

In the days of their consistent tutoring sessions, he'd found it unappealing to seek out the quick gratification of easy women and instead found every interaction with the opposite sex boring and unfulfilling.

All because of Avra.

It was all her fault.

And she was driving him mad.

"Nox, there you are."

He spun around, nearly jumping out of his skin as he reached for his dagger. But then he relaxed when he recognized Maya's face decorated in the shadows of the tree.

His hackles flared with caution as he took a step back and glanced over his shoulder. If Avra caught them out here...

And why did his thoughts immediately jump to her? He didn't care about her opinion of him. Or did he?

"What are you doing outside at night?" he asked, glancing around himself once again. Nothing stood out except the black gates and the shimmering blue ward surrounding the school. And then the thought occurred to him... Had she followed him? He tried to diffuse the situation with a jest. "Don't Sun fae sleep at this time of night?"

Rather than providing an answer, she looked up at him with big eyes and a pout to her lips. "I thought you weren't afraid of a little fun."

Ugh. He had no patience for this. Even if she hadn't been engaged, he would never entertain a tryst with her.

With a start, he realized he hadn't pursued any women since spending more time with Avra. He now found the company of women...*lacking* in comparison. There was something about her that intrigued him. Perhaps it was the hard chase. Or maybe the mystery shrouding her kept him coming back for more pieces of the puzzle.

"I'm not interested, Maya." He turned away from her, but she caught onto his elbow, her eyebrows furrowed and her eyes blazing with anger.

"You spend far too much time with that girl, you know."

He tugged his arm out of her grip. "I don't see how that is any of your business."

"It *is* my business." She fluttered her eyelashes at him and tucked a strand of straight golden hair behind her ear. "I broke things off with Brody. I can give you what you want. Forget about Avra."

As someone who had grown up as an impulsive liar, he doubted her sincerity. Some women would say anything to have him for one night. "Goodnight, Maya."

He tried to turn away again, but this time she stepped in his path and blocked the way ahead. "What do you even know about her? Have you seen her mer form? No? I didn't think so. Plus, she acts strangely. I have mer friends."

"And?"

She ticked off on her fingers. "First, they never wander off alone. Habits of a dangerous ocean. Second, they love showing off their mer form, even in the smallest ways like wearing an ocean ring on land or drinking water just to watch their skin shimmer."

"Envy is not a good look on you."

"And they can't stay away from the water for long!" she finished with a lift of her chin. "They feel dry and scaly and just can't stand it."

"Will you stop already?" Crossing his arms, he glanced toward the gates, now feeling like he was being watched. His skin prickled at the back of his neck, and he itched to reach for one of his weapons. "This has obviously become an obsession for you. What are you attempting to do? Get me alone? Or are you trying to prove something to yourself?"

Maya took a single step closer and leveled him with a hard stare. "Do you even know who she is beneath that mer glamour? Because the rest of us don't have a clue."

He couldn't stop the laughter from bubbling up his throat. "If I understand correctly, Avra has now become a *group* obsession." He shook his head in disbelief. "It would do you some good to focus on yourself rather than on her." This time, he turned a shoulder to her, and she didn't stop him. "Oh, and give Brody my sincerest regards. I don't doubt that you're still together."

"Hmph!" She stormed away, and he watched for a moment as she disappeared around the bend on her way back to the school.

But something she'd said gave him pause.

Glamour...

What if... What if the matriarch wasn't hiding at all? What if all this time, he'd been searching in all the wrong places? What if she was hiding in plain sight beneath a glamour?

His heart pounded in his chest as the new idea spun a web inside his mind. He recalled the day his father had been killed. The Matriarch had looked to be in her forties. Therefore, her glamour was more likely to be one of the professors at the school. Either that, or a staff member.

That narrowed down the possibilities considerably.

The idea grew a stronger foothold as he stepped through the academy gates and became one with the forest, shifting with each breeze and following paths through the shadows. A shimmering blue barrier drew his attention to the border surrounding the school, which only allowed those attending and approved visitors to pass through. He was the only one who could get in and out without detection. Otherwise, the Hawkers would have had a better chance at tracking down the Matriarch long before now.

Unfortunately, he'd failed time and again to find her. But now he found another chance to try again. Still, the length of time it was taking was breeding grounds for impatience. Kress was going to be furious.

Taking a deep breath of the crisp, forest air around him, he entered deeper into the trees, following the feeling of being watched. He slowly turned around, only to face the scathing glare of Kress himself.

The man stood taller than himself, several deep scars on his face giving him a fearsome appearance. Long, tangled brown hair trailed down his back and over his curved human ears, and the veins bulging through his crossed arms gave off the notion that he needed no weapons when he could crush someone's skull with his bare hands.

"You are not here to play student," Kress growled, stepping closer until he towered over Nox. "You are our youngest Hawker, and therefore, the only one who could pass off as a student." He moved closer until his menacing snarl revealed the missing tooth on his right side. "So tell me, Klaver. What in the blazes are you doing in there?"

Well, maybe he liked playing the student. So what? For once in his life, he felt like a normal person who worried about normal things like girls and grades. Growing up with a weapon in his hand had never afforded him the luxury of what others might call boring and ordinary.

But someone like him would never know what a life like that was like.

It didn't mean he couldn't pretend.

"Despite what you may think," Nox replied with an equal show of brawn, "I *have* been searching for the Matriarch. I have as much stake in this assignment as you do, remember? I'm thinking Professor Graves is hiding her beneath a glamour somewhere on school grounds." He raised an eyebrow. "Unless she managed to sneak past your careful watch."

"Not a chance. My minotaurs have been waiting in the shadows. Though…" The other man scowled. "I now have one less, no thanks to you."

Nox shrugged, not daring to apologize when he refused to lower himself into submission. "It attacked a student. I had to intervene."

Kress spat into the dirt and nodded in the direction of the academy. "My patience grows thin. We spent too long getting you into the school. Either you find a way to get me in, too, or you hurry up your search." A malicious grin pulled on the scars on his face. "She's surrounded. She'll have nowhere to go."

Nox tightened his grip on the hilt of his sword as the heat of hatred and anger coursed through his blood. While the Matriarch lived, his father remained unavenged. Nox, nor his father, could find peace when the Infernal leader still needed to be punished for what she had done. For what her people had done.

Turning back toward Darkest Star, he vowed to find and kill the Matriarch. Even if it was the last thing he ever did.

Avra was a confident person when it came to exams, but she found herself biting her round, stubby fingernails, constantly glancing at Nox's back as the minutes ticked by in silence during midterms.

She was confident she would get a perfect or near-perfect score. But what about him? Had their tutoring sessions made a difference in his academic abilities? Or would he fail this test like he did all the others?

Silently, she scoffed at herself. Why should she care what grade he received? She was using him for his unknowing protection, nothing more.

Then why did she keep glancing up from her exam? Why did she chew on the end of her quill until it resembled the sick feathers of a volcanic duck?

Taking a deep breath, she placed the remainder of her focus into finishing her exam. Unfortunately, she finished it early. She could only twiddle her thumbs for so long before sitting around felt awkward, and discomfort climbed her spine when she had nothing else to occupy her time.

Finally, she relented by turning in her exam on Killian's desk. The professor used his magic to sift quickly through the pages before writing an A at the top of the first page and handing it back. The test had been easy enough, but what about for Nox?

She slowly made her way out the door. But not before glancing over her shoulder to find Nox's gaze fixed on her. He quickly looked away and placed his focus on his test, but even then, she still felt his attention on her.

She ended up twiddling her thumbs outside on the bench in front of the building, watching as the night sky shifted slowly as the minutes passed agonizingly by. Little by little, others trickled out of the building, but none were Nox.

A terse breath escaped her lips, and she decided she couldn't handle the strain of waiting any longer. Gathering her books in her arms, she started toward the greenhouse to check on her Infernal plant when someone threw their arm around her shoulders, startling her.

A muffled scream climbed her throat, and she tried to jab her attacker in the ribs. However, the man shifted to the side, dodging the attack while continuing to hold her around the shoulders. The familiar minty, masculine scent calmed her racing heart when she realized it was only Nox, and her entire being relaxed.

"Don't sneak up on me!" she cried, this time succeeding in elbowing him in the ribs, followed by his "oof!" His grin only widened. "I thought you would have learned after the first incident."

"Oh, I *did* learn after that first incident," he said as he guided her in the opposite direction of the greenhouse. "I learned that you are easily startled, and I find that incredibly entertaining."

"Well, I don't."

He ignored her as he squeezed her shoulders while holding out his exam papers in front of him. "You are looking at the proud owner of a C!"

Plenty of red marks glared back at her on the parchment. She couldn't help but sigh in relief that it wasn't an F. He'd learned *something* at least.

"That's incredible, Nox! I'm sure you can get it up to a B by the end of the semester."

"Don't get ahead of yourself, love."

Like always when he called her sweet pet names, her face flamed up, and she was grateful to her glamour for hiding the way her red stripes might have glowed in the face of her fluster.

She was so preoccupied with her fluster that she didn't realize he'd led her to the boy's dorms, where heavy drum beats and lutes and rowdy singing flooded out of open doors leading inside. Both men and women entered and exited, many stumbling or talking in slurred voices when intoxicated.

An after-exams party, it seemed.

She dug in her heels when realizing he meant to lead her inside. "Oh, I can't." Shaking her head, she ducked beneath his arm to escape his grip. "It's against my culture to become intoxicated without…"

The sentence trailed off, and she bit her lip when she wasn't sure she wanted to share with him.

"Without what?" He nudged her with his elbow.

Releasing a deep breath, she explained, "Without the protection of several trusted guards." The explanation was weak at best, but she didn't want to reveal anything more and give away who she was. *What* she was.

His eyebrows furrowed as he cast her a funny look. "Why? You think someone will take advantage of you in your inebriated state?"

"Yes, exactly." It was tradition to always keep guards at her side. On top of that, being taken advantage of at any time provided a risk of pregnancy. Any heirs to the Matriarchy must be legitimately conceived through her laws lest the child get executed upon birth. Therefore, should she ever choose to consume a drink, she must have her *Ikshwa* and two other trusted guards surrounding her, each of them sober.

But… Her *Ikshwa* was gone. Dead. And there was no one else to protect her. No one aside from Nox.

"You won't *need* a guard, Avra. Despite what you think, most men aren't as terrible as you've been led to believe. Besides, I swear you're safe with me." The confident spark in his eyes faded momentarily, replaced by something akin to worry. "Come on. You can't truly hide away beneath your covers after midterms. Have a little fun. I won't leave your side, if it puts you more at ease."

How had it come to this? Aside from the minotaur incident, she'd had to manipulate Nox into his protection. And now he offered it freely? Was he *that* happy with his C-grade that he was willing to endure her company? On purpose?

"All right…" she replied hesitantly. "But I'll likely leave early."

A spring entered his step as he led her across the well-manicured lawn and toward the dorms, the music growing louder with each stride. They weaved through students littering the hallways as they played games, conversed, or enjoyed drinks with one another. And then Nox led her up a flight of stairs, through another hallway, and into a room occupied by seven other people sitting in a circle on the ground while playing cards.

"Nox!" one of the men cried out with a large smile pulling on dimples on each side of his cheeks. "We thought you'd be in the exam room until sunrise."

"Ha-ha," Nox replied with a roll of his eyes. "You're hilarious, Hans." He gestured to the room at large. "Allow me to introduce you to my friends. This is my roommate, Hans. And then we have Lucas, Emond, Leila, Nessie, Sam, and Hannah. Everyone, this is Avra."

"Where'd you pick this one up?" Hannah asked with a smirk, the ring in her nose shifting with the facial movement. "In the orchard pickin' the teacher's apple?" The group laughed, and her face flushed with heat. At least until Hannah reached out a hand decorated with silver and bronze Sun fae tattoos across her fingers and wrist and shook her hand. "All jests aside, I was wonderin' when Nox was gonna bring you 'round. Talks 'bout you enough."

"I do not," Nox huffed beside her. "She's jesting. Again."

Avra raised an eyebrow and stared at him pointedly. "You don't talk about me? I'm hurt, Nox. Especially when I whooped your behind with the sword last week."

Everyone laughed again, and the insult even inspired the corner of Nox's mouth to lift before he replied, "Was that what you thought that was? The way I recall it, you attacked while we were packing up, and my sword was sheathed. I suppose that's the only way you can win against me."

"You sure are full of yourself."

He snatched something from the desk before throwing a perfectly red apple in the air and catching it deftly in his opposite hand. "Ah! There it is. The apple for Professor Graves so you can kiss arse."

More laughing.

Avra playfully sneered at him as she caught the apple on his next toss and lobbed it at his stomach.

"Oof!" He caught it right before it managed to drop to the ground. But then he chuckled and set it back on the desk and addressed the group. "What's the next game? We want to join."

Nessie took a swig of water from her glass. A pink shimmer momentarily rippled across her skin, and her hair transitioned to a darker shade of pink. A Freshwater mer. "You're just in time for…" The mer glanced back and forth across the group with a devilish smirk growing across her silvery lips. "Truth or Smooch." And then she patted the space beside her while nodding with her head for Avra to join. "There's enough love to go around."

Amusement rippled through Avra's core. At least until she realized the woman was serious. "As in…kiss each other? That's highly inappropriate."

The group laughed. Again. Even Nox's mouth lifted in a grin as he sat on the edge of his desk, arms and ankles crossed.

"Surely, you're not serious," she tried again, failing to comprehend why such a game was socially acceptable. "You can't tell me you're all in the same committed relationship."

Hannah rolled her eyes and dragged her fingers through her straight black hair. "We've all kissed each other. No commitment required. S'all part of the fun."

Again, Avra glanced back at Nox, appalled that he'd take enjoyment in such an activity. Surely not… "And you are all intimate with each other?"

A sudden uproar of fierce denial attacked her on all sides as each of them contested her claim, including Nox.

All right… So none of them have slept together, but they'd still kissed one another? In her culture, Infernals usually only kissed their bonded mates. So this was…different.

The idea was a bit difficult to wrap her mind around.

"Just harmless kissin'," Hannah clarified. "You in? Or you a coward?"

With a huff, Avra crossed her arms and turned a shoulder to them. "This is a ridiculous game. Of course, I refuse to play."

"Afraid?" Nox asked with a smirk.

"No." She held her head high, trying not to reveal her underlying uncertainty, but she was sure it leaked through her indifference, anyway. "I have never kissed anyone other than my late bondmate."

The room quieted, and she felt more than one pitying stare on her back.

"Let's change that, shall we?" Nox murmured.

When she didn't answer because her uncertainty and hesitation reared its head, he hooked his finger around her pinky and pulled her toward the edge of the circle.

"It doesn't actually mean anything," he reassured. "It's just fun."

The desire to push away all her worries for one night surfaced. To spend time with her peers. To drink and laugh and play and forget everything that pressed heavily on her shoulders. But… "Kissing someone you are not committed to is considered fun?" She huffed but didn't pull her pinky out of Nox's grip when she enjoyed the small warmth emanating from his finger far too much. "I fail to understand the allure of this activity."

The others laughed, whether at her expense or because they found her amusing, she didn't know. Or perhaps they'd had a bit too much to drink as it was.

"Who never let the house cat outside?" Lucas asked, his eyes such a light blue in color that they almost appeared white. Laughter followed his remark.

Avra's mouth pressed in a thin line as she recalled her lonely childhood. She had always been expected to behave and maintain good poise in all her interactions and throughout her daily life. She'd studied and practiced and learned. But she could count on one hand how many times she'd actually had fun. Matriarchs—and even Matriarchs-to-be—were not allowed to have fun when so much responsibility weighed on them constantly.

Nox gave her finger a slight squeeze, pulling her attention to the kindness in his expression rather than a teasing smirk. "We can leave if you don't want to do this."

She glanced over the group, each with hopeful stares. They wanted her there. They wanted to spend time with her. Like friends. She wasn't entirely sure how to navigate such a situation, but she realized she wanted to try.

"I do," she said in a firm, decisive tone as she took a seat between Nessie and Sam. "I want to play. If someone would kindly explain the rules."

When Sam handed her a drink, she took a deep breath and downed the entire glass, the clear liquid burning her throat on its way down. The others cheered and shoved her shoulders in a congratulatory manner. Her *Ikshwa* was gone. No one could protect her. But perhaps she didn't want to be protected. Perhaps, for once, she wanted to throw caution into the fire and allow herself to burn.

"The rules are easy enough," Leila said as she dealt out a round of cards. "There are two matching cards, and for each round, you are paired with whoever matches your card. One will be black, the other red. The holder of the black card gets to ask any question of the holder of the red card. If the person with the red card answers truthfully, they are safe for that round. If they decline to answer or are caught lying, they have to smooch the other. If you match with yourself, you can either play those cards and are safe for the round, or you can choose anyone in the circle to question."

"That's it?"

"That's it."

Easy enough. She'd answer truthfully each round to avoid kissing altogether. That way, she'd still spend time with her peers while not committing to a single kiss.

Lucas laid down the first card—an ink drawing depicting a Sun fae holding a bouquet of flowers. The blood drained from her face when she realized it matched one in her own hand. She laid it down next to his and challenged him with a defiant stare.

"Avra, Avra, Avra," the man said, a chuckle under his breath. "I'll start us out with a simple question to ease you into the game. What's your surname?"

She clenched her jaw, her hands fisting in her lap when she realized she couldn't answer the question. Her surname was very Infernal. They would know immediately what she was should she answer honestly. Perhaps even *who* she was if they were studied on Infernal Matriarchy.

Therefore, she lied. "Dawson."

"That's a lie," Nox called out across the circle. "That's a Sun fae surname, and you're mer."

A glare heated in her eyes as she silently mouthed, *I'll kill you.*

"Oooooh," everyone chorused before slapping their knees in a rhythmic pattern and chanting, "Liar! Liar! Liar!"

Lucas leaned toward her. She balled her hands into fists in her lap. And then she let him kiss her quickly on the lips. Just like that, it was over before Hans laid down his card to match with Nessie.

She released a tense breath, her fingers aching as she relaxed her hands. *That wasn't terrible,* she thought to herself. It was nothing like kissing Yianni, which was more out of duty and respect than anything else. And this… Well, it had been pleasant like the brief contentment from inhaling the sweet scent of a flower on a warm summer's day. The kiss inspired no feelings of longing or attraction. But it was pleasant, nonetheless. Like two friends sharing a laugh.

The tension in her body melted further as she relaxed and allowed herself to live in the moment, to laugh with her peers, to tease them for their answers or subsequent kisses. Another drink helped her lose her rigid posture and laugh more freely. It allowed her to relax and lose the feelings of guilt over breaking her people's customs, over kissing someone who was not the man she had been promised to, over placing herself in danger when drinking without the steady presence of her *Ikshwa* to keep her safe.

Next, Sam matched with her and laid down his card depicting a king with a crown. He asked, "Out of everyone in this room, who would you be most likely to green your gown with?"

Her gaze immediately jumped to Nox, and the action didn't go unnoticed when the relentless teasing began. Intense heat burned her face as she quickly glanced away. "The cat!" she blurted as she pointed beneath Hans' bed.

"There is no cat!" Hans shouted.

Everyone guffawed, and she found herself subjected to Sam's kiss moments later. She barely felt it when her fluster occupied the majority of her attention, and she felt the heavy weight of Nox's stare boring into her. But she refused to glance at him again, not when her expression would surely give away what she thought of Sam's question.

She didn't get the chance to calm her fluster when it was her turn next, and her gaze jumped desperately from card to card for a match of her own. But she found no such match and ended up laying down a card with a blooming flower painted on one side. Leila laid down the same card.

What was an easy question? One that wouldn't subject her to another kiss?

"Who is taking you to the autumntide dance next week?" she asked.

"Nox."

A chill washed down her body, throwing her entire mood off balance with the unexpected information. Unfamiliar feelings tumbled in her stomach, but she recognized one over all the others.

Disappointment.

Why in the seven blazes was she disappointed?

"Liar!" Nox cried as he flicked a card in Leila's direction, hitting her shoulder, before everyone burst into laughter. "I haven't asked anyone. You just want that kiss."

"You caught me." Leila winked at Avra and pursed her lips. "Pucker up, Teacher's Pet."

A warm relief flooded through her, washing away the previous chill of unexpected disappointment. However, she was far too shy to initiate even the smallest kiss. Therefore, she pecked the other woman on the cheek and returned to her seat on the floor.

Thankfully, no one insisted she kiss her correctly, and the game continued without a broken stride.

When it was Nox's turn, he laid down a card with a man holding a magical flame in his hand. She glanced down at what remained of her own cards and shook her head. Everyone glanced between themselves, and more people shook their heads as well.

At least until a devilish smirk lifted on Nox's lips, and he laid down an exact match from his own hand.

"Skip or choose?" Lucas asked.

"Obviously choose," Nox said, his eyes flashing with amusement. "Where's the fun in skipping?"

And then his gaze honed in on *her*.

"Avra No-Surname." His grin grew larger as he singled her out. "This is more of a dare than a truth." He produced a bottle of greenish opaque water and held it out to her. "Show us your mer form. Or face a devastating kiss."

Her face both paled and heated simultaneously when she realized the bottle contained seawater. This was never supposed to happen. Under no circumstances could she allow the others to find out she wasn't mer. Even if it *was* Nox, someone whom she trusted.

Instead, she stuck up her nose at him and turned her head away. "I am not a performer. I refuse to put on a show."

Nox clicked his tongue. "You can't answer a single question honestly. I'm not sure what to make of that." His grin widened, and his eyes sparked with excitement. "Surrender a kiss, love."

Avra's heart shot to her throat. A rapid pulse thrummed at her neck. Involuntarily, her gaze dipped from his intense green eyes to the supple curve of his lips.

Chanting picked up around them. "Kiss her! Kiss her! Kiss her!"

But their voices became a quiet buzz in the back of her mind when she was overly aware of the way Nox crawled the short distance between them, scattering cards in his wake. The way his gentle fingers cradled either side of her face. His sweet breath tickling her cheek…

And then he kissed her.

It was as if she were transported back to the safety of her homeland, almost as if volcanoes erupted on all sides of her and filled her nostrils with ashy longing. The temperature rose in her core when, beneath her glamour, her stripes couldn't help but react to his touch. They warmed her body, steadily rising in temperature as he leaned into her until they fell backward on the ground together.

She felt powerless against his touch and couldn't find the will to extract herself from beneath him. The kiss grew feverish. Insistent. And she wanted more, more, more. His lips were like her first taste of the Infernal Springs, and she wanted to consume every raw piece of him until she had her fill.

The core in her chest burned with longing, with need as his gentle fingers shifted from her face and threaded through her hair. Suddenly, the kiss wasn't enough. She wanted more. She wanted all of him.

But then the cheering and whistles struck out at her suddenly, forcibly pulling her back to the present. She broke the kiss, staring back at him with a stunned expression. In all the years of her life, she'd never known a connection like this could exist. She'd never known someone could break her down and build her back up with a single, excruciatingly beautiful kiss.

And that terrified her.

She pushed against Nox's solid, muscular chest. Although he would have been much too heavy to move him off her on her own, he shifted aside at her silent request. The moment she found an opening, she scrambled to her feet and fled from the room without looking back.

A whirlwind of emotion crashed into her as the walls seemed to close in on either side of the hallway filled with hundreds of people blocking her way. She gasped for air as she weaved in and out of students, desperate to escape the confinement of the dorms.

The emotions only seemed to amplify when she burst outside and heaved in each heavy breath. Terror for a future unknown. Guilt for deceiving Nox. Shame for kissing someone who was not her *Ikshwa.*

For...for...*enjoying* herself so immensely that she'd forgotten her people, that she'd forgotten her purpose.

But what terrified her the most of all?

She was falling in love with Nox Klaver.

WELL, SHITE.

The air filled with shock, with uncertainty as Nox stared after Avra as she fled the room. He ran his thumb over his bottom lip, her kiss like a pleasant fire on his lips.

"Was it something I said?" he jested feebly, but icy shock continued to build up in his chest as he tried to make sense of what had happened.

But no… He *knew* what had happened. Only, he'd never experienced it to such a degree before. Perhaps he'd never experienced it at all. "Love" was not in his vocabulary. He'd shunned the very idea of losing control of his heart. But he'd slowly been losing it to her through every study session, every time he touched her hand or corrected her stance during combat practice, and every time she opened that pert little mouth of hers to challenge him in the most infuriatingly alluring way.

Hannah gave him a pointed look. "She didn't have n'issue until *you* kissed her. You rattled her."

And she rattled me as well.

"Stay and play s'more. Otherwise, we'll have to reshuffle."

Nox slowly shook his head as he stared at the doorway, hoping Avra might rush back in. But she didn't. "I can't kiss anyone after that. That was…" He paused, searching for the right word to accurately describe the magic he and Avra had shared with a single kiss. "*Special*," he finished, and still, the word hardly did their wild connection justice.

"Oooooh," several of them chorused before Nessie said, "Looks like someone is committed."

"I am," he realized with shock burning through his soul, and he finally tore his gaze away from the doorway and toward the stack of books sitting on his bedside table. Every relationship of his had been fleeting. Flippant. Short. A way to amuse himself for a time.

But with Avra…

He wanted more.

Her heated touch had momentarily sent him over the edge of his sanity, and for once in his life, he'd lost control. Rather, she'd had complete control over *him*. He wanted to do anything she asked of him if only to feel the wildness of her touch, of her kiss, at least one more time.

"I thought you didn't do serious relationships," Lucas teased as he gathered the cards and reshuffled. "You didn't like to be tied down to one person, or something like that."

"She changed my mind," he murmured, the right words evading him in his attempt to explain what he'd just experienced.

When the words continued to evade him, he climbed onto his bed and pulled several books and blank pieces of parchment onto his lap. Never in his life had he been so eager to read and study. But now he found excitement eating at him as he opened the pages.

"Studying now of all times?" Nessie chuckled with a roll of her eyes, pink shimmering across her skin as she took another swig from her glass of water. "Midterms are over. You can relax."

"I scared Avra away." He momentarily placed his quill between his teeth as he turned to an overly complicated subject about magic matter and began writing down his questions. "I need an excuse to see her again. She obviously won't come to me." And he didn't want to run after her now. Not when she seemed to need space.

Hans asked, "You don't think she'll show up to training practice with you?"

He paused in his writing as he considered his roommate's question. But after witnessing the flash of...of...*fear* or whatever that was in Avra's eyes, he wasn't sure of anything at all. "I'm not willing to take the chance to find out."

A smirk lifted his lips as he guaranteed an audience with her by including a note about Sun fae magic being used during the night. Knowing Avra, she wouldn't be able to help herself when she inevitably corrected him.

Like Nessie had said... He certainly was committed now, and he planned to pursue Avra to the ends of the kingdom if necessary.

"There you are!" a familiar voice called from behind Avra. The mere sound of Nox's voice spurred her heart into a panicked frenzy.

She quickened her pace.

After what had happened last night, she wasn't ready to face him. What was she supposed to do? What could she possibly say?

Therefore, she walked briskly down the cobblestone path leading around the fountain and toward the safety of the greenhouse far too distant for comfort, pretending as if she hadn't heard him. Perhaps if she'd brought her Kip Stone along, she could genuinely say she hadn't heard him at all.

"Avra!" Nox called after her again, this time closer than before.

Her heart shot straight into her throat as he grabbed her hand and spun her around. But this time it wasn't fear sending her pulse into a frenzy. It was knowing what his lips tasted like. It was knowing how his tongue teased and explored, how his warm breath felt against her mouth.

"I am in dire need of your help, I realized." He breathed hard, as if the short journey to her side had taxed him.

He handed her a piece of parchment with rows upon rows of notes and questions, the subject straight from one of Professor Graves' assigned books from class.

"Shadows below," she murmured as she scanned the long list of questions, but then her attention snagged on a note so blatantly wrong that she couldn't simply skim over it without correction.

"What is it?" Nox asked, hands stuffed in his pockets.

She tipped the piece of parchment toward him and pointed to an incorrect fact. "You are hopeless, Nox. The moment the sun descends, Sun fae are cut off from replenishing their magic until sunrise. They may only use magic at night if they have it stored within them. Otherwise, they must wait until morning."

He grinned at the ground as he shuffled his feet, and when he glanced up at her through his lashes, it was as if her stomach tumbled down a flight of stairs as it fluttered and twisted in the presence of this infuriating man.

"I suppose I still have a ways to go until that B, huh?"

"Perhaps," she replied coolly as she handed back the list. Heartache and anger punched her in the gut when her gaze dipped momentarily to his lips before she glared at the infuriating spark of mischief in his eyes. She turned on her heel and sped away from him, but he kept up with an easy stride. "I'm sure you had plenty of fun last night. How many women did you end up kissing? Five? Twenty? One hundred?"

Because she was fool enough to have allowed him to kiss *her*. It meant nothing to him. He'd mentioned it before they'd played the Infernal-flaming game anyhow. And she'd fallen for it. Stupid!

"Zero after you," he said, stopping her in her tracks.

For a long moment, she stood stupefied by the sincerity in his tone. By the lack of teasing note. He wasn't lying.

She turned to him and found the truth of his statement in his eyes. The teasing spark in his expression often waiting for something ridiculous to exit his mouth had long since disappeared, and sincerity stared back at her.

"Zero," she reiterated disbelievingly. "What? Did you grow bored of the wide selection of women throwing themselves at your feet?"

"Oh, Avra," he laughed, and sure enough, that spark returned to his eyes, and his smirk returned with a vengeance. "You overestimate the amount of attention I get from women."

"I assure you, I don't."

"Have you been spying on me?"

Another burst of anger traveled down her arms and into the hands she planted on her hips. "What do you want, Nox? Can't you go ruin someone else's day, or does it have to be mine?"

"A bit rude this morning, aren't we?" he teased. But then he hooked his pinky around hers, and she was powerless against his charming influence as he led her beneath the boughs of a willow tree, the atmosphere secluded and quiet. Several birds twittered overhead, and a small breeze wove through the drooping branches. But otherwise, it was peaceful and still.

At least until Nox managed to spur her heart into a frenzy by stepping closer until the toe of his shoe brushed against hers. The seemingly innocent touch brought her back to last night and the way he'd kissed her. The experience had been breathtaking. Magical. Terrifying.

"I have something for you," he murmured before reaching into his pack and pulling out a rectangular package wrapped in brown paper and tied with twine.

Her heart skipped with hopeful anticipation as she gingerly accepted the gift from his hand. "This is book shaped."

"Clearly, it's shaped like a box."

Amusement twitched her mouth at the corners, and she couldn't help her excitement as she pulled on the twine to unravel it from the outside. And then she carefully peeled back the brown parchment to reveal the book beneath.

She swallowed a lump of emotion in her throat as her fingers reverently caressed the hard cover and spine. *"Weapons Mastery and Finesse,"* she read the title, opening the volume to somewhere near the middle. The book was filled with illustrations of weapons, fighting stances, and dueling positions. From briefly flipping through the pages, she gathered the book could help her learn how to wield and fight with a variety of weapons.

Nox tapped the book with his finger. "I know you learn easier through the written word, so I found this for you. Thought it could help."

Finally, she pulled her attention from the pages and toward Nox's adorable half-grin. "This must have cost you a fortune." Books were expensive. And one with so many illustrations? "How did you acquire this?"

"I have my ways." He nodded toward the book. "My favorite passage is on page fifty."

Far too eagerly, she flipped to the page indicated and inhaled sharply when a folded piece of parchment fell out and flitted to the floor. She bent to retrieve it and opened it to reveal a purple Shadow Flox pressed and perfectly preserved within, the pigments staining the white parchment a colorful array of purple, pink, and yellow.

The top of the parchment read:

Go to the autumntide dance with me?

She stared at the words for far too long as a measure of shock crawled up her body and froze her limbs. Despite what Nox had mentioned, women really did throw themselves at his feet like ripe apples falling from the tree. Dozens of women would come running with the snap of his fingers.

Why would he choose *her* of all people?

When she still didn't answer, Nox pressed, "You like dancing. I like you. What do you say?"

"When did that change?" she blurted.

"When did what change?"

"You know exactly what I mean. And I deserve an honest answer. None of your smooth side-stepping, thinking I won't notice your deflecting."

He stuffed his hands into his pockets and shrugged. "I don't know when it changed, only that it did."

The answer was fair, as it was exactly what she would have said herself about him. But this was *Nox*. Everyone loved him. He had dozens of friends, and twice as many admirers swooning over his good looks and unique aura.

Why her?

"I-I-I don't know," she stuttered, thinking about the lilybane growing in the greenhouse. It would fully mature sometime in the next several days, and she could delay returning home no longer. "I'm leaving Skaad this week."

Silence echoed between them as if she'd shouted into a deep chasm and nothing resounded back.

"Going on vacation?" he asked, though the hesitancy in his tone revealed he knew exactly what she meant.

With a shake of her head, she answered, "I'm going back home. I'm needed there." She released a long breath to try to expel the hurt in his eyes from her mind but it didn't work. "I love it here. The school. The teachers. The people. It's a place I could only dream of belonging. But I don't. And I can't stay."

"Why only tell me now?"

"I never thought you cared."

Nox scoffed and rolled his eyes. "Poor judge of my character, I must say."

A part of her wanted to spill her entire self to him, to reveal the actual reason she must go. But something held her back. Fear, perhaps. Because she was falling for Nox. And should he learn that she was an Infernal, he likely wouldn't take kindly to her then.

"Well..." His hands pulled from his pockets and dropped to his sides. "Can we keep in touch?"

The thought of saying goodbye to him for good created a pit of ache in her chest. All her life, she'd always done what others wanted, what was expected of her. She'd followed rules and traditions and had given her entire self to her people. Quite literally with her *Ikshwa* as was tradition in return for his undying loyalty.

Just this once... She wanted to do something for herself. The lilybane was not ready. The dance was less than a week away. Rather than twiddling her thumbs...

"I admit I don't know the traditional dances of your people. But perhaps you might teach me."

Nox released an audible breath and smiled as he hooked his pinky around hers. "I've been told I'm a good teacher."

"By whom?"

He smirked. "You."

She feigned appall. "I never said any such thing!"

"You did!" he teased. "I heard you say it under your breath last week during combat training."

"Have you been spying on me?" she threw right back at him, reiterating what he'd said earlier about her.

"Always."

Once again, she found it difficult to tell if he was jesting or flirting. The two seemed to go hand in hand with him. However, she'd never believed the behavior would be directed at her one day. What was this? Was he genuinely interested? Or did he view her as the new flavor of the week?

But as she glanced down at the book she held in her hands, the warmth burning in her core revealed the unmistakable truth.

He cared.

If he'd gone out of his way to acquire this special gift, he must truly care.

A laughy breath escaped her lips. "I don't know what to wear. The traditional garb of my people likely wouldn't suffice."

"I think you should wear it. Just because we're on land doesn't make your traditions any less important."

On land. If only he knew.

She glanced down at the pleated skirts of her student uniform and bit her lip. Infernal clothing was beautiful in its own right, and Nox deserved to know what she was…

Besides, she planned to leave this week. Could it hurt to reveal the truth of her identity? If only to him and no one else. And then perhaps… Perhaps they could truly keep in touch. Because she didn't want to leave him.

First, she needed an elixir to drop her glamour. Then, she'd find out how deep Nox's sincerity ran.

Her attention returned to his green eyes, the black slit of his pupils thin beneath the light of early morning. Considering the post-midterm break between classes, she surmised he'd retire for the day soon.

"Looks like I'll need to find a new partner for the final project in Graves' class." He chuckled wryly and rubbed the back of his neck with a hand.

Releasing a long breath, Avra stared at the ground when looking into his eyes became too difficult. Should she have been anyone else, she would have liked to spend a few years at Darkest Star Arcane. Unfortunately, she wasn't just anybody.

"Are you trying to make me jealous?" she teased back half-heartedly. "Because it's certainly not working."

"I don't believe you," he returned with another charming smile enough to turn her insides into a pile of mush. He had absolutely no business being so handsome and charming. She both admired and hated him for it.

"I need to brew an elixir," she blurted, slowly backing away from him with his gift held against her chest. Deceiving him was no longer the morally correct option. He would understand and still like her when he saw the real her. Surely.

"It's mid-term break. Put school aside for a few days."

Her grip on the book tightened. "This isn't an assignment. It's personal."

"Do you need help—"

"No." But then she smiled. A real, genuine smile filled with hope rather than despair. And realizing she still held his list of questions, she said, "You clearly need a lot of help before school starts again next week. We'll go over your questions—"

"Don't forget dancing lessons."

A breathy chuckle escaped her. "Dancing, too." A shy smile lifted her lips as she tucked her hair behind her ear, drawing his attention to the lack of point on the curve. "I'll see you soon."

She left the privacy of the willow curtains before he could somehow change her mind to stay. She needed to prepare for her trip to Crotona. Allowing a handsome, charming man to distract her was a bad idea.

At least until tomorrow, perhaps.

But then the thought of Theo grounded her back to the earth. An insistent thought prodded at her mind, starting as an idea the size of a grain of sand and growing to the size of a boulder. Yes, she would have Lord Graves' soldiers at her back once she summoned them. But she had no *Ikshwa*.

What if…

Immediately, she shook the thought from her mind. But it insistently tugged and pulled until it forced her to confront it.

What if Nox came with her? To protect her. To keep her safe until she called upon the Shadow Lord's help?

Again, she dismissed the ludicrous idea. Journeying to the lower realm could kill Nox simply by breathing their hot, dry air. He would sooner die of dehydration than survive long enough to protect her from anything.

As she ventured along the stone path leading toward the academy, the thought refused to abate.

What if there was a way?

11

IF NOX INTERROGATED any more teachers, someone would start getting suspicious.

He kept the conversations light and appeared as if he sought learning rather than concrete information. But asking the wrong question to the right person could prove disastrous. Therefore, he treaded carefully.

It would be much easier if he could flirt the information out of them. But he *did* have boundaries there, at least.

Professor Gamlik, the Elixirs and Potions teacher, pushed her spectacles up her nose as she gazed at him nearly cross-eyed through a waft of purple smoke. Her short, fluffy gray hair had long since frayed at the ends, almost as if she'd blown up a potion too many in her career.

Due to her inability to focus for longer than a minute on the same subject, he gauged she was either not the

Matriarch or a very good actress. For some reason, he pictured the Matriarch to be more smart and cunning.

"And that is how you create a memory potion," the woman said, inhaling the purple fumes before making a disgusted expression at the odor of charred flesh. "Never a pleasant smell, that one."

"Very interesting." He prodded the smoke with a finger, declining to inhale it like she had. All his memories were best kept in his sketchbook and not at the forefront of his mind. His past hadn't always been happy.

Certain no one else lingered in the room but himself, he ventured cautiously, "I read about glamour potions in a book, and I couldn't help my curiosity. They exist outside of texts, don't they?"

This was the part where he would know for certain who he dealt with. But when the professor lacked an immediate reaction to the word, he realized he needed to take his search elsewhere. He'd spoken to three female professors and three female staff members with nothing to show for it.

"They do." She peered at him through the haze of smoke. "They can be complicated potions to make when you create a glamour from your own imagination. Much easier to duplicate someone else's appearance."

Interesting. Either the Matriarch was pretending to be someone else, or she was someone no one had known before school started. He could use that information to his advantage.

"And if I happened to take the potion outside the academy walls, for example, would I be trapped outside the borders?"

She pushed her spectacles up once more. "The barrier is designed to recognize someone's face. Theoretically, if you were to take a glamour potion outside the walls and try to get back in as yourself, your access would be denied."

"And if I had another student's face?"

"*Theoretically*," she emphasized, "you would be able to pass." She chuckled and pointed a stern finger at him. "Using such glamours could get you expelled. It's best you steer clear of them."

Nox pressed his lips together in mock disappointment. "And yet, Professor Graves teaches students how to make love potions even though they are forbidden dark magic."

"Ah…" The professor sighed in defeat. "I suppose you are correct." She rummaged through her supplies and pulled out a variety of ingredients, and he made sure to pay extra attention to everything she did. It could come in handy later. "The headmaster has informed me that you may need extra help outside of class to pass the exams at the end of the year. Perhaps I can help."

And then she taught him how to make a glamour potion—alongside a few others, which he probably should have paid more attention to. But it was the glamour concoction he was most interested in.

Finally, after exhausting himself of his attention span, he gathered the ingredients she had used over the next day and investigated further into the teachers. But the more he investigated, the more he wondered if he'd been incorrect in his theory. Unless the Matriarch was Lyyli herself—whom he would never contemplate questioning to avoid earning Killian's wrath—he started to doubt that the Matriarch was even at Darkest Star. How trustworthy were Kress's sources?

If his boss was so confident she was here… They needed to take another approach.

Which led him to brew several new potions to use for later.

When he finished potion-making to the best of his poor ability, he returned to his dorm to find Hans flipping through the pages of one of his books. His roommate nodded in greeting.

He jumped onto his bed and melted into the pillow, pulling out his own study materials, which was highly uncharacteristic of him. During midterm break, no less! He could be camping with his friends at the beach or drinking each night away. But instead, he found himself buried in books, wanting to learn and discover.

Silently, he chastised himself when, not for the first time, he remembered he wasn't a student. Not really. He was at Darkest Star to search for the Infernal Matriarch. Nothing more.

He sighed and closed his book about the magical properties of plants, picking up his sketchbook instead. A wistful melancholy hung over him as he flipped through the pages, some of the images dating back years ago. One image depicted his father frowning and shaking rocks out of one of his shoes. Nox couldn't help but grin at the memory. He and Leni had placed a pebble in one of his shoes each time he'd taken them off. It had driven him up the wall. At least until the two of them hadn't been able to contain their laughter, giving themselves away.

Another image was of him and Leni holding hands, grinning at each other as children. His friend was blind, and he'd led her by the hand across Hawker camps throughout their childhood until she'd learned to use her magic to navigate her surroundings.

They had been like brother and sister, especially as some of the only children amongst Hawkers.

Guilt returned at full force when he recalled the day he'd left her with the Hawkers. It was the same day as his father's death. He'd been so stricken with grief that he'd wanted to leave his past behind.

Pushing those feelings of guilt away, he turned to a new page, picked up a chalk pencil, and began drawing in his sketchbook. It was always the same face that haunted his best dreams. A pert mouth, intense eyes, a teasing expression. He could not push Avra from his mind, no matter how hard he tried.

His lips pressed tightly together as he smudged the chalk with the tip of his finger to create the delicate shadows beneath Avra's chin. All he wanted was to be a normal student and court Avra and shirk his studies occasionally. He wanted to prank his peers and get caught once in a blue moon and go out with his friends on fun adventures.

If only things had been different for him.

Another sigh escaped him. It was time for another audience with Kress. If he continued to fail to locate the Matriarch, his boss would take more extreme measures by attacking the school with whatever beasts he had at his disposal. People would get hurt. Some would likely get killed. He didn't want to put these people in danger. His friends. But this war would never end until they had the Infernal Matriarch in their grasp.

He'd failed. And now Kress would take his place.

A knock at the door startled him upright. He and Hans shared a confused look.

"You expecting anyone?" Nox asked, but his friend shook his head.

"I don't have plans until tomorrow night." Hans buried his face in his book, and Nox sighed when he realized he'd have to be the one to open the door.

He fixed the unruly strands of his hair and tucked his shirt into his trousers. His vest lay somewhere on the ground beside his bed, so he felt only half-dressed as he turned the handle of his door and opened it.

His eyes shot wide open when he faced Avra, who stood in the corridor with a book held to her chest. The toe of one foot hid behind the heel of the other, and the way she bit her lip between her teeth drew his attention to her mouth. Memories flashed in his mind. Of their lips locked together. His fingers buried into her hair. The warmth churning through his entire body.

The heat of her touch…

"Avra," he said in a breathy voice. Nothing smart nor witty came to mind when he was held captive by her blue-eyed stare.

"Are you busy?" she asked before glancing over his shoulder toward Hans.

His roommate quickly packed up his books into a bag and shouldered his way past him into the hallway. "I'm off to the library." Behind Avra's back, the infuriating Shadow fae winked. "I won't be back for a few hours. Try not to have too much fun."

And then Hans disappeared, leaving him alone with Avra and still nothing witty waiting on the tip of his tongue. Rather, he was dumbstruck, the clever retort fizzling out entirely in favor of deafening silence.

"Umm…Nox?" she pressed.

"No, no, no." He pulled the door open wider to invite her inside. "I'm only studying. Nothing too serious."

She laughed, her arm brushing against his on her way inside. "So you admit that you don't take your studies seriously."

With a roll of his eyes, he shut the door behind her, overly aware that they were alone. Together. In his bedroom. "I take them seriously enough." But then he swore under his breath when he realized his room was dark, and by the way Avra squinted her eyes, she couldn't see a thing.

Purple magic pooled into his hand, and he lifted his arm toward the ceiling to release it. Small, purple dots latched onto the ceiling overhead, creating specks of pulsing light. A compromise. Not too dark as to blind Avra but not too light as to irritate his own eyes.

"Incredible," Avra murmured, turning in a full circle as she gazed up at the ceiling. "They're like stars. I have never seen anything like this."

Nox stuffed his hands into his pockets and shrugged. "Just Shadow fae magic."

She turned to him, tearing her gaze away from the lights to meet his eye. "What else can you do?"

"I mostly use my magic to fight. But I have a few other tricks up my sleeve."

"Like what?"

He gestured to the ceiling with a grin on his face, but clearly, she wanted more of a show.

After the kiss they'd shared, his mind was muddled and his feelings rested on his sleeve, much to his chagrin. All his life, he had been in control of himself. Of his emotions, of his relationships, of his actions. But when around Avra? She was the one with control over him. He disliked it almost as much as he enjoyed it.

Releasing a long breath, he pulled his hands out of his pockets to glance down at his fingers. "My father taught me magic. Most of my arcane skills revolve around combat and distraction."

"Distraction?" Her grip on her book tightened, but she never moved away from him. She stood only an arm's length away. Far too close for comfort but still not close enough.

He nodded. "I can incite one's greatest fear using my magic. During combat, it proves useful. I can even bring forth someone's happiest memory if they haven't learned to block their mind from magic."

She bit her lip again. "Are you able to see the memories themselves?"

"Unfortunately, no." He moved toward his desk to grab one of his books but stopped short when she clasped her fingers around his wrist. The heat from her touch spiked his feelings into a frenzy within his chest, and he took a moment to breathe deeply through his nose before turning to face her.

The blue within her eyes was pleading, vulnerable in a way he'd never before witnessed. "I want to see a memory of my family. Before..." She swallowed, blinking rapidly as if to keep her emotions at bay.

For a moment, he didn't know what to do. He'd never seen her in such a state of vulnerability. Usually, she expressed only anger or smugness toward him. The sight of her wayward emotions made him want to do anything she asked.

"Before what?" he urged softly.

"Before they were killed."

Something akin to a dry desert climbed up his throat and settled in his mouth as he stared back at her. Ever since he'd known her, she'd been secretive, not telling him of her family or her home or her origins. Was this why? Because it was too difficult to speak of?

He unsuccessfully tried to swallow against the dryness of his throat. "But you said you were returning home because your family needed you."

"No." She shook her head. "I said I'm returning home because I'm needed there."

"By whom?"

"My people." She blew out a long breath. "I never gave you my surname because I thought you would recognize it, and I didn't want to be recognized. Not here."

Blinking slowly, he tried to recall the merpeople and their hierarchy. He didn't know much about their culture aside from what he'd learned from a few mer friends along the years. The ocean beneath was a mystery to him.

"So…" He placed one fisted hand on his hip, trying to find a delicate way to ask about what he wanted to know. "Are you some sort of princess?"

Again, she blew out a long breath before lifting her gaze from her book to his face. "Queen would be a better term for what I am."

"A queen."

"Yes."

He noticed her fingers trembling over his wrist. As if she were afraid. But of what?

"You're serious."

She nodded, and for a moment, he wasn't sure what to think. The first thought to cross his mind was that she was delusional. But then he recalled her quick distrust, her abnormal smarts, the way she'd shied away from his bottle of ocean water as if she'd wanted to hide her identity. Not to mention her over-involvement with Professor Graves and her stuffy personality when they'd first met. Surely, royalty all had sticks up their arses.

"Queen…of what?"

He tried to understand but failed abysmally. Her simple statement had taken a hold of his world and shook it like one of those snow globes he'd come across on his travels. Professor Banks taught the class *Histories of Fae Folk*, but he couldn't for the life of him remember anything the man had taught over the semester. He thought he recalled different monarchs over different oceans, but he could be wrong.

Avra pulled her gaze away and stared at the ground. "Can we talk about something else?"

"Umm…no? Not after you drop that explosion in my life. What business does a queen have here? Shouldn't you be…oh, I don't know…ruling over your people or something?"

It was the wrong thing to say because moments later, Avra burst into tears. Relentless sobs escaped her throat, and she dropped her book to the ground in favor of hiding her face within her palms as she cried.

His mouth fell open, and he stood by helplessly as she released her tears. Not once had he witnessed her in such a state. The situation must have been serious for her to drop her book of all things, one of her most prized possessions.

Wordlessly, he reached for her and folded her into his arms. Another round of shock rushed through him when she clung on tightly and buried her face in his chest. For a moment, he wasn't sure what to do, what to say, in the midst of a crying woman he actually cared about.

But this time…

The sound of her heartache cracked his resilient outward resolve. He wanted to hold her until her despair disappeared. He wanted to take away all her hurt and her pain and replace it with smiles and laughter.

He perked up at the thought. There *was* something he could do. Was it the best timing? Probably not. But anything was better than *this*.

The purple of his magic snaked out of his hand and wove around his fingers. He silently coaxed the amethyst strands up her back, over her shoulder, and allowed it to enter her head. His magic met no resistance. Either she had no idea how to block him mentally, or she didn't have the heart to try.

Threads of control seeped into her. But unlike when he tugged hard to pull on a memory so excruciatingly terrifying as to immobilize an enemy, he pulled softly, bringing forth one of her happiest memories to the forefront of her mind.

Long ago, his father had shown him what it was like, both by inspiring his most terrifying memory and by showing his happiest. For him, he'd been happiest when he, his father, and his friend, Leni, had spent leisurely time together. He recalled the time they had fished inside a boat on top of a sparkling lake while the moonlight shimmered down on the glassy surface. Croaking frogs, gentle winds, and his father's quiet humming had filled a peaceful night.

Nothing else trumped that memory, but he wouldn't doubt if studying with Avra managed to come close.

Little by little, Avra's sobs quieted and her trembling ceased. Her body relaxed against his, her sniffles transitioning into soft sighs. "Mother," she whispered. "I miss you."

Emotion clogged his throat when he guessed what sort of memory flitted through her mind. He knew exactly how it felt to see his father for the last time over and over again in his mind. Whatever memory she currently witnessed, it was doing wonders to help calm her down.

He didn't know what had upset her, but if it was bad enough to make Avra cry of all people... It must not have been good.

"Thank you," she murmured against him after her tears subsided.

"Mmm," he answered noncommittally, not wanting to divulge how much she'd come to mean to him over the last few months. He didn't like putting his heart on display and chose to avoid it whenever possible. Even for her, he was hesitant. He didn't do emotions. He didn't do attachments.

Which was why his growing feelings for the woman in his arms confused him and frightened him, even.

Not wanting to give himself a chance to dwell on those thoughts, he began swaying back and forth with her still tucked safely in his arms. His swaying turned into foot movements as he led her in a dance around the room.

"What are you doing?" she asked, her voice muffled by his chest.

He smiled into her hair and continued holding her close as he led with footwork only, and surprisingly, she followed his lead. "If I remember correctly, a certain beauty wanted me to teach her how to dance our dances."

"This form is passable. But it's not beautiful."

A snort escaped him, and he couldn't help but roll his eyes. He found this form extraordinarily beautiful, and now he wondered what her mer form looked like if this was only "passable."

"Either way, class has commenced. I expect you to make me look good on the dance floor as my partner."

This got her to laugh, and he couldn't stop the grin from spreading across his face as she lifted her head from his chest and gave him that teasing, spicy look he enjoyed so much.

"I can make *anyone* look good on the dance floor," she retorted. "Even you."

"Oooooh." He hissed between his teeth. "Good one."

He guided her into taking a step away from him and held both of her hands in his. "I'm not sure how dancing is in your culture, but Shadow fae dances are meant to intrigue."

"What do you mean?"

"I mean…" He turned her around until her back was to him and leaned closer to speak in a raspy voice in her ear. "Light touches. Wrist to wrist. Movements are not bold but wispy. Like shadows. Like mist."

He lifted one of her wrists with his own and slowly lowered it, then did so again as if their bodies were fluttering leaves carried on the wind. He lightly pushed on her waist, and she obeyed as she spun outward, but then he caught her with one arm trapped behind her back and the other arm raised once again by his wrist.

For a moment, they stayed in that position as he guided her around books, clothes, and other obstacles scattered about the room, never once glancing away from the blue of her eyes.

He reached for one of her hands, fingers lightly brushing together before the back of their wrists of their other hands touched between them. They turned in several circles, and then he pushed off from her wrist, stepping back as she spun around once, and then caught her with her back to him.

The position was brief, but it was enough to create a pit of raging desire within him. He wanted to be close to her. He wanted to taste her sweet lips on his tongue and give her an experience she would never forget.

Taking a deep breath, he pushed the desire away, barely holding it at bay as they continued dancing. Step by step. Wrist to wrist. A weaving pattern of light touches and careful movements. The purple light from his magic reflected off the creamy complexion of her skin and her big eyes filled with wonder.

"Either you are very good at following my lead," he murmured, lightly touching her wrist, "or you already know this dance."

She smiled, and the sight brought him immense relief. After her earlier episode, he thought a smile would be far more evasive. "Dancing is what I love to do. I learn quickly."

They stopped in the middle of the room, and a stream of purple magic passed between them, bringing attention to the light spattering of freckles across the bridge of her nose, to the wisp of brown hair in her face.

He lifted his fingers and gently brushed a strand of hair out of her eyes, but he couldn't bring himself to drop his hand. The back of his fingers rested on her cheek. His other hand continued to touch her at the waist.

"Avra..."

"I-I-I should go," she stuttered.

She spun around and walked briskly toward the door, but just as she opened it, he reached over her shoulder and slammed it closed once again until his chest lightly brushed against her back, until his chin rested a hair's breadth away from her cheek.

Although she didn't turn around to face him, she didn't try to leave again, either. Fast, heavy breaths escaped her as she stared at the door, but he felt her entire attention focused on him.

"Do you truly want to leave?" Because if she did, he would let her. But a part of him suspected she didn't.

"I-I-I..." She released a long breath. "Nox..."

"Admit it." He trailed a finger up her arm, to her shoulder, and traced the shell of her curved ear. "I affect you."

A shuddering breath shivered against him, and he delighted in the way his presence seemed to rattle her like hers did to him. "If I do, will it overinflate your already bursting ego?"

"Heh." He lightly brushed his lips against her ear. "Perhaps." And then he lowered his voice to a whisper. "Why don't you find out, love?"

He placed a light kiss directly below her ear, grinning in satisfaction when gooseflesh lifted on her skin. He wanted his intent to be unmistakable. To give her a chance to either reciprocate or run.

However, he was sure he could find a way to convince her to stay.

In a quick motion, he spun her around and pinned her against the door with her arms above her head. Her breaths quickened. Her eyes darkened. And the way she looked at him indicated she wanted him just as much as he wanted her.

Besides, she didn't protest nor resist.

But she still was not giving her consent.

"You are not my guardian warrior," she said with a rasp. "I cannot... We cannot..."

With one of his hands keeping her arms pinned above her by the wrists, his other hand trailed down the length of her arm and caressed the small bit of skin peeking out from the bottom of her blouse at her hip.

"I can be whatever you want me to be. I'll be your guardian warrior."

He assumed this position was last held by her late partner, though he had no idea what it meant in terms of mer tradition.

"You don't know what that entails."

When the temptation of her proved too much, he lowered his mouth to her throat, basking in her accompanying groan. She tasted sweet, like autumn florals and mysterious intrigue.

"Enlighten me," he murmured against her skin before he kissed her beneath her jaw and again on the hollow of her throat.

Rather than explaining herself, she rapidly shook her head, and he almost released her when he thought she was refusing consent. But no… That wasn't it at all.

"It's against the rules!" she protested in a breathy whisper as if trying to find any excuse to leave, her gaze darting toward his bed. "If the headmaster found out, we'll—"

"And who's going to tell him?" His fingers dug through the soft strands of her hair, and he lightly pulled back to expose more of her neck. She whimpered at the sheer anticipation even when his lips only hovered over her skin. "Certainly not me."

"Hans will return soon. We can't."

"Hans left to give us time alone. But…" He dropped her arms, leaned closer, and brushed his lips against her ear. "You say the word, and we'll stop."

He captured her earlobe between his teeth. She clutched onto the front of his shirt, and the most adorable squeak escaped her mouth.

Finally, she sighed. Her rigidness melted, and she leaned into his advances. "I-I-I don't want to stop."

Her words sparked an unquenchable heat within him of the likes he'd never felt before. He wanted her. Not just for tonight. But for always. He wanted her time. He wanted her heartache and her laughter. Her troubles and her joy.

He wanted her love.

Which was stupid and idiotic and had come with the most terrible timing, ruining everything and then some.

"This is your fault," he said, slowly untucking her blouse from her skirt until his hands lay against the heated skin on her back. Hot. Very hot. As if his touch set her on fire. If she felt his skin, she was bound to find something similar.

Her fingers clutched tighter onto him. "What is?"

"You ruined all other relationships for me." One by one, he unfastened each button of her blouse in the front, and she didn't stop him. Not even when he exposed her undergarments. Not even when he pushed her blouse over her shoulders and listened as the fabric hit the floor. "Why couldn't you just keep your tantalizing mouth closed?"

Mischief sparked in her eyes, a silently issued challenge staring back at him as if he'd just claimed he could get a higher test score than her.

"Then come close it yourself."

"Gladly," he rasped.

He cradled either side of her face and wasted no time as he dipped his head and closed the distance between them with a kiss to her lips. But it was unlike any other kiss. It was scalding in the most delicious way. It burned just like the rest of her body, and he wanted more.

He kissed her again and again until their kisses became more feverish and desperate. No longer was he able to exercise careful control when her touch set him ablaze in the most unexpected and exciting way.

Feverish delight ran through him as she shrugged him out of his shirt and slipped his belt out of its casing with a single tug. They stumbled toward the bed, all sense of control lost between them.

At least until they fell onto the bed together, and she stopped him with a hand against his chest. "Wait! I don't really look like this!" She gasped as he kissed her neck and then along her collarbones. "This isn't me. You should know—"

"You can show me your other form later." His hands slid over her hips and up her waist, to her back. "Mmmm." His lips brushed against her throat. "I'm fine with you as you are. I just want to be with you now."

And then she fully surrendered to his touch, and he completely lost himself in hers.

12

EVERYTHING ABOUT THIS situation screamed and kicked against the traditions of Avra's people. Nox was not an Infernal. He was not her *Ikshwa.* He was a Shadow fae from the upper realm, one who thrived on moist air and moonlight. This was forbidden. This was sacreligious. This went against everything she'd ever known, everything she'd grown up believing.

But as Nox held her sweetly in his arms, as he placed a gentle kiss on the top of her head…

She couldn't bring herself to feel more than a brief moment of guilt. Her people were dead or captured. Her traditions were gone along with her people. And what she desperately needed was comfort. Companionship. And she would deny herself no longer.

Even if the companionship came from *Nox Klaver.*

Oh, who was she kidding? She enjoyed his touch, his presence, more than she could possibly describe. He filled the cold, empty caverns of her heart with warmth and sunshine. If he were forbidden, then she would wholeheartedly jump into those forbidden waters despite the traditions of her people.

He kissed her temple. "I'll be leaving the school grounds, so I might not see you for a couple of days after tonight."

The sound of his voice brought her out of her ruminating, and she couldn't help the envious dip of her stomach. She bit her lip. "Are you meeting someone?"

"Mmmm." He tasted the corner of her mouth with his tongue and then kissed her lips. "It sounds like you're jealous."

"It was a simple question," she scoffed, but he wasn't wrong. And by the fires below, she wanted him to kiss her again.

"I'm meeting my father's friend," he explained. "About some work. That's it. He's not really a friend. Just an…irritating acquaintance." His fingers lightly brushed her bare shoulder. "But I won't be long."

She didn't answer when worry plagued her relentlessly. He would be gone for two days. And the dance was soon after. Followed by…

"You seem leagues away," Nox murmured as he continuously smoothed down her hair with his fingers. "What's on your mind?"

She shifted so her hand rested on his bare, muscular chest beneath the blankets of his bed, bringing them nose to nose. Her stomach flipped pleasantly, and her heart pattered with nervous delight.

"I have a lot on my mind," she admitted. "I…" She trailed off, unsure how to broach the topic. "I don't do casual relationships, Nox."

His arms tightened around her as he pulled her closer and kissed the tip of her nose. "You're not going *anywhere*. Not without a good fight."

"But I must return home."

And then his arms became rigid, and the beginnings of a frown formed on his mouth. "I thought we could keep in touch."

She wanted to tell him it wouldn't work so easily as that. Not when they each called a different realm their home. She still needed to show him her Infernal form.

What would he think?

Blowing out a long breath, she turned her attention to one of his hands and absently played with his fingers. "I thought… Well, I hoped maybe you might like to come with me."

He hesitated. "To the sea?"

Infernal stones! She'd made a mess of things. How could she have allowed their relationship to escalate like this? Based on a lie? He still thought she was mer. Would he hate her when he learned the truth?

"Listen, love," he murmured, the tip of his finger caressing the curve of her jaw. "I have legs, not fins. Otherwise, I would throw myself into the ocean and follow your every beck and call."

"Nox," she sighed his name. "I must clear something up, though I hope you might keep an open mind—"

Someone rapped on the door on the opposite side of the room, and then it swung open moments later. Hans walked inside, and Nox pulled the blankets farther over her shoulders to conceal her.

Her cheeks flamed, but she made no move to reach for her clothes discarded somewhere on the floor. She didn't want to leave yet, even if that meant subjecting Hans to the knowledge of what had happened between her and Nox.

Hans froze, but then his gaze shot toward the ceiling. "I just remembered I have to visit the professor about an assignment. I'll be back in the morning."

The Shadow fae left the room, and Avra released a breath of relief. Nox's chuckle vibrated against her.

"To be fair," he said, a grin lingering on his face, "Hans did say he'd be back in a few hours. Time simply passed a little quicker than I anticipated. Now, what was it you wanted to tell me?"

He sat up on his elbow, and the blanket pooled at his waist, revealing the black curse mark stretched over his belly and chest.

The sight filled her with dread. Her stomach dipped with disbelief.

And then fear.

No, no, no. This wasn't right. This couldn't be true. She swore those marks hadn't been there before. But it had been dark. And she'd been more occupied by things other than his chest.

But there it was. Familiar symbols and designs emblazoned on his chest. Unmistakable.

And Infernal.

The type of curse clinging to his skin was only earned when someone killed an Infernal. Nox was a Hawker. The very one that had been hunting her all this time.

Nox was a killer.

But still, denial coursed through her as she shook her head. It couldn't possibly be true. Surely, it was just a trick of the light. It wasn't real. Especially after they'd made love. Especially after their unforgettable night together.

"What is that?" she rasped. But no, she knew what it was. She only wanted him to say it.

"Oh." He frowned and glanced away. "It's nothing. Just…something from my past."

He talked about the curse as if it were nothing. As if he hadn't ended the life of one—or more—of her people. "Do you…do you know who I am?"

"Blatant change of subject." He laughed and nuzzled his nose against hers. Cold shock still prevented her from shifting away. "I know you are smart and lovely and ambitious. That's who you are. Even if you are a little mean sometimes."

Perhaps just a few minutes ago, she might have playfully elbowed him at his jest. But... This was no longer a game. Nox was hunting her. And from how it appeared, he had no idea that he held his prey within his arms.

"Otherwise," he continued, "I only know what you've told me. And I hope you'll trust me with the rest in time."

"Yes..." she murmured sadly when she realized this was it for them. No more nights spent together. No more laughs and barbs and spending time with one another without a care in the world. The Hawkers had found her. There was no running. No fleeing. There was nowhere else to go.

The only way she could survive...

Was if Nox had a change of heart.

"I should go." Her whisper barely managed to escape past the cotton clogging her throat.

"Not a chance." His arms tightened around her. "Stay with me. Just for tonight. I can see that you're getting tired."

Yes, but...

She squeezed her eyes shut and made a dumb choice. Because that's all she managed to do with Nox—make stupid decisions.

With a nod, she nuzzled closer to him and allowed herself to forget. About her. About him. Just for one night, they could pretend that the world wasn't about to fall apart around them. If he didn't know what she was, *who* she was, then he wouldn't kill her. For now, she was safe.

"I want to show you my true form." Her fingers brushed the dark, messy locks of his hair. "At the dance. Meet me there."

"But without a mer tail."

"Without a mer tail," she confirmed.

"How will I know it's you?"

"Believe me, you'll know me when you see me." Her fingers burrowed into his hair, relishing in the last bit of Nox she would ever get. "I promise you. I'll be unmistakable."

"You better show up," he said as he teasingly flicked her nose. "I'll hunt you down if I find out you left before I return to Darkest Star."

Hunt...

"Of course." The words escaped her as a croak.

How had this happened? How had all of her decisions led to this moment? To the one person who would destroy her world? She'd insisted to Lord Graves that she'd wanted Nox to guard her. She'd spent countless hours tutoring him, and more countless hours getting tutored in return.

Out of all the students at the school, how had she singled *him* out?

She buried her face into his chest to hide the way her expression crumpled with heartache. Nox was more proficient with weapons than anyone she'd ever known.

Because he was a Hawker. He'd mentioned his father had taught him everything he knew. His father had also been a Hawker. And the person he was meeting tomorrow? A friend of his father's. Also a Hawker.

They were closing in on her. At the dance, she would have more than one enemy hunting her.

She had to play her cards, to lay down her best hand.

It was the only choice she had left.

Minutes passed, and although she was tired, she forced herself to remain awake. She couldn't risk her glamour dropping sometime during the night and allowing Nox to witness what she was.

However, his grip on her soon relaxed, and his breathing deepened as he fell asleep.

Her gaze darted to his desk and the plethora of weapons scattered on top. Hawker weapons. The weapons of a killer. If she got to him first...

A breath shuddered from her lungs at the thought. She didn't want to kill him. But if she were to remain safe... What choice did she have?

She waited a bit longer for him to fall into a deeper sleep, until his arms loosened enough for her to slip away.

Quietly, she pulled on each of her discarded pieces of clothing before standing in front of his desk. Her hand shook as she reached for one of his daggers, sheathed within a thick leather casing.

This was her only chance. If she didn't take him by surprise, then she wouldn't escape his clutches alive. Not after the way she'd seen him fight. Not after how fast she knew he could move.

The curse mark on his chest stared back at her. Taunting her. Daring her to do it. To end his life. He was an Infernal killer. He'd killed who knew how many Infernals in his past? And he would do so again in his future.

As Matriarch, this was her responsibility. To protect her people. To drive back her enemies and rid her people of outside threats.

She had to do this.

But then something lying on the desk caught her eye and gave her pause. Her heart stuttered in shock when she discovered a drawing depicting her own likeness on the top page of a notebook. The lines and shading were so detailed and skilled, and with the darker color of the chalk, it almost exactly resembled her Infernal form. All that was missing were her horns, her thin, pointed ears, and the stripes on her skin.

Had Nox drawn this?

It was... It was... *Beautiful.* But the word hardly did justice for the talent and skill he possessed with a simple piece of chalk.

Momentarily, her grip on the dagger loosened as uncertainty warred within her. She turned to face Nox more fully, her gaze passing over the long, dark lashes shadowing his cheekbones. The soft parting of his lips. The gentleness of his features while asleep.

And her heart responded with a deep, throbbing ache at the thought of his blood on her hands. Not Nox. She couldn't do this to him. She would never be able to live with herself if she plunged the dagger into his heart.

Her shaking hand placed the weapon back onto the desk, and she squeezed her eyes shut as she realized what this meant.

She was at his mercy. Unless she could find somewhere to run before he returned from his short trip.

But…

She recalled the Infernal Minotaur outside the academy's gates. And before that, she remembered how easily her enemies had tracked her portal and followed her to the upper realm, how close they had almost come to finding her before Killian had whisked her away.

Running was not an option. Not anymore.

Therefore, she needed to play her best cards, and she needed to do it quickly.

On her way toward the door, she glanced over her shoulder one last time at the peaceful way Nox slept despite almost getting a dagger plunged into his chest.

No…she didn't do casual relationships, but they could never be together.

The next time they saw each other…

They would become enemies.

FOR A MOMENT THERE, Nox thought Avra was going to stab him.

But she hadn't. Then what had she been doing with his dagger?

One of the things his father had ingrained in him early was learning to sleep lightly to always ensure survival, especially if there was no one there to take watch as he slumbered. He'd woken to the sound of Avra picking up his dagger from the table. And from there, he'd feigned sleep. During the night, especially, he was a light sleeper when it was usually his awake hours.

However, what made little sense was the way Avra had stood before him with his dagger in her hands. And how she'd lingered…

The moment Avra left the room, he released a long sigh and rolled his eyes at himself. Growing up doing what he did, being who he was, had made him paranoid. Never once had she purposely tried to hurt him. Well, not counting the punch she'd delivered to his stomach when they'd first met.

He recognized the way he was trying to sabotage this for himself. For once, he'd met a woman who actually meant something to him. One he wanted to keep. The flight response within him was flaring up, but he refused to let it win.

Guilt struck him in the gut as he pulled on a new pair of clothes, hiding his curse mark, even from himself. Avra deserved to know what it was. She deserved to know what had happened and about his life growing up. If this relationship was going to work, he needed to tell her everything.

Just as soon as she tells me everything. He scoffed at the thought. They were both keeping secrets. He was not good at long-term relationships, and she was not good at short-term relationships. This would not be easy to make it work.

But he wanted to try.

The memory of Avra's warm body against his sent him spiraling into a pit of happiness he had not known in a very long time. And her scent lingering on his skin...

He felt dazed in the most beautiful way as he strapped himself with all manner of weapons before heading out of his room. He snuck through the shadows of the school property before leaving the academy grounds altogether. Thoughts of Avra distracted him, and he knew allowing his focus to drift from the task might prove dangerous, but he just couldn't help himself. He didn't want to leave her side for a single minute.

After we kill the Infernal Matriarch, he thought to himself, *I can go with Avra to the sea.*

Somehow, he'd find a way to make it work. He'd heard of charms and potions that could allow a land-dweller to stay beneath the sea for a short period of time. He was resourceful and could find a way to make it work. He was determined, after all.

Because after their night together…

He would be damned if he ever let her go.

Focus! he chided himself. He could fixate on his new flame after his mission was complete. And then he could wash his hands of this mess and travel the world again. Starting with the ocean.

Nox skulked through the night, constantly glancing over his shoulder and listening to his surroundings. Nothing out of the ordinary jumped out at him. Shrill screeches echoed above him in the trees. Several pixies chased each other around the nearby river. Wild shadow horses chomped on mice in the distant field.

But otherwise, the night was still.

He trekked across the river, soaking his shoes and his trousers up to his knees. He followed a path for a time, and when it branched off in three directions, he took the trail on the farthest left, leading toward a mountain crafted of tall trees and large, rocky crevices. At the base of the mountain surrounded by boulders half his height…

A bonfire flickered to life, illuminating the four figures lingering in the campsite. The light from the flames brought out the deep scars resting on Kress's face as well as the shine from the baldness of Conrad's Shadow fae head. Ulrich, another human, sharpened his blade for an arm on a grindstone, and Felix, a Forest fae, sat on his bedroll counting bolts for his crossbow. Never once had Nox heard Felix's voice.

Ulrich noticed him first and glared as he itched his half-missing ear. "Ah! There he is. The laziest pile of imp shite to ever walk the kingdom. We've been camping out here for months! And for what?"

Ugh, he really hated dealing with these men. But when they all had a common goal, he had no choice. "You're only envious that I could get into the school and you couldn't."

"Yeah, well, I don't look like I'm fifteen years old, do I?"

Nox rolled his eyes. He was twenty-two. Besides, he couldn't help it that most Shadow fae didn't grow facial hair. It was in their blood.

Ignoring the infuriating human, he turned to Kress, watching as the scarred man sharpened his blade with the tip of the weapon sticking into the grass. "The Matriarch is impossible to find. If you're so confident she's at the academy… It's your turn."

Kress spat at the ground near Nox's feet. "Useless. Just like your father."

Nox saw red.

His hands balled into fists, and he took a step forward. "What did you say?"

Conrad grabbed onto his shoulder and held him back from pummeling the other man with his fists alone. "Let's cool down, why don't we? We've been out here a while. Some of us want to go home. Or at least move onto the next assignment."

Nox shrugged Conrad's hand off his shoulder with a huff, and then one by one, he reached into his pack and threw glass vials of elixirs to his comrades. They each caught them deftly. Kress raised an eyebrow, and Nox explained.

"In two days, there will be a dance. Over the last couple of days, I gathered the ingredients and samples of several different male students who will not be on campus at this time. If you drink these, you will look like them. Sound like them. It will give you access to the school, and the barrier surrounding the property should allow you inside."

"Should?" Kress turned his vial around in his hand. "How long does it last?"

"One hour." And then under his breath, he muttered, "If you're lucky."

"Well, well, well." Kress's mouth lifted into a sneering grin, one that stretched his scars in the most unsightly manner. "Looks as if Klaver's boy came through, after all."

At the mention of his father, Nox's hand reflexively jumped to the ash vial around his neck. He'd been taken from this world far too soon and far too cruelly. The Matriarch would pay for what she'd done to his father. And if he was lucky, his would be the hand wielding the weapon to cut out her heart. Or take her head. He wasn't sure which yet.

By the end of this week, this would be over, and he would finally avenge his father's death.

He took a step forward, determination fueling every part of his body. "Here's the plan."

By the shadows, Nox was nervous.

Anxious energy fueled every speck of his body as he adjusted his cufflinks and smoothed the lay of his vest. Ever since returning to Darkest Star Arcane earlier that day, he'd been a mess of frayed nerves and self doubt. Which was odd for him. Because he rarely felt insecure. But now?

His heart was on the line. He tried not to care, or at least not to show it. But much was at stake with Avra.

First, he'd see her mer form—at least half of it—for the very first time. He felt sure he would love it, but he kept biting his knuckle with nervousness. They also hadn't had a chance to talk about what had happened between them. What were they to each other? Did she still want him to accompany her to the ocean? How would they make a relationship work?

At the same time, he feared her finding out about his goal tonight. He was going to take down the Infernal Matriarch, but he needed to do it quietly as to keep the knowledge out of Avra's reach. Not to mention keeping her safe from the attack entirely. The assignment could get messy fast.

He inhaled long and slow before releasing a quivering breath filled with anxious tension. Together with his group of friends from the academy, he stepped into the ballroom.

Loud music from musicians playing instruments in the corner hit him first. And then he stopped short at the dazzling chandelier overhead reflecting sparkling light off the ceilings painted with beautiful images of different cultures. He recognized the mystery and intrigue of the original Shadow Lords of Katalle followed by the golden healing magic of the Sun fae. The Forest fae woods of Andanara. The colorful sea life of the merfolk. Humans and their talent for crafting.

The last section remained a mystery to him as his gaze passed over creatures created from flurries of fire and snow.

But then he inhaled sharply when he caught sight of an image nearly hidden in the corner of the ceiling. It was a woman with gray skin and red stripes, her horns decorated with all manner of jewelry as she weaved a ball of green magic between her hands.

An Infernal.

He quickly tore his gaze away. They were the enemy. No matter how beautiful they were depicted on the ceiling of the ballroom.

"Where is she?" his friend Emond asked, nudging him with his elbow. "Your girl?"

Well, Avra wasn't exactly his girl yet. But he planned to make it official tonight.

Hopefully.

He shrugged. "No idea. She told me she would be unmistakable. I'm not entirely sure what that means." Especially because he wasn't sure what to look for. There were a lot of fae dancing and standing around talking. Plenty of them had different skin colors ranging from dark brown to blue to pink, such as his friend Nessie, who giggled with a light, airy mer voice as she accepted the hand of her partner, and he whisked her onto the dance floor.

Blue-gray skin, red fins, ashy black hair.

He repeated the description in his mind as he scanned the ballroom for any sign of Avra. Although he knew she would not have fins today, something else, such as her lips or ears, might be red.

What a strange image. He just couldn't imagine it and needed to see it for himself.

That's when the whispering started.

One by one, his peers turned to face the flight of stairs on the opposite end of the room. His brows furrowed as he glanced around him, and then his gaze trailed over numerous heads and toward the place they all stared.

His mouth fell open. His heart dropped to his toes. A viciously cold wind swept through his body until his heart felt as if ice slowly encased it in its frigid embrace.

An Infernal stood at the top of the staircase. No, not just any Infernal. Golden jewelry crowned her black horns like dripping water, the sparkling strands catching onto the light from the chandelier, indicating she was more than a simple Infernal. The shimmering ebony gown accentuated her hips and showed off her blueish-gray skin with red stripes stretching across her chest, arms, and legs with crimson jewel-like markings on the sides of her cheeks and neck. On her pointed ears lay ridges on the edges. And her lips...black, complimenting the pointed obsidian fingernails protruding from each finger. Her ashy black hair curled at the ends at her shoulders, framing her face and bringing attention to...

Her eyes.

Even from this distance, he noticed they were a familiar blue with a golden-orange star burning in the middle around the iris. And she gazed right at him, holding her head high.

The chill racing through his body became colder as the realization hit him then. He recalled the conversation they'd had in his bedroom just before they'd made love, just before he'd given his entire self to her and then some.

"*Are you some sort of princess?*"

"*Queen would be a better term for what I am.*"

There was no mistaking that hair. That body. Those eyes…

Avra was the Infernal Matriarch.

14

AVRA KNEW THE MOMENT the truth dawned on Nox. The soft green of his eyes hardened to steel. His hand dropped from his weapon, and his fists clenched at his side. Hate and hurt burned in his eyes, and she was sure her own were a direct reflection of his. She'd allowed herself to get swept up in his charms, to collapse into mush at his feet.

But he was the enemy.

And she was completely at his mercy.

Tonight, she would either die as a martyr or live only because Nox allowed it. There was no in between. Her fate was now in his hands.

And she hated it.

Overly aware of the dozens of eyes trained on her from all across the room, she slowly descended the stairs with her head held high. The thin sandals on her feet made nary a sound on the stone staircase. The sweep of her black, ashy gown only briefly skimmed the floor. But the golden, tinkling bracelets and charms around her horns marked her for what she was.

An Infernal. The Matriarch herself.

She could no longer hide. There was nowhere left to run. Therefore, this was her last card. Her best card. To stun him with the beauty, vigor, and grace of her Infernal form, of her true form, before he had a chance to draw his weapon.

She knew he'd brought other Hawkers. They watched her from bodies clearly not theirs with the same hate shining brightly in Nox's eyes. Even Lord Graves' soldiers couldn't spare her from this fate.

But…

…they might certainly try.

Her gaze jumped to the Shadow fae soldiers stationed around the room to guard the students. There were enough to give the other Hawkers pause, enough to give her a chance to speak with Nox alone.

Perhaps she should have told Killian about her discoveries about the Hawkers. Perhaps she should have sought help. But no. She didn't want anyone else to get hurt because of her. She had to do this on her own.

The hard hatred and distrust never abated from Nox's eyes as she reached the ground floor, and for a moment, she waited to find out if he would draw his weapon or offer his hand.

In the end, he lifted his hand, and she slipped her fingers into his. Wordlessly, he led her onto the dance floor amidst a dozen other couples before turning to face her just as the music began to play. His nostrils flared. His grip tightened on her hand.

And then he began to lead her in a dance. Her body felt rigid. On edge. Anticipating a sharp blade against her throat. But the only sharp blade she received was the cut of Nox's glare.

Finally, he spoke first. "You're the Infernal Matriarch."

"And you're one of the Hawkers who are hunting me."

His jaw jumped, but the steel in his eyes never abated. "When you mentioned your other form, I thought you meant... Well, not this."

Wrist to wrist. Turn. A brief touch to her waist.

For tonight, she tried to remain stoic and brave despite the chill of fear and uncertainty climbing her spine. Despite her front, her voice escaped her throat as a rasp.

"I know what you can do. I've *seen* what you can do. At least give me a fair chance to defend myself."

"Did you know before or after we were together?" he blurted, ignoring her request altogether.

"After. When I saw your curse mark." She sighed, her gaze jumping to the other "students" with hands poised over weapons. They certainly looked like her peers, but the way they watched her with vengeance in their eyes betrayed who they really were beneath their glamours. "I know what you are now. A killer."

"I kill monsters. Don't make me out to be some villain."

"I'm not a monster."

"You killed my father!"

"I have never killed a Shadow fae!"

His grip on her hand moved from her fingers to tighten around her wrist. "The Infernal Matriarch took his life six years ago. I was there when it happened."

"It was not me. I would have been on the cusp of womanhood then. I had not yet stepped into the Matriarch role."

"Then it was your *mother*." He spat the word as if it were a dirty napkin in his mouth. "You all look the same." He pointed to his chest. "Do you want to know how I got this curse? By defending my own life. That woman's *Ikshwa* attacked me, and she got away. I got this curse because I killed him first."

Ikshwa...

Her own father had died ten years ago, and since then, her mother had taken another two *Ikshwas* in that time. This must have been her guardian after her father. Her mother had said he'd fallen to Hawkers who had ambushed them in the woods. She hadn't mentioned that the Hawker who had killed him had only been a boy himself.

"I remember when my mother told me this tale from her point of view," she hissed under her voice, just loud enough for him to hear her over the music. "You attacked first. You are to blame."

He blinked slowly, shaking his head. "My father took me to the lower realm to hunt game. To introduce me to the harsh environment of your realm. The Matriarch killed without being provoked." And then he shook his head again, his glare once more cutting into her. "You should have told me! About you. About your status. About how your family was killed."

"You never asked me how they died!" she cried.

"Well, it wasn't polite!" he sputtered. "But that is beside the point! You lied to me. You said you were mer."

She gave him a pointed look. "And? I did what I had to do to survive. You—*this*," she gestured between them, "was not supposed to be a factor."

"You tricked me. You *used* me."

Holding her head higher, she looked him directly in the eye. "I did. I used you. You were the best fighter in our class. I asked Killian for you to tutor me. Not just for me to learn how to fight better but so you could spend more time with me and protect me from bloody Hawkers! I never realized you were one!"

The stripes across her body burned red with anger, enough for Nox to hiss in pain and release her hand. Now, they stood in the middle of the dance floor, each glaring at the other.

"Don't pretend to be the good guy." She poked him in the chest. He swiped her hand away. "My people were annihilated by your kind. Murdered. Men. Women. Children. I am what hope remains for those who are left, and you came to take my head."

"Your kind are *devils*. Infernal creatures of the lower realm."

"Who told you that?"

"It doesn't matter. What *does* matter is that I came for your head, to rid the world of the Matriarch."

"Then do it." She stepped closer until the toes of her sandals brushed against his boots, until she spotted the gold flecks within the green of his eyes. Many people littered the dance floor, blocking them from view of the soldiers surrounding the room. She slipped the dagger from his belt, and he made no move to stop her as she placed the weapon inside his fingers and held it against her throat. "Do it, Nox. Kill me. Finish what you came here to do."

His nostrils flared again, followed by the jump of his jaw.

But when she released his fingers, his hand fell loosely to his side while still holding the dagger.

What was he waiting for? Could he not stomach killing in cold blood? Did he want to move this outside where there would be fewer witnesses?

The stripes on her body lost their warmth as a shadow loomed over her from behind. She felt the danger far quicker than she was able to move. She turned halfway, glimpsing the flash of a silver blade.

But then Nox grabbed her arm and yanked her out of the way of the blade aimed toward her heart. He moved faster than an Infernal spark as he thrust his dagger upward and into the chest of the Hawker who had been about to kill her.

A gasp escaped her parted lips, and her eyes widened as she watched the bald, slender man fall to his knees while blood soaked the front of his shirt.

"Traitor!" the man said, spitting blood at Nox's feet before falling onto his side, his body still and unmoving. And then the screams and chaos began when others noticed the dead body, the blood. People began running, creating a dizzying effect when she was still reeling from what had happened.

"What did you do?" she shouted in disbelief through the screams lifting toward the ceiling.

"I don't know! Just get behind me, stubborn woman." Nox grabbed her arm again and pushed her behind him. With his dagger, he blocked a second attack from another Hawker with a blade for an arm from the elbow down.

"What are you doing, Klaver?" the man growled, attacking again. This time, Nox drew his sword to deflect the other blade. "This was not the plan."

"It's *Avra*." And then he and the man traded blow after blow, block after block, with a dizzying array of fancy footwork and fast blades. A click of metal sounded behind her, and once again, Nox grabbed her by the elbow and yanked her out of the way of a crossbow bolt. It shot directly next to her arm where her heart would have been moments before, narrowly grazing the fabric of her dress, and embedded itself into the blade-arm man's throat.

Blood gurgled from his mouth, and he quickly joined the first Hawker on the ground.

Avra stared in disbelief at the blood pooled at her feet. These were trained killers. And Nox had taken two of them out while protecting her at the same time.

Shadow fae soldiers jumped into action as they ushered bystanders out of the room and leaped forward to attack the remaining two Hawkers. However, the battles were short, and Shadow fae blood soon joined the others on the ground.

They had to escape, and she knew of only one thing she could do now.

She pulled several sprigs of Infernal plants tied together with twine from the bosom of her dress, but just as she attempted to throw it to the ground and speak the words to activate the portal, the black-haired man with the crossbow shot two bolts in rapid succession.

Nox deflected one of the bolts with his sword. But the second bolt ripped through the herbs in her hand and scattered the leaves and petals across the ground.

She dove for them the moment the larger Hawker with the facial scars entered into combat with Nox, each trading blows with their swords. Avra couldn't follow their movements when they fought like two lightning bolts flickering across the sky.

The man with the crossbow released another bolt, this one aimed directly at Nox. He deflected it with his weapon before continuing his fight with his other opponent.

Breathing rapidly, Avra scooped up each little piece of her scattered collection and squeezed the herbs together into a ball in her hands. The ratio had to be perfect. Nothing missing or incomplete.

The black-haired man loaded another bolt, but before he managed to release it, Nox slipped a knife mid-turn from the confines of his suit and threw it with impeccable aim and speed. It struck the man directly in the chest. He continued to fumble with his weapon until he fell onto the ground and lay still.

Taking a deep breath, Avra tossed the herbs onto the ground while simultaneously shouting in her native tongue, "Open gate!"

Wind rushed into the ballroom, tugging on her hair and clothing in a continuous spiral. Red and orange sparked on the floor like two flames weaving together until it created a bottomless ravine leading to the lower realm.

She could have jumped then. She could have left Nox and the remaining Hawker behind. But no… Nox's change of heart gave her pause. She didn't want to leave him. She *couldn't* leave him. Not now. Not like this.

The scarred man clashed his weapon against Nox's and gave it a sharp turn, effectively disarming him. His sword flew out of his hand and skittered across the marble floors before lying still.

At that moment, Avra abandoned all thought for herself, all hope for escape when Nox only held a single dagger against the scarred man's blade. She charged forward, and when the man was preoccupied with Nox, he didn't react quickly enough before she laid her hand upon him.

And shot her poison magic into him.

The man gasped, stumbling backward and dropping his sword to the ground as he clutched at his chest and clawed at his throat. Hawkers were immune to their poisons, which meant they only had seconds to react, seconds to flee.

She met Nox's gaze as he scooped up his weapon and silently asked with her expression alone, *Will you come with me?*

The scarred man reached for his sword as he began to recover from her poison and strode toward them. Without another moment of hesitation, Nox took her hand. And together, they jumped into the portal.

15

NOX COULDN'T BREATHE.

He landed on his hands and knees on dry, ashy ground, and it was as if the very atmosphere buried itself into his lungs and baked them from the inside out. His throat felt dry and parched, and he found himself unable to swallow. His eyes refused to blink, as his eyelids became stuck because of the dry, crumbly air around him.

His hands shot to his throat as panic clawed at him.

I can't breathe, I can't breathe, I can't breathe.

An incessant ringing filled his ears. Black dots shrouded his vision. His gaze darted frantically for the portal he'd jumped through, if only to return to the mess he'd created after his heart had made a terrible decision, after he'd thrown everything away to save Avra.

Stupid!

Between struggling to remain conscious and berating himself for his terrible decisions, his panic only escalated further until he thought he might faint.

Beside him, Avra groaned. But then she scrambled toward him, catching him as he began to fall backward into the chasm of darkness in his mind.

"Drink this." She pressed a vial to his mouth. "I made it for you."

He pressed his lips together and turned his head away. She was still his enemy. Surely, this was poison.

"You stubborn man! *Drink it*! If you don't, as an upper dweller, you will not survive here."

Finally, he relented when he realized he could die either way. At least a small chance of survival presented itself with whatever lay within that vial.

Therefore, he opened his mouth and allowed the cold, thick liquid to enter. Immediately, the dryness in his mouth abated, allowing him to swallow. Little by little, the rest of his body followed suit as the burning dryness disappeared from his eyelids, his mouth, throat, and then his lungs.

He heaved in a deep breath. And another. Until the ringing in his ears died down and the black dots at the edges of his vision fizzled away.

He took another deep breath, this one filled with relief. Although his head still spun, he managed to push himself into a sitting position and took in his surroundings Black, shriveled trees stretched high above them, the bark releasing the faintest scent of something akin to nutmeg. Foreign plants littered the ground beneath the trees from tall red grass to shrubs teeming with alabaster leaves.

Somewhere above him, the sun, or whatever heat source fueled this realm, rained down its red light, creating a strange, dusk-like atmosphere. Neither too dark nor too light for his eyes to adjust.

Only once had he visited this place when his father had taken him six years ago. And that visit had changed his life forever.

"What did you give me?" he asked. His voice didn't escape dry and raspy like he'd imagined it might. The last time he'd entered the lower realm, his father had given him a Hawker pendant to help him breathe in this atmosphere.

Avra sighed from where she knelt on the ground next to him, her head bowed and her hands resting in her lap. He couldn't stop himself from staring at the twisted black horns protruding from her head, and then his gaze roamed over the ashy-blue pigment of her skin and the red stripes that seemed to warm and glow in response to her emotions. They didn't glow now.

Seeing her this way was…strange. Because everything was the same. Her personality. Her voice.

The blue in her eyes…

But now her skin and ears were different, and she had horns. It was still Avra. Which was likely why he hadn't been able to drag the dagger across her throat like he'd been meant to.

He still cared for her. And that was dangerous. And confusing. And he hated himself now more than ever. For…for…*everything.*

"An elixir," she answered. "It allows you to traverse this realm comfortably. It should last for a week or two."

"I'm not staying here for a week or two," he snapped. "I'm going back."

But then he groaned into his hands when he realized he had nothing to go back to. He couldn't return to the school and put everyone in danger again. He had no family and no place to call home. Kress would surely be hunting him now, especially knowing he was with the Matriarch herself.

In the span of a few minutes, he'd destroyed his entire life. All because of what? A woman?

How typical of him.

"Then go." She gestured to the nearby trees. "I'm not keeping you here."

Nox lifted his head from his hands in time to witness the defeated hunch of Avra's shoulders, the exhaustion settled deep in her expression. If he left… Would she give up? Because she looked close to breaking.

"What time is it here?" he asked instead.

She didn't even glance at the sky before answering. "Dusk. Just like the upper realm. Our days are darker, and our nights lighter. The sky will appear the same as your realm, but with red streaks like northern lights, and two crimson moons circling through the night."

He glanced down at his hands when he caught the whiff of metal on his fingers. He started at finding blood smeared across his palms and flecks of red dotting his shirt.

He'd killed two men today and had caused the death of a third.

Yes, he'd killed before. But it wasn't what Avra surely thought. He'd taken the lives of bandits or soldiers who attacked first.

And then there was the *Ikshwa*…

No, he couldn't leave her like this. Afraid and alone and defeated. He'd killed for her. And he would do so again if he must.

He was a survivor. He could survive this. *They* would survive this.

Clearing his throat, he pulled his attention away to try to distract his confusing thoughts. "My father once told me it's dangerous in the Infernal wilds."

"Yes," she murmured. "There are other tribes, some who are not friendly with ours. There are beasts who can hunt you from the taste of your essence on the wind alone." She paused, her mouth pursed. But she continued, nonetheless. "And then there are Hawkers. Trained killers who hunt our kind. But you wouldn't know anything about that."

He glared at her. "I'm not sure I like your attitude."

"And I'm not sure I like yours." She huffed and crossed her arms, turning her head away from him. Her mannerisms reminded him entirely of the woman he'd come to know at Darkest Star. The same woman who both vexed him and fascinated him. The same woman who boiled his blood with both anger and…something else.

"Well?" He stood with his hands on his hips, turning in a full circle to survey his surroundings. "What now? We're on the run. There are beasts hiding in the shadows. We have nowhere to go."

"We?"

"Yes, *we*. I'm stuck with you whether I like it or not. I don't know how to get to the upper realm." And he couldn't just leave her, but he didn't want her to know the real reason he stayed.

She winced as she shifted her body. "I need to find my brother, Theo. I need to know if he is truly dead."

"You said your entire family was dead."

"Well, I couldn't exactly tell you about him, now, could I?" She winced again. "I couldn't risk it."

He crossed his arms. "But Professor Graves knew about it, didn't he?"

"Yes." An exhausted breath escaped her before she ceased moving. "He knows everything. I was under his protection. Until… Well, until I learned about you."

"So, you weren't really the teacher's pet. You two had an understanding."

"Yes." But then she shrugged one shoulder as the corner of her mouth twitched. "But I still enjoyed playing the student for a time."

The entire situation was backward and confusing and his mind was scattered in a hundred different directions. "Since you didn't attempt to kill me that night in my room, why didn't you run?"

She gave him an incredulous stare. "I've been training with you for months. And I just watched you take down three Hawkers by yourself. You think I could have run?" A breath shuddered from her lungs, followed by another wince. "I know your men were waiting outside the gates. That's the only explanation for that minotaur that attacked me. And your kind have tracked our portals before. I was sure you would follow. I was cornered, and I knew it."

"So...what?" He threw his hands in the air before turning away from her and planting his hands on his hips, if only to give him something to do such as scan the shadows for these beasts she'd spoken of. "Revealing yourself at the dance did not help your case."

"Didn't it?" Her infuriating smirk lifted the moment he turned to face her. "I'm here. I'm alive."

"So, you used me again."

"No. My only chance at survival was if you found a change of heart."

"You should not have taken such an enormous risk." He frowned when he realized how much he still cared despite learning of her identity. He was angry and confused. But he cared. However, he didn't want to delve deeper into that internal confession. He wasn't sure he'd like what he found.

Again, he glanced down at her, wondering why she still knelt on the ground rather than standing. If there were beasts about, they needed to find a safe place to hide. As if on cue, a shrill cry lifted into the skies somewhere above them.

"Get up," he ordered. "If you're so intent on surviving, lazing about won't help you."

She rolled her eyes at him. "Thank you for that astute comment."

However, she still didn't move.

Stomping toward her, he grabbed onto her elbow and hauled her to her feet. But then she cried out in pain and collapsed against him. Her eyes sparkled with unshed tears before she squeezed them shut as if wanting to hide her pain from him.

That's when he noticed her foot bent at an awkward angle. Dark purple bruises and swelling stood out against the blue-gray pigment of her skin.

He swore. "That's broken."

"Is it?" she replied dryly. "I landed on it wrong during the portal jump."

The survival instinct within him reared its head, especially when a bush rustled somewhere behind him.

Whatever these charred, blackened woods were, they weren't safe. They couldn't stay.

He gently set her back down on the ground and produced one of the few remaining knives he carried on his person. She didn't even flinch as he knelt to one knee beside her and cut a large seam in the side of her dress up to her thigh.

Fluster climbed his neck at the sight of her entire leg. He couldn't help but recall what it had felt like to hold it in his hand… How it had felt wrapped around him—

Stop! he chided himself as he tucked his knife back into his vest and turned his attention to her horns rather than her tempting leg. He absolutely under no circumstance could entertain such thoughts. They were enemies now. Nothing more.

Then why did he take her hand and carefully pull her onto her good foot? Why did he heave her onto his back rather than force her to walk on a broken bone?

Why did he cup his hands beneath her knees and hold her as if she were something precious rather than the daughter of the woman who had destroyed his entire world?

He shook his confusing thoughts away and focused on the path ahead, but he found it difficult when she wrapped her arms around his neck, as her sweet, floral scent filled him with heady longing—

Ugh! he internally groaned. This was going to be a long night.

"Where?" he grumbled.

Thankfully, she understood what he was asking. "If that man followed us here, we're not safe if we leave these woods."

"But they're dangerous. Besides, Kress can handle himself. We'll be better off leaving this area."

She tightened her grip on him. "I know a place not far from here. Keep going straight. And don't veer far from the path."

"What path?" Even with his Shadow fae eyes, he found nothing standing out in the waxing darkness.

At least until she snapped her fingers, and green poison shot out of her hand and sparked more poison several paces to his right. It left a thin sliver of a wispy green trail leading them forward, creating a nearly imperceptible path to follow.

"Don't use that around me," he warned as he started forward while keeping the poison a safe distance away from himself. "I'm not immune."

"But you're a Hawker."

"There's a lot you still don't know about me."

"All right."

"All right? That's it?"

She nodded, and the edge of her horn brushed against his temple like a gentle caress. For a moment, he lost himself in her scent, in her touch once again.

This was not good. He could not control the way she made him feel, Infernal or not. But he could do his best to ignore it.

"Show me where to go."

AVRA HELD ONTO NOX for as long as possible, even when agony ripped through her ankle, even when her arms shook from holding tightly to him for so long. She'd endured far worse than this, and as far as escapes went...

She was lucky to be alive.

Finally, she spotted the Ash Caverns up ahead and directed him toward them, watching for any sign that the heat would be too much for his body to handle.

However, the only perspiration that seemed to gather on his forehead stemmed from the exertion of carrying her over a long period of time. The elixir likely protected him from the hot temperatures. For now, he was fine.

Nox made several rounds through the trees, likely to hide their scent from wild beasts and to confuse their location should Kress be following them.

At last, they broke through the forest and made their way into the caverns carved into the mountainside. The rocks were a solid gray streaked with red that pulsed with a soft glow, growing brighter the farther they traveled into the caverns as the darkness deepened around them.

"This was farther than I expected." Nox carefully set her onto the ground and wiped his forehead with his forearm.

Avra squeezed her eyes shut, breathing through the pain in her foot. "You wanted to get out of the woods. This is the next best place."

"Where are we?"

Another deep breath. "The Ash Caverns. It's a network of mazes beneath the mountain."

"Then…you could lead us back out if we get lost, right?"

She remained silent, not wishing to answer that question.

"Right?"

With a sigh, she opened her eyes to find concern resting between the dark furrow of his brows. For someone who had suddenly found himself someplace unfamiliar, he was reacting much better than she'd expected him to.

"No one comes back out of the caverns if they enter too deep. Either they get eaten by some sort of beast, or they get lost forever."

"Fantastic," he breathed.

Little by little, he stripped himself of his outer suit coat, then his vest, and when he started for his white shirt beneath, she clenched her fists at her sides, unable to tear her gaze away from his sturdy frame.

"What are you doing?" she rasped.

He nodded to her foot. "Broken, remember? You need something to bind it."

"Just breathing in Crotona air will speed the recovery process."

"Yes, well, until then…"

A lump of desire and attraction formed in her throat as she watched him unbutton his shirt and turn his back to her, but she found it difficult to swallow. Muscles rippled on his back and shoulders with each movement, and his tall Shadow fae frame filled her with a sense of safety rather than fear.

Oh, what a confusing turn of events…

He ripped the sleeves off his white shirt and dressed in what remained of it once finished. But the shirt now hung open, revealing a good portion of the tattoo stretched across his torso when he turned back around.

Killer…

The simple reminder was enough for her to finch away when he reached for her. He paused and glanced up at her through his dark lashes, waiting, almost as if asking permission. And when he reached for her again, she held still and allowed him to set the bone and wrap it firmly with the fabric from his shirt.

She clenched her fists against the ground and only allowed herself a single whimper. She couldn't show weakness to him if she could help it. Not like how she'd broken down crying in his room, seeking comfort in his embrace. Things were different now. He'd killed her mother's *Ikshwa* and who knew who else?

By the time he finished tying off the fabric, her foot throbbed and burned and ached. She had nothing but the ashy air to soften her pain. No healer. No Elders. No home in which to rest. Her future remained bleak. What could she of all people possibly do? She felt helpless, with no hope in sight.

"What do you eat?" he asked. "Small children?"

"Do you torture helpless animals?" she shot back.

They glared at each other, the animosity of their upbringing shooting sparks between them. Unfortunately, the sparks weren't hatred. Not exactly. Not when she could feel the burn of longing racing through her. Not when she noticed the same burn in his own eyes. It was hatred. It was desire. It was everything in between.

"I feel betrayed," he said suddenly, averting his gaze.

"*You* feel betrayed?" she scoffed. "No, no, no. I am the one who was betrayed. Besides, you can't even look at me. What is it? My skin? My horns? Am I what your nightmares are made of?"

He lifted his gaze to glare at her as if to show defiance and prove her wrong. "This is not what I wanted. I was supposed to avenge my father. I got caught up in the student life. I made friends. I was normal for once in my life. And then you came along and shattered my beautiful illusion."

"To oblivion with your illusion!" Her nostrils flared, her jaw clenched. "Were you or were you not in Crotona during the attack on my people?"

"I was not."

The anger deflated from her lungs as she released a sigh filled with the weight of a thousand aches for her people. "Did you know about it?"

He released a similar sigh. "Not until after the fact. I am not what you think I am."

"Your curse mark on your chest tells a different story."

For a long time, they fell silent. The air around them filled with heartache and resentment. At least until she broke the silence with her voice.

"I suppose I lost myself in the illusion as well. I tried to ignore the heavy burden on my shoulders by recovering and hiding, and for once, I wanted to be someone other than who I was."

"Recovering?"

Her gaze drifted to her lap as she placed her hand over her abdomen. "I was stabbed by a Hawker. I escaped to the upper realm, and Lord Graves found me. Took me in. Provided me with a glamour. It took weeks to recover from that injury, and by then, I was too afraid to set foot outside the gates."

His attention lingered on her abdomen, almost as if he were trying to remember if there was a scar there. Unfortunately, there was. But it could be worse. She could be dead.

"You almost died?" Even his faint murmur echoed off the rocky walls. Anything louder could prove dangerous and attract the wrong kind of foe.

She chuckled wryly. "I have no idea how I survived all of that. Luck and very brave people at my side." Heartache built up within her chest at the thought. "Brave people who sacrificed themselves so the new Matriarch could live on."

Guilt piled on top of her until it felt as if it were trying to bury her alive. Very little her training had done her when she was too frightened to do anything more than hide.

After a moment, Nox spoke, "I'd convinced myself that your actions had been innocent when you'd picked up my dagger in my bedroom." His lips thinned, and he shook his head. "Now I realize you were going to try to kill me."

And so, the guilt continued to bury her. She placed her attention on inspecting Nox's handiwork on the wrapping around her foot to avoid glancing his way. "I didn't realize you were awake. I…" Another sigh. "I couldn't do it."

"Why?"

Much to his obvious frustration, she didn't answer. She *couldn't* answer when such confessions could ruin them both.

When the silence lasted a little too long, Nox pulled her out of her depressing thoughts with his conversation. If only a little. "Your magic is…interesting."

"Poison. It's all I can do."

"Hmm. It was any wonder why I never witnessed you performing magic at the school. It was because you couldn't. At least not without giving yourself away."

She half-heartedly shrugged one shoulder as she tried to find a comfortable position in which to rest her foot. No such position existed. "I do not have much of an affinity for magic."

"Or fighting," he chimed in.

"Are you trying to make me feel better?" she asked sarcastically. "Because it's working wonders."

"I'm not trying to…" He sighed. "Never mind. I'm simply attempting to understand. As the Infernal princess, or whatever you were called, I almost expected you to be tutored in all areas of your life. Not just with books and knowledge."

"It's my job." She slumped miserably against the cold, rocky cavern wall. "I am supposed to be a source of wisdom for my people. And then others in my life are supposed to protect me. My magic and fighting skills were only an afterthought."

"Should've been a forethought."

Despite wanting to throttle him, she knew he was right. All her life, she'd always done what her mother and the

Elders had told her to do. Of course, there was wisdom in that. But that wisdom had been her downfall.

Now *she* was the one who must make her own decisions.

And she had no idea where to start.

To distract herself from the pain, she closed her eyes and listened to the wind howling through the caverns, to the small creatures squeaking somewhere farther into the mountain, to the steady breaths moving in and out of Nox's lungs.

She focused on her own breathing and didn't allow her thoughts to stray, not when she wanted to think of nothing at all. She wanted to feel nothing. No pain. No guilt. No despair. Just nothing. At least for a few moments.

She wasn't aware she'd fallen asleep until Nox guided her head with gentle hands and rested it in his lap. The muscles of his legs were hard, but they were softer than the cold stone ground.

"Sorry," she murmured. She was just so...*tired*. Exhausted because it was sometime late at night. Tired because her foot throbbed and her heart ached and she was worn down from running and hiding and trying to stay alive.

"Just rest." Nox's fingers brushed lightly against her hair, almost like an accident. Because after everything that had happened between them, she doubted he'd show any form of affection toward her.

"You'll stab me."

He released an exasperated breath. "I could have stabbed you all this time. I'm quite sure it won't happen at this point."

"Quite sure is not the same as absolutely certain."

"What can I say?" The teasing lilt returned to his voice. "If you irritate me enough, I might change my mind."

"That's not funny."

"Then you have no sense of humor."

"My sense of humor is not quite as morbid as yours."

"Oh?" he asked. "I wasn't aware you had a sense of humor at all."

She pinched his leg. He only laughed quietly as if not wanting the sound to echo off the cavern walls and reveal their location to potential threats.

At last, she relented. "Just a few minutes. And then wake me."

"Mmmhmm."

She swore she felt the phantom caress of his fingers against her hair once more, but she likely imagined that, too. The warmth emanating from his body plus the safety his presence offered lulled her into as peaceful of a sleep she would ever get when they were being hunted.

However, she woke with a start at the sound of metal being drawn from a scabbard. She bolted upright, her eyes flashing open to find Nox standing in the middle of the cavern with his sword held at the ready. He faced the darkness of the cavern pointing farther into the mountainside, his gaze fixed on *something*.

A flash of fire lit up the area for mere moments, revealing the beast that stalked forward on four legs with smoke streaming from its nostrils. Pointed claws extended from its feet. A jagged tail whipped behind it, sharp as a knife. Tusks curved out of either side of its mouth dripping with flames, and with a simple shove of the beast's head, those same tusks could impale someone and burn them from the inside out with a lethal poison.

A wild caliboar.

Nox's gaze flicked from her to the cavern exit as if telling her to flee.

She refused. And because of it, he rolled his eyes in an exasperated manner, mouthing, *You'll get us killed.*

Shaking her head, she used a nearby branch to help support her weight as she limped forward and stood one step beside him. Her tail whipped around them and wrapped around his wrist, trying to get him to lower his weapon. His arm didn't budge.

"They never venture into shallow caverns," she whispered.

"So?"

"So, something is wrong." Her tail tugged on his wrist again. "Kneel down."

"Do you *want* to die? Because at this point, the only person keeping you from Death's door is me."

The caliboar snorted and stamped its foot on the ground, spouting flames from its nostrils once again. It was going to charge. And when it did, they would not escape this cavern alive.

Without another word, Avra fell onto one knee and bowed her head, avoiding eye contact. The beast's snort echoed against the rocky walls, followed by another stamping foot. It was taking Nox's stance as a challenge.

"This is my realm, Shadow fae," she hissed, her tail continuing to hold onto his wrist and urging him downward. "Like I said, you will not survive here without my help. On your knee."

"You are delusional if you think you can best this beast without a weapon. I've seen them before. My father and I defeated one years ago. It's dangerous."

A spurt of fire shot from the caliboar's nostrils, brighter and hotter than before. "They are loyal creatures. If you earn their trust, they will never leave your side." She loosened her grip on his wrist just as the creature charged forward, its lumbering steps shaking the caverns and loosening dirt and debris from the ceiling. "Trust me, Nox."

After a moment's hesitation while glancing between the two of them, he finally dropped his sword and knelt to one knee with his head bowed like hers.

The caliboar stumbled to a rumbling stop directly in front of Nox and lowered its sharp tusks. But instead of impaling him, the beast took a long, snorting sniff of Nox's hair. And then with one powerful movement, it flipped him onto his back and stepped over him, continuing to sniff him.

"Avra," Nox said in a strained tone.

"Stay still," she warned. "Don't move."

"I'd rather not get eaten!" he shot back, but he quieted real quick when double flames shot from its nostrils and narrowly avoided singeing him.

Another torturous minute passed, but somehow, it felt like a lifetime as she waited for Nox to either be accepted or impaled. But then the caliboar stuck out its dry, scratchy tongue and licked Nox from chin to temple. A breath of relief escaped her.

The creature didn't inspect her for quite as long before it licked her as well and sat back on its haunches like a well-trained canine waiting for orders.

"I think I'm going to be sick." Nox gagged as he flipped over onto his hands and knees. "That's the foulest-smelling breath I've ever encountered."

It wasn't the foulest she'd ever encountered herself, but it was high up there when caliboars tended to feast mostly on carrion. "Just count yourself lucky you're not dead."

"I don't know. I think I might still drop over dead after smelling *that*."

"Stop being dramatic." The pain in her foot still flared with discomforting agony. Therefore, all she managed was to shakily stand on one foot with her branch-crutch supporting her weaker side. "And go retrieve your new pet."

"New pet? No, no, no. We're not taking him with us."

Avra only grinned.

17

THEY DID, INDEED, take the foul-smelling pet with them, much to Nox's discontent. He couldn't argue with Avra's logic that she still couldn't walk on her own, and he couldn't possibly carry her the entire way to who knew where.

Apparently, caliboars were used in her culture like horses were used in his. And also, apparently, they were good and stuck with this creature until it keeled over dead one day. At the very least, it needed to eat a mouthful of mint leaves twice a day. At the most, it needed a complete mouth replacement and an entire change in diet. If that thing breathed in his face again, he might not hesitate raising his sword the next time.

Nox wrapped his arms around Avra's waist, helping to keep her steady as they rocked back and forth with each step the caliboar took through the caverns. He could not help but lean into the warmth her red stripes emanated, especially as the early morning took on a chill this deep within the mountains.

"Where is he taking us?" he asked, his gaze lifting toward the high ceilings painted with similar glowing red stripes that lay across Avra's skin.

He leaned around her to witness the tail end of her somber expression as she pulled out a ragged piece of clothing from within the confines of her dress. "This belonged to Theo. The caliboar is trying to locate his scent." And then she sighed. "With no body found, I believe he was captured, not killed, in the upper realm. But—"

"You can't kill an Infernal in the upper realm. Otherwise, there poses a risk that the strong poison their bodies release afterward will kill you as well."

He frowned when he realized it hadn't mattered to him at the time. He was not immune to their poison, but he hadn't cared if killing the Matriarch ended up killing him, too. As long as his original goal had been completed, he just hadn't cared.

How sad and foolish of him.

She frowned. "I don't like that you know so much about us. Especially about the death bit." She shifted where she sat and stared forward. "But yes. Theo likely was not killed in the upper realm. No one would have lived to move his body unless they was a Hawker immune to the poison. Therefore, whether alive or dead, he must be in the lower realm. And if he is... The caliboar will find him."

The large beast lowered its head and sniffed the ground, which rocked them forward until his body was flush against hers, until no space remained between them at all.

He released her waist and clenched his fists in his lap, reminding himself over and over that she was an Infernal, that she had lied to him and betrayed him. That she was the blasted Matriarch of her people. All other thoughts he attempted to dump over the side of his figurative ship, but they only seemed to stick to his fingers and cling on tighter.

They traveled through the caverns for what seemed like hours, until his legs became unbearably sore from riding the strange beast and his eyelids drooped. But then they'd shoot open whenever he heard a strange sound or when they encountered a deadly beast.

However, one look at the caliboar sent the creatures scampering away.

The consistent, steady rhythm of the caliboar's steps lulled him into a relaxed, peaceful state despite the chaos of the last couple of days. He hadn't slept well when he'd visited the Hawkers, and he hadn't slept at all during the sweet hours that he'd watched out for Avra as she'd slumbered.

But now, the weariness in his body plagued him, and despite trying his hardest to stay awake, he found himself drifting off. His head dipped lower. His hands relaxed.

And then the sensation of slipping to the side, of falling, jolted him awake. He cried out in shock as he fell the distance from the caliboar's back to the ground, taking Avra with him.

They crashed to the cavern floor in a heap of warm bodies and tangled limbs. The weight of her falling on top of him seemed to bruise the bottom half of his ribs. He coughed when the air was knocked from his lungs, and then he groaned.

"Sorry," he murmured, attempting to sit up when the movement briefly pained him. "Did I hurt you?"

Avra's horns moved side to side as she shook her head. "Startled me more like it. I thought you'd last longer on a caliboar. Seems like I was wrong."

"Excuse me?" he scoffed as he reached down and took her hands, helping her to her good foot. However, she was able to put a small amount of weight on her broken foot. It must have been healing. "I can last plenty long on a mount. I drifted off. That's all." He stalked toward the foul beast with the intent to show her, but her fingers closed around his wrist, stopping him in his tracks.

"You look exhausted, Nox. You need to sleep."

"I can't sleep. Besides, we can't keep stopping to rest when you are diurnal and I'm nocturnal. We'll lose too much time that way."

"Then we'll travel during the night when you're at your strongest."

"That leaves you vulnerable," he argued. "You need your strength, too."

She frowned. "The best warrior needs the most rest. I'm not much help."

He threw up his hands. "Not much help? You're navigating us through this twisted maze of a cavern. You need a clear mind to do so."

Wearing a scowl, she stepped forward and poked him in the chest. "Do as I say, Nox. No one denies the Matriarch."

"Well, make that one then. You'd better get used to it, love, because I almost always get my way."

They scowled at one another, their heated glares returning not even hours after their last argument. He couldn't resist the alluring way her stripes burned and how her eyes seemed to glow in anger just for him. He liked her impassioned reaction. Even if it earned him her ire.

He pointed to the caliboar. "Beasty will take watch. We'll compromise and both get rest. I will take no further arguments from you, young lady, especially because I know you didn't get a full night's sleep."

"You infuriate me!" she hissed, poking him in the chest again.

He swiped her hand away. "That makes two of us."

Using her crutch, she angrily stormed away and slumped onto the ground. He attempted to hide his grin at the adorable way she crossed her arms and the way her lower lip jutted out in a pout. He wouldn't mind kissing that pout away and replacing it with a smile.

He blinked slowly, trying to snap himself out of it before spinning around and placing his attention on his surroundings. They needed food and water and warmth, as the caverns were bound to get cooler when they weren't moving.

"Does Crotona have water?" he asked, worriedly biting his lip between his teeth. "Or am I going to die from dehydration?"

Surprisingly, he didn't feel thirsty. But it didn't mean he could make it long without water.

She replied, "The elixir I gave you should help you hold out for long enough without it. Once we're out of these caverns, we'll find you water. I promise."

All right, so he didn't need water. Yet. But his stomach rumbled from going so long without eating.

He hardly knew what he was doing in a foreign land with foreign creatures and plants, but he did his best as he collected materials to build a fire and sparked it to life. Next, he wandered around the cave until he caught a couple rat-like creatures scampering across the ground and located dark red berries growing from a small fissure in the wall.

"Food or poison?" he asked, gesturing to the berries.

Avra lifted an eyebrow. "Eat it and find out."

"I'm serious."

"They're edible. But they'll cause you to hallucinate."

"Never mind then." He tossed them to the floor, but the caliboar quickly lapped them up with its rough tongue. "Great," he muttered. "Nothing better than a hallucinating mount."

Next, he slumped on the ground on the side of the fire opposite Avra. Echoing drips and scuffling feet filled the silence as he skinned and cooked the rats over the flames. The result was tough, blackened meat nearly impossible to chew. But Avra ate hers without complaint, and she consumed it all, leaving nothing behind.

"Well…" He shrugged one shoulder. "It wasn't children, but I hope it was palatable enough."

Her answering scowl lifted a grin on his face, and he chuckled as she tossed a pebble at him, which bounced off his chest.

He glanced at his surroundings, trying to locate anything within the darkness that might serve as a softer place to sleep other than the hard, rocky ground. But it looked as if he were bound to wake with a sore back and stiff limbs. He'd endured worse. But only barely.

His eyelids drooped, but he wasn't ready to sleep yet. Not when Avra stared pensively into the flames, not saying a single word. It was never a good sign when she was quiet. What was on her mind?

Biting his lip, he located a stick and turned one of the logs to occupy his hands. But one question burned hot in his mind and refused to simmer down.

"Did you love him? Your *Ikshwa?*" He attempted to maintain a cool, uncaring mask as he prodded the fire again. Because he didn't care. Not at all.

She paused for a moment. "It's…complicated."

"How so?"

"Traditionally, when a future Matriarch is born, several male children will battle one against the other for the chance to become her *Ikshwa* as she grows up and takes her place as ruler among her people. The victor will become bonded in the Ceremony of Rites." Her mouth twisted to the side. "Yianni won the competition, and we were bonded shortly after." Another pause, almost as if she were deep in thought. "He was ten years older than me. There was nothing romantic between us. Though, he did claim me, as was his right, when I came of age."

Nox balled his hands into fists as he stared at the billowing flames. He didn't care. He truly didn't.

Oh, but he did.

"What happened to him?"

Her expression fell into her lap as she fiddled with the sharp black nails extending from each finger. "He was my protector. When our people were attacked, he was one of the first to fall from defending me. It was…" She blew out a long breath. "It was a massacre. Theo, my brother, got me out of the village. We fled to the forest. Then to the upper realm." She grimaced. "It was much like your first taste of the lower realm. I couldn't breathe. I thought I was going to die." A wry chuckle escaped her as she shook her head. "It probably would have been quicker than what waits for me now."

"You don't think we can make it out alive?"

Her head hung until he was no longer able to see the blue and orange of her eyes. "You weren't there, Nox. And I'm glad for it. My people need help. And I will die trying. That's all I can say."

Not for the first time, her attention shifted to his chest where his curse mark lay hidden beneath his shirt. And not for the first time, shame burned him from the inside out. After meeting Avra, after finding out who she really was... Well, she had to know the truth. About him.

"I never took the vows," he blurted, but then winced at the tactless way it had escaped his mouth.

"What?" she whispered.

With a sigh, he prodded the fire again and watched as wisps of orange embers floated into the sky before the ghost of its skeleton turned them white. "For all my life, it had always been me and my father, and then later my friend, Leni, came along after taking her in when her parents abandoned her. The three of us traveled together. Pops trained me in the art of weaponry. He told me that one day, I would have to defend myself, and I would need to be ready."

He paused as he tried to gather his thoughts, as he attempted to figure out what he wanted to tell her, as he tried to push the thoughts of Leni aside. He missed her. He hadn't seen her in too long. "He was a poor man. There came a time when food was scarce, and he could no longer feed us. I was only eight years old when he shut me inside a shabby cabin in the woods and told me to wait for him." Memories of that day still haunted him, because it was the day when his entire world had changed.

"What happened?" Avra asked quietly, bringing him back to the present.

He prodded the fire again. "He didn't return for three weeks. I had to hunt for myself during the daylight hours because the woods were so dangerous at night in the Shadow realm. And when he finally returned, he had an Infernal-killer curse on his chest just like I do now, and he wasn't the same man." His mouth twisted to the side. "He became a Hawker to feed us, to provide for us. The job paid well, despite the question of morality that came with it. But I'd been convinced these Infernal creatures were devils, and I grew to hate them. Especially because of how the job had changed my father. We still traveled and he still trained me, but a hardness had corrupted his soul. I had blamed the other Hawkers for his change."

"Then..." Avra released a shaky breath. "You're not truly a Hawker. If you have not taken the vows."

He shook his head and listened as the logs crackled and popped in the momentary silence between them. "I was sixteen when my father..." He ducked his head, not wanting to relive the moments of his death. But he needed to speak of it, to explain. "He was given an assignment in Crotona. It was my first time accompanying him there. He'd told me it was to hunt, but now I'm realizing it wasn't animals he was hunting."

The ash vial around his neck called to him, and he instinctively gripped it in his hand. "I'm beginning to wonder if that was *my* official initiation into the group, as I had never visited the lower realm before. I was given a pendant to help me breathe in the realm, much like the elixir you gave me earlier." A subtle ache formed in his head, and he rubbed his temples to try to massage it away.

"Your father was hunting the Matriarch," Avra finished for him. "He was hunting my mother."

Nox sighed. "I don't know, Avra. Maybe. But I don't think he would have done so with me in tow. It's more likely our encounter was an unfortunate coincidence." He glanced up to find her watching him with rapt attention. "One night, we were camping. We were Shadow fae. We heard them coming, saw them before they saw us. My father pushed me behind him when he realized *who* it was. Told me to run and not look back. But I didn't. I had never seen an Infernal before. Even at sixteen, I was just a scared little boy."

Avra's tail whipped behind her. Perhaps in agitation. Or maybe anger. He wasn't sure. "You said my mother killed your father."

He released a slow, languid breath and nodded. "Two against one, especially when one was an *Ikshwa*, was not good odds for my father. No matter how skilled he was with the blade." He squeezed his eyes shut to try to block out the memories. It did little good at keeping them at bay. "My father put up a good fight. I should have fought with him, but I was so scared. I don't..." He released another long breath. "The Matriarch poisoned him. Although he was immune, it was enough to stun him for her to finish the job. I...I was so angry. I reacted without thinking it through, without a care for myself. I tried to attack your mother, to make her pay for what she had done, but her *Ikshwa* blocked me. We fought. But the man was already injured from the fight with my father. It gave me the advantage..."

"And you killed him," Avra finished for him.

"Yes."

The memories attacked him relentlessly despite how much he wanted to push them away.

"Papa!" younger Nox had wailed, slumping to his knees as he held his father's lifeless body in his hands. Fat, warm tears trailed from his eyes and down his cheeks. "Papa!"

He heard the scuffle of feet, and through the blur of his tears, he noticed the Matriarch standing off the side. Watching him. But he didn't care. She could kill him if she wanted to. He couldn't bring himself to raise his sword again. Not when his father was gone.

Killing an Infernal always left a curse mark behind on the killer's chest, and he felt every agonizing second as it burned into his skin, marking him for what he was, for what he'd done.

But rather than finishing him off, the Matriarch grabbed her Ikshwa's body beneath the arms and dragged him away.

Nox cleared his throat. "The Matriarch must have taken pity on me to leave me with my father's dead body. To not finish the job when she otherwise could have rather easily." His hands clenched in his lap as he swiped burning tears from his eyes. "I was so...*angry*. My father was my world. The only person I had in my life. The only one I could count on. I had nothing left."

A gentle hand rested on top of his, and he jumped at the contact. Somehow, Avra must have circled around the fire and now sat next to him. Shoulder to shoulder. Knee to knee. "But you never took the Hawker vows? Even after that?"

He shook his head. "I gave my father the funeral I never expected to have to give. And then I ran. Away from the Hawkers. Away from Crotona. I left it all behind. I traveled. I lost myself. I never formed a meaningful relationship with another person again. At least until Darkest Star."

Well, there used to be his blind friend, Leni. They had grown up together like siblings. They'd once shared a special bond. But he hadn't seen her in years.

"But you never told me how you ended up at the academy."

Why was he spilling all of this to her? Why did it matter to him that she knew?

Perhaps he wanted to clear his mud-stained character in her eyes. Or maybe he wanted her to know all of him. Even the parts he kept hidden. "The Hawkers found me. Said they had a job for me. I wasn't interested. But when they mentioned killing the Matriarch..." He shrugged. "They needed someone who looked young with an affinity for magic to get accepted into the school. Since I had a history with them already, I was the best choice."

"And you took the job."

"How could I not?" He turned his head and stared into the darkness, if only to keep himself from glancing her way. "I wanted revenge. My father deserved retribution."

"I know it won't fix anything, but I'm sorry about what happened, Nox. I wish things had ended up differently for you."

"But things don't always work out the way I want."

The weight of her hand on his seemed to grow heavier as the moments passed. She was a presence he couldn't ignore. Nor did he want to.

"And, what do you want now?" she asked.

Oh, he knew exactly what he wanted. But in the grand scheme of things, it made no sense. *They* made no sense. They had no future together. They didn't belong with one another.

Unfortunately, he'd always wanted things he couldn't have. And almost always, he got what he wanted. At least for a short time. But Avra wasn't just another conquest he could use and discard.

She deserved better.

Pushing away his feelings, he cleared his throat and continued to stare at the cavern wall. "I want to help you find Theo. And…" He blew out a long breath and finally dragged his attention back to Avra, his gaze fixing on the diamond-shaped red markings on the side of her face. "And I want to start over. With us. I want to put the past in the past. I want my friend back."

"But my mother killed your father."

"And I killed her *Ikshwa*." He turned his palm around and captured her fingers in his. "Oh, Avra. I'm so sorry. I'm sure he meant something to you."

She rubbed her hand across her jaw. "He wasn't my father but my mother's second *Ikshwa*. And it's not really like that in my culture. My mother's *Ikshwa* was bested by a better warrior. You. The life he'd led was celebrated at his funeral, and we recognized his sacrifice. But he was not mourned in the way Shadow fae mourn their lost loved ones."

His eyebrows furrowed as he tried to keep up with her words. "I don't understand. Did your mother not mourn him?"

"*Ikshwas* are not chosen through a love bond, Nox. Should the Matriarch already have a guardian, another may challenge him, and the best warrior will take the title of *Ikshwa*. But challenges are only acceptable if the Matriarch allows it because sometimes, she is happy with the one she has and does not want another. But if she allows the challenge… Her current *Ikshwa* must now prove himself worthy to stand at her side once again, or he will lose his spot, and possibly his life, to his challenger."

Absently, he played with her blue-gray fingers, and he couldn't help the jolt of excitement that she allowed it. "So… It's possible for the Matriarch to have many lovers."

"Over the course of her life, yes. My grandmother only had one *Ikshwa* throughout her eighty years. I did grow fond of him. I mourned him when he died of sickness."

"I'm sorry to hear it."

"Are you?"

Nox blew out another long breath and stared down at their intertwined fingers. All his life, he'd been taught that Infernals were devils, that they were evil creatures that needed to be destroyed. But now knowing what he did about Avra…

He couldn't help but think he'd been played the fool. She was not a devil. She was just…different.

He trailed the fingers of his free hand over the sharp points of her fingernails, across the red, striated patterns on her skin, and over the smooth texture of her arm. Had he not met her in her glamour, he wouldn't have given her five seconds worth of a chance. But he had. He'd formed a friendship with her. And something more. No matter how confusing the newest turn of events buffeted him against rocky shores.

"Yes," he murmured finally. "I *am* sorry to hear it."

She placed her other hand on top of his, stopping his curious exploration of her. But when she turned her head, it brought them nose to nose, close enough for him to feel her breath teasing his skin. Close enough for him to capture the flowery scent wafting from her hair.

"Fine then." Her whisper once again caressed his face, and all he wanted was to lean in. To breathe her in. To capture her essence with a quick taste. Or perhaps not so quick. "We can start over. I value your friendship."

"And I yours."

Sure, if friends held hands and kissed and made love well into the night...

They were certainly friends through and through.

"Your turn," she said. And for a moment, confusion tapped on his chest as she placed her hands on either side of his face. But then his heart picked up speed as she guided his head onto *her* lap.

"We talked about this." Despite trying to remain awake, his eyelids drooped again. "You need to rest as well."

"And I will. But my mind is racing."

"Do you want to talk about it?" But even as he asked it, he yawned deeply, and his eyes closed entirely.

"Perhaps when I sort my thoughts out."

He gave into the gentle lull of her warmth, and despite them having been enemies, despite their past, he felt safe enough in her presence to allow himself to fade into her, to hand her the remainder of his trust and expect her to protect it.

And then with a sigh filled with warmth and relief, he allowed himself to fall asleep.

18

A PIERCING SCREAM echoed across the cavern walls, and Avra bolted upright at the same time Nox launched to his feet and drew his sword. They waited for a second scream, but all was quiet and still. Even the fire that had long since gone out.

"You heard that?" Nox asked.

She nodded, now wide awake when her heart pumped hard directly in her throat. "That was Infernal. I'm sure of it."

"What do you want to do?"

Surprise jolted her pulse faster as she glanced his way. He was allowing her to make this choice rather than ordering her about? In all honesty, she didn't want to make any decisions at all. But it was time to be the Matriarch her people needed.

Shame fell heavy on her shoulders when she still couldn't speak the words, to officially take up the mantle over her people. The doors to her power remained locked. It was as if her tongue lay frozen inside her mouth, and no matter how hard she tried to speak, the words refused to escape.

Taking a shaky breath, she answered, "We follow the sound."

She glanced at him out of the corner of her eye and realized what he was doing. He was willing to face the unknown at her side, not knowing whether enemies lay in wait or if they were safe.

He was risking his own life to protect her.

It wasn't any small gift, and she treasured the gesture close to her heart.

He helped her onto the caliboar, though she found herself able to place most of her weight on her injured foot now. Walking may still be difficult, but it wouldn't be long until the injury healed entirely.

With her good foot, she kicked the caliboar's side, and the beast slunk forward on stealthy paws. The caverns were darker than usual, and without viewing the position on the sun or moons, she guessed it was sometime in the early evening. However, the caliboar seemed able to navigate the darkness as well as any Shadow fae, guiding them in the direction they'd last heard the scream.

But then a sick dread took hold of her stomach and squeezed enough for her to become queasy as they entered a large cavern. Articles of clothing lay strewn about the cave alongside ransacked bags and discarded weapons.

She slid down from her mount and limped toward a fire pit filled with black and white ashes. She stooped low and rubbed the ashes between her fingers. Cold. This had not happened recently.

Exploring further, she recognized Infernal garb, and the curved blade of the daggers strewn about the floor indicated they were also Infernal in make.

But…

Everyone was gone. And judging by the chaos surrounding them, her people did not leave by choice.

"Breathe, Avra," Nox said as he placed one hand on her back, the other over her heart. She hadn't realized she was stumbling when her mind spun and her ears started ringing. His strong hands kept her upright, kept her from collapsing to the ground.

At last, she inhaled a deep breath and clung onto his arm.

"Where did they go?" she gasped. "Who did this?"

Oh, she had a good idea who had done this, but why couldn't the Hawkers leave her people alone? Why did they have to chase them here? To exterminate them?

"Look," he murmured, turning her around to survey the mess. "There's no blood. No bodies. Either they fled or surrendered willingly. We'll find them, Avra. I promise."

"But Theo—"

"We'll find him, too. Don't lose hope yet. We've found their trail. This is good."

"How can this be good?" Her head felt light once again, and she reminded herself to breathe. "Look at this."

"No, it would be bad if we found traces of blood or dead bodies. No bodies means they might still be alive. Don't give into despair. Not yet."

She nodded her head and took another deep breath. Who knew that Nox Klaver, a not-quite-Hawker, would be her voice of reason? He kept her grounded even when she wanted to collapse in fear and despair.

"Then who screamed?" she asked.

A cough sounded across the cavern. Her eyes flew wide open, and she released Nox to limp after it. She kept one hand on the handle of her dagger strapped to her thigh, and she felt comforted knowing the caliboar and Nox followed with his own sword drawn.

They turned a corner in the cavern, and Avra's breath stuttered with disbelief when she found one of the Elders from her village, a man named Antonis, lying on top of a bedroll with incense wafting around his body.

He was not long for this world.

In her culture, those on their deathbeds were sent to the afterlife with incense and loved ones surrounding their bed, holding hands and chanting their final farewells. However, no one remained behind to do the honors of the sendoff.

"Antonis," she murmured. Dark gray weaved through the strands of his hair around his short male horns, revealing his old age. The red of his stripes now held the faintest glow, ready to tucker out at any moment.

"Matriarch Avra," the man rasped.

She dropped to her knees and took the man's hand in each of her own. "I'm here. What happened?"

"The ones who survived the initial attack fled to the caverns, hoping to lose the Hawkers." His lungs released another hacking cough. "But some of us were injured when they ended up finding us."

"Where are the survivors?"

"The Hawkers herded everyone away. Didn't want all the Infernal dead. No, we were to be made slaves."

"To whom?"

He coughed and wheezed before lying back with his eyes closed. He spoke two words, "Siska Tribe," and they filled her with a deep dread unlike any other.

Nox must have seen the terrified look on her face, because he said, "My father had dealings with this tribe before. But they were a little more on the violent side."

"Yes," she whispered. "They are not Infernals, like us. They are closer to what you might consider a demon in the upper realm."

The creatures were Nethers. Razor sharp teeth and claws. Pointed horns and eyes that glowed red. Less humanoid than her, though they could speak and reason and form ideas. They were ruled by their appetite for bloodshed and their instinct to hoard. If the Nethers had taken her people hostage, who knew what they planned to do with them?

Antonis's wheezing fit pulled her out of her worrisome thoughts, and her grip tightened around his light gray, weathered skin.

"We thought you were gone," the man rasped before he smiled. "Our people can have hope once again." One last breath exited his mouth, and then his body lay still.

For a long moment, she stared at the Elder she had failed. Although he'd been old, he likely would not have succumbed to death should she have been there for her people.

"I should have come sooner," Avra whispered. "I shouldn't have waited so long. I was a coward. Hiding when my people needed me."

"You were injured—"

"I was a *coward!*" she cried, hanging her head. "You cannot make excuses for me. I could have found a way to return all this time, but I hadn't wanted to. I wanted to leave my mantle behind and shirk my responsibilities."

Her hands clenched on top of her lap, her shoulders shaking. But no tears came. No, she was angry. At the Hawkers. At the Nethers. At herself.

But then her shaking ceased suddenly as Nox took her hand and threaded his fingers through hers. She inhaled sharply and turned her head toward him. His attention lingered on the Elder and not on her.

"I'm not completely ignorant of Infernal customs," he said, nodding his head toward the man. "You send him off, and I'll follow."

Avra squeezed her eyes shut, a heaviness crushing her shoulders with the weight of her responsibility as Matriarch. But her burdens didn't feel quite so heavy with Nox next to her.

Taking a deep breath, she began chanting low and slow, her voice reverberating off the cavern walls and echoing in her soul. She swayed back and forth where she knelt, and Nox swayed with her. Coupled with the incense wafting toward the ceiling, it was almost as if she were at home in one of the huts, sending off another soul to the afterlife. When her mother had been Matriarch, Avra had attended many sendoffs by her side. But now it was her turn to continue the tradition.

In her heart, she promised to continue *all* their traditions. She refused to let her culture die, no matter how many of them might be left. No matter if they only survived a short while longer.

She finished the chant and prayed out loud in her native tongue for Antonis to have a safe journey to the afterlife before her arm fell slack at her side. Nox's gentle strength lent her the energy she needed to climb to her feet, to keep going.

"I…" Nox rubbed his jaw with one hand, and with the other clutched that ash vial around his neck. "I'm actually not sure what Infernals do with their dead. I don't have a shovel, but I'm sure we can find one."

She shook her head. "We prepare the bodies with oils, burn them on a pyre, and scatter their ashes in our sacred woods. Anything else is considered disrespectful and insulting. It is better to leave him here and let nature do what she will than burn his body in an incorrect manner."

He stared at her, his eyebrows pulling together.

"What?" she asked, rubbing a hand up and down her arm.

He shrugged one shoulder. "I always thought Infernals were creatures incapable of sophisticated emotion. I'm just realizing how wrong I was. How could I have gone so long believing all these…these…*lies?*"

Her gaze shot toward his chest, to where his curse mark lay hidden beneath his clothing. But this time, it wasn't with hatred or disdain. He'd been misled. Deceived. And she couldn't fault him after hearing about his past, after he'd protected himself even against her own mother.

Not quite knowing how to reply, she allowed him to help her onto the caliboar while he walked on foot. The creature had led them this far through the caverns. She felt the faintest breeze caressing her skin, indicating the exit lay somewhere close. They were almost out.

As they traveled, she couldn't help the faintest smile from lifting on her lips. She felt a new camaraderie with Nox. A kinship. A close connection. He was a Shadow fae, yet he'd participated in her traditions without a single complaint. What had happened to them? How could they have gone from enemies to friends, from friends to lovers, from lovers to enemies, and now something in between all of that?

Despite her whirlwind of thoughts, she knew one thing.

She didn't want anyone else at her side but Nox.

"Now that the secret is out in the open..." His voice echoed off the high ceilings above them, pulling her from her ruminations. "What's your surname?"

Amusement bubbled up her throat at his reference to the Truth or Smooch game they'd played in his dorm room, the game that had changed everything. "Nassaki. But you likely already know that."

"I do. I just wanted to confirm." He smirked and lifted an eyebrow. "And the most likely to green your gown with?"

She rolled her eyes. "You already know."

He bumped her knee with his elbow. "Say it. Because I know it's not the nonexistent cat."

Her face flushed with heat, and the glowing red stripes on her skin gave away her fluster. "You. Obviously."

"Even back then?"

"You say it as if it were a lifetime ago."

"It feels like a lifetime ago."

"Then yes. Even then."

His smirk only widened. "I thought that's what your look meant. I didn't like Sam kissing you so much after that."

"You got jealous, Nox?"

"Obviously," he shot back. "Naturally, I had to be the next—and last—to do so."

"You knew I would refuse the ocean water."

"No." He shrugged. "I was content with either seeing your *mer* form or receiving your kiss. Either way, I couldn't lose."

"And?" She ran a hand up and down one arm and bit her lip, realizing she *wanted* him to like her. She *wanted* him to like the truest version of herself. "What do you think of this form? What do you think...of *me*?"

Nox hummed. "You were right. Your *fae* form was simply passable in comparison."

She released a shaky breath. "Even though I'm Infernal?"

He didn't answer, but rather grinned to himself as they continued on their way.

TAKING THE CALIBOAR as their mount had been the right decision. Smaller creatures or predators kept their distance from the ferocious beast, all while it led them down a path free of Hawkers and other enemies.

The path led them out of the caverns and along a cliffside overlooking a sparkling dark blue ocean that seemed to burn like fire when the position of the sun brushed against the distant horizon.

Avra smiled to herself when she caught Nox staring at the sea, a bewildered awe in his expression. For him to admire the beauty of her realm... It was a big step. And he was taking it in a wonderful stride.

"This is a good place to rest," she said as they entered a shaded grove overlooking the water. High black and red trees towered over them, providing shade, shelter, and protection from both the elements and creatures of the night.

Several birds called back and forth to one another with squawks and whistles, but otherwise, the evening was quiet and peaceful—attributes she had not expected to find in Crotona upon her return.

Nox helped her down from the caliboar by the waist, and they let the creature roam free around the grove, knowing it wouldn't wander too far. They found a soft place to rest on a bed of moss, the trickling of a freshwater river nearby that flowed its way into the ocean.

Oh, how she'd missed Crotona. The upper realm was beautiful in its own way, but her homeland held a special place in her heart that no realm or city could match.

"How's your foot?" Nox asked quietly, the last rays of sunlight catching onto the strands of his dark hair and giving him an effervescent glow.

"It's healing."

Rather than taking her word, he reached for her foot. And she let him.

He slowly unwrapped the bindings and inspected every angle, maintaining a gentleness in each of his movements that she would never suspect a warrior like him to possess.

The intimate way he cradled her foot in his gentle hands ignited the heat within her stripes. But rather than glowing blazing hot, too heated to touch, it was a soft warmth filled with fluster and happiness and growing desire.

She shouldn't want Nox. It went against all her traditions. He was a Shadow fae. And not once in generations had Infernal mingled with fae. It wasn't done.

Her entire life had been thrown upside down and shaken up. She'd promised to continue her traditions, but where Nox was concerned...

She refused to deny their connection, to push him away because of the blood that ran through her veins. More importantly, he'd saved her life. He'd aided her. Guided her. Remained by her side even when his own traditions refused to allow it.

Although she didn't know where the future might lead, she did know she wanted him by her side. To claim him the way she would claim her *Ikshwa*. To love him the way she never thought was possible.

"It looks stable," he murmured as he began wrapping the foot once more. "But I think you need the added support for a couple more days. Just to ensure—"

His sentence cut off as she cradled his cheek in her hand, feeling the smooth skin of his face against her palm. The first time they were together, he'd all too easily seduced her. She had exactly zero skill in that department, even less than her lack of swordsmanship talent.

But she...she loved him. And perhaps that was all she needed.

"You have not kissed me once since the dorm room incident," she murmured.

She bit her lip, waiting to find out if it was because of their past, or because of the way she looked. She was not the "mer" he'd thought she was. What did he think of her now?

His breath caught, and ever so slowly, his hand lifted from her foot and cradled hers against his face, weaving his fingers between hers.

"It's not a good idea," he said, but when her expression fell, his face split into a wide, charming grin, "but that has never stopped me before."

"Why not a good idea?" she whispered, even as he knelt one knee between her legs and laid her back on the soft black moss beneath them until his striking features took up most of her view of the sky.

"I..." His expression took on a note of uncertainty. "You can do better than me. You deserve something—*someone*—better. I've only ever been good at breaking hearts, love."

"Then don't break mine."

He squeezed his eyes shut, his breath stuttering from his lungs before his hands slid up her arms and pinned them against the moss above her head. When he opened his eyes and smiled, it wasn't a playful smirk staring back at her or a devilish grin. It was true, genuine love.

She might have wept at the sight of it, but her stripes were too busy warming and cooling in rapid succession to his innocent-for-now touch.

"I won't," he whispered.

"You promise?"

"I swear."

And she believed it. She believed *him*. Although they couldn't predict what the future might hold, she trusted him to keep his word to the best of his ability. Whatever came at them… They would face it together.

"Then…where would you start?" she whispered, holding the intensity of his gaze without looking away.

He glanced back and forth between her eyes. "I would start by saying you are the most magnificent creature I've ever laid eyes on."

She rolled her eyes. "Don't lie to me, Nox."

"Have I ever lied to you?"

But she only gave him a pointed look. He laughed, and the beautiful sound spun webs of excitement through her belly.

"Fine. But I'm not lying about this. I was struck dumb by your beauty when you first revealed your Infernal form to me. And I was angry about it."

"Truly?" she breathed.

"Fae's honor."

The corner of her mouth lifted in a grin, and she shook her head nearly imperceptibly. She knew plenty of people who would never trust a fae's word. But she trusted his. She knew he wasn't lying. At least not this time.

"And then…" he continued, trailing his fingers over her wrist, down her arm, and over the grooves of each of her collarbones. "I would tell you that you are *mine*." The delicious word sent pleasant shivers down her spine. "And be warned that I don't like to share."

Her grin stretched wider across her face. "There is no one to share me with." She pushed thoughts of her people from her mind. For just a few minutes, she didn't want to shoulder her burdens. All she wanted was to remain in the present with Nox.

The calming push and pull of the ocean contrasted against the excitement weaving through every fiber of her body. The soft moss cushioned her in a gentle embrace. But the serenity of the atmosphere helped very little where her racing heart was concerned. Especially as Nox lowered his head and brushed his lips softly against hers.

The kiss was not filled with passion or lust. But love. And she returned the feeling wholeheartedly as she cradled either side of his face and returned his sweet, gentle affection.

A sigh of contentment escaped her as they broke apart. Being with him like this... It felt *right*.

"Huh," he murmured as he lifted one of her hands and kissed each finger. "I thought it might be different kissing you in this form. But it's surprisingly the same. You are really warm."

"It's my stripes," she confessed. "They grow warmer or colder depending on how I feel."

"They burned me before. At the dance."

"Because I was angry."

His mouth hesitantly hovered over one of the stripes on her arms before he lowered his head and kissed it. In response, her entire body released a warm, pleasant heat. Not hot like anger but simply warm.

"And what feeling is inspiring the heat now?" he asked.

She weaved his black hair through her fingers, admiring the way the color complimented the blue-gray and red of her skin. "Happiness. You make me happy, Nox."

"I am genuinely glad to hear it." His thumb brushed against her bottom lip, and then he traced the grooves in the sides of her pointed ears. But then his exploration paused at the base of one of her horns. "May I touch them?"

"Mmhmm." Her head turned to the side to give him better access. "Horns are for lovers."

"Is that what I am to you?" He kissed her wrist.

She gazed at him with an earnest expression and traced the strong outline of his jaw and pointed ears with the tip of her finger. "You are more to me than just a lover."

His lips moved to her palm. "Then what am I?"

Her finger paused over the tip of his ear when the word wouldn't quite reveal itself in her mind. "I don't know the exact term for it in your language. But in mine, you would be called *Shumwa*. It means '*one who holds my heart.*'"

The handsome grin of his lifted right on time. "Do I really?"

Instead of answering out loud, she took his hand and placed it over her heart, allowing him to feel the way it beat for him, the way it warmed against his touch. Although she'd never been in love before, the feeling was unmistakable. Her stripes burned for him. Her heart beat for him. And she never planned on letting go.

"You are *mine*," she said huskily, repeating his words back to him. "You belong right here. With me."

A shaky exhale broke past the seal of his lips. "I've never belonged anywhere."

"Well, now you do—"

He interrupted her declaration with a kiss and then another until the world disappeared around them and all that remained was the two of them. His fingers trailed over her hair until he hesitantly brushed against her horns. She sighed at the gentle touch.

She took his hands and guided them to her horns until he held either one securely in his grip. Another sigh escaped her at his gentleness. At the way she trusted him fully to take her horns. At how safe she felt enclosed in his arms, with the warmth of his body showering her in pure happiness.

Never in her life had she experienced such bliss in the presence of another person. But Nox...

She desperately wanted this relationship to work, and she would do anything to ensure it thrived.

As Nox deepened the kiss, she responded with love and enthusiasm until they were a tangle of heat, emotion, and hope for whatever the future had in store for him. And she realized with a contented smile against his lips…

Wherever he went, she would follow.

20

ASH, DUST, AND HEAT were beginning to feel commonplace since Nox had stepped foot in the lower realm. Although Crotona still had a long way to go to feel like anything remotely close to home, he was beginning to see its charm.

He placed his hands on his hips as he glanced toward the red-streaked navy skies illuminated by two beautiful red, large full moons. Nothing in the upper realm compared to the awe of Crotona's skies, and for a moment, all he wanted was to lay on the ground and gaze up at the foreign heavens glimmering overhead.

It wasn't home, no. But after Avra's declaration toward him, that he belonged with her... He supposed this realm would make for a fitting new home. As long as she was there with him. It may take some getting used to, but overall, he thought the sacrifice was entirely worth it.

"I have a question."

Nox turned his attention to Avra, who held Theo's shredded clothing in one hand to the caliboar's snout while stroking the fur over its shoulder. Soon, they must continue forward when the beast caught her brother's scent once again, and he planned on her riding the rest of the way. Her foot was nearly fully healed, but it didn't mean he would make her walk on it if she didn't absolutely need to.

"Hmm?" she asked.

Her bottom lip was swollen after being thoroughly kissed and then some. He lifted his hand to fix his hair to try to hide the satisfied smirk wanting to grow across his face. "When an Infernal kills another Infernal, such as in battle or a duel, do they also get the curse mark on their chest?"

He expected her to say no, so when she instead replied with a, "yes," he snapped his head toward her and shot her a look of confusion.

"You're jesting."

"I'm not." The caliboar snorted and pawed its foot against the ground to indicate that it caught Theo's scent. "Among my people, the mark manifests differently as an extra stripe from collarbone to navel. It is regarded as a symbol of strength if earned during a duel. Only the best warriors have one. Any others sporting a mark are easily recognizable as Hawkers."

"Your people will love me then," he murmured sarcastically. Though, neither of them mentioned the fact that her people might not be alive.

Avra stepped toward him beneath the willowing boughs of a large tree teaming with layers of red, billowing leaves. He inhaled sharply as her fingers began unfastening each of his buttons one by one until his entire chest lay exposed to her, including the black curse mark stretched haphazardly across his skin.

She lay a hand over his chest, and his heart beat fast in response to her warm touch.

"A curse mark like this will never disappear unless forgiven," she said in a husky tone, and when she glanced at him beneath her long, dark lashes, his heart began an erratic rhythm that he didn't care to stop.

But when her words finally sank in, it slowed in disbelief. "I thought it would remain forever."

She shook her head. "Not always." And then a burst of heat flashed from her hand and into his body, hot enough to startle him back a step. But she kept her hand steady on his chest, not breaking contact until the heat slowly died, and in its place, warmth fizzled across his skin from collarbone to navel.

His eyes widened when he found red Infernal symbols stretching in a V-shape to his belly button in a beautiful, bold design. The black curse mark had disappeared entirely, no longer angry and ugly and a symbol of shame for what he'd done.

"Why would you forgive me?" he asked, his throat clogged with emotion. "Why would you give me this symbol of strength among your people when I don't deserve the honor?"

"I am the Matriarch." Her finger slowly traced the designs along his skin. "I forgive whom I choose, and I find you deserving of such forgiveness." She glanced up again, offering a warm smile. "Now you belong with us, *Shumwa*."

Nox wrapped his arms around her shoulders and pulled her into his embrace. For many years, he'd carried that curse with shame and self-disgust, anger and hate. But now? He felt lighter. As if everything that had made him lose himself had washed away, and now he'd found a new home. A place where he belonged and felt accepted. A place where the pain of his past could no longer reach him quite so fully.

A wry laugh escaped him as he smoothed Avra's hair back around her horns. "Who knew that the Infernal Matriarch punching me would lead to this?"

She rolled her eyes at his mention of their very first interaction. "To be fair, you grabbed me first."

"You're right." He laughed again and shook his head. "I shouldn't have touched you. I was only trying to get your attention."

"Well?" She gestured with her hands to herself and their surroundings. "You have it." And then a sultry grin lifted on her lips. "What are you going to do with it?"

Half his mouth lifted in a smirk at her insinuation. His hands found her waist, and he pulled her closer ever so slowly. "Oh, I can think of a few things—"

His ears picked up the sound of a drawstring getting pulled back only moments before the whizz of an arrow. It gave him a split second to react as he yanked Avra toward him. An arrow with an obsidian tip lodged into the tree with a *thunk* where Avra's head had been moments prior.

His first thought was that the Nethers had found them. But the way the leather cord bound the arrow tip to the shaft was clearly Hawker in nature.

Several Nethers and Hawkers rushed out of the cover of the trees while others stayed back with their bows at the ready. In the space of seconds, he counted five opponents. Two were Hawkers. Three were Nethers. Two in the trees. Three armed with knives.

"Avra!" someone screeched somewhere in the distance, followed by Infernal language.

"Theo!" Avra gasped. "I recognize his voice. He's alive!"

"Go!" Nox pushed her toward the caliboar, and she wasted no time as she mounted the beast. But not without glancing back at him worriedly one last time. "I'll be fine. Find your brother."

And then he turned toward his opponents with a grin stretching across his face and his sword poised to fight. He now knew he belonged on this side of the fight, and he would do anything to protect Avra, even if it meant a few embarrassing, cursed rhymes might escape him in the process.

His new opponents wouldn't know what felled them until it was entirely too late.

Despite every single one of her instincts screaming at her to turn back, to help Nox, Avra forced herself to continue forward on the caliboar at near break-neck speed.

Wind whipped through her hair. Branches snagged on her clothing. The scent of fire and ash filled the skies. An arrow whizzed directly past her ear from behind, and she kicked the creature even faster to outrun the attacker.

And then she saw it.

A small camp lay up ahead filled with strong, wooden cages housing several Infernal, along with a few more of her people tied to wooden posts with their hands stretched behind their backs.

Unfortunately, they weren't alone.

She counted three Hawkers and ten Nethers from one sweep of her gaze alone. That didn't count those who may be hiding within the black leather tents or those waiting in the surrounding trees. There were too many opponents to take on by herself.

Unless…

Unless she spoke the words. Unless she said her vows.

But as she opened her mouth to take the power that was her birthright, to unleash a fury among her enemies of the likes that they'd never seen before, her tongue froze. With hesitation. With fear. She wasn't good enough to lead. She wasn't ready to take her mantle. Not for herself. Not for her people. Not even for Theo.

Therefore, she thundered forward with furrowed brows, feeling each pounding footstep the caliboar took toward the camp. When the first person noticed her, they began shouting a warning to the others. But it was much too late.

She hopped off the caliboar at the last possible moment, hissing when she landed wrong on her foot. But the pain didn't deter her as she unsheathed her two daggers and charged toward one of the cages imprisoning several Infernal. At the same moment, the caliboar ripped through her enemies, tossing them with its large tusks and felling them with powerful swipes of its sharp claws.

A nearby Nether flapped its wings and gnashed its long, sharp teeth. Talons slashed toward her, and despite being a lousy fighter as Nox liked to call her, she instinctively recalled all the blocks and attacks he'd drilled into her again and again and again until it had become muscle memory.

She ducked beneath the attack, twisted around quickly to gain momentum, and ripped one of her daggers through her opponent's chest. However, she didn't stop to make sure she'd finished the job when more Nethers rushed in her direction. Her weapons cut through wing membrane, tough limbs, and thick, leathery skin.

With her heart pumping fast and desperation in each of her movements, she wasn't sure if she'd been scratched or stabbed. All she knew was she needed to keep going. To keep fighting. To reach her brother.

The caliboar stood on its hind legs and released a high-pitched battle screech, distracting her opponents long enough for her to slip away and sprint toward one of the cages. The doors were locked tight with *ebony inferius* leaves wrapped around the bars. The plants were nearly indestructible, but they did have one weakness.

Fire.

She rushed toward the billowing flames of a firepit and snatched one of the unlit torches lying on the ground at the base of the pit. After sticking the torch into the flames and watching it light up, she returned to the cage and counted the passing seconds that brought her nearer to her doom. If this didn't work...

No, it *had* to.

Finally, the leaves caught fire and snapped like brittle rock. The cage door flew open. Infernals rushed out with war cries as they located makeshift weapons such as branches, wooden beams, and stakes holding up the tents before rushing forward to join the throng of chaos near the caliboar.

The extra distraction allowed her to move onto the next cage and the next until ten more prisoners were freed from their bindings.

Desperately, she glanced back and forth across the camp as she tried to locate Theo. He wasn't in the cages with the others. Where was he?

Hope lit up the dark recesses of her heart as she spotted a wooden pole sticking out of the ground across the camp, and her heart soared at the sight of familiar blue-gray skin, dark strands of hair curled around short horns, one broken in half, and red stripes that stuttered out when they attempted to glow. Theo was actively trying to use friction against the pole to break the *ebony inferius* around his wrists, but to no avail.

Two Nethers moved onto her path toward her brother. She dropped the torch and raised her daggers, her lungs heaving in each heavy breath as she glanced back and forth between the two of them. These were the very creatures that had managed to kill and capture so many of her own people with the Hawkers' help. She could not possibly best them when she was rapidly losing strength.

But still, she planted her feet and readied herself for another attack. As long as her brother lived, she refused to give up.

Before she managed to rush forward, purple magic exploded around her, striking the two Nethers like lightning bursting down from the sky. The creatures screeched with pain, their bodies convulsing on the ground as purple smoke wafted from their limbs. And then they lay still.

Avra's attention snapped toward Nox, who held his hand out in front of him with the remnants of purple wisps escaping between his fingers. Blood spattered the pale hue of his skin, and his clothing was shredded or torn in several places. But he was alive.

Momentary shock pulsed through her heart from her previous encounter with the Nethers as she stumbled past Nox and toward her brother. "How is your magic so strong?" she gasped. "I've never seen anything like that from you."

Nox scooped up the torch she'd dropped, barely flickering, and joined her at Theo's side. "Your realm has two moons. Two *large* moons, which is where I draw my power. My magic is stronger here." He dipped the torch toward the *ebony inferius* leaves, holding it aloft as if to avoid burning Theo's hands in the process. Within moments, the plant snapped and freed her brother from its captivity just as the last of the enemies were either struck down or ran for their lives.

"Where were you?" Theo gasped, pulling her into a firm embrace. "I'm so glad to see you safe. But where have you been? I came back for you and you were gone." And then he muttered under his breath. "Then again, I got captured shortly after. It was good you were gone."

"You came back for me?" she breathed, her head momentarily dizzy as she took in the new information. But how? And when? "I was badly injured." Her hand inched toward her side and rested over the scar on her abdomen. "A Shadow fae found me. Took me to a safe place."

Theo scowled and nodded his head toward Nox. "Not this Shadow fae, was it?"

"No." But then she rushed to say, "Nox helped me get back home."

Her brother's attention turned toward her wrapped foot, missing nothing, and then to Nox's ripped sleeves. "The portal jump injured you."

She nodded. "But I'm on the mend—"

A crash sounded behind her, and she spun around quickly to find another Nether rushing toward her with a weapon raised. Everything happened so quickly that she felt dizzy from the whirlwind of motion.

Nox stepped in front of her faster than she'd ever seen anyone move, ready to defend her. But before he managed to swing his weapon, a large, muscular figure leaped out of the trees, tackled the Nether to the ground, and buried his blade into the creature's neck.

After a few moments, the man stood upright with blood dripping from his chin and several new scars across his shoulders and chest. His short, pointed horns poked out of long, messy black hair, his skin a darker shade of ebony while his stripes glowed like molten amber.

The breath fled from her as the man's orange and red eyes found hers in the waxing darkness.

Breathlessly, she whispered his name. "Yianni."

21

THE ENTIRE WORLD of Crotona seemed to freeze over like a blizzard burying an entire city as a chill climbed up Nox's body and swarmed within his chest. His limbs wouldn't move. His tongue refused to work. All he could do was stare at the Infernal man Avra had called Yianni.

The man's mouth was forever curled into a snarl. The brawn of the muscles in his entire body stood out like an intimidating statue carved directly from an obsidian slab. His red and orange eyes burned like hard flames void of any emotion but anger and destruction. They were hard. Intense.

At least until they landed on Avra.

Yianni fell to his knees in front of her and kissed each of her feet, lingering a little longer over the bandage covering her injured foot. The man spoke in the Infernal language, and Nox understood none of it.

"Yianni," Avra said again, disbelief in her breathy voice. "I thought you died." She glanced back at Nox, distress in her eyes.

Was she remembering the passionate moments they'd experienced together? The kisses they'd shared?

Did she regret them? Especially now that she knew her *Ikshwa* still lived?

His fingers curled tighter around the hilt of his sword, a scowl on his face as he glared at the other man. Surely, Avra wouldn't even entertain a relationship with Nox if her beloved Yianni still held the title of *Ikshwa*. The man had claimed her. Taken her to his bed. He was still bonded to her.

But Nox refused to believe it, refused to accept it. Avra was his. Even if their differing cultures stood in the way of their future.

"I saw you die," Avra insisted.

More Infernal speak that Nox didn't understand.

Yianni next cupped her behind one knee and kissed her ankles in a more intimate manner, and that was enough to set Nox off. He charged forward and shoved the other man by the shoulders, hard enough for him to crash onto his side in the warm dirt. Yianni rolled into the attack and drew two daggers in a flash of motion. Even quicker, he rushed forward and swiped at him. Nox blocked the attack with his sword and a dagger held in the opposite hand, all while Avra screamed at them to stop.

But he couldn't stop. Not when he saw red. How dare Yianni touch Avra so intimately. How *dare* he!

Each attack became feverish, faster than the last as they traded blow after blow until his surroundings melted into a red, hot blur. This man threatened everything. His relationship with Avra. His newfound home. His sense of belonging. Nox felt powerless, as if someone had ripped the rug out from beneath his feet and trampled over him. But he refused to give up everything he'd gained since meeting Avra, and he refused to allow the man to touch her in such a way again.

The clash of blade against blade echoed against the navy and red skies as Nox found himself facing an opponent far stronger, far faster than any of the Hawkers and Nethers he'd fought combined. It took his entire concentration to fight, to prevent himself from getting caught on the other man's blade. A part of him knew he could give himself more advantage by using his magic, but then he risked Yianni using his own poison magic.

Nox likely wouldn't survive it.

His surroundings crashed into him once again as Avra's voice permeated the barrier of his concentration. "Stop! The both of you!"

And then she slipped close enough to place herself in danger of the fight.

Immediately, Nox dropped his weapons to the ground to avoid hurting her, but Yianni didn't do the same. He slashed forward again and again with inhuman speed, forcing Nox to duck each swing and leap backward to dodge a stabbing movement.

"Your Matriarch has ordered you to stop!" Theo's voice thundered, and only then did Yianni's blades fall at his sides. But his glare never dissipated.

"Never touch her again!" Nox hissed, squaring his shoulders threateningly. Although he was muscular and tall, as Shadow fae were oft to be, Yianni still managed to tower over him with height and brawn. But brawn was not the only factor in winning a duel.

Yianni replied with an answering snarl and a string of Infernal words he didn't understand.

"You don't speak my language? Or choose not to?" Nox spat at the ground. "Well, let me spell it out for you. Touch her again... And. I. Will. Kill. You."

Yianni growled and took a single step forward.

"Nox, stop." Avra placed one hand on his chest and her other on Yianni's. She lowered her voice, "He's my *Ikshwa*."

"Then tell me I mean nothing to you, and I'll leave."

"I can't..." She released a shaky breath and stared at the ground. "I can't do that."

"What you can't do is have us both. You have your *Ikshwa*. Now tell me to leave, and we'll part ways for good." He wasn't entirely sure he meant the words, but anger clouded his judgment, and he wasn't sure *who*, exactly, he was angry with.

She squeezed her eyes shut, and her chin trembled. "Don't leave."

"And I can't stay if he's going to do that. If you're going to let him." He placed his hand over hers and gently squeezed. When Yianni's mouth lifted in a snarl, and he shifted forward as if to attack again, Nox pulled out his second dagger and pointed it menacingly at the other man. "Try again, and I won't hold back."

This time, Yianni spat at *his* feet, but he backed off until Avra's hand fell to her side.

Her chin trembled again, and she lifted her head until she met his gaze. "I don't know what to do, Nox. I just don't know."

Nox pulled away when her words felt like a punch to the gut and then the heart. For years, he had belonged nowhere. At least until he'd met Avra. He'd belonged with her. He'd actually had a future to look forward to.

And now?

There was nothing.

All because Yianni had returned from the dead.

His heart ached at the thought. Had all of Avra's flowery words been a lie? Had all of her promises to him meant nothing?

He scooped up his discarded weapons and sheathed his blade, his nostrils flaring. "Then I will find a way to leave this place—"

"If you try to leave," Avra warned half-heartedly, "I will kill you myself."

He lifted his hand, and the simple gesture was enough for Yianni to leap forward as if to tackle him. But Theo restrained the man's arms and held him back. Nox gently cradled Avra's chin in his fingers, not daring to do anything more when her moral dilemma burned brightly in the distress in her eyes.

"You can certainly try, love. But we both know you are a lousy fighter."

However, hope continued to hound him, and he knew he couldn't go. He couldn't leave her, not yet. No matter how betrayed or angry he felt.

Without another word, he dropped his hand and stalked toward the dead bodies of the Nethers and Hawkers. He angrily swiped the blue stone pendant off a fallen Hawker and pulled it over his own head to help him breathe easier and stay hydrated. Next, he found a new pair of clothing on a corpse not completely covered in blood like his own that would fit him. If he were to survive down here, he could do so on his own. He'd been trained for this. He didn't need Avra's magical elixirs.

At the first opportunity, he planned to leave behind the one person he cared for more than life itself. To run when things became rough. Because that was what he was good at. It was better to run soon while he could still save some pride than wait for Avra to break his heart when she eventually rejected him for the sake of *tradition*.

But until then… He had nowhere else to go.

And perhaps… Perhaps a part of him wasn't ready to let go.

Things were bad.

But not in the sense that Avra had ever imagined they'd be. Because she'd found Theo alive and well. Many of her people were alive, and from a report from her brother, many more were farther into Nether territory.

But no. This wasn't what pressed heavily on her mind. It was her predicament with Nox. She had promised him herself. She had promised him a home, her heart. And now she realized they were not hers to give.

It was as if she were a child again, everyone else making decisions for her. No matter how hard she tried, she couldn't climb out of the pit her people had created for her without losing their trust, without smashing their hope.

Nox was an unforeseen obstacle. She hated the thought of him being ripped away from her for good. She wanted to keep him. But how could they possibly be together? She was still bonded, although she hadn't known until recently. And Nox?

Well, she feared she'd unknowingly been unfaithful to Yianni while losing her heart to another man entirely.

She raked her fingers through her hair as she stared at the billowing flames controlled within a fire pit before her. Theo had insisted she rest beside the fire while their rescued people set up tents and took inventory of rummaged supplies far away from the defeated Hawker camp.

When lifting her heavy gaze proved too much, she kept it fixed on the flames, not daring to meet either Nox's or Yianni's eye. Was she a coward? Or preventing another fight from breaking out?

Both, she decided. Even the smallest glance was sure to set one of them off, as heated as emotions currently were.

Theo sat down beside her on top of a fallen log and wrapped an arm around her shoulders—comfort she desperately needed that she couldn't get anywhere else at the moment.

Thoughts of Nox entered her mind, followed by a heavy ache lingering in her chest.

She turned her head to find Theo's usually hard and unyielding expression dull and sunken, his body thinner than she remembered. What had occurred during his captivity?

"Care to tell me about what happened with the Shadow fae?" he asked.

Avra averted her gaze and stared at the ground beside her feet. "I think anyone here can take a good, successful guess." Especially after Nox's earlier protective and jealous display in front of everyone.

After a long pause, her brother murmured, "You love him."

She nodded, peeking up long enough to find Nox setting up a tent of his own across camp, his jaw clenched and his expression hard. Oh, how she desperately wanted to run into his arms and hold him tight. To gush her feelings to him. To find comfort in his embrace and promise him the world.

But it wasn't possible. Not anymore.

"I know my heart is miniscule in comparison to the welfare of our people, but…"

"If our Matriarch is unhappy, no one can truly thrive."

She threw her hands into the air. "There is no winning here, Theo. I will lose something precious to me no matter what step I take."

And no, she certainly didn't mean Yianni. But her *Ikshwa* symbolized the hope and happiness of her people. Discarding him, especially while her people were vulnerable and in distress, would prove unwise. If she lost their faith, her people might scatter, slowly dying off one by one, and then her enemies would win. All would be for naught.

Theo glanced at Nox next, and as if feeling his gaze on him, Nox lifted his head. The hardness in his eyes dissolved into something somber, something resigned.

He didn't believe she would choose him…

The Shadow fae's attention diverted back to his task as he drove a stake into the ground with a mallet, and her heart ached all over again. Yianni wasn't supposed to be a factor. The camp atmosphere wouldn't have been so intense if he were still gone. Of course, she didn't delight in the idea of his death, as it had made her feel lost in the beginning. But Nox meant more to her.

Her brother leaned closer. "You must think long and hard about the future, Avra. Does the Shadow fae have a place with us?"

Or in other words, was Nox worth the risk? Her people likely would accept an outsider into their ranks after Nox had saved many of their lives. What she wasn't sure about was if they'd accept him over Yianni by her side.

She ran her fingers through her hair, grateful to feel her horns on top of her head rather than hidden beneath a glamour. "What happened?" she whispered. "We saw Yianni die."

Theo nodded, his tail thrashing behind him. "The Hawkers delivered a gruesome wound enough to knock him out. Then they captured him and delivered him to the Nethers." He grimaced and clarified, "Well, *us*. I got captured, too. It was as if they knew where I was going before I even knew myself."

Her poor brother. If only she'd been able to stop this from happening...

"And…" She let out a long breath, not wanting to ask but needing to, nonetheless. "What befell all the captives? Surely, you weren't to be put into cages all this time and left to rot."

With a shake of his head, he pointed to the black and purple mountain ranges near Nether territory. "They had half of our people mining obsidian at knifepoint. The other half, the better warriors, they placed in a pit to fight beasts for fun. Both Yianni and I were among the latter. Some of our people…" His shoulders slumped. "Some didn't make it out of the pit alive."

Her heart ached at the thought. The Nethers had paid the Hawkers a good sum for this? To use them as slaves?

In the long run, she supposed the cost would have paid itself off eventually.

"Avra. Come to bed," Yianni ordered in their native tongue. She glanced up to find him nodding his head toward his tent. But then she turned her attention toward Nox next, whose mouth became pinched, and his nostrils flared. Although he didn't seem to understand Yianni, he clearly understood what had been said.

Never once had she refused Yianni. This was his right as her *Ikshwa*. Tradition demanded that she acquiesce to his orders that she might trade her body for his protection. To encourage his devotion. Yes, she was the Matriarch. But refusing one's *Ikshwa* was strongly discouraged in her culture.

If she rejected her own culture, would her people lose hope? Would they lose faith in her as their Matriarch?

To prevent Nox from understanding her words, she replied in her tongue, "It has been a long road. I am not well."

"I will help make you well. Come."

Surreptitiously, she glanced at her people who surrounded her. Although their minds seemed elsewhere, she felt the weight of their attention heavily on her and Yianni. She knew if she refused, it would cause more harm than good for her people. And if she didn't...

She would lose Nox forever.

If she hadn't lost him already.

Her hands balled into fists in her lap, her arms shaking. This was not the position she'd ever wanted to find herself in. To have fallen in love with another. Only for the hands of tradition to pull her back, internally kicking and screaming while she must maintain a brave front.

What was she to do? No matter what she decided, she would lose something precious to her. But which was the greater loss?

Theo stood, pulling her away from her troubling thoughts as he spoke in Nox's native tongue rather than their own. "Yianni, now is not the time. Allow our Matriarch to rest. She has gone through a great deal of trouble and injury to return to us. Show her your respect."

Yianni replied in the Infernal tongue as he knelt to one knee and dipped his head. "I meant no disrespect. I only want to protect you."

"I know," she murmured, refusing to look at him directly lest he notice the warring conflict burning in her eyes. "And I recognize your dedication." She dipped her head, saying no more to prevent herself from digging her pit any larger than the gaping hole it already was. Theo had bought her more time. But how much more? And how much more could she afford before Nox decided enough was enough?

Yianni retired by himself, though he kept one of his tent flaps open as if wanting to keep an eye on her. Or on Nox. She wasn't entirely sure. And she wasn't entirely sure she wanted to know, either.

A gentle touch brushed her shoulder, and when she glanced up, her heart leaped into her throat when she found herself gazing back into green eyes.

Nox nodded toward his tent. "You look tired, Avra. It's for you. I'll make sure no one goes in." He paused and frowned. "If that's what you wish."

Clearly, he was referring to Yianni.

"I thought you were building the tent for yourself."

"Why would I do that?"

He gave no further explanation as he stalked across the camp to help others with their tents and to tenderly care for injured children. Although reluctant, her people allowed him to help.

Avra's heart softened as she watched him dab at the forehead of a sick child. His administration gathered a group of curious Infernal, and she couldn't help the soft smile from lifting on her lips as he spoke to her people and asked them how to say certain words in the Infernal language.

None of them seemed to know what to do with an outsider, but they appeared curious and intrigued by him. It was a good sign.

A good sign for what, exactly? With her bond to Yianni, she felt trapped and helpless. She wanted Nox to stay. She wanted him to belong. But how?

"Huh," her brother said, and she found him grinning while he poked at the fire.

"What?"

Theo shrugged, his grin lingering. "I like the way he treats you." He then gestured with a flick of his eyes toward Yianni's tent. "Your *Ikshwa* offered you a place to sleep with strings attached. Your Shadow fae did not."

"He's not my…" She trailed off, cheeks flaming. All this time, Nox had taken care of her, provided for her, protected her with no expectation of anything in return. He was much different from Yianni.

The faintest smile pulled on her mouth as she thought of their time together at the academy. For months, they'd hated each other. He'd had a rakish reputation. She'd thought he'd cared about nothing but himself.

But she'd been wrong. About his motives. About his character. The Nox he allowed everyone to see wasn't truly the Nox written in his heart.

"What do I do?" she asked quietly, her soul falling into despair.

"I can't tell you that. It's not my place. But…" He reached behind him and pulled out an old, dirty map he must have swiped from the enemy camp. "What I *can* do is help you decide the next move."

Avra wasn't ready. She couldn't do this. Not yet.

But as she stared at the map of her lands…

She realized she had no choice but to move forward. Because if she didn't, what remained of her people were doomed.

22

TO SAY THINGS were tense around camp was an understatement.

Emotions ran high anywhere from fear to uncertainty, distrust to jealousy. And Nox found himself smack in the middle of it.

Over the course of several days, he'd found little ways to help out the Infernals from setting up their tents to going out to hunt to help feed the hungry. And little by little, he earned their trust. They were not like the demons he'd been led to believe they were all these years. Rather, they were like scared little rabbits with no energy or willpower to flee should things go south.

Avra's appearance seemed to bolster everyone's hope, to place great faith in their leader to pull them out of a despairing situation. And Nox let her do it. He stepped back and watched her lead, offering what measure of help he could when possible.

But now that they'd found her people…

Things weren't the same between them. He suspected they would never be again. That didn't mean he couldn't find a place to fit. He was good at adapting.

He reached past the stiff, dead legs of a furry gray creature resembling a sheep draped around his shoulders and clasped his necklace vial tight in his hand. Anxiety and uncertainty writhed violently within him, tearing him in two. Half of him wanted to stay with Avra, to find his place and hope to wedge himself into her life.

But the other half…

Yianni still stood in his way. Avra's partner. The man she was *still* bonded to. Yianni was her *Ikshwa*. A binding and permanent fixture in her life.

Still, he'd been watching the other man closely. If Yianni so much as touched Avra, Nox would pull out his weapons. And if Avra so much as allowed it, Nox planned to leave immediately.

His quiet footsteps through the winding forest created an even wider chasm inside his chest when he realized he was alone. Very alone. No animals. No enemies. No Infernals.

Nowhere to belong…

Kress would ensure he could never return to Darkest Star without placing his life in danger. His father was dead. Avra was promised to another.

He had nowhere to go. But a part of him still held out hope that Avra would choose him, that she would discard Yianni and offer her heart to him instead.

"I am a fool," he muttered to himself. A fool for wanting a home badly enough to torment himself like this. A fool for loving a woman so much that it hurt in a way he'd never experienced before.

Taking a deep breath, he pushed everything from his mind as he re-entered camp. Several Infernals glanced up and exclaimed joy when they noticed his kill. Their red stripes pulsed with a happy glow. One of the men took the creature from him to butcher it. An older woman placed her gray hands against either side of his face and kissed his cheek to express her gratitude.

He smiled and exchanged what few words he'd learned in the Infernal tongue in the days of their encampment. Providing food was only a small offering compared to losing their homes, loved ones, their land. But it seemed like one of the only things he could do to relieve their suffering.

To the older woman, he asked in the Infernal tongue, "Where? Avra?"

He cringed at his vast lack of knowledge of their language, but the woman smiled anyway at his effort and replied with a string of unfamiliar words while pointing toward one of the tents.

His gut twisted violently when he recognized Yianni's black tent standing a little taller than the others. For a moment, hurt and distrust pulsed through his chest like uncomfortable vines.

He pushed the disconcerting feelings away and chose to trust Avra instead.

He ventured toward the tent, dread pulsing through him like his own Infernal stripes that brought misery instead of happiness. Step after step. One dreaded swallow after another.

Several arguing voices within the tent erased his uneasiness, and he pushed one of the flaps aside to find out what the fight was about.

Yianni, Avra, and Theo stood around a table in the middle of the tent, a map spread out on top that they must have taken from the fallen Nether camp. Although he didn't understand their language, he watched as Yianni dragged his finger from their encampment location toward the river, from the river toward a gnarl of black trees.

And then he recognized one word.

Estruna.

The river they spoke of had been discussed by Hawkers many times. It gave those waiting downhill from the ravine the tactical advantage while those uphill had no idea they were about to walk into a trap. Hawkers had used this length of river to scare animals before an ambush for the sake of meat for their bellies.

But if he were a Hawker, he knew he could also use it to his advantage to ambush a group of weary Infernals.

"That's a terrible idea," Nox cut in, drawing everyone's attention from the map. "Because—"

"Pale face not allowed in war room," Yianni growled for the first time in Nox's language. "Leave." He pointed toward the exit of the tent. "Now."

"But you can't go that way." He gestured toward the map on the table. "If you would be ambushed anywhere, it would be there."

"You don't know these lands." Yianni stepped forward and pushed Nox backward by the shoulders. If Avra hadn't been standing in such close quarters, he just might have fought back. "These are safe parts. Leave."

"I'm sorry, Nox," Avra murmured, setting her gaze on the ground. "Only Elders, Matriarchs, and family in the war room. It's tradition."

Family...

He clenched his jaw as he glanced from Yianni to Theo to Avra. Yianni was family. Nox was not.

"I understand," he replied coldly as he finalized his resolve. He'd tried so hard to fit in here. But it was impossible if Avra refused to make space. "I have taken you this far. What happens now is none of my concern."

He tossed the tent flap aside and stalked into the camp, grabbing a few of his discarded weapons on the way until he carried everything he'd come with, not leaving a single piece of himself behind. Not even the bloodied outfit he'd previously worn as he tossed it into the fire on his way past and only briefly glanced at the embers leaping into the sky.

"Nox!" Avra called after him. "Wait!"

But he didn't wait. He kept walking, his back turned to her. Away from the camp. Away from the one person who held the power to shatter what was left of his heart. He had to leave before she could do away with it anymore than she already had.

He ignored the murmurs of confused Infernals. He also tried to ignore Avra's pleas for him to stop as well as her footsteps racing after him. But he increased his pace to make it more difficult for her to catch up. Especially on that foot of hers.

Finally, she grabbed his arm and yanked, forcing him to spin around to face her when they'd rounded the bend of the mountain and now stood secluded beside a lake sparkling blue like gemstones in the sunlight. He noticed Theo standing a little farther down the path, his arms crossed and his back to the tree as if he weren't listening in. But he knew Theo well enough by now that the brother was always listening. Always there. Always involved.

"You can't leave!" she cried in a gasping voice as if the chase after him had taxed her. "I need you."

"Need me?" he shouted, but then repeated himself in a hissing whisper. "Need me, Avra? Every single one of your actions and words since finding your people has been the exact opposite. You don't need me. You have your *family*."

He spat out the word as if it were gritty dirt in his mouth.

"I didn't mean it like that. You know I didn't."

"Of course, you did! You have made it very clear that I don't belong here. After all your promises to me. After all your sweet words." He stepped closer and glowered at her. "You are a liar, Avra."

She shook her head, the jewelry around her horns clinking with the movement. "I just need time to figure things out. I need you to stay until then. Please."

He threw his hands into the air before fisting them on his hips and staring out toward the sea. "You are bonded to another! Practically married to the man. If you want me to stay, you must break off your relationship with him."

"I can't!" she shouted back. "It's not done. Only the Elders can sever it."

"Yeah? And where are the Elders now? One is dead inside that cave, and who knows where the others ended up?"

Her nostrils flared, and the glare he'd become accustomed to over the past several months returned at full force. "That's not fair, Nox."

"Isn't it?" Two could play at the glaring game. "You are the supposed Matriarch of your people, yet you can't even find the backbone to lead. You let everyone push you around to get what they want. But what about what you want?" His voice broke against his will, and he tried to hide his emotions by running his fingers through the locks of his hair. "What about me? Do I even factor in?"

Her eyes softened. "Of course, you do."

But he shook his head. Her words and promises meant nothing when all trust had fled. "People fight for what they want. Yet, you do not care enough to lift your voice on my behalf."

"It's not done! You don't understand. Tradition entails—"

"To the shadows with tradition! Tradition will not save your people now. You have to step up and lead and fight. *You*, Avra. And you cannot do that if you cling to the past."

Something between an angry growl and despondent mewl escaped her throat. "My people will retaliate if I reject my *Ikshwa*."

The word "my" grated on his heart. Breaking it. Shredding it. Nothing had ever felt quite so painful. Not even the worst wound he'd received in battle.

"Then you are afraid of their opinion of you." He turned away from her, and he never planned to turn back around. He'd only fooled himself into thinking this could work. She'd already hurt him enough.

"That's not…" She trailed off. "Stay. Please."

"No. Not like this."

A ragged breath escaped her. "If you leave, I might never see you again."

"And?" He solidified his heart until it was stone instead of soil. "I don't see the problem."

He was glad his back was turned to her to prevent her from witnessing the tears building up in his eyes. The heartache. He couldn't remember the last time he'd cried. But most of all, he wanted to save his pride, even at Avra's expense. For years, he'd had to protect himself at all costs. Now was no different.

"That's it?" she shouted in a raspy voice. "You're just leaving? What about me?"

How ironic! That she would throw his words back at him as if she were the victim of her own actions. It only turned his heart further to stone.

"You seem to have things handled." His heart raced uncomfortably. His hands became cold and clammy. The urge to bolt, to flee overcame him. His heart was fragile. He needed to protect it. "You don't need me."

"I do."

If he didn't run *now*, he knew he would break down. To crumple into a mess of dependency, tears, and pathetic begging. To put his heart on the line like he'd never done before. Years' worth of running kicked in, and he knew he must kick the door down lest he suffocate.

If she wouldn't let him go, he had to break his promise and break her heart.

"I don't need you, Avra."

Her stuttering breath followed his comment, but he refused to turn to look. "You don't mean that."

"I do."

He took another step but froze when she spoke in a quavering tone. "I love you, Nox. Please."

But instead of soaring upon hearing the words spoken to him, his heart shattered. If she truly loved him, she would find a way to fit him in her life. She'd made no effort at all. Yianni was her *Ikshwa*. He held the most important place by her side. And Nox? Well, he was just an outsider.

"You'll get over it." He took another step.

"That's it then? No other response?"

"What else can I say? That I'm shocked you feel this way?" He opened his mouth to continue his sentence to further hurt her, but he couldn't do it. He needed to run. Why wasn't she letting him go?

"Oh, don't act so surprised!" Her voice broke. "That I, a stupid female, fell for your magnetic charms. You knew what you were doing. You could get any woman you wanted. And you did."

"Did I?" he asked quietly. "Because the way I see it, I'm your second choice."

And when the panic within him spurred hotter and faster, telling him to flee, he could hold back no longer. This was not a safe place, where hearts burned and broken souls shattered. It was unfamiliar and hard and heartbreaking, and he could no longer stand the heat.

Therefore, he left her standing there by her lonesome. Not once did he look back as he continued forward.

He didn't know where he was going. He only knew he needed to get as far away from her as possible. To do what he did best. Fleeing and breaking hearts. His father had been his anchor in his life, and perhaps there would be no other.

For the first time in a long time, tears fell from his eyes and trailed down his cheeks at the thought of never seeing Avra again. It hurt. A lot. How could love possibly hurt like this?

Thankfully, Avra didn't follow him again, and he allowed himself to swipe his arm across his eyes to clear the path of the blurr his emotions provided. The action dropped his guard, and doing so in unfamiliar territory was the number one mistake Hawkers made just before they were killed.

He inhaled sharply when something cold and sharp pressed against his throat.

"Well, if it isn't Nox Klaver," a sultry female voice purred in his ear.

He lifted his blade blindingly fast to counter hers until they stood with crossed daggers between them. His eyes widened in recognition. His heart burned with shock. And then his weapon fell slack at his side.

"Leni," he breathed.

23

IF SOMEONE HAD told him a day ago that he'd willingly walk back into a Hawker camp, Nox would have laughed at them. Which was why shame piled high on his shoulders as he followed his friend by the hand through a maze of large gray boulders, black sand, and red, yellow, and orange flora until they reached a hidden alcove beside the beach.

He stared out over an endless ocean with one of Crotona's two red moons lifting from the horizon, glowing brighter with each passing moment as the sun descended in the opposite direction.

Awe nailed his feet to the floor when once again, he realized just how beautiful the lower realm was. Yes, it was hot and dry and different. But a good different.

"Wait." Leni's hand tightened around his, halting him in his tracks before they rounded the bend where camp stirred with clanging pots, mild profanity, and the sound of a sharpening blade. She turned toward him, her pointed Shadow fae ears poking through her straight, shoulder-length blonde hair. She stared at his chin with milky eyes, unable to make direct eye contact in her blindness but still able to navigate her surroundings using her magic.

"What is it?"

She sighed, her attention turning toward their clasped hands. The action felt natural, as he had spent a good deal of his childhood leading her around Hawker camps and unfamiliar terrain until she had gotten a better grasp of her magic. Like him, she had been rejected by her parents, though because of being born without functioning eyes. The Hawkers were the only family she knew.

Leni nodded in the direction of the camp. "They know what you did at the academy. They will be none-too-pleased to see you."

"And Kress?"

"No one has seen him for months. If you want to speak your side of the situation before he finds us, now is your chance to clear your name."

He hesitated. He wanted nothing to do with the Hawkers. Now was the chance to flee. But to where? Crotona was an unfamiliar realm, and there was safety in numbers.

His hand moved to rest over his chest where his new red Infernal mark lay beneath his clothing. What would the Hawkers think?

His jaw clenched with resolve as he clasped his father's vial in his hand. He wasn't a Hawker. He wasn't an Infernal. But he needed a place to stay until he could find a way to the upper realm. He was no fool. Navigating a foreign world on his own could kill him. He'd always been a survivor, so surviving was what he would do.

Leni's hand flickered with blue magic, the very same that allowed her to navigate her dark world, before she tugged on his hand and led him toward the camp.

Taking a deep breath, he allowed her to lead him and steeled himself for a complicated situation he needed to manipulate his way through. Either with lies, bribes, or half-truths. All without raising his blade.

Yes, he may have defeated three Hawkers back at Darkest Star Arcane, but pitting himself against at least a dozen here was suicide.

As he neared the camp, he ended up counting fifteen Hawkers eating supper, sparring with weapons, or pouring over reading materials. The leader of the group, a human man he recognized as Heath, spotted him first. The man whistled and stood, placing his hand on one of the several daggers strapped to his chest. The others in the group ceased their activity and stood, too, glancing uncertainly from him to their boss and back to him.

"If it isn't Klaver's boy," Heath said with a dark chuckle, now taking one of his daggers and twirling it between his fingers. The man's bushy blond eyebrows furrowed, his thick mustache curling up with his smirk. "The last I heard of you, you were killing your own."

Leni gave him an encouraging squeeze to his hand.

Nox planted his free hand on his hip and rolled his eyes. "Where'd you hear that?"

The leader shrugged. "People talk. Including spies."

He inhaled sharply when the man's words clicked in his mind. "I wasn't the only one at the academy."

"Nope," a familiar voice called out in the waning light. "Kress isn't always...*competent.*"

Squinting his eyes, he searched the vicinity for the source of the voice, but then his blood ran cold when he spotted a slim figure leaning against a tree with a foot propped behind him. Chin-length blond waves framed a thin face. Ice-blue eyes stared back at him with a knowing smirk playing around their corners.

Hans.

Nox dropped Leni's hand as shock burned through him like fire. Or ice. He wasn't sure when his body both burned and froze simultaneously. "You were my friend," he gasped, shaking his head.

"No one is stopping us from continuing a friendship." Hans laughed as he pushed away from the tree. "You sure did take your time finding the Matriarch, however. You dallied with her. Aided her. Trained her. Shared a bed with her. Will you have me go on?"

"I didn't know it was her," he rasped. "She targeted me." A half-truth. "And to be fair, I doubt you knew, either."

"No." He paused. "I didn't."

If the Hawkers were to attack, to condemn him to death, then he needed to know one thing first. "Why are the Hawkers here? Why the Matriarch? Why kill off all the Infernals?"

Heath continued to twirl his dagger in his hand. Nox had once seen him throw one of them with deadly precision without any warning. His nonchalant attitude was a ruse. The man was dangerous.

"This is the largest payout we've ever had," Heath answered. "We don't normally take jobs from Nethers, but they gave us a lot of coin up front. When we're done here, we will all be wealthy beyond imagination." He lifted an eyebrow. "Didn't Kress tell you?"

Nox pressed his lips together and crossed his arms. Kress had told him very little about the job, and he'd been too focused on revenge to ask questions. Stupid of him. To be fair, he hadn't cared then. But he cared now.

"And the job is…what, exactly?" He had an inkling, but he wanted to know for sure.

"Herding as many Infernals into Nether territory as we can. That has meant killing off leaders and warriors. Giving them the weaker of the bunch." He shrugged. "But kill enough of their strongest, and it's easy to control them."

A chill crawled down his spine. He'd wanted to kill the Matriarch. Not support mass genocide and slavery. This was wrong. No matter the payout. "And the Matriarch?"

Heath stopped twirling his dagger. A warning. Nox had minutes, if not moments, left to live if he didn't create a reason to spare his life.

"Bring the Nether leader the Matriarch's head, and we'd get a bonus. It seems you were just as incompetent as Kress, and then you turned on your own."

"Me?" He pointed to himself incredulously before gesturing a hand toward Hans. "Your so-called spy couldn't find her, either. Besides, I had no choice but to fight against Kress and his team." He tried to come up with a lie, quick enough to prevent suspicion. "They mentioned taking the pay from her kill and running, leaving the lot of you at the Nethers' mercy when you inevitably failed to bring her head."

The leader's hairy upper lip lifted as he snarled. "You said you didn't know about the job."

"I never said that. I wanted to make sure we were on the same page. But it seems Kress has been keeping information from you."

"And you? Were you involved with this deception as well?"

Nox shook his head, his confidence bolstered by Heath's anger turning from him to Kress. It would be easier to manipulate the man this way. "He didn't tell me until the night of the dance, when I learned he was a traitor. I had to end them. The Matriarch slipped through my fingers. I didn't realize she found a way to create a portal."

Hans interjected, "I found an Infernal herb growing in the greenhouse. I didn't realize it belonged to Avra until it was too late."

"So you admit your failure."

"It was your failure to begin with."

"Shut it!" Heath shouted, a disgruntled expression on his face as he slipped his dagger back into its sheath. "Both of you! What's done is done. If you're staying, then get some shut eye with the rest of us before we make our next move." He pointed a finger at each of them. "And stop your squabbling. I'm tired of hearing it."

The man stomped toward his tent and disappeared inside. After a few moments of stunned silence, another Hawker named Diane whistled teasingly. "You and Leni again? Some things never change."

Another Hawker chimed in. "Always holding hands around the camp. Still fancy each other after all this time."

Leni rolled her eyes. "Keep going, and I'll wedge a knife between your eyes. Slowly."

The other woman held up her hands in a placating manner. "I'm teasing, Leni. Sometimes I don't know when you're serious."

"Me neither." Leni flashed a grin unhinged enough for the other Hawker to shift with discomfort where she sat. Before the woman managed another retort, his friend once again snatched his hand and pulled him across camp and farther into the waxing darkness.

Every now and again, her fingers flashed with blue light until they encountered the trickling flow of a river concealed by long, dark reeds somewhere between brown and black. He reached out to touch one of the cattails, and it disintegrated into wispy gray fluffs like animal fur loosening from a creature's undercoat.

Everything about this realm appeared different from his own, but at the same time, he found many similarities. They weren't so different after all.

Following a lengthy stillness of simply walking the outer banks of the river, Nox finally broke the silence. "Are you going to rat me out?" he murmured.

"No." She shook her head and briefly squeezed his hand before dropping it once more. "Though, I would appreciate an explanation."

He shrugged. "What's there to say?"

Another stretch of silence passed as the skies darkened until two red moons shone brilliantly in the sky overhead. The magic within him stirred in their presence. Even Leni's blue glows appeared stronger and more prominent. She rarely used her magic for anything other than navigating her surroundings, as she preferred her weapons to her innate ability.

Cobalt magic flickered in Leni's hand moments before she led him across the small river over jutting stones and found a path leading toward a pond. The surface of the water rippled with a red-silver glow as it reflected the moons overhead.

They settled on a boulder, and he sat with one knee propped up while the other dangled over the side, the toe of his boot nearly grazing the water.

"How did you know it was me?" he asked, referring to when she'd held a knife to his throat less than an hour prior.

"I stumbled across an Infernal camp while wandering about. I was going to stake it out when I heard a familiar voice arguing with whom I presume to be the Matriarch herself." She tipped her head in his direction. A silent question.

Nox swore under his breath, and his first instinct was to reach for his weapon. But he didn't. Because it was *Leni*. "And? What of it?"

"And let's just say I'm confused which side I'm on. As are you, it seems."

"I don't know what you mean." He stubbornly crossed his arms over his propped-up knee.

She shoved his shoulder. "The Hawkers are my home. But you are my family, and I didn't sign up for mass genocide. I'm on your side." She nodded her head in the direction they'd come from. "What was that? A lovers' spat or such?"

He didn't answer.

Blue glowed in her hand once again and flickered out. Her brows furrowed as her milky eyes stared out over the pond. She seemed to see more than what her eyes didn't show her.

Suddenly, she blurted out, "Did you forget to come back for me?"

"You were taken care of," he replied quietly, releasing a long, exhausted breath.

"You left me behind."

He sighed again and hung his head. "I became someone I didn't recognize after my father's death. I didn't want you to see that."

She snorted, waving a hand in front of her face. "With what eyes?"

Chuckling in a self-deprecating manner, he briefly glanced her way. "Sorry."

"Insensitive as always." She elbowed him, and they fell into easy silence once again. At least until she commented, "You are much like the fae I remember. Perhaps a bit more rough around the edges with a gooey, soft center. But similar, nonetheless."

Several moments of uncertainty passed as he internally tried to find his footing. But each time he thought he found his feet, they slipped out from him again. "What do I do? Where do I go?"

"Where do *we* go," she corrected. "You're not leaving me behind again."

"And your so-called *home*?" He took a deep breath of the dry air resembling something between hot desert and ashy sand.

"Like I said..." The bottom of her foot skimmed across the water, only the sole of her shoe getting wet. "I didn't sign up for this. I don't care about the hefty payout. This just feels...wrong."

He nodded in agreement. It also felt wrong to flee and leave Avra to the Hawkers' mercy, but there was nothing else to do but step out of the family portrait he didn't belong in. Besides, she knew the land better than he did. If anyone could bring her people to safety, she could.

Perhaps other Hawkers might turn away from the job as well. They were nothing but glorified mercenaries. They had no stake in this job except coin.

Leni elbowed him again. "You clearly love her. You are very good at self-sabotage, you know."

He sighed and rested his forehead on his knee. "I know."

She flicked the point of his ear, and he couldn't help but yelp and cover it with his hand. For someone who was blind, she certainly didn't seem like it.

"That was for running." She rolled her eyes. "Again. Just stop."

"I'm not running."

"The moment you get a little uncomfortable, you run." She ticked off on her fingers. "There was that time with Margaret. Then Lucille. And don't get me started on that Sun fae girl from the tavern. You run and self-sabotage, and the person you're hurting the most is yourself."

"You know nothing," he scoffed. However, Leni had been by his side for years. She'd witnessed quite a bit of his self-destructive behavior. He just couldn't help himself. He was just afraid that—

He squeezed his eyes shut as he realized where his pattern of self-destructive behavior had stemmed from. His mother had abandoned him. She hadn't wanted him. It had hurt him all his life, and he didn't want to give anyone else the chance to abandon him as well.

Especially not Avra.

"So I abandoned her first," he murmured while shaking his head in frustration with himself. He'd left before she'd had a chance to hurt him irreparably.

And he'd hurt himself in the process.

"You irritate me," he grumbled to his friend. "I hate when you're right."

Leni laughed and momentarily rested her head on his shoulder. "I'm always right. But the question you should be asking yourself… What will you do about it? How will you salvage this?"

"What is there to salvage?" He gestured to his surroundings as a whole. He'd made a mess of things. If he picked up enough of the broken pieces, could he wield something back together to resemble what once was?

"Things break. People fight. It doesn't mean it can't be fixed."

Didn't it? He'd grown up with the idea that when something was damaged, it was time to toss it. Including weapons, enemies, and relationships. Even if Leni was somehow right, that still didn't change the fact that Avra was Shadows-bent on customs and tradition.

"So…what now?" Within the reeds, a chorus of crickets commenced their song. He couldn't help but wonder if they looked like the crickets in his realm or if they resembled something else entirely.

"Well," Leni mused, "if you want to fix things with Avra—"

"I meant with us. If you want out, you have to leave soon."

"And you'll come with me?"

"Wherever we go, we go together." He was done leaving the people he cared for behind. Although he was unsure he could fix things with Avra, and he didn't know if he wanted to try, what he did know was that Leni was family. He wasn't about to leave her behind again.

A large smile lifted on her lips. "Then we need to make a plan, and we need to do it fast."

24

THROUGHOUT THE YEARS of her life, Avra had been taught that crying showed weakness, and weakness was no way to lead her people.

Until now, she hadn't realized how suppressing her emotions could damage her. She wanted to cry. Needed to cry. But the well behind her eyes was empty. It had almost always been empty save for a few instances when her emotions had gotten the better of her. Instead of unloading her heartache through tears, she felt it acutely in every beat of her heart, in every deafening pulse through her ears.

"Avra," a distant voice said. It sounded far away, almost as if she were beneath water as the other person called to her.

"Avra," the voice called again. Distant. Muddled. Perhaps on a different plane or realm entirely.

She continued to stare at the empty patch of grass Nox had stood on moments earlier. Or perhaps minutes ago. Maybe even hours. She wasn't sure when the passage of time didn't exist, and only heartache and disbelief remained.

She had done this. She had known that she and Nox had stood on a fragile glass bridge they had painstakingly built together, only for her to smash it with a hammer until they fell through dark waters and into nothingness.

Their relationship had always been fragile, as if one small thing might explode her entire life and scatter the pieces. She had lost her family. Her home. Many of her people. And when she'd held the power to keep the one person she wanted most, she'd failed at that, too.

What kind of Matriarch was she?

"Avra." Again, the voice called to her, this time closer, moments before something rested on her shoulder and squeezed.

Avra blinked slowly, languidly, until her gaze landed on Theo, who stared back at her with concern resting in the orange of his eyes. Were they still standing on the path? How long had she been here?

"We need to return to camp," he urged, his hand moving to her elbow. "It's not safe out here."

Indeed, the last beams of sunlight reached for the horizon like a man desperately trying to claw his way out of his grave even as the darkness pressed down on him.

Nights in Crotona were dangerous when traveling alone. She needed company, soldiers, and fire.

But what she truly wanted…

"He's gone," she rasped. "How could he leave like this?"

"Do you want me to answer? Or stay silent?"

The knowing look in Theo's eyes told her this was her own fault. He would never say it out loud to his Matriarch, but to his sister? He just might spare the voice.

"What do I do?" She felt lost and unsure and defeated. Although she'd trained her entire life for this position, to become the Matriarch, she felt wholly inadequate to lead her people.

"I can't tell you that. It's not my place." He tugged on her elbow again. "Come on."

"But what if he returns?"

However, after several long moments of pressing silence, she realized he wasn't coming back.

"He could get attacked out there," she whispered, hands held to her heart. "Starved. Lost. Eaten. We need to send a patrol. We need to—"

Theo pulled her into his embrace, muffling her quick, panicked breaths into his chest. "He's gone, Avra. Accept it."

Her trembling limbs shivered in disbelief as the shock of Nox's departure slowly melted away and made room for inevitable grief. She had known she would lose something precious to her no matter her choice.

She hadn't realized losing *him* would pierce her straight through the heart and bleed her dry. But now she knew. Now she realized what terrible sacrifices the Matriarch must make for her people.

Pushing away from her brother, she wiped all emotion from her face and turned her back to the patch of grass where Nox had disappeared. Some things weren't meant to be.

No matter how much she wished for them.

Without another word, they returned to the camp, now with fires flickering in the growing darkness of evening and hopeful eyes staring up at her from sunken faces. Maybe she needed Nox, but her people needed her more.

It was time to move forward. It was time to lead. If no one could do this but her, then she would do the best blazing job she could. Or die trying.

Yianni approached her side from the right and held up a map to the fire in front of them. "We go along the Estruna River, and then we take our best warriors and free the remainder of our people."

Avra nodded and tapped her sharp fingernail against the map. "Estruna River it is. In a few days, we march."

Nox and Leni needed an exit strategy, and fast.

Hawkers didn't look kindly on those who had already spoken their vows and left their ranks. The deserted Hawker would be hunted down and killed. Made an example of. Although Nox hadn't spoken vows...

Leni had.

He'd had years' worth of practice of running and hiding. He could hide her for a time. But that would only work if they didn't get caught running away in the first place. They wouldn't make it ten paces without finding a knife in their throats.

A shiver raked its claws down his spine at the thought.

Nox slowly ambled around the camp at midnight, a red moon lighting his way by shedding its crimson light across the ground. He held a dagger in his hand, pretending to clean it with a small cloth while his attention lay on his surroundings. If anyone noticed him wandering about, he could claim as a Shadow fae, he wasn't about to sleep anytime soon.

But in reality... He was looking for a safe way out.

In the days that Nox had returned to the Hawkers' camp, they had repositioned Leni's tent closer to the others as well as facing it toward Heath's tent. Already, they were at a disadvantage, almost as if they expected Nox to spirit her away.

They weren't wrong.

But just for once, Nox wished something worthwhile would be easy.

Two voices caught his attention inside the tent to his left, and he paused to listen, if only to gather more information to make a successful plan of escape.

"We already have plenty of coin to live comfortably for a while," a male voice said. "If we leave now, we won't have to risk our lives for the rest."

"They'd hunt us down," a female voice responded.

"We're not leaving the Hawkers. We're simply waiting for the next job."

"I'm not willing to risk it."

Their hushed conversation became unintelligible, and Nox took another step closer, still cleaning his dagger as he eavesdropped on the conversation.

Finally, the man said, "Heath said we're ambushing them at the Estruna River. Looks like it might be a massacre. But I'm hoping we're on the winning side of it."

A cold fear clawed its way into his soul and cooled his body enough that his suddenly stiff joints threatened to collapse him. He'd been right. The river was a perfect place for an ambush. But Avra and Yianni hadn't listened to him. They hadn't believed him.

Perhaps they never would.

Unless…

Determination thawed the frozen pieces of his body enough for him to tuck his dagger away and move swiftly and quietly toward Leni's tent. There was no more time left. *Avra* had no more time. They had to move. Now. Before either of them reached the Estruna.

He'd brought very little to the Infernal realm, and most of it was strapped onto his person. Therefore, he didn't need to pack any belongings to slow him down in their escape.

He didn't knock, didn't announce himself, before he slipped into Leni's tent and easily located her with his Shadow fae eyes, lying on her bedroll with her blonde hair obstructing much of her face.

He knelt down and clasped his hand over her mouth, but not before finding the tip of her blade at his throat. Her eyes widened, but when he quietly said, "Shhh," she slowly lowered her blade.

"What are you doing?" she hissed. "Asking for some late-night tryst? I'm not interested in you that way."

"Ouch." He placed a hand to his wounded heart. "You're the only woman who has ever said such a thing to me."

She rolled her eyes. "Really, though. What are you doing, Klaver?"

He glanced toward the tent's exit and frowned before turning back to her and lowering his voice. "If we're going to escape, we need to leave."

"Now?"

"Right this second. Pack whatever you can carry. The rest you'll have to abandon."

Without a second's hesitation, she began silently stuffing her belongings into a knapsack and strapping weapons onto her person. Lastly, she tied the laces on her boots. Without the light from her magic, she blindly reached for him and narrowly missed his arm, instead brushing against air. She tried a second time and grabbed onto his forearm.

"I assume you have a plan," she murmured.

"Yes?"

"You sound uncertain."

He sighed, and he glanced over his shoulder to peer through the crack in the tent. No one stirred. It didn't mean someone wasn't watching. "The Hawkers are ambushing the Infernals this week at the Estruna River. Their scout reported that they're headed in that direction. They'll arrive within days if they continue at the same pace."

"And you're going to warn them."

He shook his head with frustration and once again glanced out of the tent flap. "I've already tried that. It didn't work."

"Then what's the point?"

"The point is that I can't stand by and watch it happen. You can either fight with me or against me. But I've made up my mind."

"And you call *me* irritating." She jabbed him in the chest with her finger. "You always poke your nose where you shouldn't. If the Matriarch made her bed, then let her lie in it."

"I can't!" he hissed, squeezing her shoulder to try to make her understand. "I have a plan. It's a foolish plan."

"It's an either 'die or try' foolish plan?" she ventured.

"Exactly. There's only one way Avra will listen to me, only one way they'll all listen to me. So I need to know... Are you coming or staying?"

"Coming. Duh."

His mouth split into a grin. "I knew you couldn't resist." And then his lips fell into a frown. "You may have to fight against those you call your family."

"*You* are my family. I'm fine to leave the rest."

Resolute determination lived in her expression, and for the first time in years, he saw her clearly for the brave, loyal woman she was. Why hadn't he returned for her? After all this time? How could he have abandoned her with the Hawkers?

"I'm sorry," he rasped. "For—"

"Save the giant apology for after our escape, will you?"

He nodded once and crept closer to the tent flap. The last remnants of a fire flickered in the dying embers of the pit. A gentle breeze buffeted the tall grass encircling the camp. One of the two Crotona moons cast a red glow over the night. The large orb in the sky illuminated far too much of their surroundings. Tonight was not ideal to attempt to sneak away from camp.

"Two Hawkers are awake in one of the eastern tents," he murmured, nodding his head in that direction despite her being unable to see the motion. "Another should be on watch. I don't know who it is or where they are."

"Probably Heath," she ventured. Although her tone of voice sounded calm, a tremor climbed down her arm and to his elbow which she held onto. "Think you can outrun a knife?"

"One of his?" A cold sweat broke out across his forehead at the thought. He'd faced death many times and lived. But that was with a chance to defend himself. Heath, however, would strike with quick and deadly accuracy. It was more likely he'd find a sharp knife lodged in his throat before he found a chance to scream.

The still atmosphere unnerved him, almost as if Heath could turn the corner at any moment and level them with a disconcerting stare. If he didn't know where Heath was, their chances at escape seemed much more improbable.

"We should have run the moment we ran into each other," he murmured. "We would have stood a chance."

"Then the problem is you," she jested. "Heath doesn't trust you."

"Within good reason. I hardly even trust myself."

He took her hand and led her to the back of the tent before pulling out his clean dagger. It wouldn't remain spotless for long.

"Run or sneak?" he asked, his heart pounding in his chest as he held the tip of the weapon to the tent fabric.

"Are the odds good either way?"

"Nope. Last chance to turn back."

She squeezed his fingers. "I have *some* morals, Nox. I'm not going to squander what's left on the defenseless." She lifted her hand as if to draw forth her magic but must have thought better of summoning the blue light as she dropped it to her side. "Heath is a formidable foe, but so are the others. I say we sneak. Better us against one than have the whole camp after our heads."

"Why did we involve ourselves in this mess?" he scoffed jokingly.

"Because we had no choice?" She grinned and shook her head. "We were children."

"Stupid children, I suppose. And even stupider adults." He took a deep breath and counted slowly. "One…"

"Two…"

"Three."

He slashed the tent vertically in a smooth movement and froze, holding his breath as he listened to his surroundings. No one stirred. No one called out or jumped into action.

Slowly, he stepped through the rip, his heart beating with hope when the forest lay only a few paces away. Next, he helped Leni out after him. Without her magic, she could still navigate her world just fine, but it took a little more time to figure out in contrast to using her magic.

They didn't have time.

He needed to be her eyes.

Using pressure to her hand, he guided her over tree roots jutting from the earth, beneath branches hanging low from above, and across a cluster of stones until they entered more fully into the forest.

The boughs overhead lay quiet, but he wasn't sure if it was because it was night, this was how Crotona was in comparison to his own realm, or they weren't the only ones within.

Until now, he hadn't realized just how much his father had protected him, how much he had sheltered him. He knew a little bit about the lower realm, but not enough to understand the way it operated. His father had also prevented him from speaking the Hawker vows until he'd come of age. By that time, his father had been killed, and he hadn't wanted anything to do with the Hawkers.

Yet, here he was. Attempting to escape a situation he'd placed himself in.

The farther they traveled through the trees, the easier he breathed. They were going to make it. They'd left at the right time. Just a bit more distance between them and the Hawkers, and they'd be free. *Leni* would be free.

As if his friend thought the same thing, she turned her head toward him with hope in her expression, a hesitant smile lifting on her lips. They were close now. Just down the hill, across the river, and over cooled, volcanic rock.

The salty sea tinged the air with the hope of freedom. Ashy, burnt earth guided their way forward. The boughs blocked out most of the sky, but he managed to make out red streaks of clouds stretching through the dark canvas like the striated marks on an Infernal's skin.

They needed to reach their destination. There was still so much to do, so much to see. Still plenty of life to experience. The Hawkers had taken so much from him. He refused to allow them to take anymore.

A whizz of something sharp and lethal sang past his ear and embedded into the tree trunk in front of him, only a few hand widths from his face. His first instinct screamed at him to spin around, to unsheath all his weapons and attack with his magic.

But he forced himself to remain calm and adopted a look of irritation as he slowly turned around to face Heath. If the man wanted him dead, he would already be bleeding on the ground.

The other man's stocky silhouette stood out against the soft red light emanating from the streaks of clouds overhead. He gripped a knife in either hand, and an intimidating glare burned from his eyes and showered him with sparks of hatred and disdain.

"Where do you think you two are going?" Heath growled. It was disconcerting the way he remained where he stood, fully knowing a single flick of his wrist could end a person's life within seconds. He was deservedly confident. Unfortunately.

"Umm…out?" Nox replied, maintaining his irritated facade. "Why does it have to be your business what we do in the dark?"

He swore he heard Leni barely holding back a gag. He wasn't sure whether to laugh or fight. Maybe he'd save the laughing for later. If they managed to escape this situation alive.

"So far from camp?" Heath twirled one of his knives between his fingers.

"Trust me, you don't want to hear us."

With Shadow fae eyes, he easily spotted the way Heath lifted a single eyebrow. "Packed and fully armed?"

"It's dangerous out here." His fingers itched to pull his sword free from its scabbard, but he knew the moment he tried, he'd find a knife to the chest. Usually, he could talk his way out of nearly any situation. This, unfortunately, wasn't among them. They all knew what he and Leni were really trying to do.

"Your father was trouble, too." Heath widened his stance, ready for retaliation. "I knew you would be no different." He slowly shook his head, never once taking his eyes off him. "I fought against the idea of sending you undercover to Darkest Star. Kress refused to heed me. Turns out I was right. You are incompetent and stir up more trouble than you're worth."

Dropping the facade entirely, Nox said, "We don't have to be enemies. We don't have to fight."

"Leni makes us a lot of coin with her useful magical abilities." Heath nodded toward her. "I don't care if you go on your merry way. You are useless to me, anyway. But I won't let you take her."

"Don't throw away your life for me," Leni murmured. "You can still go."

He ignored her. If she wanted out, he would get her out. Just another foolish thing to add onto his lengthy list of stupid decisions.

"How much coin? Perhaps we can come to an arrangement."

"Nox…" Leni warned.

Again, he paid her no heed. If he could save *one* of his "family" members, he would give his all. Especially because he knew he should have done this years ago. He wanted to make up for his long absence.

Heath snorted. "You have nothing, Klaver. A few coins, perhaps. Several weapons. Unless you have a stache of wealth your father left you, you have nothing of value to me."

"I can get close to the Matriarch!" he blurted, eyeing the man's twirling knives. "Hans downplayed our involvement." He spoke quickly now, knowing each second wasted was a second closer to a bloody death. "Send me ahead with Hans at the ambush, and I can give the Hawkers a better position to attack."

The twirling knives stopped, and a look of interest piqued the man's expression. "You are bluffing."

Nox shook his head. "The Matriarch means nothing to me. You know how much I care for Leni. I will do this in exchange for her release. I will do this, and you will let us leave when the task is finished."

Heath glanced between the two of them, and after a few moments, his hands fell to his sides, though he never relinquished his grip of his weapons. "The Matriarch still trusts you?"

He inwardly grimaced. "Yes, she does. You have a better chance with me there. Plus... I know how many men they have. How many fighters and civilians. The information is yours. For a price."

Under his breath, Heath said in a gruff tone, "The Matriarch's head is worth a fortune." The man's brows furrowed, and he planted one of his fists on his hip. "All right, Klaver. You have yourself a deal—"

With Heath's defenses down just the smallest fraction, Nox lifted his hands and shot a bolt of purple lightning out of his fingertips. But he didn't stop there. He reached forward with his magic and tugged hard, penetrating the other man's mind like a fierce jab with a sharp weapon.

Heath screamed as he lived out his worst nightmare in his mind. His knees buckled. His head snapped backward. And Nox took that moment to shoot another round of lightning, the purple crackling through the air and smashing into the man's chest, throwing him backward.

Nox gasped and stumbled on his feet, struggling to maintain his balance. His magic flickered out. Purple electricity continued to crackle along Heath's still body.

His head became light, and then he glanced down to find Heath's knife lodged directly below his collarbone, right over his heart.

"I think…" He inhaled a gasping breath. "I think I've been hit."

"You think?" Leni scoffed, but the concern pinched between her brows gave her away. Her hand lit up with blue light as she reached forward but didn't touch him. The light flickered on and off as if her magic were searching, all while he swayed on his feet, his mind dazed as he tried to figure out what to do. Despite his precaution, Heath had still injured him.

In a quick movement, Leni grabbed onto the handle of the knife and ripped it out of him. He clamped his mouth shut, his scream muffled. When the worst of the pain subsided, he folded over at the waist, breathing deeply through his nose while warmth pooled in the front of his shirt.

Blood.

"It missed your heart," Leni said as she shrugged him out of his shirt, followed by the sound of ripping fabric. He lifted a hand to protest against losing his clothing. Again.

But he continued to breathe through the pain, trying to keep the darkness attacking his mind from winning.

Leni pulled a small metal box out of her knapsack, scooped a fingerful of thick, clear liquid, and smeared it across his wound. Next, she used the strips of fabric to bind his wound by wrapping it over each of his shoulders and around his torso. Fine, so he'd have some sort of coverage at least.

"You could become a physician with that magic of yours," he jested, wincing when the simple action of speaking was enough to cause him pain. However, the balm on his wound began taking some of the pain away, and he reckoned it was aiding in healing the injury. He'd seen only a handful of Shadow fae with a similar substance. It wasn't cheap. It was more than likely that Leni had stolen it.

She paused and cocked her head to the side, giving him her full attention. "Would the Infernals allow it?"

He shrugged but instantly regretted it when the agony of his wound burned him like scalding fire, but less so as the seconds passed. "You can see what others cannot. It's a useful skill even the Infernals surely couldn't pass up."

She finished tying off the makeshift bandage, her expression thoughtful until she broke the silence with the mention of their encounter with Heath. "You know, you've always been quite the liar."

"Only when it matters."

"Mmmm…nah. I remember you lying for the sake of lying when we were children. It drove your father up the wall."

He shrugged but grinned unapologetically. "Let's go. Before any of the other Hawkers catch up to us." His gaze passed over the charred corpse farther down the path. "We've made a lot of enemies today. I'm good at that."

Leni's hand lit up blue as they picked up their pace and jogged down the path away from the Hawkers' camp. Hope once again crept into his chest and settled there like a warm blanket. They would make it this time. He was sure of it.

All too suddenly, Leni elbowed him in the ribs, and he momentarily lost his balance, stumbling a few steps before righting himself once more.

She grimaced. "Ew, by the way. *What we do in the dark?* Never say anything like that again."

"It gave him pause. It was good for something."

She cut him a scathing glare. "It was good for making me throw up a little in my mouth."

Nox grinned and lightly shoved her shoulder. She shoved him back. And then they continued creeping through the shadows, each with a dagger in either hand. If anything were to sneak up on them, they would not become easy prey.

"Are you sure you want to do this?" he asked quietly as they followed a path along a river.

"It's a bit too late to change my mind, isn't it?"

"Yes, but…" He couldn't quite explain the protectiveness he felt over her. It hadn't been there before. Likely because he'd been numb and uncaring for so long. At least until meeting Avra. "You could return to the upper realm. You don't have to dump yourself on the Infernals' doorstep like me."

"True, but it will be oh so fun."

He shook his head with exasperation. "Fine. But I warn you that they're more charming than they look."

She chuckled and poked him in the back of the good shoulder with the blunt end of her dagger. "I've heard their charm makes smitten men do dumb things."

"Yeah, yeah." He rolled his eyes and gestured with a nod to the path ahead. "Come on. We still have a lot of ground to cover."

They had to intercept the Infernals before they reached the Estruna River. They were walking straight into a trap, and even after Nox had tried to warn them…

He knew nothing he could say would sway them from their path. Not after what had happened in the war tent with Avra and Yianni.

But…

If tradition was the only thing Avra would listen to, then he would force her to hear him.

He was going to challenge Yianni for the position of *Ikshwa*.

25

AVRA HAD THOUGHT she'd known pain. She'd thought she'd known brutal, unforgiving heartbreak. But it wasn't until the man she loved left did she realize the level of ache that could truly exist.

Unfortunately, she only had herself to blame.

She had pushed him away. She had prodded him to the edge of a cliff until there was nowhere to go, nothing to do but jump.

And jump he had.

Days of walking caused her injured foot to ache, but she refused to ride on the caliboar when many others were far more injured than herself. Matriarch or not, she needed to look after her people even in small ways.

Lifting her head, she glanced at the position of the red sun burning in the sky and sighed when it was yet another reminder of traveling with Nox just as the moon would remind her of their nights together.

"I don't want this to be the end," she whispered to herself, releasing a long breath of hot air from her lungs.

Unfortunately, she'd never be able to find Nox now. She knew nothing of where he'd go next, nothing of where he'd call home, nothing of how to reach him.

I don't need you, Avra.

His words cut into her heart like spinning blades. However, they were true. Not once had he needed her like she'd needed him. What had she offered him other than tutoring that he could have very well done without?

"This way," Yianni ordered the group as they edged closer toward the Estruna river. The surrounding area provided cover with a variety of tall trees shading them from the elements. The tall structures stretched upward in a pattern of black trunks and crimson leaves with branches decorated with patterns of bright feathers and woven leather. This was a sacred site the Elders often used for Infernal rituals. It was where she and Theo had been blessed into the family upon birth, and it was where she had once planned to do the same for her own children.

But now?

The future remained uncertain.

"We'll camp here," Yianni said, jumping straight into unpacking and setting up tents.

Avra bit her lip with hesitation. Nox had said this area was a good place to get ambushed. But he knew nothing of the terrain while Yianni *did.*

Still, his warning throbbed in her chest along with the ache of his absence. Not once had his protection led her astray.

She turned to Theo and Yianni. "Perhaps we should find a place to set up camp across the river near the withering fields."

Yianni chuckled and shook his head. "Heeding the pale face's warning is foolish. I am your *Ikshwa.* I have hunted in these parts numerous times. It is the safest route."

"But if there's a chance he's right? We can't put our people in danger."

"It's the fastest path to the Siska settlement. The longer we wait, the higher the risk of us returning with no one at all. When word reaches the Nethers about what happened… We'll lose all advantage."

"But—"

"No!" He stepped closer until he towered over her. "We go this path."

Theo's hand encircled her wrist as he pulled her backward. "You are speaking to your Matriarch," he reminded.

"I am *Ikshwa*," Yianni replied, now taking a step closer to her brother and towering over *him*. "You heed *me*."

Her brother's eyes flashed with defiance, his fists curling and uncurling beside him. No higher authority existed over the Matriarch, followed by *Ikshwas* and Elders. Her brother would back down. He had no choice.

Sure enough, Theo stepped backward and dipped his head in submission. Avra's jaw clenched uncomfortably as she glanced between them. Had Yianni always been this way? In the two years of their official relationship, he'd always gotten what he'd wanted from her. Was she just as submissive as her brother?

"Set up camp," Yianni ordered the others, and despite their lethargy, each jumped to obey. "We'll travel through the pass tomorrow."

Avra watched as a flurry of activity enfolded in front of her as Infernals set up tents, managed the fire, and sharpened weapons. And as she looked upon each face…

Sunken eyes. Downturned lips. Slumped postures. No hope existed in this camp. She realized… Her mother, the last Matriarch, had failed them. But Avra didn't know how to fix it, how to boost morale. Perhaps she had already failed them, too.

She started toward one of the carts holding her own tent within but jumped when an arm shot out and blocked her path. Her gaze forebodingly traveled up a pair of muscular legs to a belt layered with a dozen knives to the red stripes pulsing on obsidian skin. A hardness lay within Yianni's eyes, his mouth upturned in a snarl.

And for a moment...

It took far too much willpower to keep herself from recoiling from him. An *Ikshwa* could be put to death for striking his Matriarch. Yianni wouldn't, surely. But the glower in his expression was cause enough to change her mind.

"I have been patient enough," he growled, nodding toward his tent. "You come. Now."

Not for the first time, she felt plenty of stares from her people around her. Nox was gone, and she felt sure he wouldn't return. Her relationship with him was over. But that didn't mean she wanted any part of Yianni touching her.

However, her people carried very little hope in their hearts. Her refusal of her *Ikshwa* might shatter what was left.

Then you are afraid of their opinion of you.

Nox's words returned with a sting along with the heavy weight of shame. For years, she had done everything asked of her with very little thought for herself. She didn't want to be that person anymore.

"No," she rasped, the word hardly audible through the thick mucus coating her throat.

Yianni's expression transitioned from a snarl to fury as his stripes burned hot enough for discomfort. She tried to take a step backward, but he latched onto her wrist and pulled her closer until his burn scalded her.

"You do not deny me." His grip on her tightened, and the camp became eerily silent as everyone's attention turned toward them. At least until the whispers started. Most of the voices were swallowed up by the nearby river. But she caught one conversation in particular that stood out from the rest.

"She is denying her *Ikshwa?* What has become of us? Of our customs and culture?"

"They died with the rest of our people."

Avra's hands clenched into fists. She knew it was important to continue her people's traditions even in the face of adversity. She knew it. Yianni knew it. And he was taking advantage of the situation by demanding her attention in public, knowing she couldn't refuse in front of their people.

Her heart trembled. It cried out in ache. What Nox never realized was how important culture was to her, how her people would fall apart without it.

Therefore, she dipped her head and forced the words from her mouth in a gentle tone. "I am loyal to my *Ikshwa.* Always."

And then her heart wept for everything and everyone she had grown to love in the past several months. Especially as the shocked silence transitioned into approving murmurs. Her mother had always said leading her people would not be easy. She'd thought she'd always known what her duties as Matriarch would entail.

But until today…

She hadn't realized just how much she would have to sacrifice.

The hardness in Yianni's eyes abated as he pulled her in the direction of his tent. But two words halted them in their tracks.

"Release her!"

Avra's heart shot to her throat as she spun around to find Nox striding toward them with determination in his expression. He wasn't alone. A female with light skin like his, short blonde hair, and pointed Shadow fae ears accompanied him. However, the woman didn't have the same slitted pupils as Nox. Instead, her eyes were cloudy and white. She was blind.

"Leave!" Yianni snarled. "You don't belong here."

"No." Nox's intense stare fixed on Avra long enough for her stomach to twist and turn with both delight and hurt, though he addressed Yianni. "This is my home, and I will not leave. I, Nox Klaver, challenge you, Yianni, for the position of *Ikshwa*. If the Matriarch will grant me this honor."

Dread pulled on the strings within her heart. Tighter. Tighter. Tighter. Until blood rushed uncomfortably through her ears, drowning out all noise except for the fear growing increasingly stronger within her. Yianni was a formidable opponent.

Nox could die.

But…

Slowly, her lips parted as the realization struck her like a blow to the chest. Nox had lied. Which wasn't uncharacteristic of him. But he'd lied, nonetheless. About everything he'd said to her.

About not loving her…

He would not have returned, he would not have issued this challenge, if she meant little more to him than a good time.

In a duel, he might not just die, but he could be brutally maimed before he succumbed to death.

The first answer to come to mind was an adamant refusal. But the fire in his eyes, the determination, stole the word from her mouth and shoved it into the deepest recesses of her soul. He wanted to fight for her, and he was willing to go through a brute of a warrior to do it.

For love.

"You are outsider!" Yianni tightened his hold around her wrist with a possessive grip. "Matriarch belongs with own kind. Not with pale elf with pointed ears."

"The correct term is fae," Nox replied coolly. "And I don't think that is for you to decide."

Finally, Nox turned his gaze to her, and it was as if a spark of connection tightened between them like a rope growing taut. Silently, Nox mouthed to her, *Forgive me.*

Her previously trembling heart eased into a bed of comfort. Nox's presence alone gave her a safe place to hang her burdens, to rest her worries. If he was willing to fight for her, then she must also do the same for him.

She gazed out over her people watching with slack jaws, their attention jumping from Nox to Yianni, from the blonde fae to Avra. "This is not any normal challenge," she said, raising her voice for everyone to hear. "Nox is not an Infernal. He is not one of our kind. Therefore, I ask if you will allow him to compete for the position of *Ikshwa.*"

Yianni stepped closer and lowered his voice, but the snarl never abated from his expression. "You cannot possibly entertain this."

She refused to answer. Her people's approval meant more to her than his.

"He saved our lives," a man answered near his tent. "We are indebted to him. He has my approval."

A woman answered next, "He carried my injured son on his back the entire journey to our first camp, treating him like his own. He is one of us." She dipped her head. "I agree. Let him compete."

One by one, her people murmured their approval, and her heart warmed to witness the love her people had for Nox, for everything he'd done for them asking nothing in return. He'd earned their respect. Now all he could do to remain at her side was to challenge Yianni for the position of *Ikshwa*.

For the sake of their relationship, for the sake of safely leading her people, she needed to allow it.

She pulled her wrist out of Yianni's grasp, and Theo helped her stand on top of a fallen log to stand taller than the rest of her people. She raised her voice. "I accept your challenge, Nox Klaver, against the current *Ikshwa*, Yianni Ariti. The rules are thus—only a single sword is allowed. The use of any magic whatsoever will result in an immediate forfeit."

Despite the flare of Yianni's nostrils, he knelt to one knee, a fist over his heart. "I accept the terms of the duel. I will earn your favor once more when my opponent has been vanquished."

The mention caused Nox's jaw to jump. "Is it a fight to the death?"

She took a deep breath and released it slowly to try to hide the tremor wanting to escape. "To the death or until your opponent either yields or is clearly defeated."

He knelt to one knee, similar to Yianni, and also placed a fist against his heart. "I accept your terms."

And with a trembling heart, she lifted her hand high in the air and closed it into a fist to seal the duel. Now, there was no going back.

26

VERY FEW THINGS frightened Nox. The idea of being forever alone. Losing someone he loved. And big brutes that could easily snap him in half like a twig.

He stared across the black sand of the dueling field with trepidation growing colder and colder within his chest, pulsing slowly through his veins like thick ice. Yianni matched him in terms of skill. But that didn't scare him quite as much as knowing that if he lost, he would lose Avra forever.

Avra drew his attention from the edge of the field, where all of the Infernals had gathered to witness the fight. She stood stoic with her gaze forward, her hair shifting around her horns with the movement of the wind. He had known her long enough to recognize the terror in her clenched fists and the worry shining in her eyes. Yet, she stood calm and poised for her people.

For him.

Several paces away, Yianni ripped his shirt over his head and tossed it onto the ground, revealing the crimson stripes burning bright across his skin.

And then his throat clogged with trepidation when he noticed the single stripe running from collarbone to navel. Yianni had killed at least one Infernal.

He recalled what Avra had told him about the *Ikshwa* trials when they were only children. Yianni had likely received the vertical stripe from killing another child at a young age.

Slowly, he unbound his makeshift bandage when it restricted his movements far too much and allowed it to fall to the ground to reveal the black curse mark on his arm...

And the red Infernal symbols marking him in a V-shape on his chest.

Several people gasped. Hissing whispers lifted into the warm, cloudy skies. But one look at the symbols, and many of them bowed their heads in respect. Others continued to blatantly stare, likely wondering about the story behind the mark. Should the mark have been black, he was sure he'd be met by anger and distrust. But because it was red, it had the exact opposite effect.

But for Yianni... It only made the man's nostrils flare with anger.

Nox rolled his shoulders, wincing when the movement tugged on his still-healing wound. It had long-since scabbed over, now beginning to scar. It would prove to be a liability in the fight. Not only that, but with the duel taking place just before dusk, his eyes couldn't quite see the full details surrounding him. Mostly shapes and silhouettes from a distance, and he really needed to focus on the objects nearer to him. He was at a disadvantage.

Unfortunately, he had no choice but to continue forward. He couldn't back out now.

"Pummel him into the ground!" Leni shouted, pounding her fist against her palm. "Show him what a real man looks like!"

"You can't even see, Leni!" he called back, a small chuckle escaping him and melting some of his anxiety.

His gaze jumped to Avra again in time to witness her mouth twitch with amusement before her lips thinned with worry once more. No, not just worry. Defeat. She already thought he would lose the battle.

Her traditions refused to allow her to express her worry, he realized. Not when he'd volunteered for this.

Well, then. If tradition was this important to her, then he must rise to the occasion.

He and Yianni turned to face Avra with a fist held to their hearts, and with one last look of despair, she lifted her hand and closed it in a fist, beginning the duel.

Faster than Nox could blink, Yianni sprinted forward, moving like a lightning bolt shooting across the sky. A flash of metal arced toward him. His body reacted on instinct as he pulled his sword from its scabbard just in time to block the other man's attack.

The force from the blow threw Nox off his feet, and he landed hard on his back in the sand. Yianni's sword stabbed downward. He rolled out of the way. The tip of the weapon lodged into the ground directly where his heart would have been moments earlier.

He rolled to his feet, barely lifting his sword in time to block Yianni's next attack, followed by a series of swift blows.

Perspiration dotted Nox's brows. True, genuine fear raced through him and clutched his heart in an iron grip. Rather than a dueling arena filled with sand, he suddenly found himself in a clearing years ago in the past, his eyes wide with terror as he watched his father face off against an *Ikshwa* at his front and the Matriarch at his back. His father had hardly been able to keep up with the rapid movements of the man's sword, and Nox had watched, frozen, while his father was injured and then cut down by the Matriarch.

If Pops, one of the greatest warriors he knew, the man who had trained him with the sword, could fall...

So could he.

The present squeezed him with unforgiving talons. His mind rushed back right as Yianni dealt him another blow against his weapon. He barely deflected it. But as his memory flashed back and forth between past and present, a tremor shivered down his arms. His palms became clammy. His mind recalled with perfect clarity the moment his father had succumbed to death at an Infernal's hand.

This time, it wasn't rage shooting through him like fiery embers. It was terror that he would meet the same fate.

Yianni struck three times against his sword, and on the third blow, his weapon flew from his hands, skittered across the sand, and buried itself halfway beneath the soft, black substance.

His first instinct was to reach inside him for his magic. He fought fiercely against the compulsion and instead scrambled backward, away from the other man's next attack.

Without a weapon, he had little chance at winning the duel.

I can't do this! His mind screamed at him over and over to protect himself using magic. To flee. To save himself. And the longer he dodged attack after attack, Avra became a miniscule thought, a vague idea in the back of his mind. He had to survive. It was what he was best at. Even if it meant running and leaving everything he cared for behind.

Nox scrambled through the sand, attempting to claw his way to his feet. But he felt trapped. No matter which way he ducked or turned, the flashing blade was already there, ready to take its kill.

He rolled to his feet and ducked beneath Yianni's next swing. His frantic gaze darted toward the trees, toward a path of escape. Yianni stood in his way.

"No matter how long mouse runs, where mouse hides," Yianni said with a snarl on his face, "cat is superior hunter. Cat always wins."

Death. Blood. Ashes.

His breaths escaped as shallow rasps. His ears rang. His hands became slick with fear. The shouts from the audience died into a distant ruckus, almost as if he stood at one end of a tunnel and everyone else stood on the other.

Yianni swung his sword, and this time, Nox wasn't fast enough to completely dodge it. The tip of the weapon caught on the cord of his necklace, snapping it off his neck. The vial of his father's ashes fell into the sand.

For a moment, it felt as if the world froze around him as he stared at the vial, at the reminder of his father. He'd given everything, sacrificed so much so Nox could have a good life. He'd stood between Nox and the Matriarch and her *Ikshwa* fully *knowing* he might not make it out alive. All to protect him.

And now Nox was the only thing standing between Avra and her *Ikshwa*, with no one else to protect her but him. If he ran now, he'd doom her to death. An extremely violent death.

Just like his father knew he might die protecting someone he loved, Nox accepted he might as well. He had to try. Even if the possible outcome terrified him.

But if he did nothing… No one would.

His pulse slowed. His breaths evened out. His hands became steady and fortified with strength.

"An opponent is just an opponent," his father had once said. *"Everyone has a weakness."*

And Yianni had already shown him his.

He spun and ducked beneath Yianni's blade again, this time with skill rather than desperation. He goaded, "I heard you received your red mark by killing a sickly Infernal. That takes next to no skill."

As expected, Yianni's expression contorted into a snarl. "I bested opponents with great skill. I am strongest in clan."

The Infernal swung his sword but with anger now clouding his judgment. The power behind the maneuver proved too much, and the momentum caused him to swing too far. It gave Nox an opening—albeit small—to sprint past Yianni and skid to a less-than-graceful stop next to his disarmed weapon.

He picked it up, finding no time to brush the sand off the hilt. He twisted around, braced himself on one knee, and placed the flat end of his sword on his opposite palm of the one gripping the handle. He barely blocked Yianni's next attack, his arms shaking with protest against the blow. The blade of his sword slipped, slicing across his palm.

He hissed, but despite the pain, he followed through with the block and refused to drop his weapon.

He tilted his sword to the side, and Yianni's weapon slid downward, away from him. Before the Infernal could attack again, Nox fisted a handful of black sand and threw it into Yianni's face, momentarily blinding him.

In a single heave against the enemy's weapon, he shoved Yianni away, causing the bulkier man to stumble backward. It gave him enough time to find his feet and adopt a defensive stance.

The crowd roared excitedly. Perhaps many of them disliked Yianni more than they let on.

Despite wanting to meet Avra's eye across the arena, he kept his entire attention on his opponent as they traded strike after strike, blow after blow. Rather than finding himself only on the defensive, he took an offensive position and fought with ferocious speed. Not only did Avra's life depend on his success, but the future of the Infernal people desperately needed a Matriarch who could lead without an *Ikshwa* stepping in where he shouldn't.

Yianni's eyes watered as he attempted to keep them wide open despite the gritty sand. It brought them onto a more equal dueling field. He needed to end this fight and fast.

"I met an Elder a short time ago," Nox said, grinding his teeth as he thwarted a powerful blow aimed at his chest.

"He told me you were a coward who couldn't fight his own battles."

Of course, it was a lie. But the bait worked incredibly well as Yianni's stripes heated into a molten red, and steam wafted off his skin. The man's attacks became a blinding fury of powerful blows, but they were disorganized and sloppy.

"Spend as little time as possible fighting an opponent," his father's sage advice came to mind. *"You'll run less risk of depleting your own stores of energy and conserve more for the next fight."*

But as he searched for an opening to wound his adversary, he found none. Yianni's attacks may be disorganized, but he was still fierce and skilled.

He barely felt the sting of the slice across his palm when the heat of determination pumped through his blood. Block. Stab. Swing. Block.

It was a dance of fire.

It was a dance of death.

"There is no honor in battle," his father had taught him while training with the sword early on. *"There is only life and death. Therefore, you must use every tool at your disposal."*

Nox feinted to the right, but Yianni wasn't fooled, calling his bluff with the sharp end of his sword. He blocked the blow and crouched low to duck beneath the next attack. But instead of springing directly upward to continue the fight, he pulled one of his shoes off and chucked it toward his opponent's head.

The unconventional attack surprised Yianni, and he lifted his blade to block the shoe, giving Nox the small opening he needed.

He swung his blade at the Infernal, slicing the man from rib to rib. Black blood oozed out of the wound. But instead of felling his opponent, the injury only seemed to anger him.

Yianni released a war cry and brought his sword above his head, swinging downward. Nox sacrificed the block he could have made for the smallest opportunity of action, not protecting himself from the blow.

The Infernal's blade sliced through his upper arm as he reached for the man's trousers, giving them a firm yank. They pooled around his ankles, revealing the undergarments lying beneath.

Yianni attempted another swing, but the movement pushed him off balance. He stumbled forward, and with his pants around his ankles, he crashed into the sand.

Nox quickly pulled off his second shoe and threw it. Yianni instinctively lifted his sword to deflect it, and Nox used that opportunity to swing with all his might.

His sword bashed into his enemy's weapon. The heavy blow caused it to fly out of Yianni's hand and hurtle into the sand ten paces away.

Before his opponent could scramble away, Nox placed the tip of his sword over Yianni's heart. "Do you yield?"

"Foul play is grounds for disqualification."

"Says who?"

The man didn't answer, but only replied with a loud snarl.

Nox breathed heavily, perspiration dripping down his body from the heavy exertion expended during the fight. He swayed on his feet, still reeling from his previous wound and now his new wound on his arm. His grip on his sword felt weak, as he had pushed every last muscle in his body to their limits and then some.

But it was done. He had won.

Yianni lay bleeding on the sand, fury painted across the sharp features of his face. Cheers lifted into the sky, and one by one, each Infernal fell to their knees and pressed two fingers to their lips as a sign of respect.

His attention lay fixed on Yianni as he adjusted his grip on his sword, keeping it held aloft of the man's breast. The fight wasn't over until someone declared it, but with so much noise and commotion, he couldn't hear any such announcement.

"You are filthy sharp-eared elf." Yianni spat in the sand. "You have no business with Matriarch. She is *mine*. She always been *mine*. And I refuse to allow outsider to take her from me."

Nox's grip on his sword tightened. A man wounded of his pride was the most dangerous creature of all. "And I refuse to allow you to lead her to her death. If this is the only way to save her, then so be it."

"She doesn't need you saving her." The man spat again, this time with a tinge of black blood with it. "It's *my* job."

"And you have been doing such a great job of it," he replied sarcastically. "Leaving her in the upper realm. Staying away when she gets cornered by Hawkers. Leading her straight into an ambush." Nox leaned closer, his nostrils flaring with anger. "I think it's time someone else takes up the mantle."

Yianni snarled, and in a motion quicker than he could follow beneath hazy sunlight, the Infernal slapped either palm against the flat sides of Nox's sword. He pulled away too slowly when the light of dusk disoriented his senses.

Green wisps of poison magic shot out of Yianni's hands and up Nox's sword. He swore and dropped his weapon, but it was too late.

He stumbled backward and tried to flick the green away from him, but the poison only latched tighter onto his hand, climbed his arm, and seeped into his body.

First, his skin heated as if someone held a flame beneath him, and no matter which way he turned, it followed.

Second, his lungs seemed to harden, and each breath he took became a struggle of raspy, choking gasps.

Third, a sinewy darkness closed in on him, and he was powerless to stop it. He was a creature of the night, but even he couldn't command the shadows latching onto him and pulling him under.

He clutched onto his throat as he collapsed to his knees, and then he fell forward face-first into the sand moments before the darkness crashed over him entirely, and Death welcomed him with open arms.

27

"NOX!" AVRA SCREAMED.

She'd never moved so fast in her life as she hurtled over another audience member sitting in front of her, sprinted over hot sand, and dropped to her knees in front of him. His eyes rolled backward. His body started convulsing. The poison was quickly making its way through his body.

He'd been poisoned.

And he was not immune.

Theo, followed by at least a dozen other Infernal, placed themselves between her and Nox and Yianni, forming a tight line with their bodies.

"Death or exile?" her brother shouted through the chaos.

Avra lifted her head for a split second and met Yianni's eye through a gap in someone's legs where he lay on the sand clutching his wound. He'd broken the rules of a duel, shaming himself in the process. The Infernal who might just have killed the man she loved. But instead of anger when she looked into his eyes, she felt pity and disappointment. He had protected her for most of her life. For him to fall in such a manner? To disgrace himself to such a degree?

She turned her head away and replied, "Exile. If he shows his face again, next he chooses death."

The group of Infernals formed a tight semicircle around Yianni, linking arms as they hissed and advanced on him. Yianni struggled to his feet and backed up as her people chanted "disgraced" in their tongue, driving him off.

She didn't check to make sure he left as her attention returned to Nox. They needed to get the poison out of his body and quickly. Otherwise, he was not long for this world.

"Help me lift him!" she shouted with panic as she looped her arms beneath his and pulled. He was too large and heavy, even just to drag a short distance.

Theo and another Infernal took Nox from her, lifting him in a single strong heave. She and Leni followed helplessly as they rushed him to the healer's tent and set him down on a bedroll, where he continued to convulse.

He'd won the duel. But he still might die.

Her hand flew to her mouth at the thought, and a sob escaped past her fingers.

Theo stepped in front of her, blocking her view of Nox, and squeezed her shoulders. "You must maintain hope. You are no use to him if you break down now."

She released a shaky breath and nodded. Her brother was right. Nox needed her strength, not her weakness.

When he stepped away, her gaze found the healer as he mixed several ingredients within a wooden bowl. "What can I do?"

The healer handed her the bowl, bidding her to stir with a dip of his head, before he knelt before Nox and hovered his hands over his body.

Green wisps of poison lifted from Nox and into the healer's hands. She'd seen it done before to a human woman who had found her way to Crotona and couldn't bear the heat nor the poison of their magic. The woman hadn't survived. But Avra needed to hold out hope that Nox *would*.

When the wisps ceased lifting, Nox's body stopped convulsing, but his skin became paler and paler by the minute as if he lay within the very grip of Death's claws. He would not make it.

No, he *had* to.

Taking the bowl from her hands, the healer asked her to lift Nox's head as he forced the purple-brown concoction into his mouth and forced his jaw to remain closed. Next, he massaged the Shadow fae's throat to get him to swallow.

His face remained pale, and his body limp.

"Will he survive?" she asked, barely keeping her panic at bay. She wanted to break down into sobs, to scream at the heavens, to slap his face until he somehow found consciousness. But none of that would help. None of it would change the outcome of his fate.

"I don't know," the healer answered honestly, his expression grave. "All we can do is bind his wounds and wait."

But there *was* something she could do. Even in unconsciousness, she could reach him.

She took his uninjured hand in hers and began singing quietly in her language. It was a song of love, of admiration, of hope. And outside the healer's tent...

Her people sang with her.

For what seemed like an eternity, Nox's body burned and fluctuated with unbearable heat and ache. One moment, the jaws of darkness held him in a vice-like grip, and the next, he floated on a peaceful, golden lake, weightless and without pain.

He lay on top of the lake, staring up at a sky filled with bright, silvery stars. They winked and twirled and glowed, pulsing with light. It was peaceful. Familiar. Beautiful. He recalled gazing up at a similar sky with Avra at his side.

His heart jolted with the memory of her, and he blinked rapidly as he tried to grasp onto reality, but it kept slipping through his fingers.

His body fell through the golden lake as reality continued to prod him with icy fingers. It felt as if he waded through thick sludge instead of calm, serene water as he trudged toward the edge of the lake. But no matter how far he walked, the shore only seemed to grow farther away.

A melody called to him in the distance. Quiet and slow at first, and then it grew into a chorus of voices. It filled his ears, his soul. But the song didn't come from the shore. It came from *beneath* him.

His brows furrowed as he shifted his gaze to the molten gold surrounding him on all sides. His fingers sifted through the odd substance, and he lifted it to inspect it closer to his face. Rubbing it between his fingers, it appeared to be something between golden dust and molten metal. Bright but not burning. Thick but not suffocating.

A part of him wanted to lay back in the gold and gaze up at the sky in eternal bliss, but the song continued to prod at his soul, keeping his mind in focus. Avra. Where was Avra?

"If one does not have something to fight for, then he is a poor man, indeed," a voice said somewhere above him in the stars.

Nox's attention snapped heavenward, and he realized with a start that he recognized that voice. "Pops?" he shouted.

Again, his father's voice floated through the skies, drowning out the music, *"The most precious of all life's gifts is breath. Don't waste it on words meant to sow hatred."*

His hand shot upward as if he could grab onto a star and use it as an anchor to climb toward the voice. If he jumped, he felt sure the sky would carry him away toward his father and into a blissful sleep.

But...

Again, his fingers sifted through the thick gold lapping against him like water. The longer he focused his attention on it, the louder the music became.

Wait...he recognized one of those voices. He'd heard it before when sending the Elder off to the supposed next life.

Avra.

Memories of her flashed across his mind. Their rivalry toward one another. Their friendship. Their love. And the final memory passing through his head was a clear picture of her eyes. Blue and orange. Unique and beautiful and pleading.

He reached out for her, but in the span of a moment, she vanished beneath the golden lake.

An ache of longing took hold of him and shook violently. He wasn't ready to lose her, to relinquish everything he had fought for.

He needed Avra. And she needed him.

Therefore, he took a deep breath and dove beneath the golden water.

Only to resurface on the opposite side with a gasp. His eyes shot wide open as his mind became disoriented by the sudden change of scenery. Instead of silver stars, he stared up at leathers sewn together to create a tent. Instead of a pool of gold, a woven blanket covered him where he lay on a fur bedroll.

His disorientation only grew worse as flashes of silver swords and snarls of hatred filled his mind, and then he remembered the vial of ashes he'd dropped in the sand.

"Father," he wheezed, fighting with the blanket and losing. "Father!" He tried to sit up but someone pushed him back down with a gentle hand to the chest. Avra's black horns first came into view, and then her pert mouth. Finally, he was able to focus on her eyes, and a rush of calm rested over him. He was safe. She was safe. And they were together.

"We have him," she murmured soothingly, dangling the vial by the cord in front of him, intact and unbroken. "He's safe."

She pressed the vial into his hand.

He blinked several times, fighting off an ache growing stronger in his head by the second. Something didn't feel quite right. He felt as if he'd been run over by a horse. Or perhaps even that caliboar that seemed to love him so much.

As he slowly recalled the fight with Yianni, he took stock of his injuries. His hand stung. His arm burned. An ache pulled on his shoulder. But otherwise, he was intact and alive and—

At last, he recalled Yianni's poison seeping into his body. It was the last thing he remembered. He should be dead. But he wasn't.

"Am I *Ikshwa*?" he mumbled, almost incoherently. But he needed to know. He couldn't be sure if he'd fought back using magic near the end. He also couldn't be sure that Yianni had lost the fight.

"Not yet." She dabbed at his forehead, cheeks, and neck with a cool cloth. "You must first be anointed by the Elders. But... We had no Elders. Therefore, I decided to appoint two in the instance that we never gain back what we lost."

"Who?"

"Theo and one other. They are ready to anoint you when you recover."

The news elated him, but only for a moment when his entire body ached, and he wanted nothing more than to close his eyes and succumb to sleep.

"I am a liar," Nox murmured, wincing when speaking pained him.

"And?" She lifted an eyebrow. "That's nothing I didn't already know."

He chuckled but instantly regretted it when his lungs seized. He coughed and sputtered and struggled for air. Despite the pendant hanging around his neck, he found it difficult to breathe when his throat seemed to close up entirely.

Avra and another male Infernal helped to lift him into a sitting position before she placed a wooden cup against his lips. The moment the liquid touched his tongue, he realized it wasn't water when the bitter taste caused another fit of coughing. The liquid spluttered from his mouth and onto Avra's shoulder.

"Try to drink," she cautioned. "It's an antidote to the poison still clinging to your body. We must administer it every two hours."

His shaking hands covered her own over the cup, and despite his coughing and wheezing, he attempted to choke down the contents even when his body tried to reject it.

Somehow, he managed to swallow a small portion of the concoction all while his lungs continued to seize. Avra comfortingly stroked his cheek as slowly, his coughing died down, replaced by utter exhaustion. A part of him regretted not training to endure the lethal Infernal poison like other Hawkers, but it had involved torturing a living Infernal into releasing their magic, and he'd wanted no part in that.

The male Infernal took the empty bowl, set it aside, and exited the tent, leaving the two of them alone. Only then did Avra turn her glare on him.

"Nox, you took an enormous risk. I don't appreciate that."

"You don't appreciate that I fought for you?"

"You don't understand." She sighed and wrapped her hands around one of his. And then his heart warmed when she kissed his knuckles with her soft black lips. "Yianni was the best of the best. He defeated friends and enemies alike to gain the position of *Ikshwa*. He was the greatest warrior in our clan. Until you."

He blinked several times to push away the throbbing ache in his face. "Was?"

She nodded. "For breaking the rules of a duel, I could have put him to death. But we have seen enough bloodshed." She paused. "I exiled him instead."

Relief washed over him, and a sigh escaped unbidden from his mouth. "I can't imagine him stepping down from his post easily."

"They never do. The shame previous *Ikshwas* carry over losing a duel can cause plenty of contention within the clan, which is cause enough for exile. They can be…prideful."

Nox scoffed playfully. "I'm not at all prideful."

But she only lifted her brows. "How often have I heard you boast of your skill with the blade?"

Speaking, let alone laughing, hurt too much. Therefore, he settled for a smile before allowing his eyes to drift closed. "I am a liar," he tried again as he lifted her hand to his cheek to show some sort of affection in his weakness. "I have never said these words before. I am uncomfortable doing so. But I need you to know…" He cracked his eyes open to find her orange and blue gaze fixed on him, giving her full attention. "I love you. And…and the thought of living without you hurts. I know I'm just a Shadow fae. I know I'm not what you had in mind for your future. But—"

She halted his words with a kiss and then another until the heat growing in his body threatened to overwhelm him. He'd gone far too long without kissing her, and he felt as if he needed to make up for lost time.

His hands snaked up her arms, over her shoulders, through her hair, until he lightly brushed the base of her horns with his fingers. The coarse texture was a stark contrast to the soft strands of her hair, and whereas it was once strange and foreign and a bit unnerving, he now found her differences comforting and lovely.

When they pulled apart, he released a long breath and melted exhaustedly onto his bedroll. "I never thought you'd kiss me again."

The soft, gentle touch of her fingers once again stroked his cheek. "And now I will never kiss another but you, my brave *Shumwa*. I am loyal to my *Ikshwa*."

He grinned. "I'm not your *Ikshwa* yet."

"In the hearts and minds of our people, you are. Including mine. You have earned this place beside me."

The guilt piling up on his shoulders over the last several days caved in. "Forgive me. For not respecting your traditions. I shouldn't have asked you to choose between me and Yianni. I realize now that it doesn't work that way."

"It doesn't." She sighed and rested her forehead against his shoulder. "But I should have recognized the way I was hurting you, and I'm deeply sorry." She lifted her head, glancing questioningly between his eyes. "Are you sure this is what you want? This is not the upper realm. It's hot and dry, and my people are diurnal. I fear you will be miserable here, especially in the long term."

Unfortunately, he could give no reassurances. He could give no promises or solace. All he had to give was his heart, which was a terrifying prospect in and of itself. "I've traveled the world. I've experienced many different climates and cultures. But not once have I lost my heart to another. Until now." He turned his head to kiss her palm. "This will be another adventure, and I look forward to experiencing it to the fullest."

A spark of hope lit up Avra's eyes moments before she kissed his cheeks, his chin, his eyelids, and nearly every other part of his face. He tried to reign in the joy that wanted to escape him as a laugh and instead allowed only a sleepy grin.

But then she pushed away from the cot suddenly and crossed the tent in several strides. She lifted the flap enough to reveal his friend Leni laughing as she sat in a circle with several juvenile Infernals nearby, playing a game with a pair of dice.

"And where does your friend fit in with all of this?"

Avra's tail twitched back and forth with possible agitation and uncertainty. He could think of only one thing going through her mind...

"Leni is as close to a sister as I've ever had. You don't need to worry about her. *Nothing* has ever happened between us nor ever will. But…I'd like her to stay. She needs a new family."

Finally, her tail ceased twitching, and she turned to smile. "Then we welcome her into our fold. However, this path is dangerous right now. I hope she is making this choice wisely."

"Believe me. She wouldn't have come otherwise."

As if feeling their attention on her, Leni's hand lit up blue, and a large grin split across her face as she lifted her head. Her gaze missed him entirely, but it was close enough. "Only you would pants someone in the middle of a heated battle, Nox!" Her laughter lifted into the skies, and several others joined in. "That has to be the most entertaining battle I've witnessed yet."

"How do you know?" he jested feebly. "You can't even see."

She grinned. "I can see just fine." Her hand lit up blue again before she returned her attention to the game at hand.

Avra's attention turned to the sky as she tilted her head upward, her neck long and slender and beautiful. He couldn't help but admire her graceful form, the light pulsing of her stripes, the elegant curve of her horns. It still felt surreal to go from hating Infernals to loving them. To loving *her*.

His fingers moved to weakly grasp the vial necklace he held in his good hand. The previous Matriarch had killed his father. It was heartbreakingly unfair. But now he had a chance to find the peace that had been missing from his life for years.

"It's almost time," Avra murmured, still gazing up at the sky. "When the moons are at their highest position, you will be named *Ikshwa*."

28

NOTHING WAS WORSE than watching the man Avra loved struggle with something as simple as walking, and not being able to do anything to help him.

Nox stumbled on his feet toward her, and remaining where she knelt on a woven rug proved difficult when all she wanted was to rush to his side and support some of his weight. Thankfully, two other men helped support him on either side as he approached the ritual circle.

Firelight from several torches danced across the circle, illuminating the sacred weaves of rope and feathers draped across the trees and the hopeful anticipation lingering on dozens of faces of those forming a circle around them.

The power of her people filled the skies, amplified beneath the sacred weaves and the holy ground beneath her.

Her brother knelt on her right and another appointed Elder on her left. A torch billowed behind her, casting heat and light with a burning anticipation to match the pulsing of her stripes. Shadows danced across Nox's face, the firelight giving him a warm glow to his otherwise pale skin.

Rather than his hair clinging to his skin with sickness and perspiration, the large curls framed his face and brushed against his neck like delicate waves lapping the sand. Even recovering from the poison, he was strikingly handsome. And judging by the sighs around her, she wasn't the only one to think so.

"Kneel," Theo commanded Nox, who slumped exhaustedly to his knees on the rug before them. She'd heard from her mother that it wasn't uncommon for *Ikshwas* to receive their title in a state of sickness or injury, especially after winning a duel. But Nox didn't hide his state as well as an Infernal might have.

His vulnerability was endearing, and his strength admirable.

The healer brought a wooden bowl filled with blood, placed it before Theo, and bowed as he stepped back. Nox's eyebrows lifted high as he questioningly glanced from the bowl to Avra.

"This blood belongs to the *gheshti*," her brother explained. "They are sacred animals that we only hunt for certain rites and rituals, this being among them."

Theo and the second Elder chanted in the Infernal tongue to purify the blood. And then she watched as her brother dipped his fingers into the bowl and smeared the blood from Nox's forehead, down his nose, over his lips, and to his chin. The second and third stripes of blood followed a trail over each eye and down his cheeks. The fourth stripe began on one cheekbone, over the bridge of his nose, and to his other cheekbone.

Next, Theo also anointed her, speaking in the Infernal tongue as he instructed them to hold hands.

Although Nox didn't understand the language, she helped him by taking his hands and faced his palms upward while she rested her hands on top of his, palms facing downward. Both Elders chanted again while a woman quietly interpreted their words in Nox's tongue. But instead of blessing the blood, they blessed the bonding between Matriarch and *Ikshwa*, that their union would prosper, that they would multiply with offspring of their own.

Theo charged Nox with the task of protecting his Matriarch, even unto death. That her life was more important than his own, and his job was to serve, provide, and protect. They charged Avra with giving all of herself, even her body, to her *Ikshwa* in return that they might prosper together in harmony.

The Elders finished the ceremony with more chanting, joined in by the others in her clan. Voices were filled with healing. For the land. For their people. First, they must rebuild and reorganize, and then they must strike. With new Elders and a new *Ikshwa*, they were well on their way toward their objectives.

The chanting and drums ceased suddenly, filling the sacred ground with total silence in reverence to the new bond created tonight. The two moons rested at their highest point in the sky, the moonlight blessing their union without a single cloud in sight.

A good omen.

After a minute of reverent silence, her people one by one began approaching and placing gifts at their feet before bowing away. The gifts ranged from plants to flowers to food. And then Theo approached and draped a sacred weave around both of their shoulders to signify the new bond.

Music, drums, and chanting picked up again as some Infernals started dancing. Others stood to create a path back to the tent she would now share with Nox. Her mouth twitched as she fought a grin, hardly believing they were now bonded. Only a few weeks ago, she never believed something like this could happen.

She took Nox by the hand, and despite his weakness, they made their way down the path and ducked beneath the flap of their tent. Cheers erupted behind them, followed by more music and the merriment of dancing.

She and Nox shared a look of amusement before they broke into laughter. The simple love and friendship in their bond sparked warmth in her heart. Warmth and happiness and joy.

"I can assume what's supposed to happen now," he said as he slumped onto the bedroll and lay his head down as if he could no longer keep it upright.

"Mmhmm." She joined him and snuggled into his side, draping an arm around his waist. "The celebrations will last all night, but they will not expect us to emerge from our tent. And if we do..." Her eyes sparkled mischievously. "We will be teased and congratulated in equal measure."

He paused for a moment, and she lifted her head to find him biting his lip. "And if we don't consummate this...bond tonight?"

"No one needs to know. That's only our own business." She sighed in relief. Of course, she would not refuse her *Ikshwa* under any circumstance, but Nox was in no state for revelry.

Another pause allowed the music outside to drift into the tent, seemingly growing louder by the minute. And then he spoke, "I don't understand. Are we engaged? Or married?"

Describing her culture to an outsider was no easy task, as it was simply...different. "We are bonded. You are mine. And I am yours. Woman and guardian. Bondmates." Her fingers traced the red markings on his chest. She enjoyed the cooler temperature of his skin. "It does not quite compare to marriage in your culture, as *Ikshwas* can often change if there are enough contenders and if I allow it. Bindings can be broken, but not without leaving a mess of hearts—or bodies—behind."

"And if there are other contenders, will you allow it?"

"Never," she replied fervently, lifting up on her elbow to rest her forehead against his. "I am forever content with the *Ikshwa* who has chosen me."

Because without his choice to fight for her, she'd had no power to claim him for herself.

He ran a hand up and down her arm, providing the comfort and companionship she had craved for a long time. "I understand that in your culture, you cannot and will not refuse me. But I am not that kind of man, and I will *never* be that kind of man. The choice to be intimate must be mutual or not at all."

Her lips parted as she stared at him, at a loss for words. Her bond with Yianni had been miserable. But her bond with Nox was nothing of the sort.

"I'm glad you're here with me," she whispered. "I know you've sacrificed a lot—"

"I've received more than I've sacrificed. Believe me."

Again, the pounding drums and laughter outside the tent filled a happy, comfortable silence, and she took that pause to trace the shape of his face with the tip of her finger. His cheekbones. His jaw. His nose. His eyebrows.

"I love you," she whispered, now tracing his lips.

He kissed her fingers and offered a weak but sincere smile. "You are my every breath."

A smile lifted on her lips as she allowed herself to live in this momentary bliss and forget the rest of her worries. "I notice you haven't lost your charm."

"I may be a taken man for once in my life," he teased with a pinch to her arm, "but my charm is one thing you can't take away from me."

She chuckled, kissing his cheek before she reached for the vial of antidote resting on a mat beside her and pressed it into his hand. "One last dose."

This time, he was able to drink it himself. Although the antidote was no magical cure, it was enough to improve the hue of his skin and lend life to his eyes that had been absent since the poisoning incident.

He set the vial aside, coughed once, and grinned as he closed his eyes. "If my father were still alive, he'd surely be having chest pains if he knew where I was now."

"My mother as well." She laughed and shook her head. So much had changed. Once upon a time, her people might have shunned Nox. But desperate times called for desperate actions. Yianni would have led all of them to their deaths. Many of her people had known it but had been unable to speak up, likely for fear of what Yianni might do to them.

Nox was a rather welcome change in comparison.

"Nox?" she murmured when he didn't answer.

She lifted her head in momentary panic, but then relief rushed through her to find his breathing deep and even, his eyes closed in sleep.

"Whatever happens," she continued in a whisper, "I want you to know that you are the best thing to have ever happened to me."

His breaths remained even, but she swore he answered with a twitch of his fingers against her own.

She wrapped her fingers around his and kissed his knuckles. When their situation appeared hopeless... It just might be the last time she could do it.

29

ALL THIS EFFORT…just for this?

Nox was insane and he knew it. And perhaps a little bit lovestruck. But as he stared with a hard expression at the map stretched across the table in the war tent, he received confirmation that he'd done the right thing. The map revealed the path the Infernals had planned to take and their next moves to fight for and recapture their people and land.

It would have been an absolute slaughter.

He ran a hand over his mouth in disbelief that he had walked away from this, that he had nearly abandoned Avra and her people to this idiocy. Good riddance to Yianni. Truly.

With a light brush of a cloth, he erased the black, chalky line leading from their current position, along the Estruna River, and toward the back of Nether territory. Should the

Infernals, by some miracle, have made it past the river, they would have found themselves trapped between two enemies with nowhere to flee.

A massacre.

"If not along the Estruna, then where?" Theo asked, hands on his hips. His tail twitched back and forth in agitation as he glanced from the map, to Avra, and then to Nox.

"The Hawkers will be waiting along the river," he answered as he swiped the rest of the chalk away with the brush of his hand. "Just past the rocky outcrop. You have two choices here. Meet them head on with our own little ambush, or evade them entirely. Either way, we will still have to fight them."

"You're sure about that?" Avra crossed her arms, her brows furrowed with worry. "Can we convince them not to fight?"

"How much coin do you have?" he jested.

By the sour look on Avra's face, she didn't appreciate his humor.

He shrugged and answered truthfully. "They have a hefty reward waiting for them. Some might be able to be convinced to turn away, but otherwise, we will have to exceed the reward money from the Nethers lest we meet them in battle."

Avra rubbed her temples and sighed. "I've seen them fight. We don't stand a chance with our numbers."

"Then we take a smaller group through here…" Chalk scratched against parchment as Nox drew a new black line starting from their location and leading over the mountain path.

"Our people will get lost in the mountains," Theo argued.

"Not with Leni as our guide. She can see things the rest of us can't."

"Can we trust her?"

"She's about as trustworthy as me."

The other two shared an amused look before Avra finally answered with a jest of her own, "Which depends on what direction the wind blows."

"Ha-ha." He rolled his eyes and smoothed out the corner of the map where a wrinkle resided. "Leaving the weaker behind is a great risk, but it's necessary. A fighter must stay behind to guard them."

With a nod toward the closed tent flap, Avra said, "I believe the second Elder is capable of the feat. What will be our plan of attack?"

Nox tapped his finger against the map in contemplation. "Lord Graves offered you his soldiers, no? Would now be a good time to call in reinforcements?"

Avra reached into her pocket and pulled out a small glass orb that swirled with a faint black mist. "We only have one chance to use it. We need to make sure we do this correctly."

For what felt like several minutes of staring at the map until his eyes ached—or perhaps that was a side effect of being poisoned—he learned the land and the terrain, recalling the bits he'd already explored with Avra.

To his surprise, she reached across the table and took the chalk from his fingers, drawing a new line on the map. Then, she lifted her head to glance between him and Theo. "I have an idea."

Conspiring against Hawkers intent on making big coin was a dangerous game to play.

Both Leni and Nox had discussed the Hawkers' strengths and weaknesses, their numbers and motivations. Despair and hopelessness threatened to weigh Avra down, but she brushed it aside and focused on what she could control.

Their numbers were few, especially when they'd left most of her people in the mountain pass with Leni and the second Elder. But perhaps a small ambush team was exactly what they needed.

Avra silently lifted her hand, signaling for her team to stop behind her. She crept over several stacked boulders with a rough, scratchy surface until she peeked over the side and into the valley below. Towering trees drooped vines like spiderwebs across the Nether village, the tall boughs blocking out most of the light in the early morning dusk. Pools of a tar-like substance bubbled within pits of the swampland, an acrid stench wafting upward like rotten sulfur and the carnage of dead carcasses.

She resisted the urge to plug her nose. She'd need her hands free for fighting. Avoiding the gag-worthy smell was not possible.

She squinted her eyes, trying to peer past the spiderwebs of trees and the bubbling pits. The silhouettes of dwellings resting on little more than twigs to keep them suspended over the boiling pits stood out in the darkness, but otherwise, her Infernal eyes could not make out the rest of the details. Her quality of vision didn't matter so much when she had a Shadow fae for an *Ikshwa*. Nox had led them through the darkness this far. Now it was her turn.

As she returned to the group, Nox sidled up next to her as if the action was as natural to him as breathing. He remained close to her side, and she rejoiced in knowing he took his role as *Ikshwa* seriously. She was his charge to protect, and she silently promised to return the favor whenever she could. They were a team.

He leaned closer and whispered, "What are the odds we break in, rescue the Infernals, and escape without notice?"

She raised an eyebrow. "None? Odds are more likely that they know we're coming."

A playful smirk lifted on his mouth, and she braced herself for something either infuriating or charming. One never knew what to expect from him. "What are the odds you'll stay behind while we do the dirty work?"

"Also none." She grinned and lightly elbowed his ribs.

He sighed. "It was worth a try." And then he nodded in the direction of the village. "I don't like the sound of this."

Beside them, Theo commented quietly, "There are no sounds."

"Exactly. They already know we're here."

"Matriarch Avra?" Theo asked, placing his hand on her shoulder. The questioning look in his eyes was unmistakable. He was asking about her dormant power.

Regretfully, she shook her head. She felt the raw power bubbling underneath the surface of her skin, but it was as if it were hiding behind several locked doors, and she had none of the keys. Her mother had always told her that when it was her turn to become Matriarch, she would know how to unlock those doors. But as it were, they felt infinitely out of reach.

Theo nodded in understanding and dropped his hand. "You said you had a plan."

She answered, "It looks like they already know we're here. We need to brace ourselves for a fight while finding the location of the prisoners—"

"They're in the furthest dwelling," Leni said, seemingly appearing out of nowhere. Avra muffled a startled cry.

"Leni!" Nox hissed. "You are supposed to be guarding the Infernals in the mountain pass."

Her hand flashed blue before an unworried grin lifted on her lips. "I've never been good at following directions. You know this, Nox."

He sighed and pinched the bridge of his nose. "Fine. You said they are in the furthest building. Are you sure?"

The Shadow fae nodded. "I sense Nethers and Hawkers waiting behind the dwellings." Another flash of blue light. "There is something strange about the land. It feels…hollow."

Theo murmured something unintelligible under his breath. "They set traps for us. I should have thought about that."

"What kind of traps?" Nox asked.

Avra gestured with her hands as she replied, "The kind where you fall in a hole and get impaled by sharp pikes. Nethers are notorious for using them to hunt game and people alike." She turned to Leni. "Where are they? Can you feel them?"

After another flash of blue light, Leni nodded. "There are six of them. Holes in the earth. If we weave around the goop, we'll fall into the holes. They're covered by…" More blue. "Foliage, perhaps. I can't exactly tell."

"Are our people alive?"

At first, Leni didn't answer as her magic flared blue for far too long. But then darkness caved in on them once more as the light dissipated. Hopefully, the enemy didn't spot the light from their positions below. "Some of them are moving. Others are not. There are a lot of them. Too many. Piled together. I can't tell how many survivors there are."

Avra focused on breathing deeply to prevent panic and fury from setting her blood ablaze. "How many are guarding them?"

"Two." Leni shook her head. "No, three. It's difficult to tell from this distance."

Crossing her arms, Avra recounted the terrain in her mind, and then she mentally reviewed everyone's strengths, all while the others looked to her for guidance. This was what she had been trained for her entire life. And finally, she felt like she was ready.

"Leni, you'll guide Theo around the obstacles to take out the guards and free our people. You must remain unseen." Next, she turned to her beloved *Shumwa*. "Nox, I know your magic is powerful here in the lower realm. You will create a distraction so large that everyone can't help but be lured to the battle. And when they come, the rest of us will fight, and we can utilize the Shadow fae soldiers at our disposal."

Nox nodded. "I can do that, but something that large might deplete my magical stores entirely now that it's morning."

"Understood." She frowned when she realized he was still at risk for another Infernal poisoning. He could not battle near the others. "You will need to fight by yourself. You can't get too close to me."

"I can't leave you unprotected," he argued.

"And my poison magic is one of the only weapons I can use. You won't survive exposure a second time with no healer around."

"Then you and I will free the prisoners instead. No magic needed."

"But I *do* need your magic. I need you at the rear."

He pinched the bridge of his nose again, but with his other hand, he hooked his pinky around hers as if to say he would follow her lead. "And you will be where? The middle of the fight?"

"Surrounded by other Inferals." She grinned. "The Hawkers want me so badly? Someone has to be bait."

"I hate you," he grumbled.

"We knew this would not be easy. But you came along, anyway."

"I'm having second thoughts."

She pinched his side, earning a faint yet worried smile. She knew by now that he wouldn't choose to be anywhere else.

"We have only moments." She crept forward, and the others followed. "Our enemies will be momentarily blinded by Nox's magic, and by the time they gain back their bearings, we all must be in position." She took a deep breath and let it out slowly as she glanced over her shoulder. "Ready?"

Each nodded in affirmation while Nox took the lead. With his nocturnal eyes to guide them, he led them discreetly down the path with Leni following directly behind to alert him to upcoming obstacles and once more warning their team of the locations of the traps.

Her heart pounded fiercely in her chest like war drums reverberating through the air. The fate of her people hinged on their success today.

When they momentarily stopped, Nox reached toward her to squeeze her hand. Their fingers slowly slid apart as he moved forward and she stayed behind. His warmth lingered long after he disappeared around the corner by himself, his last touch a final farewell should things go wrong. It wasn't enough. It would never be enough. But she knew he loved her. He'd sacrificed so much for her, and that would sustain her through whatever came next.

A deafening silence filled the swamplands, so quiet that the faint ringing in her ears were like crashing boulders and her pulse like the thundering strides of a caliboar.

As if on cue, her new caliboar friend nudged her with one of its tusks, ready to be ridden into battle. Had this been any other battle, they'd have plenty more warriors and caliboars. Today, it was a small battalion. They'd never had so much to lose.

Almost without warning, purple lightning streaked across the sky, and she forced herself to look away from the dazzling effect lest their distraction become hers as well. She wasted no time as she swung up on the caliboar and kicked its flanks.

The jarring impact of its lanky stride nearly threw her, at least until she settled into the creature's motion. Screams lifted into the air as Nox's magic struck their hidden enemies with magnificent force. She charged directly into the purple light, and like traveling beneath a bridge in the pouring rain, Nox shielded her from his own magic, allowing her to pass without injury.

With several warriors flanking her, they charged into the fray of battle just as Nox's magic flickered out like the wind snuffing a flame. The enemy was effectively blinded and could barely even lift their weapons before her small team charged through and cut them down. And when they moved far enough away from Nox, they used their poison magic.

"This is for my people!" she cried, lifting her dagger into the air. The warriors fighting at her side cheered, releasing their battle cries before engaging the Nethers once more.

She recalled everything Nox had taught her during their training sessions together. How to block. How to remain steady. How to fight with swift precision. Riding on top of a mount proved more difficult to fight, but when the beast tackled the enemies and dug its sharp claws and tusks through them like sand, she had the advantage.

However, the battle became more difficult when Hawkers emerged with gleaming weapons and fierce expressions. War cries lifted into the air on the opposite side of the battlefield, and like the fierce warriors they were, the Hawkers began striking her own people down.

Determination stole through her as she moved faster, struck quicker. This battle would not be without bloodshed, but she wanted to prevent as much death on her side as possible.

Through the thick darkness, she heard more shouts and war cries near the back of the field. Although her eyes could not make them out, she recognized the Infernal tongue. Leni and Theo had freed their captive people, and now they were racing to help. Raw determination from wounded and weak Infernals wouldn't be enough. Now, they needed soldiers.

She turned the caliboar around to find a safe place to summon the soldiers away from the hidden traps, but just when she was about to kick the creature into a run, something large and heavy slammed into her and threw her off her mount, pinning her to the ground.

Her eyes flashed open wide when she found herself staring at a Hawker with a triumphant grin stretched across his face. A flash of silver glinted beneath a ray of light breaking through the heavy darkness. She lifted her hand to strike him with her poison, but his weapon moved with deadly speed.

Only a half a second before it pierced her, Nox tackled the man off her, twisted the dagger out of his hand, and pierced him with his own weapon.

"You all right?" he gasped as he staggered to his feet. He reached out a hand to help her up but seemed to think better of it when the green poison of her magic still lingered.

She nodded and pushed herself to her feet, silently cursing when she realized she'd lost one of her daggers in the attack. Silently, Nox handed her one of his own as if sensing her need, and then he spun around, cutting a path through the emerging Hawkers while keeping himself between her and the enemy.

She wasted no more time as she pulled the small glass orb from her pocket and tossed it with all her might. The glass shattered against a rocky hill, opening a swirling black portal to their realm. Only moments later, Shadow fae soldiers began pouring out with armor and weapons, striking down their enemies with control and precision.

When she turned back to her mount, a Hawker dropped down from one of the buildings sitting on stilts and swung her blade in her direction. Avra ducked beneath the attack and leaped backward. But too late, she realized she'd stepped on one of the hidden traps.

The ground caved beneath her in a flurry of mud, straw, and leaves. Her hands scrambled to find something to grab onto to break her fall. She desperately grabbed hold of vines stretching across the walls, preventing herself from getting impaled by the sharp pikes bursting from the ground and threatening to skewer her alive.

Her feet slipped against rocks coated with some sort of oil. Her breath faltered. Her heart pounded. And then she heard the screams of her people above her, the fighting and desperation, unable to do anything but cling on helplessly to prevent her own death.

If she did nothing, they might all die. If she did nothing, no hope remained for her people.

Her panic and hopelessness slowly dissipated as, one by one, the locks within her slid open like a punch to the gut, and she felt the way appear to the deepest recesses of her soul. She was the Matriarch. And her people needed her.

"From dust to ashes," she grunted, pulling herself up one vine at a time as she spoke the words of the Matriarch. "I call upon the ancient powers to render my soul." Another grunt, another vine. "The power passed from Matriarch to Matriarch." Her hand slipped, but she clung on tightly and continued her climb. "To consume and burn with the eternal flames of my ancestors." Her foot found a sturdy step between two tangled vines. "I am their protector, their leader, their Matriarch. I take this power upon myself, to be your Infernal vessel." And then she climbed the rest of the way out of the pit and stood on unshakable feet. "From dust to ashes. To fire and flame."

Power swelled within her, rushing through her and filling the previously vacant gaps of magic in her body. Her stripes burned red before they became translucent, sliding beneath her skin like snakes and pooling in her core as burning embers.

The power of her ancestors bent to her will, ready to be used in the service of her people. Power. Radiance. Burn. Her people would persevere.

She was fire. She was heat. She was the Infernal Matriarch.

And she would free her people from the chains that bound them.

30

IT WAS AS IF the entire battlefield stopped to stare as Avra came into her powers as the Matriarch. Her body shimmered black like obsidian, and rather than red stripes racing across her skin, her core heated a bright crimson like magic pulsing through the heart of a crystal.

Nox gawked in awe, as did many of the Infernals fighting by his side, when the hot tar in pools of onyx obeyed her whims. With the flick of her wrist, the tar burst into the air and obliterated enemies, trees, and buildings in a hot mass of sticky goo.

Steam rose upward from the earth, and little by little, the ground melted like a forge consuming hard metal. Or perhaps lava beneath the earth slowly climbed from the pits of its existence and claimed the surface, cutting a path from one end of the battlefield to the other until Nox nearly lost sight of Avra through the rising smoke.

Heat scorched the very air he breathed. Toxic fumes clawed their way toward him in a rush of red, green, and gray. It ventured close but shied away, almost as if Avra's magic recognized him and refused to hurt him.

Several enemies lost all color in their faces while others fled entirely. Those who remained choked on the toxic fumes in the air or were swallowed by lava and tar shooting upward, grabbing onto their legs, and consuming them whole with nothing but a scream left in their wake.

Cutting through the thick fog, the orange in Avra's eyes glowed fiercely to match the red in her core. She was beautiful. Powerful. Magnificent. She was the Matriarch that whispered fear in the hearts of her enemies. With that sort of power, it was any wonder she'd been trapped for so long with the Hawkers closing in on her tail. Now she was untouchable. And her enemies knew it.

Nox lowered his guard.

It was a stupid mistake, one his father had drilled in him to never do during a fight, even if he was confident in the outcome of the battle. The moment he lowered his sword the smallest fraction, something whizzed through the air in his direction. He reacted too late.

A bolt slammed into his upper thigh. Pure agony ripped through skin and muscle, momentarily blinding his senses as the pain and momentum of the attack stole his balance.

He crashed onto his good side, barely catching himself with the hilt of his sword against the ground. His knuckles scraped against rock. His wound seeped hot, sticky blood.

Before his mind could wrap around what had happened, a flash of metal caught his eye through the thick smoke surrounding him. He dove to the side, ducking beneath the attack and rolling to his feet.

Even at a time like this, his father's voice filled his mind. *Your body is capable of a lot when wounded. Keep fighting. Your body will carry you through the rest.*

With a single glance, he recognized the bolt by the hawk etched into the wood and knew that if he left it in, he'd risk death should his enemy have enchanted the weapon like he'd witnessed several times in the past. Therefore, he grabbed onto the shaft sticking out of his leg, and with a strong heave, he ripped it out and threw it on the ground. A cry of agony escaped his lips.

His watery eyes glanced up to find his next opponent snarling at him from beneath the mask strapped over his face that blocked out the smoke and poison from Avra's magic.

Kress.

"This is the part where you beg for your life," the man spat, warily circling him but keeping close enough that Avra could harm Nox if she tried to intervene with her power. "And the part where I promise you that you'll feel every agonizing slice of my blade as it rips through you and tears you apart."

Nox limped on his bad leg as he turned with Kress's movement, never turning his back to him and always keeping his weapon between them.

"It's over, Kress." He wearily lifted his sword, his body exhausted from fighting, fighting, and fighting some more. "Even if you kill me, the Matriarch will not allow you to walk out of here alive."

"Oh, but the sweet revenge will be worth it. If I must die, you're coming with me, Klaver!"

Kress slammed his sword downward. Instinctively, Nox braced himself on his injured leg and lifted his sword to block the blow. His leg folded beneath him. Kress kicked him in the stomach, and he flew backward and landed hard on his shoulder. He lifted his weapon and blocked the next attack aimed at his neck, holding the position with shaking arms.

In battle, it didn't matter who was strongest if one had been fighting longer than the other. Nox had very little energy left to spare, especially when his body was still recovering from Yianni's poison, and the wound in his thigh made it nearly impossible to think of anything but burning agony.

He'd fought Hawkers. Then Heath. Yianni. And now Kress. This was not the battle he wanted to claim him. Not when he'd fought so hard and gained so much. He couldn't lose it all now.

Avra. The Infernals. His new home. He hadn't had a home in a long time and people to call family. This wasn't where he wanted to die. This wasn't the end for him.

He shoved against Kress with his weapon, giving him a large-enough gap to roll onto his feet. Ignoring the pain flaring in his leg, he slammed his weapon down on Kress again and again, his opponent blocking each blow with an expert maneuver.

I can do this, he thought to himself with each gasping breath. It was only one more opponent. It was the last obstacle in his path before he reaped all that his sacrifices had sown.

Keep the battle short and swift.

Kress circled around him once again, and Nox dared to test his weight on his injured leg once again. It held. But not without a fiery pain shooting to his foot. The heat of the battle would sustain him long enough to fight.

Only one more opponent.

He placed all of his focus on Kress as they fought sword against sword with the intention to kill, to end this battle once and for all. No one else intervened, but with others' attention on finishing battles of their own, he doubted anyone could see them through the smoke, anyway.

There was no one to help him. Not even Avra when she was busy driving off the remaining Hawkers. He was on his own.

I can do this, he told himself again. He'd fought more difficult enemies than Kress, and the Hawker was the last link in the chain binding Nox to his prison.

Destroy the last link, discover true freedom.

Kress fought ferociously as if only seeing fury and revenge in his eyes. Nox had taken away so much from him. Hawkers. Coin. Wealth. If he was intent on dying in the process of killing Nox, then he'd give it his all. This was not going to be easy.

But as Nox battled sword against sword, he also battled the pain and weariness in his body. It wanted to collapse, to give into the temptation to lie on the ground and remain still. Despite the temptation, he continued to fight, even when his body heavily protested.

In an expert maneuver that Nox couldn't evade, Kress twisted his sword out of his hand, and it skittered against black, rocky ground. He dove for it, not allowing a single moment to give his enemy an opening.

I can do this! I have to do this!

He snatched his sword, but the weariness of his body refused to act quickly to block the next attack. Even as he lifted his blade, he knew he wasn't going to be fast enough to save himself.

But then someone stepped in front of him and blocked the attack with a dagger of their own.

Nox stared wide-eyed at the back of Leni's blonde hair, her arm raised to block dagger against sword. But then horror raced through him as the back of her white tunic slowly stained red. Kress's dagger in his second hand stabbed through Leni, the very tip of the weapon emerging on the other side between her shoulder blades.

But in her second hand was another dagger striking upward through Kress's abdomen.

Kress pulled his weapon out of Leni and stumbled backward. She collapsed to the ground. Her dagger still protruded from the man's body.

"Leni!" Nox screamed, his voice nearly deaf to his own ears when he could hear hardly anything against the rage pulsing through his blood. Fury gave him the strength he needed to push himself to his feet, and in only two swings, he struck Kress down and stabbed his weapon directly through his heart.

Disbelief clouded Kress's expression before his head became limp to the side, and the light exited his eyes in death.

"In death you shall burn, and to life to never return." He silently cursed his rhymes and spun around, away from Kress.

He skidded on his knees to a stop beside Leni, hardly feeling the pain in his thigh. One look at her pale face and unfocused eyes, as well as the blood pooling quickly across her chest, and he knew it was too late.

"Why?" he choked, grasping onto her hand. Panic flared within him when she didn't squeeze back. "You shouldn't have sacrificed yourself for me. You should have... You should have..."

She drooped her head to the side and gave him the faintest smile. "And let you have all the glory? Not a chance." Her eyelids fluttered before remaining half-open. "I could be a healer." Her grip grew weaker on his hand. "Or a baker. I've always wanted to bake."

"You're terrible at it," he replied huskily, but the insult caused another flicker of a smile to grace her lips.

Her breaths grew more rapid as she struggled to find his face with her cloudy eyes. "I'll say hello to your father for you. I'm sure he's missed you fiercely."

"I beg you. Stay."

"Now it's my turn to leave," she jested. "I'm going to have all the adventures I never could before. And I'll be able to see all of it. With eyes that work."

Nox bent over her hand and pressed her fingers to his forehead. "You'll have to show me all the sights when we see each other again."

"I will." Another flicker of a grin. "I promise."

One last breath escaped her lips. Her head fell to the side. Her cloudy gaze became empty and lifeless.

Finally, her entire arm fell limp. Her chest did not rise again with breath.

He stared at her now lifeless form in disbelief. Only seconds ago, she'd been alive. Only minutes ago, they'd traded jests. They'd only had a few days together. And now she was gone in the blink of a blade.

This couldn't be real. It was impossible. It wasn't…

Gentle arms wrapped around his shoulders from behind, and he felt one of Avra's horns brush against the side of his head. "I'm so, so sorry, Nox. I wish I could have done something."

"This isn't your fault. It isn't…it's not…" He gripped her arms and turned his head to bury his face into her shoulder, her skin and stripes now back to normal. "She was too young." His voice was muffled by the clothing she wore. "She's younger than me."

Her soft lips kissed the top of his head and then his temple. "She died in battle. That is the greatest honor any Infernal can grant themselves. She was one of us. And we will honor her dedication and sacrifice as if she had been ours all along."

With an ache growing steadier in his chest, he closed Leni's eyes with his fingers and murmured a quiet farewell. He'd never been religious. He'd never believed in anything other than the visible and tangible world around him. But just this once, he wanted to believe that he might see her again. Just this once, he had to believe it wasn't the end.

Because accepting that this was it for them hurt far too much to comprehend.

Unable to face his grief, he stood and turned his back to his friend. He could not allow himself to grieve. Not now. Not yet. Especially when so many others still needed his help.

"It looks like I need to start exposing myself to Infernal poison to become immune," he commented as his gaze passed over pockets of green, wispy magic from the aftermath of the battle. "I won't last long here, otherwise."

"No, you won't."

He blew out a long breath and glanced over the dozens of Infernal tending to their wounded or dead, and others tearfully reuniting with loved ones. Shadow fae soldiers began returning to their own realm almost as quickly as they had arrived, likely to avoid as much exposure to the dry climate of Crotona as possible. "I still have so much to learn about your people."

"And now you have time to learn it. Besides..." She brushed a kiss across his temple. "You are my *Ikshwa*. These are your people now, too."

"Are...are you sure?"

Instead of answering out loud, she nodded her head in the direction of other Infernals, many of whom bowed their heads and pressed their fingers to their lips in respect for both of them. Not just for Avra.

He was a Shadow fae. But they treated him like one of their own.

Although he felt as if he wore a mask that didn't quite fit his face, he nodded to the Infernals in acknowledgement. Their largest issues were over, but many more still remained. If they looked to him and Avra for hope, then he would remain unfaltering, because...

He was done running. All his life, he'd run away and dismissed all his problems, all his feelings, all his burdens. But now he wanted them all. He wanted to shoulder these burdens. He wanted to take care of these people. He refused to falter. This was exactly where he needed to be, what he needed to do.

Therefore, with Avra at his side, they joined the others. And got to work.

Nox sat on a cliffside overlooking the Infernal village on one side, and the other side boasted a beautiful ocean stretching across the horizon where the dusk met the sea in a kiss of blazing orange and red. His legs dangled over the edge of the cliff as he attempted to capture the horizon with his chalks, hardly doing justice to the colors nearly impossible to replicate.

But it was another place he'd discovered, another adventure he'd experienced. This time with his father and Leni beside him.

In his opposite hand not holding the chalk, he held two small vials of ashes in his palm, one belonging to his father and the other to Leni. Although his friend had promised to show him the sights in the afterlife, nothing held him back from showing her the sights in this life. There was still so much to see, so much to do, so much to explore. He wanted to experience it all. With his loved ones at his side.

A brief gust of wind rushed over the pages of his sketchbook and through the small, open shelter he'd built behind him crafted of black leather and wooden poles. He'd set it up at a slant to protect from the harsh sunlight and provide a small measure of shade while still giving him a fantastic view of his new home. Crotona.

He flipped the page in the notebook as his mood took on a somber tone. His fingers flew across the page as he drew and shaded and captured the memory of Leni before his mind might somehow forget. He portrayed her large smile, her foggy eyes, her thirst for life, missing no detail. And then he drew his father next to her with his arm around her shoulders, pride shining in his eyes.

He felt it in his heart. If there truly was an afterlife, he knew his father would be proud. Of him. Of Leni. Their little family of three. Well, now four with Avra joining the fray of misfits.

Speaking of Avra…

He heard her stir behind him where she lay on a pile of blankets and pillows within the shelter. The tinkle of the jewelry around her horns was a comfort to his ears, easing his worries and reassuring him that she was here and she was safe.

"You really do wake with the dusk," Avra croaked behind him, and he turned his head, a grin lifting on his face as he watched her rub the sleep from her eyes. Up here on the cliffside overlooking the village was as much of a honeymoon as they were ever going to get when now was not quite the time to leave her people to fend for themselves.

Plus… He was sure no one wanted to hear them *truly* consummating the union closer to the village. That was for them alone.

He rested his cheek on his fist as his gaze skimmed over the mess of her black hair and the revealing clothing she wore for her *Ikshwa's* eyes only. For him. "It won't be easy to break my sleeping habits." He clicked his tongue and shook his head, his gaze traveling appreciatively from her horns to her feet. "You'd better turn right back around. Looking like that, I just can't resist you."

She froze as she stared back at him, and when she tipped her head to the side questioningly, he realized his mistake.

"Shadows," he hissed, dropping his hands into his lap. "I didn't mean it like that. You get a choice, Avra. You always get a choice. I'm only teasing."

"Oh." She laughed and knelt beside him, piercing him with those beautiful blue and orange eyes of hers. "This is not because of duty, you know." She ran a finger over his lips. His jaw. His throat. "I want to be close to you."

"There is no duty," he replied huskily. "This is not my right. It's a privilege. You can refuse any time you want."

She slowly shook her head in disbelief. "I'm not sure I can easily get used to that. You're different, Nox. But I love that about you. I love *you.* I'm glad we met all those months ago."

"It's not a meeting one easily forgets," he jested. "Getting punched in the gut right where it hurts. You left me a reminder of yourself for days."

Soft laughter escaped her as her exploration moved to his collarbones where she traced patterns over his skin. "I had to make sure you didn't forget me."

"I could never."

Her levity sombered as she glanced down at his sketchbook. "I'm sorry about Leni."

"Me too."

A peaceful pause passed between them, and despite everything that had happened in the past several months, he knew things would turn out all right. Especially now that they were together, and nothing could tear apart Matriarch from *Ikshwa.*

"What do we do now?" he asked.

She lifted her head and planted a soft kiss on his lips. The sweet scent of her, the softness of her mouth and her skin and her hair… He rejoiced in knowing that they could show each other affection without culture nor custom to hold them back. In her culture—in *their* culture—they were forever bonded. Nothing could make him happier.

"Now?" she asked, gazing with hope shining in her eyes unlike the fear and hopelessness and hardness that had existed when they'd first met. "Now we rebuild." She lifted his hand with hers, placing finger against finger. Palm against palm. "We rebuild. We grow. We thrive."

"Together," he whispered.

With a nod, she reiterated, "Together. For now and for always."

His heart lifted at the turn of direction of his thoughts as he threaded his fingers through hers. "The semester at Darkest Star is not quite over."

With an exasperated chuckle, she shook her head at him in disbelief. "You can't mean to return."

"If we have enough ingredients for the portals to travel back and forth, I don't see a reason why we can't rebuild while continuing our education."

"But I'm the Matriarch, Nox."

"And I am your *Ikshwa.*" He gave her a mock severe expression as he placed his free hand over his heart. "I take my care of you seriously, and what you need is to finish your semester at school. You'll never forgive yourself, otherwise. You'll always regret not completing your classes while you still could."

He pulled her close by the shoulders into an embrace, delighting in her following laughter. She placed a hand against the base of one of her horns as if trying to reorient herself.

"But we've missed so many days of school as it is. Surely, Killian will fail us."

"The headmaster placed nearly his entire army at your disposal." He grinned and chucked her chin. "He's already eagerly studying Crotona's indigenous plants and taking samples back to his realm. You think *that* man will fail us?"

She chuckled and rolled her eyes. "Fine, perhaps not. But we've missed plenty of schoolwork. Not to mention the final project in Professor Graves' class."

"Don't worry about the project." His fingers lit up with the purple glow of his magic. "I have an idea."

AFTER EVERYTHING THAT had transpired, after all the vows he'd made and responsibilities he'd taken up, Nox had never truly believed he'd ever see the upper realm again. Therefore, it felt surreal to stand in the garden circle at Darkest Star Arcane, breathing in cold, humid air on the very last day of school for the semester.

Even more surreal, he held the hand belonging to a beautiful woman with a look of challenge and excitement on her face as she gazed at the building up ahead.

Avra no longer wore her glamour and instead showed off her graceful Infernal form, drawing plenty of awe-filled and curious stares from the students around them. Many of them had likely seen her at the dance in her Infernal form, so they knew who she was. What she was. No longer afraid of the unknown the Infernals presented. And like himself, they seemed to find it difficult to look anywhere else in her presence.

The gold and pink sunset hues of dusk welled over them like a slow and languid river, inciting his awe not for the first time since they'd periodically visited the upper realm for classes. Being away from this realm most of the time filled him with a strong longing to visit, but each time they returned was better than the last.

"I'm not ready for this to end," Avra said in a breathy voice that had nothing to do with difficulty breathing the upper realm's air. At least not with the pendant she wore around her neck that did opposite for her what his did for him in the lower realm.

He squeezed her hand and offered an encouraging smile. "You may be the Matriarch, but that doesn't mean your exploration of the world has to end. As *Ikshwa*, I demand periodic leave to visit some of my favorite places in the upper realm."

She grinned and elbowed him in the ribs. "You are such a bad influence on me. What will our people think?"

Our. It truly felt good to belong somewhere.

"Our people love me. Admit it. I've managed to charm them all."

Laughter escaped her, and she attempted to elbow him again. He sidestepped and pulled her into the momentum of her movement until their lips met in a kiss she clearly hadn't expected from the way she inhaled sharply, and her eyes flew wide open.

But then she leaned into the kiss and pulled herself closer to him.

Not too long ago, he could never see himself in a committed relationship. But now? Beside Avra was the only place he wanted to be.

They broke away all too quickly. If not for passersby, he would have happily spent the next hour kissing Avra senseless.

Later, he promised himself. After their presentation of their final project, and after they returned home to Crotona. Then he was all hers.

"You really do abuse your *Ikshwa* privileges," she whispered, her gaze darting to his lips.

"And you enjoy every moment of it," he murmured, hovering just out of reach.

She pinched his side, and he couldn't help but grin from ear to ear as he took her arm and looped it through his. They continued forward and entered the building ahead. Each time he stepped into one of the Darkest Star classrooms, he couldn't help but tense up, his eyes scanning every nook and cranny for potential threats. Kress and Heath were dead. What was left of the Hawkers had disappeared. And they hadn't heard a peep from Yianni, nor did they expect to. He was a man deeply grounded in their traditions, and Avra had said she doubted he would show his face again and further embarrass himself in front of the clan.

Still, he felt ill at ease knowing he now stood between the Infernal Matriarch and those who might mean her harm. Taking on the hefty responsibility of *Ikshwa* often weighed on him, especially when he took her somewhere by themselves. But there was no one else he'd rather protect with his life.

Professor Graves greeted each student as they walked into his classroom. When his gaze landed on them, he gave them a sad, regretful smile. "Is there any way I can convince the two of you to stay for the next semester? Your generosity of allowing me to study your realm has more than made up for tuition costs at Darkest Star. A full scholarship is on the table."

Beside him, Avra bit her lip and gazed longingly at the classroom beyond the professor. She answered, "Believe me, I want it almost more than anything, but I have been absent by attending classes too much as it is."

What Nox knew she didn't say was that the constant jumping from realm to realm was exhausting for her when her body didn't acclimate easily to the more humid temperatures in the upper realm. The pendant she wore helped, but the journeys were easier when they were spaced farther apart.

Besides, her duties as Matriarch made it difficult to live the student life, anyway.

"Well, the offer continues to stand if you change your mind." He gestured them inside, and they took a seat near the back of the classroom in the farthest corner to give him the best vantage point. At first, they'd fought about this, as she preferred the front of the classroom. But he'd insisted her safety came first, telling her she could sit at the front, but he'd have to sit at the back to keep watch.

Much to his satisfaction, she'd given in and stayed in the back with him for the remainder of the semester. The thought warmed him that she favored his close proximity to her favorite seat in class.

When everyone took their seats, and the professor began his last lecture of the semester, Nox reached across the space between his desk and Avra's and took her hand, giving it a brief squeeze. He wasn't quite ready for this chapter of their lives to close, but he looked forward to discovering new open doors and adventures awaiting them.

"Without further ado," the headmaster said, his arms folded behind his back, "I will call you up group by group to present your final projects. The original assignment was to recreate something from nature using magic and sustain it in a classroom setting. Royce and Vivien, you'll present first."

Two by two, their classmates presented their projects, anywhere between a volcanic failure that exploded something akin to jelly all over the front of the room to a controlled ball of sunlight and nutrients that helped plants grow at a quicker rate.

Finally, he and Avra stood in front of the class. They pulled the curtains together to block out the blue, magical lights weaving through campus outside until darkness closed over them.

He lifted a silver ball that fit inside the palm of his hand, the metal weaving together to create an intricate, spherical pattern.

"There are many ways to store magic," Avra started out, stating facts as if she'd found them inside a book at the library. "Crystals. Stones. Weapons. Inside this sphere..." She took the ball from his hands and shook it gently, creating a soft rattle. "...lies an obsidian stone from the Infernal realm, which is capable of holding a great deal of magic. Coupled with a steady stream of magic captured inside under the right conditions and a functional design..."

"You can recreate the night sky," he finished for her.

He took the sphere from her and twisted it halfway until it clicked twice.

Light shot out of the sphere and encompassed the walls and ceiling of the classroom. The placement was purposeful, imitating the night sky when standing in the middle of the academy garden and staring up at the heavens above.

With another click, the stars shifted around them until they floated between desks and over people's heads. Their classmates exclaimed their awe as they reached out to touch a star or two, their fingers passing right through the small specks of magic.

Right here in his hand, he held one of the most important places in his life. Darkest Star Arcane. The place where he'd met his soulmate. The place where he'd found himself. The place that had set him free from the anger in his heart.

No matter where in the world or between the realms he found himself, he'd always have this place with him, forever burning like stars in the night sky.

He glanced at Avra, and his heart thrummed with admiration at the way she gazed up at the makeshift stars, at the way the light sparkled in her blue and orange eyes.

With her book smarts, she had been able to figure out the placement, sustainability, and patterns of the upper realm night sky. With his magic and her instruction, he was able to create it. And now, as it sparkled over their heads like shimmering diamonds, he realized neither of them could have done it without the other. Together, they could create something magnificent and beautiful.

After a few more moments of gazing at their creation, he finally spoke. "We call this..." He dared not speak too loudly as to disturb the quiet and awe of the atmosphere. "...A weave of starlight."

"Incredible," Professor Graves said as he gazed up at the "stars" in awe. "Well done. A most promising end to the semester." When Nox retracted the stars, tucked the sphere into his vest pocket, and they took their seats, Graves clapped his hands together. "That concludes the last class of the year. I hope to see your familiar faces in one of my classes next semester. I'll be calculating grades within the next couple of weeks, so expect a letter from me soon. Class is dismissed."

Everyone filed out of the building, and with it, Nox experienced a sense of loss. Loss for the normal student he could have been. But he'd gained so much recently that it hardly mattered. A family. A home. A purpose.

And sweet, sweet Avra.

A somber smile rested on her face as she followed his lead down the path, likely feeling some of the mixed emotions unraveling in his own heart. An end to a difficult but rewarding chapter, but with the hope of the next chapter to begin anew.

"Should we head back home?" she asked.

He shook his head. "Not just yet."

A grin lifted on her lips as if relieved to hear it. She flirtatiously bumped him with her shoulder. "Where to, *Ikshwa?*" The sweet trust in her gaze told him she'd follow him anywhere, and he knew he would do anything to remain worthy of that trust.

Instead of answering her question, he only grinned as he took her hand, led her down the cobblestone path weaving through the gardens, past the academy gates…

And onto the next new adventure.

ABOUT THE AUTHOR

Sydney Winward is an award-winning fantasy and paranormal romance author who dabbles in the occasional historical fiction. She loves building complex worlds filled with magic, strong characters, and emotional stories.

Sydney is the author of the Sunlight and Shadows Series and the best-selling Bloodborn Series, and when she's not writing, she's reading, thinking about stories, or going on adventures with her children. She lives in Utah with her husband and three amazing kids.

www.sydneywinward.com